NOVA ROMA 2

QUAESTU PRO NOVA TERRA

Anderson Gentry

Cover Design by John Ladebauche

Printed in the United States of America
First Printing 2023
ISBN 978-1-944644-39-0
E-book ISBN 978-1-944644-40-6
Library of Congress Control Number: 2023932945

Fiction-Alternative History,
History-Ancient Rome, History-North America

Crimson Dragon Publishing
Willow, Alaska
www.crimsondragonpublishing.com

Contents

INTRODUCTION

*I know that the acquisition of Louisiana has been
disapproved by some … that the enlargement of our territory
would endanger its union … The larger our association the less
will it be shaken by local passions; and in any view is it not
better that the opposite bank of the Mississippi should be settled
by our own brethren and children than by strangers of another
family?*

— *Thomas Jefferson in his second inaugural address, March
4th 1805*

In *Nova Roma 1: De Itinere in Occasum*, we saw the formation of
a second Roman Republic in the New World as, during the height of
the second Roman Civil War, the Optimate Senators led by Consul
and General Pompey Magnus fled Julius Caesar's advancing army and,
with two legions, sailed for Hispania—and instead landed in the place
we know as South Carolina. As that story drew to a close, we saw the
beginning of the growth of the republic with the addition of several
new provinces.

A land as vast as North America invites exploration and
expansion. It is reasonable that a merchant society like Rome would
seek expansion, precisely as the Roman Republic and later, the Empire,
did in our timeline. Therefore it stands to reason that the Nova Roman
republic would do so as well.

Consider the differences between our timeline and the world of
Nova Roma. There can be no purchase of new territory from European
powers, as those powers did not yet exist; so there will be no Louisiana
Purchase, of which Thomas Jefferson spoke in his second inaugural
address. The Purchase, perhaps Jefferson's most impressive legacy, made

the youthful United States a continental power, and opened a wealth of resources and land to the growing American nation.

It stands to reason that the Senate and people of Nova Roma would seek to do the same.

Another piece of Jefferson's lasting legacy is the Lewis & Clark expedition, in which the young American government first explored and documented the extent of the Purchase and beyond. After eighty years of growth and consolidation, might not the people of Nova Roma also feel the need to explore?

Through most of our history, mankind has been a race of wanderers. There is something deep within us that drives us to see what lies over the next hill, beyond the next valley.

Several things will influence this next step in the Nova Roman saga.

First: North America is divided by a great boundary. The Mississippi River is a legacy of the last Ice Age, a continent-spanning river the Chippewa called *Misi-ziibi*. The Cheyenne called it the *Máxe-éometaae*, while the first Spanish explorers in the South called it the *Río del Espíritu Santo*. The Novan natives of Nova Roma I call it the Mesizibi, and that is the name that the people of Nova Roma have adopted as the Republic's territory expands into that region.

Feeding the Mississippi is another great river, the Missouri. It was the Missouri that Lewis & Clark followed west, and it is the Missouri that became a major highway to the West for generations of pilgrims and settlers. A third navigable river, the Platte, led west to where Denver and the other cities of the Front Range now stand.

The story of the first steps the Nova Roman republic will take into this great land, the American West, will begin as it did in our timeline, along these three rivers. For people without highways or railroads, rivers are not only a reliable means to travel but also to navigate; if you follow a river upstream, you can follow it back down. The early exploration in any new land always begins along the waterways. Look even today at the placement of towns and cities in the American West to see the influence navigable rivers had on the growing nation. Today we have St. Louis, at the confluence of Mississippi and Missouri; Omaha, near the junction of the Missouri and the Platte; the city of Denver lies on the South Platte, the town of North Platte, Nebraska is near the union of North and South Platte. The Platte, the Missouri, the Mississippi, all of the major cities of the plains lie somewhere on or near those or other major rivers.

Second, the new Romans spreading out from their capital of Pompeius are not the only emigrants to have left Europe in the wake of the Roman Civil War. As we saw in Nova Roma I, a group of Caesarian loyalists followed them. They were only a few, twelve Roman cavalrymen, led by the historically-renowned centurions Lucius Vorenus and Titus Pullo. After losing the Battle of Pompeius these other Romans fled north, there to change their name from Roman to Reman and found the Five Seas Nation. That nation of ironworkers, soldiers and traders now contend with the Roman civilization to their south for control of a continent.

Further complicating the saga is the southern civilization of the Maya, who were at their peak at this time of history. Thus the first phase of expansion west begins with an edge of unfriendly competition that was not present in our timeline.

For those interested in how this exploration played out in our history, I can recommend several works.

The *Journals of the Lewis and Clark Expedition* are available in a 13-volume set, but if hard copy is your goal I recommend you find it in a local library; the only bound volume of this I have found comes from the University of Nebraska Press and runs into four figures to purchase. The Journals are available online, sponsored by the University of Nebraska Lincoln, at http://lewisandclarkjournals.unl.edu.

For a beautiful depiction of the countryside, flora and fauna of the American West, I recommend Hal Borland's *High, Wide and Lonesome: Growing Up on the Colorado Frontier*. His one well-known work of fiction, *When the Legends Die*, is another great piece of Western storytelling. Borland was born in Nebraska and spent much of his youth on a homestead near Burlington, Colorado.

Another interesting and rather encyclopedic work is Denis McLoughlin's *Wild & Wooly: An Encyclopedia of the Old West*. *Wild & Wooly* is a great compilation of legends, facts, stories and more-or-less accurate accounts of events and life in the post-Civil-War West.

Finally, in fiction, James Michener's benchmark *Centennial*, while somewhat dated (his presentation of the natural history of dinosaurs in particular is badly obsolete) remains a bright, compelling view of the exploration and settling of the west, particularly the plains and mountains of central Colorado.

Living as I do in the American West, I am well acquainted with its appeal and its mystery. The West is a land of wide open places; desolate plains, rim rock badlands, deep forests, mountain meadows, alpine tundra and great desert basins. It is a country of endless variety. In its pristine state it is a hard land; it is a truism here in Colorado that the mountains, like the sea, will try to kill you if you lack the respect they deserve, and even today, here in civilized, 21st century Colorado the mountains claim the lives of the careless almost every year. It is a beautiful land, but a land that even now requires preparation and proper equipment to travel in. Consider then the courage required of the first explorers who explored this vast land on horseback, in wagons drawn by oxen or even on foot, with nothing more than they could carry with them.

The story of the West is a story of adventure, of exploration, of legends. The West always appealed to those hardest hit with wanderlust, and in its time it also appealed to those with other reasons to avoid more civilized environs. All of those figure in our timeline's history as well as the still-unfolding history of Nova Roma, whose explorers will now be taking their first steps into this land of legend.

To Mom and Dad, who taught me to love exploring.

NOVA ROMA 2

QUAESTU PRO NOVA TERRA

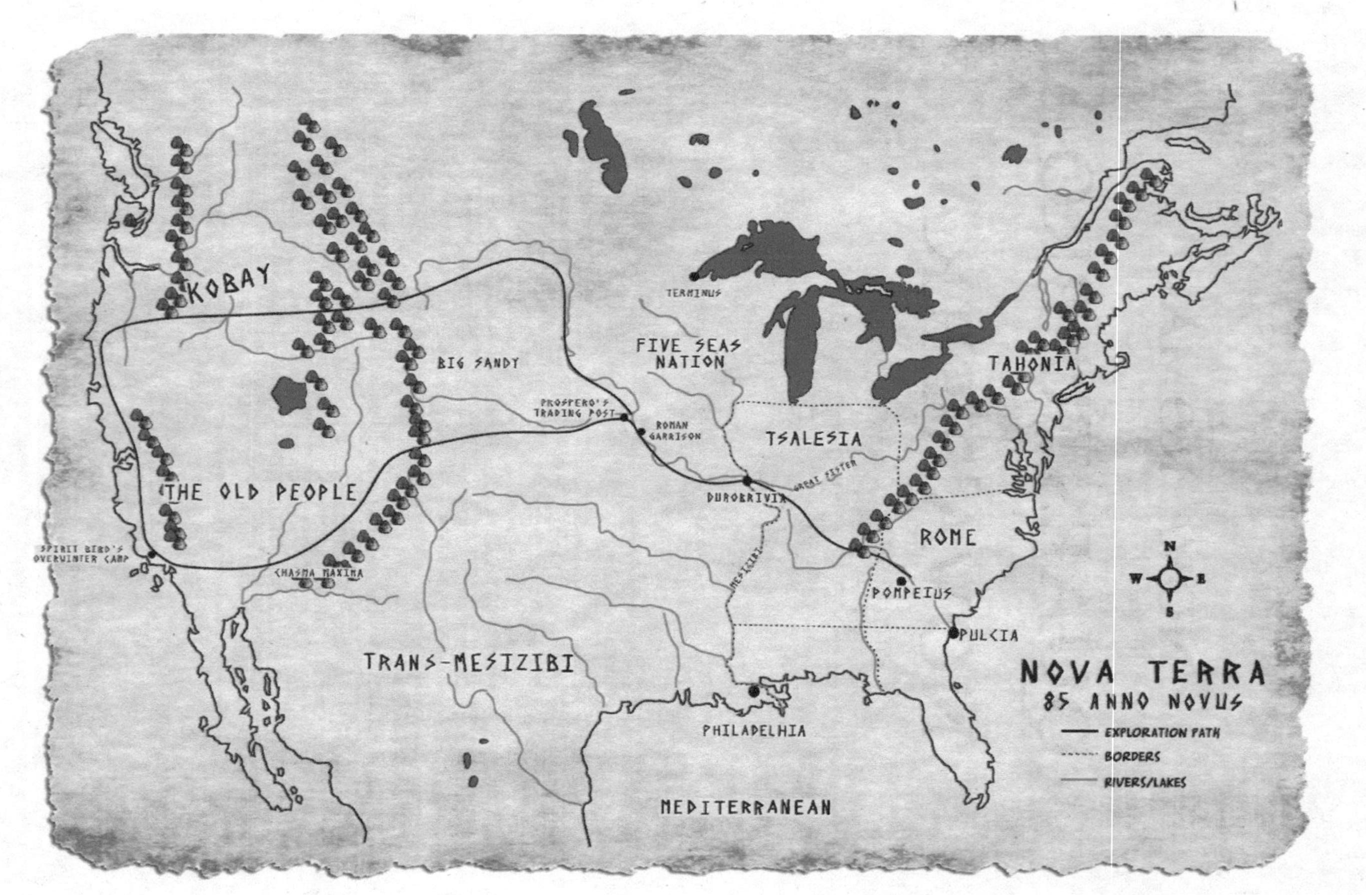

KOBAY
TAHONIA
BIG SANDY
FIVE SEAS NATION
TERMINUS
PROSPERO'S TRADING POST
ROMAN GARRISON
TSALESIA
GREAT RIVER
THE OLD PEOPLE
DUROBRIVIA
ROME
SPIRIT BIRD'S OVERWINTER CAMP
CHASMA MAXIMA
POMPEIUS
MESIZIBI
PULCIA
TRANS-MESIZIBI
PHILADELHIA
MEDITERRANEAN
NOVA TERRA
85 ANNO NOVUS
EXPLORATION PATH
BORDERS
RIVERS/LAKES
N
S
E
W

DRAMATIS PERSONAE

Expedition Members

Tribune Flavius Arcadius Tahonius: Leader of the expedition, former commander of the Second Tahonian Legion, where he held the rank of Legate. Arcadius is currently serving in the Roman Senate as Tribune of Mars from the province of Tahonia, an elected office in which he is representing the interests of the legions and legion veterans.

Centurion Ursus Tacitus: A silent giant, matched by no soldier in all the legions for size and strength: First Spear Centurion from the Second Tahonian Legion, now serving as Optio (second-in-command) of the expedition. Tacitus is a member of the Evocati, soldiers that have served one ten-year term in the legions and re-enlisted for a second decade. As a First Spear Centurion Tacitus was third in command of the Second Tahonian Legion, having commanded the prime cohort in the legion.

Legionary Manius Octavius Taurinus: A common legionary, Taurinus is known throughout the Second Tahonian for his tracking skills.

Legionary Faustus Marius: A highly skilled archer, Marius is a lighthearted man, always joking.

Legionary Marcus Albium Bubonius: An experienced physician and naturalist, keenly interested in the sciences as well as the flora and fauna of the West. Bubonius is also an Evocati, in his third decade in the legions.

Legionary Valerius Fortis Caninus: Caninus claims to be grandson of the Nova Roma hero Canis Magnus. He shares his grandfather's love for fighting, carousing, and womanizing.

Legionary Cominus Quintus Corvus: Corvus is one of the Roman Army's best slingers, and has been an instructor in that art for most of his decade of service.

Legionary Atius Lupus Minimus: Minimus, an accomplished forager, scrounger, and sneak thief, is imprisoned and awaiting punishment for theft when selected for the expedition.

Legionary Celerius Dorotheus: Often used as a messenger due to being the Second Tahonian's fastest long-distance runner. In a sprint, Dorotheus can outrun many a good horse.

Legionary Marcus Plancius Varus: The Second Tahonian's most creative craftsman, known for his endless tinkering and innovation with legion equipment.

Legionary Quintus Alces Sanctus: One of the Legion's staunchest Stoics, long-standing friend of the physician Bubonius, and also an Evocati in his third decade. A solid, experienced soldier and a deeply religious man.

Legionary Junius Marcus Aurelius: Younger than the common run of legionaries, Aurelius is a master swordsman, often carrying two light, slim gladii custom-made for him. Accomplished at fighting with either or both hands.

Joining the expedition in the Trans-Mesizibi

Julius Spotted Horse: The expedition's scout, hired shortly after crossing the Mesizibi. Spotted Horse is an unkempt, ragged, unsavory man, but is also a former cavalryman, an accomplished horseman, and has already crossed the continent several times.

Bright Water: A young Novan girl living in a small village near the western ocean. Bright Water, though young, has already gained some skill in healing and has extensive knowledge of plant life in the area.

Ochee: A young orphan boy in a warlike, xenophobic tribe in the northwestern forests.

<u>Romans</u>

Quintus Tiberius Pompeius: Great-grandson of Pompey Magnus, sitting Consul of Rome and the last of a great line. Pompeius suffers from an affliction of the lungs that makes him weak physically, but does not affect his mind; he has ambitions to bring the land of the Trans-Mesizibi under the eagles of Rome.

Gregorius Lucius Brutus: Grandson of Marcus Junius Brutus, Senator of Rome, who shares Consul Pompeius' vision of Western expansion.

Marius Falto: An informal leader of the Collegia of Rome, Falto is in fact little more than the leader of a gang of thugs. The Collegia control much of the transport of goods and the common crafts of the city of Rome, and Falto controls the Collegia.

Drusilla Secunda: Owner and operator of the Raven's Roost, a popular inn in Rome's Aventine district. The Raven's Roost is a gathering place for many of Rome's merchant class as well as members of the Roman government, which provides Secunda with a secondary trade as a broker of overheard information. She is the primary steward of Rome's careful balance between the nobles and the tradesmen.

Septimus Flavius: Master of the Trident, a large Roman freighter, regularly engaged in trade with the savage tribes on the east coast south of Mayan lands.

Legate Maximus Decimus Meridius: Commander of the Thirteenth Cisalpine Legion, selected by Rome to establish the first garrisons in the West.

Prospero: A fat, oily, garrulous man, Prospero is an ambitious merchant from Durobrivia, who moves west to the first Roman garrison to establish a trading post.

Publius Aquilus Aurelius and Antonius Caius Aurelius: Senators from the southern province of Cadovia, known as the Golden Twins. Staunchly opposed to Consul Pompeius' proposed western expansion.

Manius Gracchus Macrinus: A budding shipbuilder with many new ideas to revolutionize Roman naval architecture. A native of the port of Pulcia, Macrinus is struggling to find financial support for the construction of his first ships.

Remans

Marcus Aquilonius: Imperator of the Five Seas Nation, which borders Rome on the north. The Five Seas Nation holds most of the land around the five great inland seas, and also holds the prairie lands west of the Mesizibi as far south as Durobrivia.

General Hirtius Varus: Commander of the combined armies of the Five Seas Nation.

Marcus Malleolus: Legate and commander of the Third Legion of the Reman Army. Chosen to lead a party of Reman cavalry on a western expedition.

Artorius Atricolus: Legate and commander of all Reman forces in the Trans-Mesizibi.

Gaius Vorenus: Centurion, commander of a detachment of Roman cavalry assigned to the lands north of the Great Sister River.

Novans

Leaves-In-Wind: Elder of a tribe of Trans-Mesizibi nomads, widely respected for his intelligence, judgment and ability to think deeply about the ways of his people.

Yap: An elder and chief of the Kobay, an insular and warlike tribe of the northwestern forests.

Spirit Bird: Chief and shaman of a tribe near the western ocean. Grandfather of Bright Water.

Primus Long Dog: Elder brother of Julius Spotted Horse, and a primary leader of a band of plains nomads that is rapidly adapting to the arrival or Romans and Roman trade—particularly in transportation. Long Dog has aspirations to begin breeding horses for trade to the other plains tribes.

Mayans

Double Bird: King of the Mayan nation. An intemperate man, who is growing increasingly uncomfortable with Roman expansion and Roman trade with the savage tribes to the south of Mayan lands.

Smoke Monkey: Brother of the Mayan king and Mayan trade envoy to Rome.

Pacal: Smoke Monkey's son and interpreter, fluent in Latin and experienced in trade negotiations with Roman merchants.

PROLOGUE

Winter — Somewhere in the Trans — Mesizibi

Leaves-in-Wind was growing old.

His people had always lived along the river the Romans called the Great Sister, after spending the summer pursuing bison and other game in the hills and on the open prairie to the west. Leaves-in-Wind had seen over sixty winters spent in the same place, on the inside of a wide bend in the river the Romans called the Big Sandy. The last two winters he had seemed to feel the cold more keenly.

It was late. Outside the pale winter sun had already set, and the band's shelters were immersed in the deep winter night, under ice-chip stars. It was still and cold outside, but Leaves-in-Wind's shelter had a stout bison-skin cover and a good fire; he was warm.

The old man sat near his fire now, an old bear pelt wrapped around his skinny shoulders, his long gray braids hanging down on his chest. He picked at the last bits of meat left from a roast duck his son Gray Fox had killed that morning and brought to him as a gift. Leaves-in-Wind had always liked eating the big ducks with green heads. His son knew this. He was a good son.

Outside, the wind rattled the hide covering of Leaves-in-Wind's round lodge. Dark Eyes, his fourth wife, snorted in her sleep, rolled over and pulled her bison-skin robe more tightly around her thin shoulders. Leaves-in-Wind watched her dispassionately. In winter there was little else to do but eat and sleep, at least for old men and women; it was no coincidence that many of the band's children were born in the autumn, nine months after the prairie winters confined people to their lodges.

When Gray Fox had brought the duck, he mentioned again the men from the east. He was fascinated by the new people in the east. Most of the younger people of Leaves-in-Wind's band were fascinated by the strange people called Romans, the people that had appeared first in Leaves-in-Wind's generation.

Winter gave Leaves-in-Wind time with little to do. As old men do, he spent much of that time pondering his memories.

Forty summers before when Leaves-in-Wind was a young man, a trading party from the Tsalee, east of the great border river, had brought news of the people of Rome. "They come from some distant land across a great expanse of water," the Tsalee trade chief had told Leaves-in-Wind. "They have built a great city of wood and stone across the mountains to the east of the Tsalee lands, and are building another at the place where the two great rivers Mesizibi and Great Sister meet."

"How is it that they are able to do this?" Leaves-in-Wind asked.

"They use special tools," the Tsalee said. He drew a knife from his belt, but the knife was not of flint or obsidian. "This knife is a Roman knife."

Leaves-in-Wind examined it. "What is it made of?"

"Iron," the Tsalee trader explained. "It comes from the earth. The Romans know how to work iron. They know how to tame great beasts and make them work for them. They even ride on their great beast they call 'horse.'" The young man was enthusiastic about new things, as young men often are.

"A man from the north came here last summer," Leaves-in-Wind had said. "He spoke of more people that ride on beasts and work this 'iron,' men called Reman. Are they cousins of the Romans?"

"They are related, but they are not friends."

Leaves-in-Wind shook his head. "It is all very strange. Men should not change so."

"The Tsalee are now joining these men of Rome. We will be as one people with them and learn all of their ways." He held up the iron knife once more, then put it back in the leather sheathe he wore on his leather belt. "Rome is the future. Make no mistake about it."

"That is all very well," Leaves-in-Wind told him. "The Tsalee, we know who you are. You are people of towns, people of farms, and people of trade. For many generations you have come west to trade with the peoples of the plains, and we have both grown richer from the trade. We know these things. Our people, though, we are not people of towns or farms. We live on the prairie. We follow the game in summer, and live along the river in winter. We have no reason to join with these Romans. You Tsalee will become Romans, and that may be a good thing for you. It will be a good thing for us to remain as we are."

"That is your choice to make," the Tsalee trader had agreed. "But no people can remain as they are forever. Even the gods change in time."

That final statement bothered Leaves-in-Wind more than he cared to admit.

Many years after that, another trader had told of the great Roman town that sprang up on the confluence of the two great rivers. Leaves-in-Wind was still young enough then for a long walk, so he and two others from his band walked from their summer camp down the Big Sandy and followed the Great Sister River from there down to the junction. There they talked a local villager into rafting them across to the eastern bank where none of them had ever been before. It was then that they saw the Roman town.

It was as the Tsalee said. Great lodges of stone and wood lay in neat rows, separated by pathways paved with flat stones. A great road of the flat stones ran away from the town to the east, and another to the south. Most amazing, in the center of the town stood a huge lodge made of stone, with great pillars on the front supporting an overhanging angled roof. People of all sorts were gathered in the open area before the building trading and arguing. Leaves-in-Wind traded his necklace of carved antler disks for a Roman knife of iron. A passing Tsalee who spoke a few words of their tongue told them the name of the great lodge: "That is the capitol building of the province of Transalpine Tsalesia," he explained. "The Provincial Council meets there."

His words meant nothing to the men from the prairie. They had their own councils, but they met rarely, and had no set place to do so. Only the Romans had such strange customs. "When we go into council, we meet under the sky," Leaves-in-Wind observed. "Only under the sky of Man-Above can the People find true wisdom."

"The Romans think otherwise," one of the other men pointed out. "And the Romans' gods give them the knowledge to make tools of iron and the wisdom to build great towns of stone. They have many gods—Jupiter, the father of gods, Mars, their god of war, Vulcan, the god who taught them to make iron. You can see for yourself the knowledge they have gained from their gods. Who are we, after all, to question this?"

To this, Leaves-in-Wind had no answer. He spent the day walking through the city, watching its people. The Romans never seemed to stop moving. They set up small structures to trade goods for small silver and gold disks that seemed to have no use. One man walked about the city carrying pieces of rolled-up deerskin, stopping periodically to look at them and shout at the passerby; a Tsalee told him the man was passing news of various events to the crowds.

In between the stalls and buildings, children tumbled about, shouting, playing games, and chasing each other about. *So many children*, Leaves-in-Wind thought.

In all his days, Leaves-in-Wind had never seen so many people. He was a man of the prairie, of the wide-open spaces west of the river, and the crowds made him uncomfortable.

As the day drew to a close, they returned to the river and crossed back to the west on another raft, this one carrying another trading party. The Tsalee traders headed off to the south, while Leaves-in-Wind led his people towards the Big Sandy River.

"The men of Rome are bringing many new things to the country," one of the men said.

Leaves-in-Wind was already known as a wise man in those days, well-regarded for his ability to think deeply about the ways of their small band and the other people of the prairie. "It is very strange," he said, "that men could live so. Do you remember all the hard edges of their town, and all the sharp corners? That is not how men are meant to live. On the prairie there is the roundness. One day is as the next. The sun rises and sets. Summer always gives way to winter and then summer returns." He motioned as he spoke, his hands describing great arcs in the air. "The great herds of bison go south and north and south again. The birds fly south and north and south again. The lodges of the people are round, like the day, like the year. Everything that there is in the world is a great circle. That is how Man-Above shaped the world. That is how things should be."

"That is how things will always be for us," one of the others said confidently. "These Romans, they are welcome to their towns by the river. There is nothing they will want on our hills and prairies."

"That is true," Leaves-in-Wind agreed. "But there are so *many* of them."

Now, many years later, Leaves-in-Wind was beginning to discover that the man was wrong. Men of Rome, with their new Tsalee allies, were appearing west of the great river, some afoot, some on horses.

The old ways were changing. Leaves-in-Wind did not know what would happen next.

Pompeius — 81 Anno Novus — Januarius

In the eighty years since the Founding, Pompeius had grown into a substantial city, easily the equal of anything the powerful Mayan nation had produced. The cream of Roman society, transplanted to a new world, wasted no time in reshaping that world.

The Nova Roman capital was the crowning jewel of the Republic reborn.

Set in the heart of the primary province of Rome, Pompeius now encompassed all four hills of the great meadows along the Tiber River, originally discovered by the fabled hero Canis Magnus. The four hills now had names — the Capitoline hill was the site of the original buildings, and the expanded Senate and Council of Plebs buildings still stood there, along with the thriving Forum and the majority of the city's temples to the various Roman gods and goddesses. The Senate building had grown into a massive edifice of white marble quarried from the hills in western Lustria. Massive white pillars supported the portico above white marble steps in the front of the massive, gleaming structure. The Senate building was the pride of Pompeius, and travelers from all of the provinces made an effort to view it.

The Council of Plebs met in an equally impressive building next to the Senate. Instead of white marble, the Council building was built of granite trimmed with hardwoods from the Tsalesian Alps. On the opposite side of the Forum lay a smaller building constructed of varied stones from the several provinces; this building housed the Consulate offices and meeting areas.

To the south of the Capitoline hill lay the Catonian hill, covered mostly with the houses and villas of the city's more prosperous residents, including most of the Senators and many representatives to the House of Plebs. The Aventine hill lay to the east, a mixture of family dwellings, workshops, inns, taverns and small, household industries; larger industries, including such diverse elements as forging, tanning and carpentry, and the Collegia that controlled them occupied the Servian Hill to the west.

A massive and beautiful wall of white stone surrounded the four hills, with heavy oak gates at north, west and east; the traditional soldier's camp, the Field of Mars, lay between the city and the Tiber. Farms surrounded the city and spread out along the paved roads that formed the arteries of the new Republic.

In the year 81 Anno Novus, the great-grandson of Pompey Magnus ascended to the Consul's chair of Nova Roma, and set the Republic on a course that would reach across a continent.

Consul Quintus Tiberius Pompeius was a small man, thin, with his Novan mother's thick black hair and his Roman father's quick intellect. His body was not robust; a childhood affliction of the lungs had left him pale and unthrifty, dependent on a cane to assist him in walking about the city. But the weakness of his body in no way impaired Quintus Pompeius' mind or ambition — or his vision for the future of the Republic.

"We stand here in the Senate building of a Republic founded

by my great-grandfather and his companions," he announced to the assembled Senate and the Council of Plebs on the day of his ascension to full Consul. "Those brave men set out in ships to sail to another land, a land called Hispania, there to raise an army to confront the would-be tyrant Julius Caesar who descended on old Rome with an army of his own. Instead, the gods themselves brought them here, to the new world. Who can say why the gods act as they do? But clearly no other force could be responsible for so great an event, and with the mandate of Jupiter, Neptune and Mars so clearly made, Pompey and the others set out to form a new republic. Old Rome may have fallen into tyranny and ruin, but not here! Oh no, not here, not us! Our republic thrives, and expands through the peaceful avenues of trade and enterprise."

"We stand in a city named for Pompey Magnus, surrounded by people brought under the eagles of Rome by my grandfather, General Gnaeus Pompey Novus. We stand in a Senate chamber that, in the four score years since our ancestors came to these shores, has seen the likes of Marcus Porcius Cato, Ursinus Quadrus Tranquilus and Lucinius Cassius Tahonius seated in its rows."

"I stand before you, Senators and Councilors, you who represent not only the province of Rome within which our capital rests but also the provinces. Among those proud lands are Attepia of the forested hills to our west; Lustria, that vast land of forests, hills, and marshes to the south; Tahonia, that place of rivers and forests to our north, stretching as far as the Three Sisters. Among the provinces are Cisalpine Tsalesia and Transalpine Tsalesia, and our newest province of Cadovia, which proceeds from Tsalesia south to the sea and west to include the great delta of the Mesizibi."

"To our north, in the lands around inland seas the people of that region call the Mother of Waters and the Father of Waters and the smaller seas, called the Three Sisters, lays the Reman Five Seas Nation. That country was founded by enemies of Pompey Magnus and the Optimate Senators that we count as our founders, and they remain unfriendly even now."

"On our western border lays the great river Mesizibi. Beyond that border are open lands peopled with nomadic tribesman, and vast herds of bison, and the people of our western provinces speak of mountains far greater than our own Tsalesian Alps. They speak of great deserts, and a western ocean beyond the mountains."

"It is the destiny of Rome to expand to that far ocean, to the northern forests, to the deserts in the south. During my consulship I propose to begin to realize this destiny. I propose to embark the people of Rome on a journey of discovery that will see Roman cities and Roman citizens in every corner of this vast continent."

His speech had been greeted with polite but cautious applause. All of the Senators and Councilors knew, as did the Consul, of the two stumbling blocks to Rome's manifest destiny: The Five Seas Nation to the north, and to the south, the great cities of the Maya.

The only way the people of Nova Roma had to expand was west. That meant crossing the great river Mesizibi.

His speech finished, Pompeius yielded the floor to the Lesser Consul, who was to preside over a debate on funding for yet another trade mission to the Maya. Pompeius had already made his opinion known on the matter—he was not in favor of spending the Senate's gold on yet another negotiation when trade was already brisk and required no government assistance. That being so, he picked up his cane and made his way slowly towards the Senate doors, intending to spend a few moments in the late-winter sunshine. The weather would grow hot and humid all too soon, even here in the hills above the low country near the coast; Pompeius meant to enjoy the mild winter weather as much as possible. As he made his slow, halting way out of the Senate building, he could hear the bustle of the Forum already about the business of the city.

Outside, he found a tall, lean man in a Senate robe waiting. "Consul," Senator Gregorius Lucius Brutus greeted him.

"Senator," the Consul replied. Fifteen years older than the Consul and far more sophisticated in business matters, Brutus was likewise the scion of a proud old Roman family, and in the new world his family was also a wealthy one; Brutus' grandfather, Marcus Junius Brutus, had made a small mountain of gold on the initial trading arrangements with the Tahona to the north and the Maya to the south. Senator Brutus was one of the Consul's most trusted advisors on trade issues; Pompeius was a firm believer in the principle that success in a field of endeavor led to credibility.

"A few moments of your time, if you would, Consul?" Brutus asked. "Share a jug of wine with me, perhaps?"

Pompeius nodded to the older man. Brutus's grandfather had earned a reputation for brusqueness and ill temper; he had been widely known as a sour, unpleasant man. His grandson Gregorius was his opposite in every way. Senator Brutus was friendly, extroverted, generous, and good-natured.

Grapes were still unknown in the new world, but several vintners were now producing passable wines from blackberries, persimmons and even the petals of the common yellow flowers that sprouted willy-nilly in every clearing. The inn Brutus chose was known for a wine produced from those flowers and flavored with the fruit of a tree the people of the southern province of Lustria called 'asimina.'

Brutus and Pompeius took seats at a low table in front of the inn. The two men sat quietly for a moment while the innkeeper, recognizing the Consul and the Senator, hurried out of the back of his shop to greet them.

As Brutus exchanged pleasantries with the innkeeper, and exchanged some coin for a jug of wine, the Consul sat and watched the activity about them.

Consul Pompeius loved the Forum.

The heart of Nova Roma's capital was always a busy place, with business starting early in the morning and lasting until well after dark. The broad, open, stone-paved plaza was surrounded by shops and inns, with the temple of Mercury on the eastern side, the temple of Concordia on the west and the Senate and House of Plebs building on the north.

When the innkeeper was finished fawning over the Consul and the Senator, and they were finally left in peace with a jug of wine and two fired clay cups, Brutus looked keenly at Pompeius.

"I was very interested to hear you speak of the western lands," Brutus said. "Very interested indeed. It is a topic that has been much on my own mind of late."

"Has it now?"

"Quite so. Consul, have you ever thought of how best to approach those lands? Our westernmost province of Transalpine Tsalesia extends as far as the Mesizibi, and the Tsalesian people of that region do not explore much past the western bank. A few traders occasionally go forth, but never more than a few days walk from the river; the plains nomads have little desire or wherewithal for trade."

"Yes, I have learned as much from the Tsalesian Senators. Lupus Rubieum Parum told me much of those great plains past the river. He says they are vast, empty grasslands, peopled only with a few bands of nomadic huntsmen."

"Just so. And there are great mountains beyond the prairies as well, so I'm told; and eventually another ocean. There is another great river that joins the Mesizibi at Durobrivia; the locals call it the Great Sister."

"And more still than that," Pompeius guessed.

"The Five Seas Nation share a border with those lands as well," Brutus reminded the Consul.

"A fact that is never far from my mind," Pompeius admitted. "But how to encourage trade into that area? There are so few people, and by all accounts the people that live on the plains are very primitive; they grow no crops, they produce no goods. There is no reason for trade missions to the area, and we know nothing of what resources may be available or even what those lands may look like—plains, rivers, or mountains."

"Exactly so. That, Consul, is why I propose to find out."

Pompeius looked at the Senator. "How?"

"A party of exploration, of course. You may know my cousin, Flavius Arcadius Tahonius, formerly the commander of the Second Tahonian Legion? He now serves as Tribune of Mars from that province."

The Consul nodded. "I know him by reputation. A distinguished soldier."

"I propose to approach him about leading a party of soldiers on a mission of exploration. I would of course support the mission financially, but if soldiers are to carry out the mission, the Consulate has to agree and officially prepare their orders."

"And is the Tribune willing?"

"He is my cousin," Brutus nodded. "I have known him since we were small boys. I am confident he would jump at the chance to etch his name in the scrolls of our history with a mission like this. Further, I am of the opinion that the best soldiers of Nova Roma's legions would compete for the chance to go on the journey."

"We cannot authorize any soldiers proceeding west of the Mesizibi without the advice and consent of the Senate. I would recommend you present the matter to the full Senate in the next session, but I think you know I will speak in support."

Brutus smiled. "I had hoped you would, Consul. I think this mission very important; either we make use of those lands, or the Remans will. Or, maybe, even the Mayans. Better we do it, neh?"

"Of course. I think the Senators from the western provinces will agree enthusiastically. They have the most exposure should the Remans move into the plains across the Mesizibi. I wonder why they have not yet brought the matter before the Senate themselves?"

"They are only two, three generations into the Republic," Brutus said. "We two, you and I, we are of the old Roman blood. Well, mostly," he amended; his own mother was half Roman, half Tahonian. "My grandfather was Marcus Junius Brutus, Senator of Rome. Your great-grandfather was Pompey Magnus, General and Consul of Rome. We are descended from the original party to come here from Rome, and our families have long histories in the old Republic. What seems obvious to us, the native-born are still learning."

"One hopes they will learn quickly." The Consul thought for a moment, mentally reviewing the Senate's schedule for the days ahead; he carried it effortlessly in his head. "Day after tomorrow," he said, "we will put the matter before the Senate."

Terminus — Capital of the Five Seas Nation

The Five Seas Nation was a land built on iron, furs, and fish. The inhabitants called themselves 'Reman' and revered the names of the fabled centurions Lucius Vorenus and Titus Pullo, their founders, and almost every Reman claimed an ancestor among them or one of the other Roman cavalrymen that had journeyed to a Tsalee town in the forest. It was impossible, of course, even had the original Romans had all of the stamina of Apollo, but it was part of Reman legend all the same.

The Five Seas Nation capital was known throughout Terra Nova as The City on the Edge of the Forest. A day's march north of the westernmost reach of the great inland sea known as the Mother of Waters, the city had sprung from a Tsalee town that had been the final destination of the Roman renegades Pullo, Vorenus and their detachment of cavalry, after their flight from the Battle of Pompeius.

That town was gone now, swallowed by the first Reman city. The original party of Caesarian loyalists had given it the name Terminus, signifying the end of their journey. The end of their journey had, however, been the beginning of a second great nation north of the one founded by the Optimates—Caesar's enemies.

Pullo, Vorenus and their men brought two world-changing things to the Tsalee town: Iron and horses. The hills east of Terminus were the source of an ample supply of iron ore. The big German-bred horses of the Roman cavalry adapted well to the cold, wet, forested environs—environs which, over several generations, had given rise to a more compact, shaggier line of equines more suited to the forests. Now tough, shaggy Reman ponies were sought after by travelers in those regions as well as explorers bound for the vast forests to the north.

Together, with their horses and their embryonic iron industry, the Roman men had founded a nation that now extended past the Mother of Waters to the Father of Waters, the long, phallic sea to the southeast, and the Three Sisters, the smaller seas to the east of the Father. The Five Seas Nation held the land on both sides of the Father of Waters south to its tip, and all the land north of the Three Sisters.

East of the Three Sisters lay the Nova Roman province of Tahonia. The boundary between the Five Seas Nation and Nova Roma was, in that region, somewhat undefined; in recent years there had been some border scrapping between the legions of both nations.

To the west of Terminus lay largely undiscovered country. To the north lay only the vast boreal forest.

Now, eighty years after the arrival of the Romans in the area, Terminus was the center of the northern iron trade. While the inhabitants were almost of pure Novan stock—the Roman blood of the founders having been diluted a great deal—the Five Seas people took great pride in their civilization, their laws, and their Roman-styled culture. They spoke a patois of Latin and Tsalee that was fast becoming the standard language spoken from the Mother of Waters to the delta of the Mesizibi.

Only in the southernmost reaches of the Five Seas Nation's territory was there much land suitable for farming, but the Remans never went hungry. The vast northern forests were teeming with game and, more valuable still, with furbearers. Pelts of lynx, mink, marten, fox, beaver, and fisher-cat were highly valued by the people to the south, not only Roman but Mayan as well. Fleets of Reman fishing boats worked the Five Seas, and dried fish was another valuable commodity.

Last but not least, there was iron.

Tools of iron and weapons of steel were the Five Seas Nation's primary source of hard currency and trade goods from the south. In years prior, the reputation of Reman iron and steel had suffered by comparison to the goods produced by Nova Roman blacksmiths, but along with a marginally republican government the Five Seas people had also developed an unusually competent network of agents within Nova Roma, and the Roman techniques for steelmaking leaked north.

Now, if a tribesman from the prairies or mountains to the west wanted a good steel dagger or gladius, he had more than one option as to where to obtain one.

For ten years, Marcus Aquilonius had served as Imperator of the Five Seas people, the fourth to hold that title since the Imperatorship of the famed First Spear Centurion Titus Pullo, soldier of legendary Caesar, formerly of the 13th Gallic Legion.

While technically an elected position, the Five Seas Nation had no written constitution that limited how long the Imperator could serve, or that limited his powers; the position amounted to an elected monarch, chosen for an unnamed term by the Council of Chiefs, whose members were made up by the various village and town chiefs. In practice, the Imperator served until the Council turned him out; in practice, he served for life, or until he weakened enough to be overthrown. Old Titus Pullo had held the post until his eighty-first year; Aquilonius planned to surpass that record.

It was a system that combined a large portion of anarchy with a touch of totalitarianism, but for the last eighty years, it had served the people living around the Five Seas.

Marcus Aquilonius was the grandson of Octavian Suetonius, the Roman cavalryman and Caesarian loyalist who had brought his father's knowledge of ironworking to Terminus. The Roman blood was diluted now; Aquilonius was a tall man as his grandfather had been before him, but his ruddy face, high cheekbones and long black hair revealed his Novan blood.

As Imperator, he had offices in the large wooden Imperium buildings, on the floor above the large chamber where the Council of Chiefs met. This morning the office's window shutters were thrown open to admit the late winter sunshine despite the usual Januarius cold, a cold which was only partly held at bay by the fire roaring in a stone hearth near the Imperator's desk.

But if the Remans were accustomed to anything, they were accustomed to snow and cold.

Aquilonius enjoyed the sights and sounds of the Suetonian Furnaces, a league away, the massive ironworking district originally founded by his grandfather. The glow of the furnaces and the hammering of better than a hundred smiths formed the beating heart of Terminus. Reman wagons took the products of the furnaces as far as the Five Seas Nation's ports on the upper Mesizibi, where Reman ships transported tools and weapons of Reman steel as far as the Mayan cities, far to the south. Trade with Nova Roma was less brisk—the Romans had an ample iron and steel industry of their own—but Reman furs were well received in Nova Roma, so as tense as relations were at times, trade with Pompeius and the various Roman provinces still went on.

The furnaces lay to the east of the Imperium building. Aquilonius turned and walked across his offices, all the way to the western side of the building; his offices were expansive. On the opposite side, Aquilonius had a fair view indeed, of the rooftops of Terminus' residential areas, of the Forum to the north, and to the west, beyond the city walls, the vast expanse of boreal forest.

It was unfortunate, Aquilonius thought, that Terminus formed essentially the western boundary of the Five Seas Nation. That, however, was about to change. Aquilonius was about to make the western expansion of the Five Seas Nation the first priority of his term as Imperator.

He knew the attempt at expansion would cause conflict with the Romans to the south. Truth be told, he looked forward to it. Rome had had their way on the continent long enough, Aquilonius maintained to all who would listen; it was past time for the people of the Five Seas to be ascendant.

ONE
PLANS

Soldiers of all ranks love to tell stories; the legions have a saying that tales grow wings whenever more than two soldiers gather. A favorite topic of storytelling among the legions of Nova Roma, even those from my northeastern province east of the Three Sisters, was the vast territory beyond the great western river Mesizibi.

Those lands were rumored to be not only vast but forbidding. Rumors and tall tales popular in the legions described enormous expanses of prairie peopled by scattered tribes of nomads; strange beasts, empty deserts, mountains larger by far than the familiar Tsalesian Alps. But as much as the legions spread rumors, nobody ever seemed to have been to those lands first-hand. I personally spoke with one legionary from Transalpine Tsalesia who claimed to have crossed the Mesizibi and traveled a short distance up the river known as the Great Sister, and he claimed there were regular ferries across the Mesizibi for trading parties, but when the great adventure to the west began, that was all the information I had at my command. What lay beyond the Mesizibi was, for the most part, a mystery—one I was to be tasked to unravel, with a small party of men and a few bags of supplies.

—Flavius Arcadius Tahonius' Trans-Mesizibi Diaries

Pompeius

Flavius Arcadius was always a little nervous meeting his cousin, the Senator of Nova Roma from the province of Tahonia, in his official capacity. Even after his election as the Tribune of Mars from his home province of Tahonia, he regarded the Nova Roman Senate chambers with some awe. "Fitting," his cousin Brutus once told him, laughing as he spoke, "that you should be filled with awe—you are just a Tahonian farm boy, after all."

Being dragged before the Consul for a personal audience did not do Arcadius' nerves any good, either.

"Relax," Gregorius Brutus told Arcadius for the tenth time that morning—this time at the door of the Consul's modest villa on the westernmost hill of Pompeius, in the Catonian neighborhood.

"Easy enough for you to say," Arcadius replied. "You deal with these people on a daily basis, cousin. Not me."

The Tribune was well turned out for the meeting. His bronze breastplate shone like the sun; he wore his best Tribune's helmet with its tall fore-and-aft brush of black horsehair. He had spent the evening before polishing his equipment, oiling leather, and even cleaning his soldier's boots. Nervousness aside, he knew he cut a good figure; he was tall, lean, with closely-cropped black hair only beginning to show a few strands of gray as he entered his thirty-ninth year. His face spoke eloquently of his mostly Novan blood—ruddy, high-cheekboned, strong; but his nature, his personal bearing, his training, were all Roman.

Even Brutus was surprised when the Consul himself answered the knock at the door. Consul Pompeius wore only a simple robe of deep red, and he was smiling as he leaned on his cane in the doorway. "Friend Brutus," he greeted them, "and this must be Flavius Arcadius Tahonius, soldier of Rome, legate and Tribune of Mars." He shook

Arcadius' hand warmly. "This is a pleasure indeed. Your reputation as a soldier precedes you."

"The honor is mine, sir," Arcadius said. He saluted, then took off his helmet and bowed.

"No need to be so formal, Tribune," the Consul said, smiling. "This is just a friendly discussion. Come in, both of you. I have servants preparing some refreshments."

The men proceeded through the house into the open atrium in the center. Arcadius admired the setting; a small fountain bubbled into a pool in one corner, and the square area was bordered by several small trees and shrubs. A small stone table surrounded by benches sat in the center of the area. Several platters rested on the table, along with three handmade wooden cups and a flask of wine.

"Baked songbirds," Consul Pompeius said, indicating one of the platters, "dried persimmons, and fresh-baked bread. Please, be seated, help yourselves."

They did so. Arcadius was not fond of dried persimmons, but he had a soldier's fondness for fresh bread. The small loaves were still warm from the kitchen.

"Tribune Arcadius," the Consul began without preamble, "I'm sure you are curious as to the nature of this summons."

Arcadius swallowed a bit of bread. "I admit I am, Consul."

"Are you familiar with the western lands, beyond the Mesizibi?"

"I have never been there, sir. I have heard tales of those lands. I have served alongside soldiers from Transalpine Tsalesia, and I have listened as they told of the great plains beyond the rivers, and of mountains beyond those."

"And, supposedly, there is a western ocean which lies even beyond those far mountains."

"Even so, cousin," Arcadius agreed with the Senator.

"What would you say to leading a small party of men to explore those regions?"

Arcadius almost jumped off the bench in surprise. "Me, sir?"

"You," Pompeius chuckled. "Your cousin was most persuasive in his recommendation of you for the task."

Arcadius shot a look at Gregorius Brutus, who was wearing an expression of sternly repressed amusement. "He must have been, sir."

"You have led a legion," Consul Pompeius went on. "Soldiering in a time of peace makes it difficult for a soldier's service to stand out, but you've managed. Your troops had the lowest rate of disciplinary actions of any of the sixteen legions of the Nova Roman army. You also had the lowest rates of desertions and unsanctioned absences. In the one action you've seen, that scrap along the border with the Five Seas Nation, you and your men performed admirably. Your service was outstanding enough that the veterans and soldiers that reside in your home province saw fit to elect you Tribune of Mars."

Arcadius could only nod.

"I was thinking," Pompeius said, "to assemble an expedition consisting of one man from each of the sixteen legions. For political reasons…" He stopped. Arcadius was frowning. "You disagree with that idea, Tribune?"

"I must, sir," Arcadius shook his head. He took a deep breath, then went on. "With respect, Consul; as a Senator and Consul, your own career has been distinguished indeed, a credit to your family line, but sir, you don't know soldiers. Such a group would be a matching of strangers. This expedition… If I am to do this," and he admitted silently to himself that the idea excited him, "I must be allowed to select my own men. I would prefer to take men that have served together before."

"Men from your old legion?"

"Yes, cousin, I would start there."

"Sixteen men?"

"No more than a dozen," Arcadius said, thinking hard as he spoke; he had several candidates in mind already. "A dozen men. Two dozen horses. A team of bison and a freight wagon for supplies, and two teamsters to handle it."

"There are no roads beyond the Mesizibi. We do not even know if there are any ferries large enough to freight a wagon and team across."

"Then we will leave the team and wagon there, at Durobrivia, Consul," Arcadius said, "but even traveling to the Mesizibi is a considerable journey in itself. There are good roads through the Tsalesian Alps to Durobrivia, but it is a long journey even so."

After eighty years in the new world, horses were still scarce enough to be highly valuable. "You must have two horses per man?" Brutus knew he would be paying for those horses and his resources, while considerable, were not unlimited.

"I would prefer three per man, in truth, but two should suffice; such a journey may well be harder on horses than on the men. Each man will ride one horse and lead the second, which will carry a lighter load of personal gear and supplies. Alternating the mounts will give each horse one day of relative ease in two."

"He makes sense," the Consul told the Senator.

"What would be my goal, sir?"

"Your physical goal is the western ocean. You are to find at least one route through the plains and the mountains to the sea, and to identify navigable rivers en route. Your secondary goals are to make a record of the usable resources, flora, fauna, and peoples of the lands you will pass through."

Arcadius sat thinking for a few silent moments, while his cousin regarded him keenly. "You're already thinking of the men you will bring on this journey, are you not, cousin?"

Arcadius smiled. "I am," he admitted. "I have several men in mind even now."

"Prepare orders for them," the Consul ordered. "Senator Brutus will see to the horses, the bison and wagon, and your supplies. I want you to start west as soon as practical."

Terminus

"Imperator?"

Marcus Aquilonius looked up to see his personal clerk. "What is it?"

"General Hirtius Varus is here, sir."

"Send him in."

The senior general in overall command of the Five Seas Nation's four legions of infantry and six cohorts of cavalry swept into the room and saluted.

Aquilonius leaned back in his hard wooden chair and regarded the General. The tall, lean soldier wore the uniform of Reman army officers; a polished iron breastplate over a thick black leather tunic, heavy quilted cloth trousers, heavy black leather boots and a long cape of black leather trimmed at the collar with wolf fur. The general held his polished iron helmet with the tall fore-and-aft crest of raven feathers in his left hand. His high-cheekboned, bronzed face was expressionless, but his black eyes shone with intelligence. He had been the top man in the Reman army for ten years now, and had made a name for himself by organizing a series of raids and forays in the forests of northern Tahonia, with the goal of pushing Roman troops out of the region. It had yielded mixed results: The Tahonian legions were hard, tough men, wise in the ways of those forests. But he had done well enough to gain the Imperator's attention, and that had been his key to ascending to the role he held now: Commander of all the Reman army.

"General," Marcus Aquilonius greeted him. "Please, please, take a seat."

"Sir." The soldier sat on the edge of a wooden chair across from the large table that served the Imperator as a desk. He sat upright, straight-backed.

"Will you have some water? Some Roman wine, perhaps?"

"Thank you, Imperator, but I am not thirsty."

"As you wish." The Imperator leaned forward, placing his elbows on the table before him and peered keenly at the General. "What do you know of the lands to our west? Not the immediate west, mind you. The plains and beyond."

"Very little, sir," Varus replied. He shifted in this chair. "Nobody does. Our trade ships work the Mesizibi, as far south as the Roman port of Durobrivia, and even farther. There is a rapidly expanding port town on the great delta where the Mesizibi meets the sea. The Romans are calling it Philadelphia after some ancient city known in the histories of old Rome. Our trade missions to the Maya go to that port. Some few of our traders work the plains on the western side of the Mesizibi and some way up the river the Romans call the Great Sister, but there are no organized missions; just irregular traders operating on their own."

"And you have spoken to these traders?"

"I do strive to stay informed of events on our borders, sir."

"It is those borders that concern me," Aquilonius mused. "Nova Roma expands by the year, it seems. Their province of Tahonia lies to our east. Their Tsalesian provinces and the province of Attepia borders us to the south. Now they hold the southern provinces of Lustria and Cadovia."

"But for north and west, they have us contained," Varus agreed. "But sir, to the north is a vast land indeed—and rich in game, furs and fish."

"And to the west?"

General Varus shrugged. "We know of those lands only at second and third-hand, sir. The tales are several: Vast prairies. Tribes of nomads. Great herds of bison, of which we obtain all we need from the Roman breeders. Nothing, sir, of much use."

"Except another border along which the Romans can hem us in," the Imperator pointed out.

"This is so."

"We can do nothing about the south and east," Aquilonius continued. "At least not in the foreseeable future."

The General replied with a single Tsalesian word common in the northern groups of the Tsalee League, a single word that, roughly translated into Latin, meant 'it can't be helped': "T'achee." It was an unquestioning acceptance of Fate, common among the Reman people, strangely typical of the people of the cold northern lands.

"It is bad enough that we have no access to the Atlantic, except via the Mesizibi, through Roman territory. I am determined that the Five Seas Nation will not be further hemmed in, General, neither to north nor west. To that end, I want you to send an expedition west, to explore those plains and what lies beyond."

Hirtius Varus had expected just such a statement; his own thoughts frequently ran across similar lines. "Sir," he began, "I would make some recommendations, if I may."

The Imperator nodded. "I had hoped you would. Go on."

"One would think to send a considerable force west," Varus

began. "This has been the object of considerable discussion among the commanders of several of the legions. Legate Malleolus in particular claims it prudent to send no less than a full cohort of infantry, accompanied by cavalry scouts."

"You disagree," Aquilonius said. He had not obtained his current position without a facility for reading people.

"I do, sir." He sat for a moment. "Sir, I would send no more than a small party of cavalry. Ten men, perhaps; I would certainly send no more than twenty."

"Explain."

The General leaned forward in his chair. "Sir, this would not be—*will* not be, I should say—a military expedition. We do not as yet seek conquest. Indeed, conquest may not be necessary, if those lands are as empty as rumor would have it. No, Imperator, this would be an exploratory mission, through empty, unknown lands. The men will not be able to carry enough supplies to sustain them for a journey that will take months, if not years. They will have to hunt and fish along the way."

"Granted."

"The expedition will have to be led by a man capable of establishing relations with any people he meets along the way. He will have to be someone familiar with mapping new territories, so he can return with information useful for follow-up missions. A man of legate's rank, at least, an experienced man, a man of determination and grit. I have a man in mind; in fact I just named him: Marcus Malleolus, commander of the Third. He is a solid man, if a bit inflexible. But he will follow your orders, Imperator, even to the ends of the earth."

"Well enough. Arms? What say you?"

"Swords. Weapons for hunting—bows or javelins. No more than

that. There is no reason, sir, to weigh them down with arms of war; the journey will be hard enough."

The Imperator sat for a few moments, thinking. "Very well," he said. "See to choosing the men and equipment yourself. I wish them to leave as soon as weather permits. Their goal is the headwaters of the Great Sister, then through to the western ocean. I intend to lay claim to all lands north of the Great Sister for the Reman people."

General Varus stood and saluted. "As you command, Imperator."

The Reman military was nothing if not efficient. Five days later, ten Reman cavalrymen under the command of Legate Marcus Malleolus departed from Terminus, bound for the Roman city of Durobrivia.

Pompeius — the kalends of Martias

The sky in the east was barely showing signs of the coming dawn when the men gathered outside Pompeius' gate, in a field next to the Attepian Way. It was a cold morning; spring was still only a promise. Breath plumed from the men's mouths as they spoke softly among themselves, and in the dark sky, the last stars still glittered.

Senator Brutus and Consul Pompeius walked down the hill from the Attepian Gate to see the expedition off, and found Tribune Arcadius in conversation with an enormous man in a centurion's uniform.

Brutus looked at the centurion with some amazement. The man was a bronze giant. He had a wide-jawed, high-cheekboned face with a hooked, aquiline nose. He held his helmet with its side-to-side brush of red bristles in one enormous hand, uncovering a head of close-cropped, raven-black hair. His shoulders looked as broad as a bull bison's above a chest that may well have been chiseled from a block of granite, with very little of the block removed. His arms were huge, bulging with muscle. The man towered over his superior, being well over a head taller than Tribune Arcadius.

As the Senator and Consul approached, Arcadius looked up from a scroll he was reading. "Ah," the Tribune said, saluting. "Good morning, Consul—Senator."

"Good morning indeed," Consul Pompeius replied. "Senator Brutus and I wanted to see you off."

"Good of you, sir," Arcadius said.

"Would you be as kind as to introduce your men?"

"Of course." Arcadius barked an order, and the men gathered in formation.

"Men—soldiers of Rome. You know on whose authority you are here, but I am honored to present the men themselves in person: Consul Quintus Tiberius Pompeius, Consul of Nova Roma, and Senator Gregorius Lucius Brutus, our patron and benefactor."

In unison, the soldiers rendered the sharp Nova Roman salute: The right fist to the heart, then the right arm snapped smartly outward to display an empty hand, palm downward.

"Consul—Senator ," Arcadius went on, indicating the giant that stood at attention now, helmet in place, in front of the rank of men. "This is my second-in-command, First Spear Centurion of the Evocati, Ursus Tacitus." This was a man who had spent more than the usual decade in the Army; *Evocati* indicated a man who had volunteered to serve beyond his first term of service, and therefore a soldier to be respected.

"A fitting name," Consul Pompeius said, looking up, up, and up at the giant's expressionless face as he shook his hand. The man was as big as an old boar bruin, and every bit as intimidating. His hand felt as though he could easily crush rocks.

"Sir," the giant rumbled. His voice was like distant summer thunder.

Arcadius led the Consul and Senator to the rank. The first man they approached was unremarkable in appearance, other than his bearing; he radiated confidence. "Legionary Manius Octavius Taurinus," Arcadius introduced him. "Legionary Taurinus is the best tracker in the Second. I think this man could track a five-day-old fart through a forest fire."

"Sirs," the legionary nodded.

The next man had a long, heavy bow and a quiver full of arrows on his back, in addition to the issue gladius on his belt. "Legionary Faustus Marius," Arcadius said. "Best man with a bow I've ever seen."

"Best in the legions, are you?"

"Best in the world, sir," Marius said, his eyes twinkling. He was a small man but wiry, with a face that wore what was apparently a perpetual wide grin.

Arcadius coughed sharply, sending Marius back to attention, then moved on. "Legionary of the Evocati, Marcus Albium Bubonius," he introduced the next man.

Pompeius noted this man, of all the group, looked the most completely Novan, in spite of his standard legion uniform and equipment. He was tall, lean, with long black braids hanging down from under his helmet. He was also obviously the oldest man in the group, judging by the strands of gray that infiltrated his black hair. His status as an Evocati—a man who had served his decade and re-enlisted—spoke volumes of the man's dedication. "A white owl?" the Consul asked, referring to the soldier's name.

"My father was leader of the Medicine Society in my town, sir" Bubonius replied. "I was born in the depth of winter. As I drew my first breath, a great white owl flew over our lodge. Among the Tahona the white owl is a great omen, and my father took that as a sign I would be a great healer." He frowned. "He was not pleased with my decision to join the legion. He was less pleased when I joined the Evocati. I am nearing the end of my third decade in the legion."

"Legionary Bubonius is a competent physician in addition to being a dedicated soldier," Arcadius explained. "One of the best physicians I've ever heard of, in fact. Where better for him to use his skills than in the army?"

"Where better, indeed," Senator Brutus agreed.

"Legionary Valerius Fortis Caninus," Arcadius introduced the next man, a big, broad man, not as large as Centurion Tacitus but big, obviously strong, with a nose that looked to have been broken more than once.

"Caninus," Consul Pompeius mused. "Are you a relation of…?"

"Canis Magnus, hero of Rome?" the man asked, smiling. "I am his grandson, sir, first son of his second son Castor."

"You'll do well, then," the Consul said, "if you're half the man your grandfather was."

"Legionary Cominus Quintus Corvus," Arcadius moved down the rank. Corvus had the long leather strap of a sling wrapped around his waist. "One of the best slingers you're likely to see."

"Legionary Atius Lupus Minimus," Arcadius said of the next man. The Consul and Senator, for the first time, looked at the man before them with some skepticism. The man was as small and thin as Centurion Tacitus was huge; his face was thin, gaunt, and the top of his legion helmet only came to the shoulders of the men on either side of him.

"All of the men seem to have some special skill or talent," Pompeius asked the man, struggling to find a tactful way to ask *what in Pluto's name are you doing here?* "What is yours?"

"He is a thief, sir," Arcadius offered.

"A thief?" The Consul's face registered some incredulity, which Tribune Arcadius answered with a broad grin. "Sir," he said, "Legionary Minimus is probably the best scavenger, scrounger, and forager I've ever seen. There is no village or town he can't sneak into and out again unseen. There is no purse he can't pilfer unnoticed, no kitchen he can't raid without raising an alarm. It occurred to me that his talents may be useful." Arcadius carefully omitted the fact that he had managed to get Lupus Minimus released from imprisonment for thievery to bring him on the expedition, and in so doing probably spared the man's right hand from removal.

"Indeed," the Consul said, his voice guarded.

"Next," Arcadius said, "is Legionary Celerius Dorotheus. "Legionary Dorotheus was in great demand in the Second Tahonian as a runner; in a sprint, he can outrun a good horse." The man was lean, long-legged; he put Pompeius in mind of a deer, built for running and jumping.

"Legionary Marcus Plancius Varus, archer," Arcadius moved on. "He has a knack not only for archery, but for crafting arrows suited for a variety of purposes."

"Legionary Quintus Alces Sanctus, also of the Evocati," the Tribune said, indicating a tall, ascetic-looking man, like Bubonius rather older than the others. "One of the Second's notorious Stoics, a follower of old Cato, and I will say, as incorruptible as the man himself."

"Another Evocati," the Consul observed.

"Legionary Bubonius and I joined the legions together," Sanctus explained. "We grew up together in the same village in Tahonia. For three decades we have served the Republic."

"Well done, both of you." The Consul slapped the veteran on the shoulder. "On behalf of the Republic, I extend the gratitude of the people of Rome." He moved on to the last man.

The Tribune continued: "And finally, Legionary Junius Marcus Aurelius, one of the fastest swordsmen I've ever seen." The Consul and Senator were startled again; the legionary looked to be little more than a boy. But they did not question Arcadius' judgment.

The young man carried not one sword but two, sheathed in an unusual arrangement of scabbards on his left hip. Something about the handles looked unusual; the grips were longer, slimmer than usual.

"My own design, sirs," Aurelius said helpfully. He placed a hand on one scabbard. "May I?"

Consul Pompeius nodded. The boy drew a long, slim, glittering blade. "Made by my uncle, Petrus Robertus of Tahonia," Legionary Aurelius said, "to my own specification. It is lighter and a little longer than a legion blade. He has long experimented with different techniques in steelmaking. This blade is deeply laminated, folded and forged over a hundred times. It is time-consuming, but produces a superior blade."

"A lighter, stronger sword. Faster, then, as well?" Pompeius made a mental note of the name; he would send someone up to talk steelmaking with him.

"Much, Senator," the legionary agreed. "And, since we are traveling light, with no scuta or pila, it is no hardship to bring both."

"Aurelius is adept at fighting with either hand," Arcadius explained, "or with both at once."

"Thus two swords," the Consul replied. "Well, Tribune, this is a worthy lot you have here." He turned to face the Tribune and extended his hand. "We won't keep you any longer. Good luck. You have our utmost confidence, and our best wishes. May Juno, Diana, and Mars smile upon you on your journey."

Tribune Arcadius took the offered hand and shook. "Very grateful, sir. We will do Rome proud, I promise you."

Senator Brutus shook Arcadius' hand next. "Good luck, cousin," he said, grinning.

"*Gratias*," Arcadius said. The scope of the task he was about to undertake suddenly crashed down on him. "I expect we'll need all the luck we can get."

"You're the very man for the job," Brutus assured him.

Arcadius nodded. "We'll see if you still think that when we return." *If we return*, he added to himself, silently.

The Tribune turned to his men as the Consul and Senator walked away. He stood silently for a moment. Centurion Tacitus stepped silently to his side.

"Well, men," he began, feeling the need to say something momentous, but unable to think of anything suitable, "see to your personal gear and horses. We'll be on our way."

While the men were making last-minute checks of horses and gear, Arcadius examined the supply wagon carefully. The load—preserved foods, tents, extra clothing and some trade goods—was well-secured in the open bed, covered with heavy leather tarps and tied down with stout hemp rope. The bisoxen—bison bulls castrated after reaching full size and strength to make them tractable, in the manner of old-world oxen—looked strong and healthy. The hitches and tack were new and looked to be of good quality. The teamsters had been hired locally around Pompeius, and while all were experienced in managing the difficult and unpredictable bisoxen and the lumbering freight wagon, they were unremarkable otherwise. Arcadius had told them they would most likely not be proceeding past the Mesizibi, and would be set at liberty at Durobrivia.

Next, he inspected the men, with Centurion Ursus Tacitus at

his side. The ten soldiers of the Second Tahonian Legion were all fit, strong, alert, their equipment well organized and in good condition. Their horses looked healthy and strong. *Cousin Brutus knows his horses*, the Tribune told himself. *He chose well.*

"Very well," the Tribune said. "Mount up, men. We have a long way to go. No sense standing here any longer."

Leather creaked, steel and bronze clacked and rattled as the men climbed on their horses. Arcadius trotted to the head of the formation, accompanied by Centurion Tacitus, who was mounted on a massive black stallion, one of two such Senator Brutus found to carry the giant.

The men formed up in two columns, with six riders ahead of the wagon and six behind. Each man rode one horse and led another. As the sun broke over the eastern horizon, the column moved onto the paving stones of the Attepian Way and headed west.

This early in the year, the mornings were chilly even in the pleasantly temperate environs of Pompeius. Arcadius wrapped his heavy red soldier's cloak tightly around himself as the road took them out of sight of the four hills of Pompeius. This early there were no citizens on the road, but that would soon change. Trade between the city and the provinces was brisk, and now in late winter there would be caravans moving out of the Attepian hills bearing Reman furs, Attepian timber, dried fish, and salted meats from Tsalesia. All manner of trade goods moved on the Roman roads.

"My grandfather said in the old world, all roads led to Rome," he said, looking over at Ursus Tacitus. "I can only imagine old Rome, but it seems the case here that all roads lead to Pompeius, neh?"

The big centurion grunted an affirmative, and lapsed back into his normal silence. Arcadius made a wry face. He had chosen Tacitus as his optio for a number of reasons; his strength, his unswerving loyalty, and not least of all, his size. In the past the giant's massive, brooding presence alone had been sufficient to make armed aggressors back down.

But as a conversationalist, Ursus Tacitus was disappointing. *Never was a man more aptly named*, Arcadius thought.

Behind him, the Tribune heard the clopping of horses' hooves on the paving stones, the soft conversation of the men and the heavy breath of the bisoxen. The plodding beasts pulled the wagon at the pace of a fat man walking; it promised to be a long trip to the Mesizibi.

"Fourteen mille to the Primus Magnus aqueduct," Arcadius tried another tack. "With that wagon's pace, that will make a good day's march. Good ground for a first night's camp, as well."

Tacitus grunted again. Arcadius shook his head. The man was not disagreeable; just silent.

Farther back in the formation, the men were engaged in speculation, as soldiers do.

Legionary Faustus Marius leaned over in his saddle. "How many Novan women, do you suppose, will yield up their virtue to the grandson of the Great Dog of Rome?"

"More," Caninus laughed, "than will to you, that much is certain. Was *your* grandfather a hero of Rome? I think not."

"None of the girls will have ever heard of Rome where we're headed," Marius reminded Caninus.

"They will have by the time we're done."

Behind them, Legionaries Quintus Sanctus Alces and Marcus Albium Bubonius traded a look.

"Young men," Alces muttered.

Bubonius smiled. "Were you so very different in your youth, old friend?"

"Men of the legions seldom marry," Alces replied thoughtfully.

"Perhaps because of just this? The soldier's life is one of wandering, and in war he may be gone from home for months, even years. What impact does that have on Roman society? How many young women surrender themselves as virgins to the houses of Diana in despair of finding a husband?"

"How many young wives would be left as widowed mothers if the young men of the legions all married and fathered a few brats before heading off to war?"

"Children," Alces pointed out, "are a gift, not a burden."

"Perhaps you are right," Bubonius agreed. "I never felt the lack of a wife, myself. I have enough to occupy me in the legion, and there are always willing women about. But, my friend, remember; as you just observed, young men will be young men, and the legions no doubt leave an ample supply of half-Roman bastards wherever they go. I suspect this trip will be no exception, judging from our young comrades' conversation."

The formation marched on as the rising sun lit up the landscape before them. Behind them, the Nova Roman capital faded away into the morning haze.

TWO
MEETINGS

A journey that was to prove long and arduous began in a very mundane manner; a simple movement of a very small body of cavalry, on an established, well-managed Roman road, through settled country. There was even the luxury of a wagon carrying tents and ample supplies for the journey, and occasionally even an inn where one could pass the night.

In every mille of the journey to the Mesizibi, the beneficent influence of Roman society was manifest. Traders of every sort traveled the roads without fear of robbery or brigands, confident that they traveled under the protection of Roman arms. The paved roads serve as the arteries of commerce, and the citizens of Rome are free to travel them and engage in such trade as suits them. Villages, towns and farms were much in evidence throughout the trip to Durobrivia.

That the country is well watered and well forested facilitates the development of a wilderness into civilized country. But in the trans-Mesizibi, everything would prove to be different. Not only was that country wild and untamed, it proved to be a far more difficult land than we imagined. It proved not too difficult, however, for trained soldiers of Rome to traverse.

—Flavius Arcadius Tahonius' Trans-Mesizibi Diaries

Cisalpine Tsalesia

"The mist makes the mountains look as though they were shrouded in smoke, does it not?"

The Roman party was enjoying a brief halt in a meadow where the paved road crested a low pass in the mountains, the boundary between the provinces of Attepia and Cisalpine Tsalesia. The view was spectacular; a wide, forested valley lay before them, with more mountains in the distance. Legionary Bubonius' observation was apt. In the spring sunshine, wreaths of mist ran in swirls across the wooded mountainsides.

"You have a poetic heart," Quintus Corvus observed.

"One doesn't need a poetic heart to see that," Bubonius replied. "Only the same two eyes the gods gift to every man."

Nearby, the Tribune was consulting a rough map of the region. "Once we cross over into Transalpine Tsalesia, it will be all downhill to the flat lands, then on to Durobrivia. Another five days, maybe six."

Centurion Tacitus answered with a customary grunt. "The wagon?" he unbent enough to ask.

"We'll leave the wagon there at Durobrivia," Arcadius replied. "That party of Tsalesian cavalry confirmed what we suspected; the road ends at Durobrivia, and we'll be doing well to find someone to raft men and horses across the Mesizibi. Then, we will be on to the plains, where at least it will be faster traveling for men and horses."

Tacitus nodded agreement.

"That venison should be ready," Arcadius said, nodding towards where the men were gathered around a fire. "Get yourself a good meal, Centurion. Good thing Legionary Marius is as good a bowman as he claims, eh? We'll move out as soon as the men have eaten."

Tacitus nodded again, and moved away silently, a massive, brooding presence.

The men traveled on, spending the next several days moving through some of the richest country Nova Roma had to offer. Nights they spent in the large tents carried in the bison-drawn wagon or, occasionally, as guests in the barracks of a legion camp on the outskirts of a town. Rolling hills led into low mountains. They climbed steadily along the winding road, through great groves of trees and grassy meadows, until they arrived at a pass denoted with an engraved stone marking the border between Cisalpine Tsalesia and Transalpine Tsalesia. The country opened up some after that; as the Roman road moved down into low, rolling hills, the forest became punctuated with more open meadows and even some considerable stretches of prairie. Local towns and villages became more common, and the men were able to barter for domestic turkey and swine to supplement the meat they took hunting and the bread prepared from flour carried in the wagon.

"I never imagined there were so many people in Tsalesia," Quintus Alces Sanctus commented one afternoon as the cavalrymen rode past yet another village. "So many little ones." Children from the village ran from the collection of small villas and shops and followed the walking horses and plodding wagon, laughing and teasing the soldiers.

"Years ago, there likely were not," Marcus Albium Bubonius replied, smiling as a little girl waved to him from the side of the road. "My father always said when he was a boy, Tahonia was only a few scattered villages, and the original five tribes of the Tahona wandered from season to season through the forests, hunting and fishing. Then came the men of Rome, with their iron and bronze, their horses, bison, roads, and farms, and all changed—almost overnight, to hear the old ones tell it. Now children no longer starve to death in the long winters; our houses are solid and warm, our bellies are full of maize,

Roman bread, bison, and pork. We trade with people as far away as the Maya in their cities far to the south. Who ever imagined such a thing—before Rome?"

"It is an amazing modern era we live in," Alces agreed.

"And much the same happened here, I am sure."

On the fourth day after crossing the provincial border, the road crested a small rise, and the sprawling, bustling river port city of Durobrivia lay before them.

"I will have to stop to confer with the Provincial proconsul's offices," Arcadia told his optio. "I want someone here to know where we are bound, when we passed through and when we hope to be back."

Tacitus grunted his assent.

On the Mesizibi

The big freighter was larger than the typical run of riverboats working the Mesizibi; large enough for a dozen men and horses, plus personal baggage and additional trade goods and general cargo. At the stern flew a red banner with the black silhouettes of two ravens, facing each other: the banner of the Five Seas Nation.

Legate Marcus Malleolus stood at the prow, watching as the ship approached the Roman port city of Durobrivia. When ordered to take a party of exploration west, he had at first resisted the order to stop and inform the Romans who he was and where he was going; but the Imperator was firm on that point, and on reflection it made sense. He had only a dozen men, and the Romans could, if they desired, send a considerable force after him.

"There will come a time to provoke a confrontation with Rome," the Imperator had told him. "This is not yet that time."

The Reman commander wore the heavy black leather cuirass, black cloth tunic and leggings, wolf fur cape and polished iron greaves and helmet of a Reman legate. His men were similarly attired, differing only that their polished iron helmet lacked the fore-and-aft crest of raven feathers that marked a legate's rank. They bore bows and lances for hunting, and gladii for defense.

This was the party assigned to lay a Reman claim to lands beyond the great river, and in so doing place the Five Seas Nation directly athwart Nova Roma's agenda in the new world.

Durobrivia — the Provincial Capital

To one accustomed to the white marble Senate and Council of Plebs building in Pompeius, the granite-walled, dark wood-trimmed building housing the Transalpine Tsalesia Provincial Proconsulate was a trifle plain. But it *was* the center of authority for the province, and so Tribune Arcadius made it a point to stop and pay his respects. He filed a report with the Proconsulate's clerks informing the provincial government as to the purpose of his expedition, the names of his men, and that they traveled with the authority of the Consul in Pompeius. With this done, he took his leave and headed for the entrance.

He found the hulking figure of Centurion Tacitus waiting for him in the building's courtyard. "Sir," the optio said in his deep, rumbling voice, "you'd better come outside."

"What is it?"

Tacitus inclined his head towards the Provincial Council building's big wooden doors, outside of which lay Durobrivia's Forum. "We aren't the only party heading west, sir."

"What? Who else … I'm sure the Consulate only sent one party west." Arcadius followed his optio out into the spring sunshine to find his question answered by the party of men who stood waiting as their leader haggled with a vendor of cotton cloth.

The sight of the leader alone would have given their origins away.

He was a tall, lean man and even in the warm spring day, he still wore a heavy leather cuirass and a long, flowing black cape trimmed with wolf fur; a polished iron helmet with a crest of raven feathers revealed him to be a legate in the Reman army. Nearby stood at least a dozen men in the black uniforms and polished iron accoutrements of soldiers of the Five Seas Nation. A group of dark, shaggy northern-strain horses were tethered behind them.

"Remans," Arcadius muttered.

The Roman tribune looked at his own party. Horses tethered safely to the side, his men were gathered in a tight little knot, watching the Reman party, who returned the Roman soldiers' attention. Arcadius noted the poses of both parties; relaxed but cautious, hands not on weapons but near them.

Arcadius decided to grasp the bison by the horns.

He placed his own tribune's helmet with its fore-and-aft brush of black horsehair firmly on his head and strode through the Forum, which had gone strangely quiet as the residents watched the silent standoff between Roman and Reman soldiers. Approaching the Reman legate, he announced himself in a loud, clear voice, with what he hoped was a commanding tone. "Salve. I am Flavius Arcadius Tahonius," he stated, "Tribune of Mars to the Senate of Rome from the province of Tahonia and former commander of the Second Tahonian Legion. And you are?"

"Marcus Malleolus," the Reman answered. He looked Arcadius up and down. "Legate of the Third Legion of the Mother of Waters Province of the Five Seas Nation."

"What is your business in Durobrivia, Legate Malleolus? Why does the Five Seas Nation send an armed party of cavalry into Roman territory?"

"Nova Roma and the Five Seas Nation are at peace, Tribune,"

Malleolus replied coolly. "We are on a peaceful mission of exploration, and carrying only personal arms. A Reman freighter brought us down the Mesizibi, and since we are bound west, we were obliged to stop at Durobrivia, as it is the only place where one might find ferries to carry men and horses across the great river."

"Bound west, you say? To what end?"

"With respect, Tribune, that is none of Rome's business. The lands west of the Mesizibi are not under the eagles of Rome, nor are they under the ravens of the Five Seas People. Those lands are free for the peaceful passage of all, and that is precisely what we intend to do—pass peacefully through them."

Arcadius felt as though he had just been force-fed a cup of vinegar. The man was right; Rome had—as yet—no claims on the lands west of the river. Further, Reman ships routinely worked the Mesizibi as far south as the port of Philadelphia, under a treaty drawn up a good twenty years earlier.

"You are right, of course," he admitted. "You must forgive my ill temper, Legate; you will admit, however, that even in peace, our nations are not on the best of terms. It was a surprise to see you and your men here."

"I assure you, Tribune, we mean no mischief. I have presented myself to the provincial proconsul, and *he* has no objection to our presence. As soon as I can negotiate with this scoundrel for cloth to replace some tentage lost in a storm, we will be crossing the river and will be on our way west."

"I leave you to your business, then," Arcadius said. He turned and nearly bumped into the hulking figure of Tacitus, who had been standing conspicuously close by. "Centurion," Arcadius ordered, "have the men stand to. My business with the Provincial Council is complete; we will cross the river and head west."

"Sir." Tacitus turned and shouted. "All right, you lot. In your saddles! We move."

Arcadius leaped on his horse and led the men off at a trot. He was suddenly and unaccountably anxious to be across the river and on the way.

A winding path led down the steep slope from the main city to the docks where freighters working the great river loaded and unloaded their wares. On the north end of the dock district, several large, flat ferries were tethered. Large hemp cables stretched across the river, and teams of bison on either side powered great windlasses that supplied the power to move the heavy craft across the channel of the Mesizibi. Arcadius released the wagon and teamsters; from now on his men would sleep in small shelters and subsist on hunter's fortune. The ferries would only carry five horses and men at a time, so Arcadius sent Tacitus across with the first party, intending to remain on the eastern bank and cross with the last group. As the centurion loaded the first group aboard the big, flat wooden craft, Arcadius ordered the other men to water their horses and stake them in a nearby meadow to let the animals feed.

When this was done, Arcadius and the men stood on the wooden docks and watched the Mesizibi.

"So this is the fabled Mesizibi. Never seen the like, have you?" Lupus Minimus muttered softly.

It was an amazing sight. Tahonia was a land of forests and rivers, and the party had followed and forded several rivers in their journey through Attepia, as well as Cisalpine and Transalpine Tsalesia.

But none of them had ever seen a river like this.

"It doesn't even flow like a normal river," Quintus Alces Sanctus observed. "Look at the water." He pointed out into the heavy brown water of the channel. "It is like a giant moving lake, not like a river at all."

"The provincial proconsul told me that the people who live along the river call it Brother," Arcadius said. "They take so much of their living from the river in fish, turtles, waterfowl and whatnot, that they consider it very nearly a relative. Now with so much trade moving up and down, it has only become more important to the people in this region. And on the other side, the Great Sister will become just as important to trade coming east. And," he reminded the men, "the folk hereabout may still be Tsalee in many ways, but they are citizens of Rome, and have been for near unto six decades now. They are as much good Romans as any of us under the law. Remember that."

"Sir, our friends are crossing as well."

Arcadius looked upstream, following Faustus Marius' gesture. The Reman party was loading men and horses aboard a similar ferry a few hundred paces away.

"Well," the tribune grumbled. "I suppose we'll be seeing them on the other side."

"Here comes a freighter," Alces Sanctus said. "How will it get past the cables that pull the ferries?"

As the men watched, that question was answered. As the freighter approached the heavy hemp rope, two men at the freighter's bow used a clever arrangement of a long pole with a forked tip to snag the cable and push it under the ship's flat keel, allowing the small ship to pass over. Oarsmen on the deck rowed the ship on downstream.

"Clever," Arcadius approved.

Nearby, Legionary Plancius Varus was seated on a large chunk of driftwood, fiddling with several arrows and a length of cord.

Legionary Caninus walked over to observe. "What are you about, then, Varus?"

"You'll see," Varus grinned. "Those boys gave me an idea." He nodded towards two boys who had just pulled a large, heavy brown fish ashore, one of the curious, whiskered bottom-feeding fish common to the big rivers. "I think we'll eat fish for supper, is that all right?"

Caninus shrugged and walked off to watch the river.

The sun was growing low in the sky by the time Tribune Arcadius crossed with the last party of men and horses to find Centurion Tacitus had, as he expected, the men organized and in good order on the far bank. "We'll move a ways inland away from the river," Arcadius ordered, "and make a camp. Best to get away from the water—insects will be bad at night near the river."

Tacitus nodded his agreement. Several of the men were already scratching insect bites.

"At least the evening meal is decided. Who but Legionary Varus would have thought to tether cord to a barbed arrow and use it to hunt fish?" Arcadius watched as Varus loaded two large, heavy fish on his second horse. "He is a clever one."

"He is that, sir," Tacitus agreed.

"To your horses, men! We'll move on," the tribune called out.

The party of Romans took to their horses and headed west, climbing slowly away from the river onto higher, open ground.

The Reman party's passage had not gone without causing some concern in another quarter. Before sunset, the proconsul of the Transalpine Tsalesia Provincial Council sent a legionary on a fast horse on the road east towards Pompeius. The man bore only personal gear and a sealed scroll. He had strict orders: Place the scroll directly in the hands of the Consul of Rome.

An experienced messenger, the legionary estimated he could make Pompeius within ten days.

Next morning

The Roman party had ridden on until after dark, and passed a short and uncomfortable night wrapped in their red soldier's cloaks, sleeping on the sandy ground near a small stream. In the morning, after a cold breakfast of hard maize biscuits, the party saddled horses and prepared to move on.

"We are in *terra incognita* now," Tribune Arcadius told his optio. "I want scouts sent out ahead of the main party. We'll rotate the duty, so each man will do scout duty one day in five."

"Sir," Centurion Tacitus agreed. He turned to where the men were climbing into their saddles and pointed to the first two who caught his eye. "Caninus, Minimus. You will scout today. Hand off your spare horses. Ride on ahead."

Both men saluted, untied the lead ropes for their spare horses from their saddles and passed them to the men behind them in line.

"The Great Sister is to our north," Arcadius told them. "Just over that ridge, I should think. Keep the river course in sight, and stay on the south bank. I reckon that Reman party is moving up the north bank. We'll stay well clear of them for now."

"As you wish, sir," Legionary Caninus replied. Spurring their horses, the scouts cantered off.

The morning was already growing warm. Arcadius led the men out of the small valley their stream ran through and into open, rolling hills. A line of large trees was visible to the north along the river; to the south lay open, grassy hills spotted with oaks, hickories, and maples.

"We'll make better time now without the wagon," Arcadius observed.

Beside him, Tacitus grunted an affirmative. Arcadius shook his head and concentrated on watching the horizon.

North of the Great Sister

The Reman party likewise got an early start on their first day west of the Mesizibi. It took them longer to move out, having erected tents during the night. As each man from the horse-poor Five Seas Nation had only a single horse, the mounts were burdened with tentage and personal effects in addition to their riders.

"At least there would seem to be enough fodder for the horses," a Reman legionary observed, looking at the rolling green hills. "Hopefully that will stay true all the way."

"Hopefully," another man agreed. "We're carrying enough of a load for them."

Legate Marcus Malleolus swung into his saddle. He heard the men but paid their remarks little heed. Their concerns were not his; they were only, after all, common soldiers. They would follow his orders as unquestioningly as he followed the Imperator's.

Waving a hand in the air, the Legate shouted at his men to move out. They cantered off upstream, following the northern bank of the Great Sister into the undiscovered country.

The south bank of the Great Sister

Late in the afternoon on the first day, the scouts rode back to the column. Arcadius was surprised to see two skinny young Novan men trotting alongside the cantering horses, easily keeping pace with the mounted soldiers.

Legionary Caninus led them in. He stopped his horse in front of the Tribune and saluted. "Ran into these two about a league ahead, sir," he explained. "They've been watching us most of the day. They have some Latin; they say they get Tsalee traders out this way sometimes, picked up our lingo from them."

"Traders, out here? Already?" Arcadius shook his head in surprise. "What do they want?"

"They're offering to have us pass the night with them. About forty in their band, near as I can tell. They're nomads; this is rather farther east than they usually get."

Arcadius looked at Tacitus. "Centurion? What do you think?"

"Perhaps they can tell us something of the country, sir," the giant offered. It was a considerable speech for him.

"Very well," Arcadius decided. He looked at the older of the two Novan men. "Lead on, young man."

The two young men led the Roman party to the encampment. Tribune Arcadius looked the collection of tents and rude huts over, deciding the place only deserved the term "village" if one applied the word in the most generous way possible. "Dismount," he ordered. "We'll lead our horses in. No sense in startling anyone."

Arcadius led the men into the center of the rough circle of dwellings and held up a hand, halting the column. A gathering crowd of locals spilled out of huts and hide tents as several young men trotted towards them from the thin line of trees along the river. The men wore loincloths and knee-high, soft leather boots; several had feathers, bone beads, shells, or some other decoration in their long black hair. The women mostly wore deerskin dresses that stopped above the knee, although several wore only finely worked, beaded leather skirts; their bare chests drew stares from the Roman men.

An old man came out of one of the huts. One of the young men that had led the Romans to the village spoke with him, then ran to a low, crude tent and shouted something at someone inside. The other spoke to Arcadius in his rough pidgin Latin, waving an arm at the old man.

"That old man, he Leaves- in-Wind. He says to tell you we have man for guest," he said. "Stay with us last five days. If you want guide, he take you west. He knows plains, mountains. He knows people that live there."

"Who is this guest of yours, then?" the Tribune asked.

The Novan shrugged. "Wanderer. Hunter. This man, he has no town, no village, no family. He bring in wapiti to share, so he stay while we eat it. Many like him on the plains."

"But he knows the way west?"

"You ask him. He comes now."

A small figure emerged from the tent, stretched and yawned, then ambled over to where the Roman tribune stood. He held up a hand. "Salve," he said. "Nice day, eh Chief?" he asked in passable Latin. He looked at the column of soldiers. "Don't see much Roman cavalry this side of the big river. Don't see many Romans at all, really."

"Except you, unless I miss my guess. Part Roman your own self, neh?" Tribune Arcadius looked the man over as he spoke. What he saw did not impress him.

The would-be guide was a head shorter than Arcadius. His build was hard to determine, wrapped as he was in an enormous bison-skin wrap even in the warm sunshine of late spring, but his face was lean to the point of gauntness. An apparently perpetual grin revealed stained yellow teeth, of which several were missing. He wore his thick black hair in a long single braid, which hung to the small of his back. A single turkey feather secured at his right temple with a thong formed his only headgear. He carried a rolled blanket, a bow, a quiver of arrows, and a sheathed Roman gladius. Filthy leather leggings, knees worn out, dangled over a battered pair of soldier's boots.

Arcadius looked pointedly at the boots. "I am Tribune Flavius Arcadius Tahonius," he said, "Tribune of Mars from the province of Tahonia, former commander of the Second Tahonian Legion, traveling under the authority of the Consul of Nova Roma. Former soldier, are you?"

The man's grin grew broader. "Yes, Chief," he said. "Did my time, yes I did. My sixteenth summer I walked over to east of the big river, joined up, did my decade in the legions. Third Transalpine Tsalesian Cavalry, I was. None better on a horse than me. I can hit a running hare with an arrow loosed from the back of a galloping horse, four times out of five."

Arcadius ignored the brag. "What's your name?"

The man spat something out in what was presumably his native tongue. "Julius Takasus T'Aquus," he said. "You would say, Julius Spotted Horse. My grandfather, he was Marcus Tiberius Agrippa. Walked all the way out here from Pompeius, he did, took a woman of the plains to wife. Their first-born was my mother."

Arcadius decided to forgo asking the man why his grandfather fled the province of Rome for exile on the far plains; chances were he was better off not knowing. At any rate, the man was not responsible for his grandfather's infractions. "You've been across the plains, then?"

"Three times," Julius Spotted Horse replied. "Twice up to the headwaters of the Great Sister, over the mountains and across as far as the western ocean. Once down the Big Sandy to its headwaters, then through those mountains into the deserts beyond, then on to the sea."

"The Big Sandy?"

"Another river, Chief." Spotted Horse scraped a patch of earth bare with his boot. Kneeling, he took a short knife from his belt and scraped at the earth, producing a rude map. "See here, the Sister, she runs due east-west along this stretch we're on here, to join the Mesizibi. But about three-or-four days ride headed upstream, she turns north. For, oh, another three days on a good horse, she goes on almost due north, before she swings northwest. Just before she turns again, you hit the Big Sandy, flowing in from west by southwest. The Big Sandy has its headwaters in the mountains to the south. The first big range of mountains run along north to south, out there; the Sandy hits them in the south, the Great Sister runs farther to the north."

"And you have to cross the mountains either way to get to the western sea? Is it the same sea in the north and in the south?"

"Yes to the first," Spotted Horse nodded. "As to the second, I've no idea—I didn't ride up the coast any distance either direction. I would guess it is, it's a bloody great big ocean, but I don't know."

Arcadius silently noted how the man distinguished his opinions from his observations—one of the hallmarks of a good scout. "You know these routes through the mountains, then?"

"No one knows the high passes like I do, Chief, except maybe the people who live in those regions."

"How many of those people are there? Are they hostile?"

Spotted Horse turned his head and spat a long stream of smelly brown liquid into the dirt. He looked thoughtful for a moment. "Anyone says he knows for sure how many Novans live on the plains or in the mountains, he's a liar. There are no cities, no towns of any size. A few villages here and there, maybe. The people on the plains are nomads, like these folks here. They never set down anywhere for more than the few months over winter. Best guess is there's no more than a few thousand. In the mountains, people are even thinner on the ground. It's rough country, hard to live in. And hostile? Chief, people there are like people anywhere. Some of them are friendly, some are nasty, some are stupid, some are clever, some are cowards, some aren't afraid of Jupiter himself. Depends on how you treat them, mostly."

"An honest answer," Arcadius admitted. "Have you a horse? Could you lead us to the headwaters of the one of these rivers and on through to the other side? Rome would compensate you for the service, of course. Does the pay you received in the legion suit you?"

"I have a good Reman pony," the man said. "Traded for him last time I was north. He's as good as your Roman horses, I'd say, for where we're going—not as big, but he doesn't eat as much and he's tough enough and to spare. I'll lead you through the mountains and beyond; as far as you want to go, if you're paying in good Roman gold. But a legionary's pay? Well, Chief, to be honest, I'm worth more to you than a common soldier, neh? How about half again a legionary's pay?"

Arcadius didn't flinch; he was prepared to offer twice the normal soldier's stipend. "Done. You'd best be a man of your word, though."

"Nobody knows that country like I do. Nobody you'll find around here, anyway." He scuffed a boot over his map. "It's not like I'm busy at anything else, just now." He grinned up at Arcadius, revealing a mouthful of stained teeth with one incisor missing. "Sure, then, Chief, I'll be your guide."

"Which is the easier route? North or south?"

"Depends on whether you prefer to freeze or starve, Chief," the guide chuckled. "Northern mountains are higher, steeper, the passes harder to negotiate, but the forests are heavier and there is more game. You want to move smartly on that northern route, though; winters are bad in that high country. Once you cross, there is another great river you can follow to the sea. On the southern route down the Big Sandy, there are still many high passes and winters are hard, but once you move through you enter into deserts, and those lands can be spare indeed. There are supposed to be a few small towns in those deserts, but I've never seen them, just heard rumors. Once you pass through the desert there are more mountains, then great, green valleys—prettiest country you'll ever see, rich country, good farmland if I'm any judge. Then the sea."

"Good lands there, in the south?"

"Only passed through them the once, but better than good, I'd say. I'm no farmer, but the land there looks like any crop would do well, as long as you plant near water; it's a dry country. I passed through the deserts late in the year, and spent the winter within sight of the ocean. You could hardly call it a winter. No snow and the weather barely got cold at all. There is plenty of game about, too. A man would have to work at it to go hungry there. If there were more people and even a few towns, I would not have come back. But I have to admit, civilized country does have its advantages." He tapped the handle of his sheathed gladius, forged of good Roman steel.

Arcadius faced a dilemma. He knew the Reman party was somewhere to his north; following the northern route would allow him to keep pace with them, but he had not the manpower to do more than note their location. Following the southern route would allow the Reman party to make uncontested claim to the northern lands as far as the sea, but would allow him to plant the standards of Nova Roma on the shores of the western ocean in the beautiful lands Julius Spotted Horse described.

"We'll follow the southern route," Arcadius decided. "Once we get to the sea, we'll decide where to go from there." He looked at the guide. "Can you be ready to leave at first light?"

"I'll be ready, Chief."

SPQR
THREE
ENCOUNTERS

Several days after crossing the Mesizibi were spent in travel from the environs of Durobrivia to the junction of the Great Sister and Big Sandy rivers. If Durobrivia came into being because of one river junction, it seems likely that one day another city will arise at the junction of the latter rivers, as both are navigable at least to small craft.

During these days our guide proved to be valuable indeed. While a disreputable character on first appearance, he proved to be familiar with the people of the trans-Mesizibi, knowing at least a few words of the various languages. More valuable still, he was fluent in the unspoken sign language that served as a patois between the tribesmen of that region, and readily instructed our soldiers in its use.

Our constant concern was the Reman party we knew also to be in the region. The primary goal of our mission was to facilitate the expansion of Nova Roma into the western lands beyond the great river, and one does not have to have a window into the mind of the Consul to know he also intended to preclude Reman expansion into those lands as well.

Nobody could have expected that a simple act of thievery could have such impact on the fate of nations.

—Flavius Arcadius Tahonius' Trans-Mesizibi Diaries

The Great Sister

As spring began to move towards summer, the Roman party made their way across the hilly wooded country west of the Mesizibi, following the Great Sister west. Ten days passed before, as the guide predicted, the river's course took a turn north and proceeded through increasingly open environs, the forest giving way to gently rolling hills and stretches of prairie. Without the burden of the wagon drawn by the plodding bisoxen and in the open country, the cavalrymen made good time, sometimes moving over thirty mille in a day. As they traveled, they ate well; the wooded hills teemed with turkeys, deer, and grouse, while waterfowl were plentiful along the Sister and her tributaries.

Sixteen days out of Durobrivia, Julius Spotted Horse looked around at the countryside and made an announcement: "I know this country—I remember that creek there. We'll be at the Big Sandy late tomorrow, maybe the day after."

"Are you sure?"

"As sure as can be Chief," the guide answered Arcadius. "Mind you I was walking last time I came through here. But yes, maybe forty, fifty mille to the fork."

"Good. We'll push on until close to sunset, maybe we can get there tomorrow."

That evening the scouts rode in towards sunset as usual, just as the main body was stopping to make camp for the night in a grassy swale. Legionaries Atius Lupus Minimus and Manius Octavius Taurinus had drawn the duty for the day. Both men dismounted and made their report.

"There were signs of a band of hunters in the region," Taurinus told Tribune Arcadius. "Some tracks, and scuff marks where they killed a deer and dragged it off. And sir, that Reman party, they are just across the Sister from us. Just as we were coming back we topped a hill, and from there we could see them making camp for the night. They already have several fires going."

"Working their way up the other side of the river," Arcadius mused. "Are they keeping pace with us on purpose? No, there's no reason for them to do so. More likely they are just traveling as we are, day by day."

"Most likely, sir."

Arcadius nodded. "Very well. See to your horses, you two. Sanctus and Bubonius killed a deer earlier, so we'll eat well tonight."

The scouts unsaddled their horses, brushed the dust and sweat off them, and picketed them in a stand of good grass. As was usual when they had scout duty, their spare mounts had already been tended to. With the horses seen to and venison cooking, Lupus Minimus squatted at the fire next to Taurinus.

"You remember where that Reman camp lies across the river, don't you?"

"Of course. What kind of tracker would I be if I could not first find my own way back and forth?"

"Tribune Arcadius," Minimus went on, "he worries about those boys, doesn't he? Seems clear he'd rather they weren't on their way west like us."

"True enough," Taurinus agreed easily. "But it's not like we can do anything about it. Our numbers are more or less evenly matched, and those men are soldiers no less than we."

"You are right. We can't attack them. No reason to, really; as you pointed out, they are soldiers, no more or no less than we."

"I know you by now, little thief. You've got something on your mind."

"I do." Lupus Minimus explained briefly.

Taurinus let out a barking laugh. "Well, I'll go along," he said. "A bit of a lark, but if it works…"

"It will," Lupus Minimus said. "I'm as good at this as you are at tracking, Manius. Trust me."

"Trust you? Never. But go along with you? This time, yes."

They waited until the other men were asleep, then slipped out of camp. Cominus Quintus Corvus was on watch on a small hill nearby; the adventurous pair whispered their plan to him before slipping away into the night. Carrying two lengths of stout hemp rope, they moved silently through the grass and down through the poplars to the river.

"Lucky for us the moon won't be up for hours yet," Taurinus observed.

"Dark as a cave," Minimus agreed.

Crossing the Sister proved to be the tricky bit, but Taurinus was a strong swimmer, strong enough to trail a stout rope behind him. The current was on the sluggish side this far up the Sister, and several sandbars made possible wading rather than swimming.

Minimus secured the rope on the west bank and then followed. The current carried them some ways downstream, but the pair managed to come ashore less than a mille from the Reman camp.

"Now comes the tricky bit," Minimus told his comrade. "They'll have a man on watch, too."

"Sneak past him?"

"Easy enough going in," Minimus whispered. They were concealed in a patch of brush in a draw that led from the riverbank up to the flat ground where the Reman camp lay. "Not so easy going out."

"I don't like the idea of killing the sentry," Taurinus said. "The Tribune, he stressed that we're at peace with the Remans, at least legally. We are soldiers of Rome, he is a soldier of the Five Seas Nation. That may well mean war, Minimus."

"I have no intention of killing him. I just need you to find him; I'll do the rest."

Taurinus lived up to his reputation, finding the Reman's sole sentry wrapped in a blanket, seated comfortably at the base of a small tree. Most amazingly of all…

"I can't believe he has a fire going," Minimus breathed. The two Roman soldiers were a few hundred paces away, concealed in tall grass. "He won't see anything beyond the firelight."

"I suspect he's not the brightest light himself." Taurinus looked over at Minimus. "Up to you now, Legionary."

Minimus smiled briefly, showing a flash of teeth in the darkness, before wriggling away through the grass. Taurinus rolled on his back, fingers laced behind his head, and watched the stars move slowly across the sky. He was on the edge of falling asleep when the thief returned.

"You didn't kill him, did you?"

"No," Minimus whispered back. "He'll have a sore head tomorrow, but he won't die."

"Good. Let's push on."

They didn't dare stand now. Instead they wriggled through the grass like snakes, working their way slowly closer and closer to the Reman tents and past them to their target.

As was normal practice, the horses were picketed in a meadow a short distance away from the Reman's tents. Taurinus and Minimus moved silently from horse to horse, calming them with whispers and silently fastening a length of rope to the bridles they all still wore. The horses were typical Reman mounts: Compact, stout, strong, with the shaggy hair common to beasts bred in the cold northern climes.

Minimus lead the lead rope back to where Taurinus stood holding the two most tractable beasts.

"Let's be off, then," he grinned. They mounted the two lead horses, bareback, and quietly led the string away at a walk, into the darkness, towards the river.

Next morning

What in the name of Pluto is that horrible noise? Tribune Arcadius rolled over in his narrow tent and threw the blanket off. Pulling a tunic over his head, he rolled out from under the heavy waxed cotton lean-to and stood up. The sun was barely up, and there in the low beams of the early morning light was an impossible sight.

Centurion Ursus Tacitus, the notoriously silent giant, was laughing.

No ordinary laugh, either. The giant was bent almost double, hands on his knees, laughing uproariously, a deep, booming laugh that seemed to shake the very earth. All around, the men were clambering out of low tents, rising to their feet, staring at the giant in amazement.

All except Lupus Minimus and Manius Taurinus, both of whom looked oddly smug.

Arcadius walked to the centurion's side. "Centurion!" he said. "Tacitus! What is it?"

The centurion stood to attention. Tears of mirth were streaming down his broad, bronzed face. "Sir," he chuckled. "I apologize for losing my composure. But look at the horses, sir."

"The horses?"

Arcadius looked up. The horses had been tethered for the night to a line strung between two low trees; two for each man, and to the side was Julius Spotted Horse's gray Reman gelding, and behind that...

"What the..."

A dozen shaggy Reman ponies were staked neatly behind the

Roman horses. One of them was lazily cropping at the lush spring grass.

"Minimus!" the Tribune roared. The slight, skinny legionary rushed to present himself and saluted, a repressed grin on his face.

"Do you know anything about this, Legionary Minimus?"

Minimus looked at the string of horses. He looked back at the tribune with an expression of amazement. "They must have broken loose from their owners during the night, sir. Who knows what may have happened?"

"Broken loose," Arcadius repeated. "And staked themselves just next to our own horses?"

"Only the gods know what goes on in a horse's head, sir. In fact, I'll wager that's exactly it. Perhaps the gods wanted us to look after them."

Arcadius grinned suddenly. "Just so," he said. "The gods work in their own mysterious ways, neh? That being the case, we can hardly leave these horses here, can we? We'll have to take them with us. Minimus, see to rigging them with lead ropes, we'll tether them with the spare saddle horses. Centurion, get everyone moving, we'll move out as quickly as possible. No fire this morning. We'll move at the gallop! I want to cover a lot of ground today."

Laughing, the men scattered to gather their gear.

Across the river

"All right, cut him down. Throw some water on him."

Two Reman legionaries rushed to cut down the careless guard that hung, unconscious, by his arms from a small tree. Another man slowly coiled up the flog he had used to administer twenty lashes to the man who had allowed the horses to be stolen.

Legate Marcus Malleolus looked around at his men with an

eloquent expression of disgust. He would have rather ordered the guard crucified, but he couldn't spare a man now, even an incompetent one.

"We'll move out," he ordered. "All of you, gather what you need. Personal weapons, sleeping rolls, and food. Leave the saddles and horse tack."

"Sir," a legionary asked softly, "in which direction? Without our horses…"

"We have orders. Our orders are to proceed to the headwaters of the Great Sister. We will carry out those orders." Malleolus fixed the man with a glare. "We will march west. You are all soldiers. You do remember how to fucking march, don't you?"

The men chorused a low affirmative: "We do, sir."

"Good. Do you have any other questions?"

"No, sir," the first man said. Reman army discipline was harsh and unforgiving, and questioning authority was discouraged — sternly.

"Good. We'll move." Malleolus placed his iron helmet on his head. "Up the river."

The men of the Five Seas Nation packed their gear quickly. They abandoned their horse tack where it lay and marched away westward, slowly, into the sea of grass.

Pompeius

Consul Quintus Tiberius Pompeius read the message from Durobrivia for the ninth time that morning. He was still in a quandary. *So the Remans are pushing west*, he thought. *I don't know why that surprised me. It is as obvious a move for them as it is for us.*

Two courses of action are possible. One, to concentrate our expansion into lands south of the Great Sister. That would still bring an inestimable amount of land under the eagles of Rome. The other: Deploy legions to block Reman expansion west, and risk war.

Pompeius did not want to be remembered in the histories as the consul who let all of the West north of the largest navigable river fall into the hands of an unfriendly power. On the other hand, he did not want to be known as the consul who started a war, even though he knew his own nation's strength, and that Rome would likely emerge victorious. *A poor use of resources, war; it would hamper our expansion. The Founders intended the Republic to grow peacefully, through trade and industry, not through conquest.*

He frowned. Even though the man himself was known only as a distant legend in the new world, the term "Caesar" was used as a pejorative in Nova Roma, a demeaning term for a bully or a brute.

Still, there always comes some time when decisive action is required. A handful of garrisons established now will secure a vast amount of land for Rome.

The Consul called for his personal aide. "Send for General Commodus."

On the Big Sandy

The Big Sandy lived up to its name, being in early summer as much sandbar as river. On the first full day the legionaries followed the course of the prairie river, Legionary Quintus Corvus won a silver denarius in a wager with Valerius Fortis Caninus by galloping his horse across the river and back; the horse's belly barely got wet in the crossing.

In the open country, the cavalrymen were able to spend most of the increasingly long daylight hours in the walk/canter/trot pacing that experienced horsemen knew covered distance most efficiently. On the prairie they fell into a daily routine: Rise at sunup, breakfast on leftovers from the previous evening's meal. A detail filled water bags at the river while the others struck the small soldier's tents. The men assigned as scouts saddled up and rode out early, well before the others were ready to move. The men then rolled up the bedrolls and packed gear on the pack horses, and assembled the horses that weren't carrying riders that day into a lead string. Then, riding horses were saddled and either Tribune Arcadius or Centurion Tacitus led the men on their way.

Walk/canter/trot, until midday, when they stopped for a short rest. At midday the scouts returned to the main body and made their report about conditions ahead, and shared in the midday meal.

If game was spotted the procession would halt while hunters attempted a kill. Game was quickly dressed, cut up, packed on one of the pack horses so the men could push on. The afternoon passed in the same manner as the morning, walk/canter/trot, until the sun grew low in the sky. Arcadius would call a halt at a likely camping spot, tents would be pitched, and cook fires started. When the scouts rode back to the main body and made their afternoon report, whatever meat was available was cooked. The men ate, spoke and joked for a while, then they slept.

The next day the process was repeated. And the next day, and the next. Always the party rode with the Big Sandy at their side.

After several days, the Sandy forked, with a major branch going off to the northwest. Arcadius spent an hour in conversation with Julius Spotted Horse, and when the scouts returned, looking for the party at midday, he sent them down the south fork, moving west by southwest. The main party followed.

Along the way there were scattered Novan villages, and bands of nomads were seen walking, dragging their personal possessions on travois. Legionary Sanctus traded a silver denarius for a deerskin vest, carefully and intricately decorated with porcupine quills, and wore the vest every day thereafter: "It feels like it brings a portion of these people of the great plains with it," he said. "It feels good." He and Bubonius were adapting to the plains in another way; both were letting their hair grow. The Tribune frowned at it at first, but there was no strict regulation on the matter, and older men of the Evocati were traditionally allowed some such small liberties. He let the matter go, even when the two older men began wearing their lengthening hair in Novan-style braids.

The days of early summer passed, and the Roman soldiers felt as though they were in a journey not overland, but across a vast sea, a sea of grass and low trees, of creeks and beaver dams, of deer and turkey, of sun, dust, and wind. Day by day, they moved on, a dozen soldiers of Rome, in a wilderness immense beyond imagining.

Pompeius

Consul Pompeius looked down at his courtyard from an upper window. His 'guests' sat in the courtyard below, engaged in soft conversation.

I've never even seen a Mayan before, Pompeius realized.

The two visitors were small, rather stout, dark men. Their outfits were outlandish by Roman standards; the two men wore long capes decorated with bright red and yellow feathers and knee-high boots of some pale fur. The older man wore an enormous headdress of long red, white, yellow, and blue feathers. The younger wore only a single band of bright yellow feathers around his head.

Pompeius' servants had seated them, served light refreshments, and assured them their master would be with them momentarily. "The young one speaks Latin," his senior houseman had informed the consul. "He is a senior official who has been on trade missions into our territory many times. The older man's name translates as 'Smoke Monkey.'" The houseman repressed a snicker. "He is the younger brother of the Mayan king, Double Bird."

"Did they say what they wanted?" Pompeius looked down again. He found the visitors' appearance fascinating; the Maya rarely came this far north, preferring to stay in their deep forests, far to the south.

"They did not, sir," the houseman replied. "They just asked to speak with you. General Commodus escorted them here himself, sir, and some of his men are outside the villa's front gate."

"Very well. They must have good reason for coming all this way to Pompeius. I suppose I'll go see what that reason is."

It took some time for the consul to negotiate his own stairs with his walking stick. When he finally limped into the courtyard, the Mayan guests stood. The younger nodded respectfully, while the older stepped forward, gave Pompeius a stiff-armed embrace, and spat out a stream of what was, presumably, Mayan.

"I am your friend," the younger man translated. "I am another you. I greet you in peace."

"And I, you," Pompeius agreed. "Please, sit. I do not stand so easily." He smiled at the visitors as he seated himself on a carved wooden bench.

"I am Pacal," the translator explained. "For ten years now I have traded with the Roman ships at the mouth of the great river you call Mesizibi. Tools of Roman steel are in great demand in our lands."

"As Mayan gold is here in Rome," Pompeius added.

"Even so," Pacal agreed. "Because of my familiarity with Roman talk and Roman ways, our king Double Bird asked me to accompany his brother Smoke Monkey here to speak to you."

Pompeius inclined his head to the older Mayan. "Tell Smoke

Monkey I am pleased and honored to receive the representative of the Mayan people. On behalf of the citizens of Rome I welcome him."

Pacal blinked at the veiled reference to the status of the 'Mayan people,' who were considered little more than serfs by the Mayan nobles. Pompeius knew this, and Pacal knew he knew this, and likewise knew the Roman Republic's official views on the matter. He decided to let that drop, and withheld that part of the consul's remarks from his translation.

After sampling the refreshments and exchanging a few more meaningless pleasantries, the Mayan noblemen got to the point: "Smoke Monkey wishes to speak of Roman shipping along the east coast of the Mayan nation," Pacal translated the older man's next statement. "The great king Double Bird has heard that Roman ships are moving down the coast, even past Mayan lands."

"That's very likely," Pompeius agreed easily. "We are a people of commerce. Roman merchants are very good at smelling a profit."

"Smoke Monkey wishes to express his brother's concern that you allow this trade. He worries that Roman steel will find its way to the savage tribes that live in the jungles of that region."

Pompeius shrugged. "Very likely he is right. It is not for me to say where free Roman citizens may or may not go. Neither I as Consul, nor the Senate, nor the House of Plebs may compel Roman citizens to stay at home if there is trade to be made in the south. Also, the seas are free for all to navigate; these traders are not taking caravans through Mayan territory, I take it? I presume you make no claims as to the ocean off your coasts."

Pacal conferred with Smoke Monkey, and then agreed the Roman parties they were concerned about traveled by sea, not by land.

"There is very little I can do," Pompeius repeated. "Our merchants and ship's masters are free to go where they please. And, as you have agreed, the seas are free for all to travel." Neither of the Mayans were familiar enough with the ins and outs of such negotiation to realize that they had in fact agreed to no such thing.

Smoke Monkey spat out a stream of Mayan. His earlier, friendly demeanor was gone now. "Smoke Monkey asks if you speak true—you have so little control over your people that you allow them to venture forth among savages? Do you not know there are tribes in those jungles that make meals of men?"

"Our *citizens*," Pompeius coolly replied, stressing the word *citizen*, for which he had noted there was no Mayan equivalent—Pacal's translation relayed that single word in unchanged Latin—"are free people. They are free to go where they wish, to trade with whom they wish. If they place themselves in danger, they alone are responsible for their decisions, and the consequences."

After receiving the translation, Smoke Monkey looked thoughtful. "Your ways," Pacal translated after the older man had thought for a moment, "are not our ways. It may be that neither of us realizes how different our peoples are. Our king Double Bird suspected this may be the case."

"Then your king is indeed a wise man," Pompeius agreed.

"And if, as you say, the seas are free for the passage of all, and if, as you say, your people answer only to themselves if they place themselves in harm's way, perhaps we are hasty in coming to you to protest the trade missions moving past the Mayan nation."

Pompeius grew wary on the instant. "Perhaps you are. And perhaps we should seek to agree, we two great peoples, on steps to be taken to ensure the seas remain free for passage and trade for the citizens of both sides." He had noticed that the word *citizens* annoyed the Mayans, and so repeated it. *Not diplomatic, perhaps*, he thought, *but there is some small satisfaction in it all the same.*

"What do you mean?" Pacal demanded, without waiting for the older man's reply.

Ah ha, Pompeius thought. He has more authority himself than he lets on. I wonder how accurately he translates? I need to find a Roman who speaks Mayan, to assist in these discussions.

"Here in the Republic," Pompeius explained, "The Roman Army protects trade missions, travelers, and all those who travel within the Republic's boundaries. All citizens travel our roads, our countryside in peace, without worry, knowing that Roman arms protect them. Our people trade in peace, in confidence, knowing Roman law protects them. That is our way."

"Roman law for Roman people," Smoke Monkey replied through Pacal. "But our ways are different."

"That much is certain. Do your people send ships out to trade on the seas?"

After receiving the translation, Smoke Monkey recoiled slightly. "We do not," he said. "The sea is dangerous and unpredictable."

Pompeius almost laughed, remembering his grandfather's stories of the great storm that brought Roman people to the shores of the new world. "That it is," he agreed. "Dangerous enough as it is, without adding to those dangers. But just as Roman arms protect our people within the Republic, so should Roman arms protect our tradesman on the open seas."

The Mayans looked perturbed. "You would send soldiers out onto the seas?"

"Are we not agreed the seas are free for the passage of all?" Pompeius asked. "Does that not include ships of the Roman fleet as well as private tradesmen? As you pointed out, do we not have an obligation to protect our people who may be treading on dangerous grounds? You did point out that some of the southern tribes may be dangerous. Perhaps our merchants should be protected in their journeys."

Smoke Monkey received the translation, looking as though he had bitten into a green persimmon. He was a member of the highest level of Mayan aristocracy, the brother of the king; he was not used to the ease with which an experienced politician could turn his own words back on him.

"We have much to consider," Smoke Monkey replied at last. "I will return tomorrow to speak with you again."

"I will be glad to receive you," Pompeius said. "Perhaps you would care to visit our Senate and meet some of our civic leaders."

"Perhaps."

Pompeius escorted the two Mayans to the villa's front gate, where a half-dozen Roman soldiers waited to "escort" them back to their lodgings. Pompeius closed the gate, then turned to see his houseman, and behind the houseman…

"Senator Brutus," the Consul said. "You could scarcely have chosen a better moment to visit."

"I had intended to confer with you regarding funding for the legions you intend to send west across the Mesizibi," Brutus replied. "But I see you have had guests, and we may have something more interesting to discuss?"

"So it would seem." Pompeius led the Senator back to the courtyard and motioned for the older man to sit down on the bench the Mayans had only just vacated.

"So, which matter shall we discuss first, Consul? Money or Mayans?" Brutus' eyes twinkled at his own joke.

"Money," Pompeius decided.

"As you wish. I have two pieces of news. The Senate agrees to fund two military expeditions west to establish garrisons at the junction of the Great Sister and another river that comes into it from the west. Also, they agree to fund one more garrison farther up the Sister."

"Good," Pompeius clapped his hands together.

"However," Brutus continued, "there is only funding available to send one legion to these destinations, accompanied by one century of cavalry."

Pompeius frowned. Asking for five legions for the plains was excessive, he reminded himself. In matters like these, if you request twice the numbers you wish for, you may receive half of what you need. But I didn't even get that. One legion, and a century of horse? Will that be enough?

And what will the Five Seas Nation send west? How many legions?

"You have been warning me of the state of the Treasury," he said after a moment. "I presume things have not improved since the Senate gave an accounting last month?"

"It has not. There are several factors involved, but the primary cause of the reduction in the money supply is due to the fact that we have encouraged citizens to move into the sparsely populated lands west of the Tsalesian Alps. Our citizens have responded with dedication and courage, but settlers breaking new land for farms do not engage in commerce that generates tariff money, nor do they engage in commerce among their own fellow citizens to the extent that people in the settled towns and villages do. Therefore our annual levies are reduced."

"You warned me of this, of course, when I was still Lesser Consul. I maintain that encouraging the migration was the right path to tread; we need citizens on those lands to make them fully ours."

"I agreed with you then and still do," Brutus agreed. "And I foresee a time—not too far in the future, perhaps, when we will encourage settlers to move across the great river into the plains."

"Which is why I want Roman troops in that region to protect them," the Consul stated.

Brutus selected a dried persimmon from a bowl, dropped it in his mouth, chewed and swallowed. "And your unexpected visitors of this morning? What are they after, this far north?"

Pompeius quickly and expertly summarized the conversation he had conducted with the Mayan representatives. "And so we face another dilemma," he concluded. "We can either attempt to restrict our trade and exploration into the great lands to the south, or we can increase our navy to protect the shipping lanes where they pass Mayan territory."

"They threaten us?" Brutus asked, his face a study in amazement. "The Mayans have always been correct, but polite, and they are always open to trade. Roman steel for Mayan gold, a steady flow in both directions, neh?"

"They do want trade, but yes, they do not want us trading with the tribes to their south," Pompeius agreed, "obviously, they do not want Roman steel in the hands of those peoples. They also admit they do not venture forth on the seas. They may, however, send troops of their own south to interfere with our traders when they go ashore." He thought for a moment. "It would not surprise me that they do not much want Roman steel in the hands of their own people."

"They may send troops south, you think? They are much closer to those lands than we," Brutus pointed out.

"I am not certain they have troops to send. They have no citizens as we know the word, and no army as such, from what I am given to understand. Their nobility trains for battle as a matter of status and ceremony, but do you think they have a Gaul or a Carthage in their background? Or even a Pompeian War? For that matter, the Alligator People my grandfather spoke of may well have been more formidable in battle." He reflected on that for a moment. "It really doesn't matter. We have no troops to send that far in any case. But if we put soldiers—some sort of marine infantry, perhaps—on the navy's ships, perhaps even offer to put some on the merchant ships themselves, we may still afford the traders some protection. All this will cost money, of course."

"It will." Brutus thought hard for a moment. "Will you speak to the full Senate and the House of Plebs on the matter?"

"I will."

"I thought as much. I'm inclined to support you, Consul. But I must be honest; I don't know where we will find the gold to pay for it."

"We may not have to," the Consul said. He had a thoughtful look on his face; a look that made Senator Brutus sit up and take interest.

"You're thinking of something," the Senator observed.

"I am. It may be a daft idea, but it might be one that will help protect our shipping, put coin in the pockets of some of our discharged soldiers, and save some Treasury money at the same time."

"Can you give me any details?"

"I'm thinking of trade, Senator; free enterprise, of course. The very blood in Nova Roma's veins. Do you know Marius Falto? Chief of the Servian Collegia?"

"By reputation only," Brutus sniffed. "He's a thug, Consul. It was his men largely responsible for that big brawl in the Servian district last month."

"Even thugs can be useful," Pompeius replied. "And as you point out, Falto has men at his disposal—men of harsh business. Men that could put their talents to better use, if merchants were willing to pay them and feed them."

"And, of course, that gets some of his rougher characters out of Pompeius in the bargain, neh?" Brutus was grinning now.

"Even thugs can be useful," the Consul repeated. "If those thugs are away being useful on a ship far from here, then so much the better."

"Two birds with one stone," Brutus agreed.

"Indeed," the Consul replied, smiling at the Senator's unintended reference to the Mayan king. "Let's hope it delays any conflict with the Maya for a while. We can't afford it—not now."

The two men sat quietly for a few moments, sipping contemplatively at cups of blackberry wine. It occurred to the Consul that, in a life with few close friends, that the older Senator had become one of the few real confidants he had. Perhaps, then, the man would be open to hearing something else that had much been on his mind.

"We expand so fast," he began, "that it's almost frightening. I feel we are riding on a runaway horse, and all we can do is hang on for dear life and see where the horse decides to stop."

"Indeed," Brutus agreed. He looked at the younger man expectantly, his politician's instincts telling him the Consul was leading up to something.

"I remember my grandfather talking of old Rome that was, the ideals in which it was founded. He knew the first heroes of Nova Roma personally, you know. Even Marcus Porcius Cato and Marcus Tullius Cicero themselves, as well as your own forebear."

"And I would say we have not only realized those ideals, but exceeded them in almost every way." Brutus set his cup down. He laced long fingers together. "We grow through trade and exploration, but our citizens also know they travel the provinces safely, protected by Roman arms—arms borne by soldiers that answer to the Consulate, and ultimately to the people themselves."

"The people, yes," Pompeius said. "We have all but done away with the concept of a born nobility—the idea that a man holds a place in society based on what his forebears did in their lives, who they were."

"And?"

"And yet we sit here in the Republic's capital, a city named for my own great-grandfather; one of the last of the born Roman nobles. I admit I hold my own position in part because of him, and because of my grandfather."

"You hold it no less due to your own distinguished service in the Senate," Brutus added generously. "My friend, you would have risen in the Senate and, I believe, to the Consul's chair even if your father and grandfather had been common drovers or swineherds."

"I thank you," Pompeius said, inclining his head for gesture to match speech. "But you do see the symbolism of the thing, yes?"

"The city around us? Pompeius? You would change its name? To what?"

"The answer seems obvious, does it not?"

The Forum

The two Mayan nobles walked quickly away from the Consul's villa. Having arrived the evening before when the city's activity was drawing to a close, they had seen very little of the life of the great town, and so by unspoken agreement they walked through the bustling streets to the Forum, where they both goggled in amazement at the bustling, shouting, haggling, pecuniary spectacle of the Forum.

"Amazing," Smoke Monkey breathed. "There is nothing—nothing like this in our country. We have our markets, yes, but this…" He stopped to examine a stall offering Reman furs. "Look at these black furs," he exclaimed. "Have you ever seen the like?"

Pacal stepped forward and spoke to the merchant in Latin. "The furs come from the nation to the north, the Five Seas country," he explained to the older Mayan. "Some animal called a 'fisher-cat' or some such. I'm not certain I understood him properly."

Smoke Monkey removed a heavy gold necklace. "Ask him how many of the furs he would trade for this."

The Roman merchant's eyes opened wide at the heavy, glittering gold chain. After a round of gesticulating, hectoring negotiation, Pacal settled at the pelts of five of the fisher-cats and ten more of red fox, another animal unknown in the Mayan country. "He offered a puma pelt," Pacal said to Smoke Monkey, "but we have those in our own country."

"Well done," Smoke Monkey said. He took the soft pelts and ran his fingers through the luxurious fur. After a moment's admiration, he handed the pelts back to Pacal, who stowed them in a satchel he carried. The Roman merchant insisted on sharing a cup of some fiery clear liquid with the Mayans before they left, to seal the bargain. The drink made Smoke Monkey's head spin.

The brother of the Mayan king looked around the Forum again. "So much goes on," he breathed. "These Romans … they are never satisfied. They will never be satisfied. They have more soldiers than we have nobles, they have steel, and they have the great boats that go on the ocean. Such … arrogant presumption! To trade steel to the savages in the south—what sensible men would do such a thing?

"My uncle Double Bird will not stand for it," Pacal snapped.

Smoke Monkey looked around once more. He laid a hand on the younger man's shoulder. "My son," he said, "my brother Double Bird will stand for it. He will have to stand for it. These Romans have steel. They have ships. We have gold, of which the Romans have little, and we can trade for steel, but we have none of that metal in our own country. We do not know how they build their great ships. We do not know how to make steel for weapons. We do not know how to build legions of soldiers, as they have." By necessity, he rendered the words *legions* and *soldiers* in Latin.

"But the day will come," Smoke Monkey continued, quietly; one never knew if one of the bustling Romans might know a few words of Mayan. "Perhaps not in our time or our children's time, but the day will come. The Maya were a great people long before the men of Rome came to this land, and in time we will learn enough of the ways of Rome to deal with their presumptions as they deserve."

"The Maya have not made war in many generations," Pacal pointed out. "We have not the arts."

"We will learn the arts," Smoke Money said. He felt suddenly the part of an ancient people, a people that were struggling to adapt to a suddenly changed world—which is what the Maya indeed were. "We must learn, or else the men of Rome will overrun us."

"Perhaps there is another way."

Smoke Monkey looked at his son. "You are already thinking of something."

"I am. Look around you, Father. Look at all that goes on here. We worry about the warriors of Rome, but the real problem may be the merchants of Rome. It is merchants who are sending ships past our coasts, not warriors."

"This is true," Smoke Monkey said thoughtfully.

"Perhaps we should learn those arts as well. The Romans value gold. We have gold, Father. We have a great deal of gold."

FOUR
ELEVATIONS

Prior to this expedition, the western mountains were only known to the Roman people as a myth. Stories of the great, cold peaks of the west filtered back from the Tsalesian provinces and points farther west, carried forth by traders, hunters, and fur trappers.

They were only stories, and in the manner of stories, they were often dismissed as mere exaggerations. We were all familiar with the forested, misty peaks of the Tsalesian Alps, spreading from near the easternmost of the Five Seas in the north to the swampy lands of Lustria in the south. Our grandfathers told us stories of the great Alps of Italy and Gaul in the old world, but again, those were only stories, and old men are noted for their capacity to embellish.

Our own guide, hired to help us find our way through these very mountains, told us in plain language what to expect. Once again, we did not give full credence to his words, which caused the guide no small amount of frustration. They were, we thought, only stories.

Nothing in any of the stories prepared our expedition for the Alps of the west.

—Flavius Arcadius Tahonius' Trans-Mesizibi Diaries

South fork of the Big Sandy

For several days after the decision to move down the south fork of the Big Sandy, the Roman's travels were unpleasant. A cluttery spell of cold rain and thunderstorms moved through the Big Sandy's broad valley, resulting in wet, unpleasant journeying. The small lean-to shelters the cavalrymen had packed were not sufficient to allow for drying tunics and gear at night. It was difficult if not impossible to start fires.

Finally, after five days of wet weather, a morning dawned bright, warm and clear. After their first hot breakfast in almost a week, Tribune Arcadius led the men into a golden morning in the low, rolling plains just south of the river. They moved off to the southwest across a rolling, beautiful sea of grass, spread out like a green-gold ocean under the summer sun. Arcadius led his men out, away from the line of trees that marked the course of the south branch of the Big Sandy. There, under the vast dome of sky, he felt suddenly carefree.

Exulting in the morning, the sky, the grass, the glorious day, he shouted over this shoulder: "Gallop! HAH!"

The two columns of riders kicked their horses to a gallop. The well-trained mounts replied instantly, bounding forward.

Arcadius held a hand up over his head, snapped a signal. The riders fanned out into a broad wedge, simulating an attack formation. The two men wrangling the spare mounts formed up with the horses, safely inside the wedge.

Another signal from the Tribune sent the men into line. "Line of battle, to arms!" he shouted, and the men drew swords and leaned low over their mounts' necks. Beside Arcadius, Centurion Tacitus looked keenly at his commander.

"Good training time, eh Tacitus?" Arcadius grinned. He pointed his gladius at a rounded hill, standing like a sentinel above the prairie. "That hill!" he shouted. "We'll take that hill! **ATTACK!**"

Whooping, the Roman cavalrymen charged up the hill. At the crest, they stopped suddenly.

"Jupiter's balls," Arcadius said softly.

On the far side of the hill they had just mock-charged was a vast expanse of open ground, gently rolling, giving way to some low hills to the southwest. But it was not the vista of open plain that amazed the Roman cavalrymen.

On the prairie before them was a herd of bison, but not like the small, scattered herds found in the east.

"How many?" Tacitus asked no one in particular.

"Thousands," Quintus Alces Sanctus said. "Tens of thousands. Maybe thousands of thousands. I've heard there were great herds of bison on the plains, but in all my days I never imagined anything like this."

Only a few hundred paces away, the nearest bison stared up at the line of mounted men. Apparently not seeing them as any threat, the animals quickly went back to grazing. Beyond them, a heavy dark mass of bison covered the plains, stretching north and south as far as the eye could see. A cloud of dust rose above the animals, obscuring the far side of the herd. Birds followed the animals and even perched on some of them.

The herd had other followers as well. "Look there!" Arcadius and the others looked to where the sharp-eyed Faustus Marius was pointing. A mille or so away, a pack of five or six large gray wolves was shadowing the herd. The wolves were taking obvious care to remain a short distance away from several large mature bulls that were forming the herd's rear guard. "Waiting for an old or sick one to fall behind," Marius guessed. "Anyone want a wolf pelt?"

"Summer is not the time for pelts," Marcus Bubonius pointed out. "The fur is too thin. Wait until winter if you want prime wolf pelts." As they watched, two of the bulls detached from the herd and made a short rush at the wolves, shaking their shaggy heads and bellowing. The predators faded away into the grass.

"Marius," Arcadius ordered, "and Caninus. Ride down there and see if you can take a young one to eat. Keep an eye out for those wolves, they'll still be about. If you can bring one down, we'll take the kill back to the river and camp for a day or two to smoke meat before moving on. Only one, mind you, we'll only take what we can eat." He looked at Tacitus. "May as well take advantage."

"Sir," Tacitus grunted agreement.

"Bet you the tongue I'll strike the fatal blow," Caninus grinned at the archer.

"You have a wager," Faustus Marius agreed. The two legionaries pulled their heavy legion bows from where they hung on their saddles and spurred their horses towards the herd.

Julius Spotted Horse walked his pony over to where the Tribune watched the hunt. He was less bemused by the sight than the others; he had seen the great herds before.

"Summer now, Chief, but winter will come soon enough. Nothing's better than a bison-skin robe for cold weather."

"No doubt of that," Arcadius said. "We used to trade for them in Tahonia. Winters there were long and cold. I don't want to stop long enough to work hides, though. None of the men are trained as tanners, and while it only takes a few days to smoke meat to cure it, I know it takes longer to work hides to wear. Are there any locals on these plains with whom we might be able to trade for robes?"

Spotted Horse shrugged. He leaned over his horse and spat another stream of brown liquid from the herb he chewed; he seemed to have an endless supply of the stuff. "Possible," he said. "I won't guarantee it. The tribes this far out are nomads. One never knows where or when they'll appear."

"We aren't carrying any trade goods, sir," Tacitus pointed out.

"Of course we are," Arcadius said. He turned to the guide. "How many bison robes do you suppose the tribesmen hereabouts would trade for one or two Reman ponies?"

"Well, now that's a good question. Many of the little plains nomad bands reckon bison robes as money, or as near as makes no difference, so they keep some about for trading. As to the horses, even odds whether they would want to ride them or eat them. If the latter, I'd say you wouldn't do that well in trade. If you can make them see the value in horses as a riding animal; better still, if you offer to trade that one stallion in the group and one or two mares, you may be able to start a horse trade out here."

"It's good country for horses," Marcus Albium Bubonius said. "Open country, all this grass."

"If there are even any locals about. We'll have to find them first," Arcadius said. He liked the idea; he wasn't looking forward to taking the dozen extra horses through the mountains. "Look there!"

On the plain before them, Valerius Fortis Caninus had managed to cut a young cow loose from the herd and drive it towards Faustus Marius, who galloped alongside the beast and was loosing arrows into its neck and chest. The young cow was strong; it took four arrows, one in the neck and three in the lungs, before it collapsed and slid to a stop in a cloud of dust.

Two of the big herd bulls were watching the scene unfold. One of them started walking towards the fallen beast. "Forward!" Arcadius waved the men forward. "Let's gather the kill up and withdraw, quickly. I don't think the rest of the herd will look kindly on us taking one of them."

The Romans galloped down the hill to claim their prize. Two of the men stood watch, nervously eyeing two large bison bulls who observed the butchering of the young cow from a hundred paces or so away, while the rest quickly skinned, dressed, and quartered the slain beast. The soldiers loaded meat and hide onto four of the spare horses, following which the Romans cautiously withdrew to the river.

"It will take several days to smoke all this meat." Julius Spotted Horse observed. Tribune Arcadius looked across to the guide, who had spurred his horse alongside the party's leader.

"No doubt," Arcadius agreed. "Are you concerned with the time spent here?"

"No," Spotted Horse said. His mouth was already watering at the thought of fresh roasted bison hump steak. "But a settled camp and smoking fires will draw the attention of any Novan tribes in the area."

"Is there any reason I should worry about that? What odds they would be unfriendly?"

The guide laughed. "Chief, I'd be more worried about the friendly ones than the unfriendly ones. Anyone thinking of being hostile will likely be frightened off. Nobody out this far has even seen soldiers of Rome before, and these nomads are more cautious than anything else. But the friendly ones—well, you will want to make sure they don't arrive with their whole tribe and make themselves at home in our camp when they smell smoking bison meat from a mille or two downwind."

"I had not thought of that," Arcadius conceded. "Best to cross that bridge when we come to it, I suppose."

The cavalrymen spent three days feasting and smoking bison meat. Only one group of Novans showed up in that time. Drawn by the smell of smoking meat, the three grinning young men appeared as though by magic out of the prairie at sunset on the second day and passed a night with the Romans. They went away in the morning with a gift of bison meat, after leaving directions to their band's summer camp with Julius Spotted Horse.

"Good I could talk to them," he began. "They speak a dialect of the lingo of the people around the country up by where the Big Sandy meets the Sister. I've spent enough time in that area. If we run into their people, I can talk to them."

"Would they be interested in trade?"

"Many bison robes they have in their camp, Chief," the scout reported. "They reckon them as coin, near as they have the idea, just like I told you a few days since. Did you see the way those young bucks looked at our horses? There's trading to be done there. These people, I'd wager a talent of silver that they'd like to have a few horses. Any extra knives or anything else made of iron, they'd trade for those as well. Seems word of iron tools has spread this far; Jupiter only knows how."

"Remans," Ursus Tacitus growled.

"Very likely," Arcadius agreed. "Or maybe just wandering traders from Durobrivia. We are not the first Romans to pass this way," he added, indicating their scout with a nod.

"Too bad it's a native village and not a real town," Marcus Varus groused. He was examining a bit of smoked meat. "What I'd pay for a piece of good Roman bread!"

"We were lucky to run into them at all," the scout added. "They spend most of their time west of here, in the foothills of the first mountain range. They come east onto the plains in summer to take some bison for meat and hides. We caught them on their summer hunting trip."

When the bison meat was smoked and packed away, the Romans packed up and moved on. The Novan camp was a half-day's ride away.

The cavalrymen followed Julius Spotted Horse across the prairie. They rode west by southwest, crossing two ridges from the meat-smoking camp. They crossed the path the bison herd had taken, marveling at a mille-wide path of earth beaten bare, and the turf torn by thousands upon thousands of hooves.

The day started out warm and quickly grew hot, with no trace of wind, which was unusual indeed on the open plains. The sky was an unbroken expanse of pale blue above them, and the plains around them an unbroken sea of grass. When they struck a small stream threading its way across the prairie, the scout led them west, following the watercourse.

"Good farmland, do you suppose?" Marcus Junius Aurelius asked as they rode up a long, grassy slope towards yet another low ridge. "The grass grows good and thick. Good land for maize, maybe?"

"Thinking of turning to farming, Marcus?"

"Not really, but it does look like good land for it."

"Too dry for maize," Marcus Bubonius opined. "Maize crops will fail even back in the home province of Rome when a year is dry. Look at the country here; it hasn't rained in ten days or more, and it doesn't look like it rains much. See how the grass is already yellowing in the sun. No, this is country for drovers, not farmers. Bison obviously do very well indeed."

"Something to keep in mind," the swordsman remarked. "In a generation or two, there will be Roman towns on these plains—you see if there won't."

At roughly midday, they found the Novan camp on the outside of a large, broad bend in the creek. Perhaps a dozen Novan families had set up some broad, low, round hide shelters. A broad lane separated the huts into two groups, and in the lane five small, naked children ran back and forth, throwing what appeared to be the skull of a small animal and chasing each other with a good deal of happy shrieking. Small smoky fires sent tendrils of smoke up from the huts. On one end of the lane two women knelt, scraping at fresh bison hides with scrapers fashioned from antlers.

Julius Spotted Horse led the Roman party to the edge of the village. He motioned for them to stop. The children had ceased their chasing and shrieking to stand, gaping in amazement at the mounted men. The women scraping at the bison hide stopped and likewise, stared. Another woman emerged from one of the huts, grabbed two of the children and disappeared back inside.

"Well, then," Arcadius began. Julius Spotted Horse held up a hand.

"Hold on, Chief," the scout warned. "Let's be still a moment, neh?"

A tall Novan with streaks of gray in his long black hair emerged from one of the huts. The local was bare-chested; lean and rangy, he wore only a clout and leather leggings. His face was chiseled, hard-looking, and he was frowning at the Romans.

"A tough one, he is," Arcadius heard one of the legionaries mutter.

Julius Spotted Horse slid down from his pony. He faced the Novan and, holding his right hand aloft, softly spoke a few words.

The older man spat back a few syllables. He picked up a long lance that was leaning against his hut and shook it at the scout. When he shook the lance, a collection of what looked like animal teeth hanging from a length of sinew rattled ominously; the lance looked as much a badge of office as a weapon, but it nevertheless had a nasty-looking fire-hardened point.

Tribune Arcadius laid a hand on his gladius. "Marius," he said softly. The archer was quietly nocking an arrow to his bow. "Hold, now."

Undeterred, the scout spoke a few more words, slowly. He made a sign, locking both hands together and holding them out in front of his chest.

The Novan lowered the lance, but held his frown.

The sun beat down, hot; the air was still. Somewhere nearby a bird called. Arcadius felt a trickle of sweat run down his back under his red soldier's tunic. He was keenly aware of all his surroundings; the dust in the narrow lane between the huts, the vast expanse of pale blue sky overhead, the faint chuckle of the stream flowing over a riffle nearby, the wooden handle of his gladius. He realized suddenly how tightly he was clutching the sword. Releasing it, he shook his hand to relieve his cramping fingers, then wiped his palm on his tunic. Before him, Julius Spotted Horse and the old Novan stood, staring at each other.

Impasse.

A shout rose from the far side of the tiny village. With a great sense of relief, the Tribune recognized the three young men that had visited the Romans' camp on the prairie, running towards them with broad grins on their faces. One of them stopped and spoke quickly to the older man, who nodded and laid his lance aside. The older Novan turned back to Julius Spotted Horse and raised his right hand in the apparently universal Novan sign of peaceful greeting.

Arcadius let out the breath he didn't realize he'd been holding.

"It's all right, Chief," the scout said over his shoulder. "Have the boys dismount. I think it's the horses that spooked the old man." He looked back at the flint-eyed old Novan, who was staring at the mounted Roman cavalrymen. His face was inscrutable, but his eyes were widened just a bit, barely — only barely — revealing his amazement.

"It's one thing to be told of something strange and new," Quintus Alces Sanctus observed, "and yet another to see it for yourself."

"Indeed," the Tribune replied. "Dismount, men. Marius and Faustus, see to tethering the horses nearby in good grass. We'll see if there's any trading to be done here."

Julius Spotted Horse spoke to the three younger men for a few moments, then returned to the Tribune with the three youngsters in tow. "They knew we were coming, but the horses were a shock even so," he said, confirming what the Stoic had opined. "They have bison robes, footwear, carrying cases of rawhide, all ready to trade. Seems they've had a couple of good seasons, and so plenty of goods in camp. And I was right — they want iron and horses." He spat some of his foul-smelling chewing weed into the dust. "Right anxious for horses, the young chaps are, now that they've seen us ride them."

"Very well," Arcadius decided. "We'll stay a day or two and trade."

"Fitting, that is. The business of Rome," Alces Sanctus reminded them, "is business, after all."

The balance of the day was spent accustoming the Novan nomads to the horses and to the Roman men. Julius Spotted Horse took the men aside and issued a stern warning regarding the Novan women. "These bands, they're just one big extended family, see. The girls that are of age are either married, good as these people have the idea, or promised. If you lot try to upend one or more of them, it will cause trouble."

"How do you know that?" Valerius Fortis Caninus demanded.

The scout pulled up his tunic to show a long, jagged scar running up his left thigh. "I've got another on my chest. One of those bloody black glass knives these plains people carry. I tried to sweet-talk a girl in one of these camps myself, you see."

"What happened?"

Spotted Horse grinned evilly and tapped the handle of his gladius where it hung sheathed on his belt. "Three-fourths Novan, I am, but the one-fourth Roman in me drove me to join the legions, as you already know. The bastard took me by surprise and cut me good—but I had my sword. I opened him up like gutting a fish. And then I had to run into the prairie in the middle of the night, as though the very Furies themselves were after me. And, you know, they were. That group hunted me for a good ten days. Hopefully I'll never see them again."

Tribune Arcadius spoke up. "Point taken," he said. "Men, consider that an order. We're here to trade. You'll have to pursue native girls some other time."

With evening drawing on, the Roman party set up their low tents a hundred paces or so from the village and gathered around their own fires to cook the evening meal. The three young men from the prairie joined them briefly, and made it plain through the medium of Julius Spotted Horse that if nothing else, they wanted horses.

The next day, the trading began.

An amazing variety of goods appeared from the low hide huts: Tanned bison robes with the heavy, shaggy fur still on, scraped smooth and soft as fine cotton, rectangular carrying cases made of rawhide cured hard as wood, dried bison and venison jerky along with softer fare of finely chopped deer meat, mixed with berries and leaves and dried. "Tasty, this," Centurion Tacitus allowed after sampling the latter.

An agreement was struck at last: All but one of the string of Reman ponies went to the Novan tribe, including the one stallion and ten healthy mares. Julius Spotted Horse was allowed to keep the last mare as a spare horse. "We still have the mountains to cross," he pointed out, "and it can be hard on horses."

In exchange, the Romans obtained two heavy bison robes for each man, and a dozen heavy rawhide cases packed tight with jerked meat and the ground meat concoction. The old Novan who had confronted them the first day, intuiting that Tribune Arcadius was the group's leader, presented him with a beautifully decorated tunic of dark yellow tanned deerskin, covered with fine white beads carved from deer antler and trimmed with wolf fur. Arcadius didn't need the scout to tell him what the appropriate response was, and so presented the old Novan with a small axe made of fine Roman steel and a spare red soldier's tunic from his pack, which caused the Novan chief's face to light up.

"Good trade there, Chief," Julius Spotted Horse observed.

That evening the Novan tribe presented the Roman cavalrymen with a huge feast of bison and venison. After the meal, a bonfire was constructed in the middle of the village and the successful trades celebrated with much laughter, dancing and singing. The old chief delighted the children of the tribe and amazed the Romans by producing a small leather bag of white powder that produced a huge flare of pale purple flame when tossed into the fire.

"Vulcan beneath us," Marcus Bubonius breathed. "I have to have some of that." Grabbing Julius Spotted Horse, he engaged the man in an excited conversation that ended with the old Novan laughing and pointing vaguely to the southwest.

"What was that all about?" Quintus Alces Sanctus asked when his old friend came back and sat beside him.

"I'm not sure what this is, but I want to know more," he said. Bubonius displayed a small wooden case in which he had some of the gray-white powder, a gift from the Novan chief. "He says he gets it from a series of caves in the hills to the southwest. As near as Spotted Horse can get out of him, it leaches out of bat shit. I'm sure that must be wrong, but I intend to find out."

"Why?"

"I'm sure this stuff is useful. That's what we're out here for, neh? To find useful places, people, and things, for the betterment of Rome? Well, I don't know to what use I can put this white powder, but I want to see where it comes from and if we can make it somehow. It would be useful for starting fires ...and maybe..." His voice trailed off as he looked up at the stars.

Beside him, Sanctus chuckled. "Always the physician, you," he said. "If there's a powder, potion, or paste that someone might use to cure a boil, a cough, or a headache, you'll want to know about it."

"A task I'm bound to by Meditrina Herself, I remind you."

"And one that we're all the better for," his friend agreed.

Pompeius

Marius Falto was a short man, squat, hard-muscled, with a broad, scowling face that wore a seemingly perpetual stubble of black whiskers. He kept his black hair cut in a stubble, and went about his business in the Nova Roman capital city dressed in a tradesman's rough tunic. He appeared to be a minor artisan or craftsman, while he was in fact the head of the Servian College that controlled the movement of grain, fruits, and vegetables in and out of the city by the simple expedient of controlling the teamsters and shipping wagons — nothing moved in or out of Pompeius without the various Collegia and, therefore, Marius Falto getting a percentage.

It was a source of no small annoyance to Falto that he received no such percentage from goods moved by water. The Matutian College controlled the Pompeian docks and also the docks at Durobrivia and Pulcia.

This had been the source of several minor turf wars between Falto's group and the Matutian College, with the other minor Collegia taking sides as seemed to suit their interests at the moment.

None of the Collegia had expected the Consulate to take any direct interest in their affairs. But the Consul of Nova Roma had done precisely that, summoning Marius Falto to a meeting in the Senate hall, no less.

Falto was unsure what to make of the summons. He needed advice, and on this early-summer morning, found himself making steps towards the Aventine hill, to seek the counsel of one of the few people in Pompeius he trusted.

Drusilla Secunda stood out in Pompeius. She stood out not only by being the proprietor of the Raven's Roost, the largest inn and tavern in the Aventine district, but also by being the only woman to own such an establishment in all of the city.

Drusilla Secunda stood out for another reason. A great-grandfather from Cisalpine Gaul left her a legacy of curly ash-blonde hair, an increasingly uncommon sight in a people, Roman though they be by name, in whom jet-black Novan hair was increasingly the norm.

She was a small woman, slight of build and slim, with a restless, nervous energy that had her bustling about her inn day and night, interceding with unpleasant customers, overseeing sometimes unreliable employees, and haggling with suppliers of foodstuffs, beer, and wine.

Drusilla also served as an unofficial confidante and sounding board for many key people in the Aventine—including Marius Falto. She looked up as that worthy walked through the door of the Raven's Roost.

"Marius," she called from where she was cleaning up behind the inn's small serving counter. "Early in the day for you to be all the way over here on the Aventine."

"Need something to set me up for the day," the Collegium chief replied. "Have you any of that blackberry wine?"

Drusilla Secunda poured the deep, dark red-purple wine from an earthenware pitcher into a small, fired clay cup. "Here you are, then. Just opened this barrel this morning."

Marius Falto took the cup and sipped. "Fine batch," he complimented the innkeeper; whatever his undisputed control over the Servian College and his influence over the other Collegia, he knew the value of staying in Secunda's good graces. She had her ear to the ground on goings-on all over the province of Rome.

Drusilla leaned on the counter and propped her chin on her hands. "So," she repeated, "What brings you over here?"

"The Consul has invited me and the other Collegia chiefs to a meeting," Falto said. He sipped again. "Said it would be worth our while to hear what he has to say. Said we'd profit by it."

"When is this meeting?"

"This afternoon," Falto said. "In the temple of Concordia." The small temple on the western side of the Forum was the traditional place for making marriage and business arrangements; in Rome, no such agreement could be made without the blessings of the Concordian priests.

"Serious, then," the innkeeper observed.

"And well timed. I've too many men idle. Idle men cause trouble. Trouble is bad for business. And when my men get in trouble, I have to deal with them, and too many of them are harsh men. Harsh men must be dealt with harshly when they get out of line, or they start getting ideas."

"Ideas that they might be able to be top man themselves," Secunda suggested.

"Some, yes," Falto admitted.

"So, will you go to this meeting?"

"Can't hardly refuse an invite from the Consul," Falto said. "Still…it's a bit odd, isn't it? The Consul himself, taking notice of the affairs of the Collegia? That's never happened before. The quality doesn't worry much about what the Collegia are up to, as long as goods keep moving into the city."

Ah, Drusilla Secunda thought. *He's fishing for something. He knows half the Senate dines and drinks here regularly.* She decided to give the Collegium man a little of what he seemed to be looking for: "Maybe he has something for your harsh men to do. The Senate has to know about some of the trouble you've been having."

"I've kept things quiet," Falto objected.

"Still. It's hardly news that the Collegia have been scrapping among themselves. The whole of the Aventine talks about it. A lot of the shop owners, artisans and so on are worried—bad for business, you know."

As if on cue, one of the Servian College men ran into the inn. "Chief!" he shouted. "Three of the boys were in a big fight with some of the Matutian College men. Soldiers involved, too. Big mess."

Falto looked at the man, then back at Drusilla Secunda. "As though the gods themselves heard you," he snapped. "All right," he told the messenger. "Show me. I'll sort those bastards out." He drained his cup and rushed out.

Drusilla Secunda allowed herself a slight smile. She knew that, come evening, one of her regular guests would be Consul Pompeius' houseman. She planned to send him back to his employer with a message.

FIVE
FALL COLORS

Crossing the plains would later be acknowledged as the easier part of the journey. One day in late summer the mountains came slowly, dimly into view, distant giants.

On first sighting we thought that two, perhaps three days would see us into the western Alps. But we underestimated the distances involved, fooled perhaps by the clearer air and open country of those climes. It was not for several days that we finally ascended into the low hills that formed a rampart before the giant mountains whose white-capped peaks urged us onward.

As on the plains, each day brought new varieties of flora and fauna to the attention of our journey of discovery. New peoples came to our attention as well, some nomads like the plains folk, some more settled. Although most were friendly, some of the Novan locals were hostile to our advance, and some few even sought to prevent our passage.

Those peoples had not reckoned with soldiers of Rome before. Small party though we were, we bore the discipline and the steel of Rome with us.

But, in the end, it was not the peoples that would change the very history of the Republic, but another discovery entirely.

—Flavius Arcadius Tahonius' Trans-Mesizibi Diaries

The foothills

On the urging of Julius Spotted Horse, Tribune Arcadius decided to abandon the lower fork of the Sandy and proceed up a tributary creek into the hills. "Passed this way before," the guide had said, "I think. It's been a couple of years ago now. But there's a pass across this first big range of mountains."

The pass Julius Spotted Horse remembered was still several days journey off, and the Tribune pushed his men hard; he wanted to be well across before winter hit. As they climbed, higher and higher, the open, brush-covered country gave way to trees, grassy meadows, and streams. One afternoon they climbed through a broad valley lined with dark pines on the one side, and on the other....

"Have you ever seen such trees?"

At the head of the column, Tribune Arcadius cast a curious look at the normally silent giant at his side. He looked past the centurion at the mountainside, where a vast, glittering cascade of gold spilled down the slope. It was an amazing sight, like a vast curtain of gold coins, sparkling in the bright sunshine, moved by the breeze.

"I have," Arcadius said, "as have you; these trees, they are much like the birches and aspen of Tahonia. But I've never seen them cover an entire hillside like that. And the way their leaves quake in the breeze, it's as though molten gold was poured down the mountain."

"Beautiful," Tacitus said.

"Yes, but it's a sign winter is coming," Legionary Faustus Marius said from his horse just behind the Tribune's. The legionary pulled his heavy bison robe tighter around his shoulders. "It's already cold here in this high country. Cold as a tavern-keeper's heart, it is."

"All the more reason to keep moving." Marcus Plancius Varus said. "After all, it's not like you're going to find any taverns, or brothels, or other places to debauch yourself hereabouts, neh?"

"More's the pity," Marius groused.

"What's your complaint with tavern-keepers, anyway?" Cominus Quintus Corvus wanted to know. "My father keeps a tavern, I'll have you know."

"No generosity," Marius replied. "Never knew a tavern-keeper to stand you even one drink on the house."

"Never met anyone you ever bought a drink for, either," Varus jibed. Marius, grinning, reached across his horse and lightly tapped Varus on the shoulder with his fist.

The cavalrymen shared a laugh and cantered on, seeking the high pass, leaving the valley of quaking aspen behind. Behind them, the sharp whistle of a wapiti bull rang out over the autumn landscape. They rode on up the broad valley, following the water course as it climbed, higher and higher.

On the third day the streambed rose into a high, wide basin fringed with spruce, and Tribune Arcadius called a short halt. "Two more days to the pass," he told the men, quoting Julius Spotted Horse. "It will be a hard crossing, so we'll spend two days here to hunt, rest the horses, and rest ourselves before we make for the pass."

The setting was a beautiful one. The stream was small this high, bright, clear, and cold as it chuckled over its rocky bed. Several small rivulets flowed through beds of short willows, and Tacitus led the men to a large, flat grassy area near one of the rivulets, a few paces from the main stream. On the south side of the basin a small stand of aspens stood, mostly bare now, while the other slopes were covered with thick, dark spruce. The white trunks of the aspen stood out sharply against the dark spruce. It was late in the day, the sun low above the snow-capped peaks to the west, and a sharp chill was in the air. Patches of snow stood in shaded places, but the sky was clear, the sun bright.

This place will do for a couple of days, Arcadius thought. *Plenty of water, plenty of wood, should be game about. We'll smoke some meat, rest up before trying the high pass.*

"Dismount," Tacitus ordered.

"Nights will be cold, this high," Ursus Tacitus observed as he swung down from his big stallion.

"Nights have been cold for some time now," Arcadius replied. "Plenty of down wood about for fires. We'll build the fires up high and keep a fire watch."

The men dismounted and started setting up camp, all the while observing their surroundings closely in the manner of experienced soldiers. Only the physician Marcus Albium Bubonius seemed moved by the surroundings; after dismounting, he stood for a long time, holding his horses' rein in one hand and gazing around the basin.

"Beautiful," he breathed. His breath fogged as he spoke, and rose into the still mountain air.

"It is that," Quintus Alces Sanctus agreed. "But there will be ample time to look about when your horse is seen to and your shelter is up, old friend."

"Of course," Bubonius said, shaking his head as thought to clear it. "It's just that…Gods beneath us, look at that!"

Sanctus looked. Bubonius was pointing not at the wide-open space of the basin but down, at a patch of wet near a rivulet, where there was a bear track.

"Not like any track I've seen yet," Sanctus said. "Taurinus!"

The tracker walked over, bringing several of the others with him. "What is it?"

"Look here."

Manius Octavius Taurinus squatted to examine the track, laid in a patch of sand. "A bear, sure enough," he said, "but not like the black bears of Tahonia, or any of the brown ones we've seen in these hills. No, this is a different sort of bear."

"What sort?" Tribune Arcadius had heard the shout for the tracker and walked up, curious.

"A big one, sir," Taurinus said. "Look here — the bears we're used to, some of the big old boars will leave tracks nearly this large, but the claws generally don't show, and the shape is different. This track is squarer, and you can see the marks of the claws, longer and heavier claws than our usual sort of bear. This is some kind of bear that must live in these mountains hereabout, but not in the east."

Arcadius thought about that. Crossing the plains, they had on occasion seen bears in the distance, some quite large, but they had not been close enough to see any differences between them and the bears they were accustomed to in the east — and the smaller brown bears of the mountains looked very much like the eastern blacks, the only difference being in color. The physician Bubonius opined that they were just a variation on the same animal, but this bear was clearly something different.

"How old is the track?"

"He went through here yesterday, maybe the day before, sir," the tracker replied. "Bear that big, he probably won't stay in any one place long. He'll need to keep moving to find enough to eat. And, if he's like the bears we know, he'll be eating all he can now to fatten up for winter."

"Very well," Arcadius said. "We are bound to run across new creatures in a land this vast. All of you, we have work to do before dark. See to the horses, get the shelters up. We'll gather more wood than we have been bringing in the last few nights. We'll build fires up high and stand watches. Keep bows and gladii to hand."

The first night in the high basin passed without incident, but in the morning a discovery would be made that would shake the little expedition, and would in time go on to shake the very foundations of the young Republic.

Pompeius

"O Conscript Fathers," Consul Pompeius began, speaking to the full Senate in session. "In these recent years the expansion of our Republic has been much the debated topic in these hallowed chambers." He took a deep breath and struck a dramatic pose. "Even as we discuss the subject here, some of the bravest soldiers of Rome are exploring those lands, having left homes and families behind to venture into the great unknown wilderness beyond the great river Mesizibi."

"But our concerns lie not only in the west. Our Republic has neighbors to north and south. To the north lies the Reman Five Seas Nation, with their extensive ironworks, fur trade and rich fishing grounds in the great freshwater seas. To the south, we are bordered by the Maya, who hold great cities in their jungle south of the Mediterranean and who are increasingly reaching north to trade for Roman steel. And to what use might they put this steel? Relations with the Maya, as with the Five Seas people, are at best tense."

"To the west we have a vast wilderness. All of you here in this august chamber know that we have an expedition exploring those regions even as we speak, and all of you here in this august chamber know as well that the Reman people of the Five Seas have also sent soldiers into that region. How long before the Maya also expand into those Western lands?"

"Only days ago, I came before you, proposing to send several legions into the plains, to garrison key river junctions. On that day I also proposed to place soldiers on the ships of traders plying the seas to the south, to protect them against any possible hostiles. And you, O Conscript Fathers, reminded me of the Republic's fiscal difficulties that will prevent both of those activities." He struck a dramatic pose. "But today, I bring news! News of a bargain, O Conscript Fathers, with the leaders of the city's Collegia, struck under the auspices of the priests of the Lady Concordia. The principals of the various Collegia have agreed to provide men and arms to protect the ships of the merchant fleet in return for…a small consideration, a small portion of the profits of trade with those southern regions."

As he spoke, he caught the eye of Senator Brutus, who sat at his place in the Senate, an inscrutable look on his face. With the expense of only one expedition to fund, Brutus had promised the Consul enough votes to fund the Western garrisons.

The plains would be under the eagles of Rome before the year was out.

The western mountains

There was a hard frost on the ground when Quintus Alces Sanctus awoke with one of the complaints of a man entering middle-age; a full bladder. He rolled over and opened his eyes.

The sun was just peeking over the low ridge to the east. The meadow where the cavalrymen had camped was a-sparkle as though the gods had scattered a million diamonds on the grass. Ice crystals sparkled in the morning sun, everywhere, and even the Stoic in Sanctus warmed to the beauty of the mountain morning. The inevitable little gray birds were everywhere, flittering and calling to each other, and this morning they were joined by a small tit very similar to the tsikadee of the East, but these, Sanctus noted, were smaller, with a white stripe over the eye interrupting the black cap. He made a mental note to tell Marcus Albium Bubonius about them; the physician was keenly interested in anything new, be it rock, plant, bird, or beast.

With a yawn, Sanctus unwrapped himself from his two heavy bison robes. He found his boots, shook them out to evict any possible unwanted guests and pulled them on, wincing at the cold leather. Next, he picked up his water bag, hoping to rinse the night's fuzz from his mouth, only to find it frozen solid.

Muttering an oath, he headed for the stream nearby. The perimeter fires were still burning, and the swordsman Junius Marcus Aurelius was sitting by one of them, alert and on guard but mostly shivering, waiting for the sun to warm him. Sanctus nodded a greeting to the legionary as he passed.

With a soldier's discipline, he walked some way down the stream before making his morning water. With that essential chore done, he walked back up towards the camp and, after he reckoned himself far enough upstream, went to the stream to drink.

He stopped on a small gravel bar, where the stream formed a small, clear pool. He bent and cupped up a handful of water, but as he brought it to his mouth, a sparkle under the clear water caught his eye.

"Juno's mercy," he breathed.

Without realizing what he was doing, he raised his hand to his mouth and drank, although later he would remember only thirst at that moment, never satisfying it. Then he reached down, into the numbingly cold water, and picked up the glittering object that had caught his eye.

He examined it carefully. It was what he had thought—indisputably, it was a small chunk of what appeared to be pure gold, stuck to a larger chunk of quartz.

"About a gold aureus worth," he muttered to himself. "And if it's here, it had to come from somewhere…" He looked upstream, following the course of the stream with his eyes, as it wound higher, eventually disappearing into a narrow canyon between the spruces to the west. Then: "Tribune!" he called. "*Tribune! Centurion!* Anyone, come quickly!"

Sanctus turned the nugget over and over in his hand, oblivious to the sound of pounding feet behind him until his old friend Bubonius spoke.

"Old friend," the physician said, "what is it?"

Sanctus held up the nugget.

A few seconds later, the stream was filled with Roman soldiers, turning over rocks, splashing in the shallows, plunging into the few deep pools.

Tribune Arcadius and his optio had been off some distance to the west, looking at the path towards the pass, but came running at the shouts from the soldiers. "What is all this?" Arcadius shouted. "What's going on?"

The men, deaf even to stern Roman discipline, ignored him.

"Sons of Dis," the giant centurion muttered. He drew a breath and let out a roar, a roar befitting a man of his mass, one that seemed to shake the very stones and trees of the valley: "*Stand at attention, you stupid bastards!*"

That broke through. The soldiers snapped to attention, even in the middle of the stream. Water dripped from tunics and belts.

"I'll ask once more," Arcadius snapped. "What's going on here?"

"Gold, sir," Quintus Alces Sanctus said. He held up the nugget. "There, in the creek."

Arcadius strode forward and took the nugget. "You men," he barked, "are soldiers, sworn to the service of Rome by sacred oath! You are on a mission for the Consulate of Rome. Need I remind you that anything we find, even gold, is the property of Rome? You, Sanctus, and you, Bubonius," he pointed at the physician, who stood knee-deep in a pool, water dripping from his tunic, "I expect better of you older men. You aren't children! You are soldiers of the Evocati!" He turned and shouted at the men. "None of you are children, damn you! You are soldiers of Rome!"

Finally, the authority of the Tribune sank in — backed up, no doubt, by the giant centurion who stood at his side. The men, rather crestfallen, shambled out of the stream.

"We will note this location," Arcadius grated. "We will report it to the Consulate on our return to Pompeius. And as for now, we will prepare to move on. Varus, Aurelius, saddle your horses and scout the trail to the west. Spotted Horse, go with them. Caninus, Taurinus, you are on hunting detail — get your bows and bring in meat. The rest of you, back to the camp!"

"You heard the Tribune," Tacitus said. Somehow his voice, quiet now, was far more threatening than the roar he had let out moments before. "Get your asses moving, or by Pluto's prickly ass I'll give you a damn good dunking in your golden stream!"

In the end Arcadius decided to move on after one day in the valley, driven in part by concern over the weather and partly by the distraction offered by the golden stream. As the soldiers packed their horses and prepared to move out, the Tribune was certain that several nuggets were probably hidden away in the men's personal gear, but he also knew that a prudent commander did not give orders he knew would not be obeyed. The men broke camp and moved out in good order with no more than the usual soldier's complaining, and that would do.

Julius Spotted Horse had identified a pass to the west as the best place to cross, and there was enough snow to make the crossing uncomfortable. "Get used to it," the scout warned them as the cavalrymen descended into a broad valley dominated by rough mountains all around. "There's at least one more high pass ahead, maybe another few days west. Then we drop down and eventually head into the desert."

Centurion Tacitus chipped off a few words from his paltry daily ration: "We'd best move quickly, then, sir."

"Agreed," Tribune Arcadius said. "We'll move as quickly as the country and the horses will allow."

After the initial drop from the pass near what the men were still calling Golden Creek, the trail climbed slowly to another range of mountains. The cavalrymen crested the second pass eight days later and followed a wide valley down into gentler country at last. At the urging of Julius Spotted Horse, the party turned south, away from the winter that was swiftly moving in.

Pulcia

Two big freighters, the *Star of Lustria* and the *Trident* were loading on the Pulcian docks, a mixed lot of iron implements, furs, cloth, and a few weapons, bound for a trip south past Mayan lands to the rapidly growing Roman trading posts along the coast.

Septimius Flavius, master of the *Trident*, was on his deck supervising the loading when a party of ten large, rough-looking men approached his ship. One of them waved, indicating a request to come aboard.

"Come on, then," Flavius called.

"Salve, Captain," the man greeted Flavius. They shook hands. "Sextus Memio. Marius Falto sends his greetings. Said you'd be expecting us."

"You'll be the cargo guards, then," Flavius agreed. "You're

right—we were expecting you. Tough boys you have there, I expect. Have you weapons and such?"

"Former soldiers, all my lot," the Collegium thug agreed. "We brought swords and bows. The Maya don't have anyone that will get on board your ship past my boys. Neither do the tribes to the south. I'll wager my boss's share on that."

"Good. Things have gotten tense a time or two the last few trips," the ship's master admitted. "Well, your men look like they'll do. Bring them aboard. My man Quintus here will show you where to stow your gear, where you sleep and so forth."

The Collegium man nodded and beckoned to his men, who shouldered packs and filed aboard. For their efforts they would receive their meals, a berth to sleep in, and ten percent of the proceeds of the trading mission in gold—of which Marius Falto would take half.

Pompeius

"And so the first lot is off on the trade ships," the Consul said, with an even, measured tone. He had been walking slowly around the courtyard of his small villa, leaning heavily on his walking stick, as his guest sat on a bench and watched.

Senator Brutus looked keenly at Consul Pompeius. The Consul was paler than usual. The cool autumn air usually helped his affliction of the lungs, but not so this year; Quintus Tiberius Pompeius's lips were a pale blue, and his breath came hard. Pompeius stopped his pacing; even that slight effort had him gasping. Finally he sat down, facing Brutus.

The Consul's term was up in the spring, but Brutus wondered if the man would live so long. He was fading away before the Senator's eyes.

"Two birds with one stone, as you said," Brutus said. "Some of the rougher sorts of the Collegia out of the city, and our trade ships protected."

"It sets a precedent," the Consul went on, "and it is one I am not sure I am comfortable with."

"How so?"

Pompeius frowned. "The Roman Army has always answered to the Consulate. That is how it should be. Our Founders made it so, and who are we to differ with the wisdom of Cato, Cicero, and my grandfather? But with this adjustment to our thinking, this measure to kill these two birds, have we broken the pact they made with the people of Rome?"

"How do you mean?"

"We have established near half a legion of naval infantry, outside of the command of the Consulate, outside of the control of Rome, and operating in foreign waters, in foreign lands. A foreign legion, as it were. It troubles me, friend Brutus. Have we broken faith with our forefathers? Have we betrayed the trust they left us?"

"Should these men have to fight," Brutus pointed out, "they do not fight for Rome; they fight for coin. If coin will entice them to fight, then coin will entice them to peace, when the time comes."

"A pension, then," Pompeius mused. "Rome will have to support these men when their task is done."

"In all candor, Consul, I do not think their task will be done in one lifetime. The Maya are an ancient and powerful people, and as we have seen, they have ample resources of their own. And what's more, they are not a stupid people. How long before they begin building ships of their own?"

Pompeius smiled weakly. "You do nothing to ease my mind, my friend. All I hear you say is that we will have to maintain this foreign legion for generations to come."

"The ship's masters and the merchants that sponsor them are supporting them, as it happens. Not a single brass oboul from the Treasury goes to their pay."

"They operate under the sanction of Rome. It troubles me, Senator. It troubles me. It seemed like a good solution at the time, and maybe it still is. Sometimes a bad solution is better than no solution at all."

The more Brutus considered the question, the fewer answers he had for the Consul.

DESERTS

> *It has long been taken as an accepted fact that the plants and animals that surround us were placed on the earth in the very beginning, and that little has changed since whatever gods shaped the various lands placed the animals and plants in their places.*
>
> *Our travels through the Trans-Mesizibi were enough to make one wonder about the assumptions the people of Rome have held for so long. Take for example the common field lark found in meadows and grasslands from western Tahonia and Rome and on through Cisalpine and Transalpine Tsalesia. In the trans-Mesizibi there is a field lark that is identical in form, but its call is completely different than the eastern lark. There appears to be no reason that the western birds should have a different call than the eastern.*
>
> *And yet there must be some reason for the differences.*
> *—Reflections on the Flora and Fauna of the Trans-Mesizibi,*
> *by Marcus Albium Bubonius*

In the West

With the worst of the mountains behind them, the Roman cavalrymen proceeded southwest.

"This is an amazing country," Marcus Albium Bubonius observed one warm afternoon. The cavalrymen rode slowly in column of twos through a surreal landscape of red, twisted rock, interspersed with dry valleys. Only a few bushes and low trees broke the stony landscape. "Look at the colors in those rocks. Amazing," the physician repeated.

"Amazing and barren," his old friend Quintus Alces Sanctus muttered. "No water. No game."

"See, those are the thanks I get," Manius Octavius Taurinus complained. "I led Marius to a group of deer only two days since, and he killed two. We still carry their cooked meat."

"You couldn't have led him to a baker, could you have?" Valerius Fortis Caninus chimed in. "I'd trade…oh, Minimus, for a chunk of fresh bread."

"And he'd steal it from you," Atius Lupus Minimus shot back.

A cloud of dust ahead marked the rapid approach of a horseman; it was the scout Julius Spotted Horse. "There's a stream a mille or so ahead," he called. "Good water, some trees. Should make a good camp for the night." He leaned to one side and spat a stream of brown juice into the yellowing grass. "Been a party of hunters though there, I'd say a few days ago. No other signs of people about."

'Very well, we'll make camp there. Lead the way," Arcadius replied.

The stream the scout had discovered was barely a trickle, but there was enough water to fill water bags and make a stew of dried deer meat and some tough cactus that the men had discovered were edible if the spines were carefully removed and the pads boiled for at least an hour.

Once his shelter was set up, Marcus Albium Bubonius wandered aimlessly around the area, as usual looking at the plant life, the rocks, and the birds that called in the brush. A low rock outcropping caught his eye, and he knelt next to it, looking at the bands of color running through the rock. He picked through the loose stones on the ground.

"Anything interesting?"

Bubonius stood up, a small rock in his hand. "Quintus," he greeted his old friend. "Nothing in particular, just this." He tossed the stone to the Stoic. "I've seen the like before, back in Tahonia."

"A stone shaped like a clam?"

"Yes. Gods know how or why."

Sanctus picked over the shelf of rock. "Ever seen one like this?" He held up a flat chunk of stone.

Bubonius looked the slab over. The surface was flat, dull gray, and the outline of two small fish showed in the center of the slab. Looking closely, the physician could see the faint tracing of fish bones.

"Not like that, no."

"How would a fish get into a rock?"

Bubonius turned the stone over in his hands. It was nothing exceptional; just a flat slab of rock, except for the puzzling outline of the two small fish.

"I have no idea," the physician admitted.

An hour later the flat stone had become the object of some speculation among the men, who all came to examine it as Bubonius sat by the fire, using his dagger to carefully chip the excess stone away from the edges of the slab, away from the two fish.

"Vulcan beneath us," Faustus Marius commented. "I bet that's it, in fact. Vulcan himself, having a bit of a laugh with us. Who else could put a fish in a stone?"

"Don't mock the gods," Sanctus warned.

"Fish," Cominus Quintus Corvus observed, ignoring the Stoic's warning, "are the province of Neptune, not Vulcan. Why would Vulcan mess about with fish?"

The discussion evolved into a debate on the influences of various gods and goddesses that went on for some time, through the evening meal. Tribune Arcadius listened with some bemusement as the men argued good-naturedly about the cause of the fossilized fish, until the scout Julius Spotted Horse spoke up.

"None of your Roman gods are responsible for this," the little scout opined. He pulled a small leather pouch from his satchel and extracted a big pinch of his foul-smelling dried leaves, which he stuffed in his mouth.

"Who, then?" Bubonius asked. He had finished his chipping, and now held what was left of the slab, only the small portion immediately surrounding the fish.

"My mother used to talk about the trickster god that walks the plains," the scout explained. "He takes the form of the little wolves that cry by night, and he plays tricks on the people of the plains. He chases game away, steals food, pinches children in the night and makes them cry, that sort of thing. His name is Coyote, and he's the one that put your fish in the rock." He sounded very sure of himself.

Bubonius looked across the fire at his old friend Sanctus.

"It's as good an explanation as any," the Stoic offered. "His people know the gods of their own land best, I suppose."

The physician looked down at the rock again, then got up to stow it carefully with his gear. *But why*, he wondered, *would any god do such a thing, trickster or not? What is to be gained by putting fish in a stone? There must be some other explanation.*

In the morning, the cavalrymen broke camp and proceeded on to the southwest. The Tribune sent legionaries Celerius Dorotheus and Junius Marcus Aurelius ahead as scouts, and the men moved out at the walk to ease their horses in the dry, dusty land.

Every rock outcrop caught Bubonius' attention. He wanted to stop and examine every bit of stone, and knowing he couldn't was an endless source of frustration.

"Gold," he muttered to himself, "strange deserts, powders that explode into flame, fish in rocks. The Consul said we were going on a journey of discovery. What will we discover next?"

A few days later, they entered lower, flatter country, and a spell of clouds and rain moved in. The desert bloomed, yellow and blue flowers everywhere, and ....

"Toads," Manius Octavius Taurinus complained. "Thousands and thousands of toads." The tracker, for some reason, had a pronounced dislike for the warty little amphibians. It was remarkable, as the little toads hopped everywhere from puddle to puddle, trilling and chirping all night.

One morning Julius Spotted Horse rose before dawn, saddled his horse, and rode off to the west. "We'll stay here for the day," the Tribune announced as the men ate breakfast, "so Varus, take Caninus out and see what you can find in the way of game. Spotted Horse has asked for a day to scout to the west, he thinks he knows the area. So get some rest, see if your horses need any attention, and report any sign of people you find in the area."

The men enjoyed a relaxing day lounging around their camp. Julius Spotted Horse returned at sunset. "We should turn west tomorrow," he reported. "We've come farther south than I suspected, but from the top of a ridge to the west I saw a range of mountains that I think I remember."

"More mountains," Marcus Varus groaned.

The scout jumped down from his horse. He patted the tough little Reman pony on the neck, and set about removing the saddle. "Don't worry about these," he said, "they are really more like hills than mountains. No steep climbs, no snow."

"Well, that's something," Varus admitted.

"How much farther to the sea?" Tribune Arcadius asked.

Julius Spotted Horse laughed. "Weeks, longer," he said. "Chief, we've come a little over half-way from the Mesizibi. We've got a lot of dry country ahead before we hit that good land by the coast."

Arcadius frowned. "By the time we get there, then, we will have been traveling for close to a year," he said.

"That long?" Centurion Tacitus asked.

The Tribune held up his rolled-up journal, where he had been documenting their journey. "We left Pompeius on the ides of March. We're well into the days of winter now; Januarius begins in a few more days. So, if it's eight weeks to the ocean, when we get there we will have been traveling about a year."

"At least another year before we get back to Pompeius," Faustus Marius said softly, "and that's if we turned around today. More like two years."

There were several long faces around the fire that evening. Julius Spotted Horse was oblivious; he was a solitary creature of the plains. The rest of the men …the Tribune had chosen them in part because none of them, even the two older men, left any family behind, and when approached every one of them had volunteered for this expedition, knowing it would be a matter of years.

But on that night they found themselves a year from home, in a bleak desert, surrounded by an endless chorus of toads, with the prospect of two or three years more travel ahead.

The Tribune felt it as much as any of the others. He walked away from the fire, a hundred paces or so into the desert, and looked up at the sky. All of the stars were there, the same familiar stars he remembered from Tahonia. But like all the men, he missed the deep forests, the broad rivers, and the tall grass meadows of home.

"Two more years," he said softly to himself. "Maybe three. Three years in unknown lands."

Still, this was the task he had, given to him by the Consul of Rome himself.

In the morning, the men broke camp, saddled their horses and rode off west.

Philadelphia

"Philadelphia," Titus Anno was telling his group of visitors, "now rivals Pompeius as a major city in Nova Roma. Since all traffic coming down the Mesizibi has to be transferred to oceangoing ships here before proceeding down to Mayan lands, to points south of there or to the Mediterranean ports in Lustria, the ports are always active, day and night, throughout the year. There are four yards now building ships. Grain, iron, coal, and all other manners of goods flow through Philadelphia. We," he concluded his brief speech, "are the new nexus of trade in the Republic."

Anno was rewarded with light applause. His twenty or so guests were gathered in Anno's large stone and wood villa that sat on a hill overlooking the expansive delta of the Mesizibi where it met the Mediterranean.

In the last decade, Titus Anno had become a major factor in Philadelphia shipping and in Philadelphia politics. In a little over fifty years, the city had grown from a few warehouses and docks on a few hectares of reclaimed swamp to a booming metropolis of almost forty thousand residents. In fact, Philadelphia was the only Roman city to rival Pompeius in population. The last ten years had seen almost all of that growth.

Two factors were responsible: Increasing trade with the Maya, and the beginnings of trade with the coastal tribes on the coast south of the Maya's peninsular homeland. Fishing was a factor, and some enterprising types were beginning to harvest the shrimp that abounded in the Mediterranean, but shipping was the lifeblood of Philadelphia.

Titus Anno was the heart that pumped that blood.

Summers in the port city were almost intolerable, hot and muggy, but now in winter the city was pleasant. This evening was cool and clear, a good night for Anno's levee. His guests were gathered on the broad stone-paved open courtyard that afforded guests a splendid view of the busy port below. Anno circulated freely through the throng of drinking, laughing guests, all of them local businessmen, shipping factors, shipbuilders, and their wives, until he found the man he was looking for.

"Quintus Bubo! *Salve*, my friend. The very man I hoped to see tonight."

"Is that so?" Quintus Bubo was an older man, tall, lean, ascetic, humorless. He also controlled well over half of the shipping that moved down the Mesizibi from Durobrivia and points north.

"Indeed," Anno said. He took the older man's arm and led him to a quiet spot in the courtyard overlooking the river. "Are you aware of the new trading posts people are talking about up the two big rivers, the Great Sister and," he troubled his memory for a moment, then snapped his fingers, "the Big Sandy! That's it. Have you heard of them?"

"Rumors," Bubo said. "Nothing more."

"I've heard more, my friend. Merchants in Durobrivia are already talking of nothing else. Given some time, perhaps two years, perhaps five, and the flow of goods out of that region will be amazing."

"What goods?"

"Grain," Anno said. "I'm told those plains are ideal for wheat. Dried and preserved bison meat and hides from the great herds of those plains. Who knows what else of value is out there?"

Bubo thought about that for a moment. "What did you have in mind?"

"You control the majority of the shipping on the Mesizibi," Anno said. "I control the Philadelphia ports and much of the shipping in the Mediterranean. Between us we could easily expand shipping up the Great Sister as far as it is navigable, the same for the Big Sandy."

"That," Bubo pointed out, "will cost. I don't know about you, but I have every oboul invested back into barges, men, and facilities. I don't have the gold at hand for a major expansion just now."

"Nor do I," Anno agreed. "But I want you to meet a friend of mine." He drew the shipping man to a small knot of people who stood under a large oak tree, talking in low tones, and extracted two small, dark men in remarkable yellow and red feathered capes. "Quintus Bubo," he said, "This is Pacal, from the Mayan capital Uukil Abnal, and his father, Smoke Monkey. They have a large treasury of gold, and are looking for a place to invest it."

"Indeed? How interesting," Bubo said. He extended his hand to the older Mayan, who studied the Roman palm for a moment and then, remembering the Roman custom, took the offered hand and shook.

The high desert

"Sweet Juno," Arcadius breathed.

"How are we supposed to cross *that*?"

The sight before the Romans was staggering. Not in all of their journeys to date had they imagined anything like this. The desert around them was as it had been for the last several days: Flat, dry, forbidding, dotted with cactus, inhabited mostly with reptiles and the strange, quick, long-legged, high-crested birds that fed on them.

But before them was not just a canyon. It was an impossibly vast chasm, a gap in the earth like none other.

"Did you know this was here?" Tribune Arcadius demanded of their scout.

"I've heard stories," Julius Spotted Horse breathed. "But honestly, Chief, I thought they must be lies. He stepped to the edge and looked down. "Gods beneath us," he muttered.

"Dismount," Centurion Tacitus ordered the other men. "Stake your horses." The men still a-horse dismounted, took long iron pins from their baggage, drove them into the hard desert soil and fastened their reins to them. Then they came forward to join Arcadius and Julius Spotted Horse at the rim.

"Chasma Maxima," Tacitus said softly. Arcadius glanced at the giant; other than orders to the men, those were the first words he had spoken in days.

"This must be an ancient land indeed," Marcus Bubonius said. "Look at the bands in the rocks. What gods are there that shaped such a place?"

"Vulcan, judging from the weather," Cominus Quintus Corvus complained. The day was indeed warm, still, and dry—just has had been the several days previous.

"Don't joke," Quintus Alces Sanctus warned. "The gods powerful enough to shape a land like this must be powerful indeed. This is their country; it's not wise to mock gods in their own place."

"Only the ill temper of a god could have made this," Bubonius agreed. He looked down into the canyon. "Long ago, from the looks of it—look, the rocks along the edge are weathered. Whatever cut this rift in the rocks did so hundreds of years ago."

The gash in the desert was perhaps a mille across, and perhaps that deep. It had a harsh, unforgiving beauty; bands of red and yellow rock formed the sharply sloped walls, and far below, the line of a river glittered in the midday sun.

"What now?" one of the men asked, somewhat rhetorically.

"That river down there," Tribune Arcadius pointed, "must come from somewhere. I suspect it's the same river we followed out of the mountains. We should have hit it before now, if it had not taken this turn west. It must have cut this canyon by flowing here through times beyond measure; look, you can see the layers of rock that the water slowly wore away. If we go upstream we'll find a place where the river is smaller and can be crossed. If we go downstream, we'll come to a place where the country flattens out, even if that happens to be where this river meets the sea."

"Sir, one of our goals is the western ocean, neh?"

Arcadius nodded to the group's physician. "Yes, Legionary Bubonius; that is one of our goals." He turned to Julius Spotted Horse, who still stood staring, open-mouthed, at the grand canyon. "What say you, guide?"

"Makes as much sense as anything, Chief," the man said at last. "I didn't come this far south before. I crossed rivers, even canyons, but nothing like this." He looked thoughtful. "The rumors I told you of back at Durobrivia, of people living in towns in these parts?" He waited for Arcadius' nod before pointing south. "As I recall they were said to be south and west of here, where the hills give way to flatlands and yet more desert."

"Towns, then? Not cities?" Arcadius was worried about stumbling into an offshoot of the powerful Mayan nation, but so far had kept that worry to himself.

"Villages, maybe towns," the guide assured him.

"Very well," Arcadius decided. "Downstream, then. As soon as we can cross, we head due west."

"Mount," Tacitus ordered. "We move."

The men took to their horses and moved slowly south, their mounts' hooves raising small clouds of dust with each step.

"Sanctus, he said the canyon must have been the wrath of an angry god," Corvus asked the physician. "You said it happened long ago—hundreds of years, you said. How about that river down in the canyon? Rivers cut valleys in the earth. The Tribune said as much. Could that river have cut the *Chasma Maxima* there, as the Tribune said?"

Bubonius thought about that. "A good question," he said slowly. "I suppose a river could cut such a canyon, but I'm not sure if the very land is old enough for the time it would take."

"How old is the world?" Corvus wanted to know.

"No man knows for sure," Bubonius replied. "Many thousands of years, certainly. Maybe many thousands of thousands."

"So, if the river was there at the beginning, couldn't it have made the *Chasma*?"

"Perhaps," Bubonius said. He was beginning to grow uncomfortable with the direction his train of thought was taking. "But I would say it's not likely. If that river cut this great canyon, why have not other rivers done so? Why has every river not cut such a gap in the earth?"

"The land is not the same from place to place, neh? Things change." A simple man, Corvus was not overly troubled by the question; he shrugged, kicked his horse, and rode ahead.

Bubonius, ever the natural philosopher who considered himself a man of reason, was more disturbed by the direction his thoughts were taking now. He rode in silence for a while, thinking. He looked at the land around him with a new perspective. This cactus and the next looked much alike, but not exactly. Why not? The tiny buzzing hummingbirds came in many varieties, but in Tahonia there had only been one kind. Why? In Tahonia the very crows had a slightly different call than crows hereabout, but both birds were alike in every other discernible way.

Why, the physician wondered. *Things change. But does everything change? Do birds and beasts change? Do men?* Another thought came to mind; *men of largely Roman stock still grew beards, while men of mostly Novan stock had little or no facial hair. Yet both kinds of men were still… men.*

Why?

For the moment, the Chasma was forgotten.

They rode south, following the Chasma, staying on the south rim as it turned west. After several days they left the canyon, proceeding through some low, rocky mountains and into yet another expanse of desert.

"Not much farther now," Julius Spotted Horse kept saying. "Better country soon."

"I thought you said you passed through north of here before," Legionary Caninus objected.

"I did. I remember how long it took," the scout replied. He leaned off his horse and spat a stream of brown into the dust. "And I know the country. See those hills ahead? We get past those, I'll bet you a gold piece that there's better country."

"So you say." Caninus sounded skeptical. "For all we know, this desert goes on forever."

Durobrivia

The chief newsreader of Durobrivia was a weathered, skinny man with leather lungs named Gaius Artorius. When he marched into Durobrivia's Forum lugging his heavy wooden stool, the bustle of activity in the city's center of commerce abated so people could hear what was new. Artorius dropped his stool in front of the Council building, climbed up on it, unrolled a scroll, and began to bellow out the news.

"News from the Senate of the Republic!" he shouted. "A motion put forth by Consul Quintus Tiberius Pompeius," he thumped his skinny chest dramatically as he pronounced each word of the Consul's name, "and passed by popular acclaim by the House of Plebs and the Senate of the Republic, the name of the capital city has been changed. No longer will the city be known as Pompeius, but now it will bear the name of the primary province. All hail the city of Rome, capital of the Republic!" He rolled the scroll up and stuffed it back into his satchel, extracted another. "The Consulate of Rome announces that a legion of the Roman Army will be sent onto the plains, along the Great Sister River, to establish a garrison. The purpose of the garrison will be to protect citizens of the Republic that travel onto the plains, seeking trade and new lands to settle. Good lands, rich lands, are available in the Trans-Mesizibi, and now Roman arms will protect those lands."

Artorius rolled up the second scroll and stowed it away. From memory, he bellowed the name of his sponsor: "Today's news is sponsored as a public service by Quintus Bubo, trader and shipping agent. Quintus Bubo provides the most reliable shipping available on the Mesizibi, from the Five Seas Nation to Philadelphia. Quintus Bubo provides true Roman services for true Romans."

He clambered down from his stool, picked it up, and stumped off to deliver the news again at his next assigned spot.

In the desert hills

"...then her husband showed up."

Arcadius was half-listening to Valerius Fortis Caninus bragging to Marcus Plancius Varus where the two men rode along behind him. The grandson of the famous Great Dog was telling of another in his interminable line of feminine conquests.

"What did you do?" Varus asked.

"I knocked the man arse over heels, grabbed my tunic and jumped out the window," Caninus said, laughing. "I was in the alley, bare-arsed, holding my tunic and belt, middle of the night, and ..." The bragging legionary's voice trailed off at the sound of hoofbeats approaching, fast. Centurion Tacitus held up a hand, signaling the column of cavalry to halt.

A horse and rider appeared over a low ridge, approaching at a gallop — Legionary Manius Octavius Taurinus, one of the day's assigned forward scouts. "Legionary Taurinus," Arcadius hailed the man. "Report! What is it?"

"A town, sir," the tracker panted. He patted his lathered horse's neck. "Bloody big town, a bunch of buildings cut into the side of a cliff and more scattered across the desert nearby. There's even a road of sorts, leaving the town and leading off south. Two, three hundred people, I'd say. Some fields on the flat in front of the town, no horses or wagons. Men and women are out working in the fields. No weapons that I could see. They didn't see me."

"A town? Out here?"

"Yes, sir."

Tribune Arcadius sat for a moment, thinking.

"Centurion Tacitus? Your thoughts?"

"Farmers, sir," the giant said. "Best to be cautious, but if there are civilized folk about, wouldn't Pompeius want to know?"

"True," Arcadius mused, remembering his conversation with the Consul, almost a year earlier now. "We'll go in," he decided. He turned to face the column. "We're going into a town," he called to the legionaries. "Let's impress them with the power and glory of Rome. Everyone in full uniform, cloaks and helmets, everything in order. Dismount and get cleaned up."

"There's a stream yonder," Tacitus pointed. "May as well take the chance to wash, sir." Like most Romans, he was in the habit of bathing regularly, and in this dry country there had not been all that many chances of late; the men were growing odiferous.

"Indeed," Arcadius agreed. "Men, follow me."

An enjoyable hour was spent splashing in a pool in the stream, after which the men unpacked the pteruges, greaves, red soldier's cloaks, and bronze helmets most of them had not worn since crossing the Mesizibi, months before.

Tribune Arcadius was fastening his greaves on his forearms when he saw the giant Tacitus approaching. The centurion had cut a long pole from the small trees near the stream, and to it attached a banner which he had apparently carried all the way from Pompeius. It was a banner with which Arcadius was very familiar; a long red banner, upon it the eagle of Nova Roma, black with white head and tail. Below the eagle was a legend:

LEG TAHON
II

"The banner of the legion, sir," the giant rumbled by way of explanation. "The eagle—the actual carved eagle, sir—it had to remain with the Second, of course. But nothing says we can't bring a banner along."

"Agreed," the Tribune replied. He turned to the men. "Mount up," he called. "We'll ride into the town in column of twos. Look sharp. They may be peaceful. Then again, they may not."

Julius Spotted Horse, looking as disreputable as always, trotted to the head of the forming column on his Reman pony.

"Do you think you'll be able to communicate with them?" Arcadius asked the scout.

"Maybe," the scout admitted. "Maybe. The sign language used by almost all the plains people drifts some as you move west. Last bunch we ran into, it was hard to understand them. That was days ago. Who knows about this bunch? These aren't plains nomads, Chief; they're townspeople."

"You'll try?"

"Of course," Spotted Horse agreed easily. "Nothing to lose by trying."

With a flourish, Tribune Arcadius motioned the cavalrymen forward. The column moved out at a trot, led by Legionary Taurinus, who led them down a broad valley, which gradually opened out into a large, dry flat.

They rounded a last outcropping of rust-red rock, and the town lay before them.

The base of the Novan town was against a large, overhanging rock outcrop that extended for several hundred paces in a shallow arc. The raised area just in front of the red sandstone bluff was covered with low buildings that looked to be made of a mixture of stone and compacted earth. The row of larger buildings backed up to the cliff itself, looking almost as though they had grown out of the rocks. Smaller buildings of similar construction were scattered in what seemed to be random fashion down the slight slope, giving way to fields of melons and maize. Past the fields, a line of low trees and bushes revealed the course of a small stream. A broad, beaten path led off to the south; the road Taurinus had described.

"Our arrival," Legionary Alces noted quietly, "has not gone without notice." The Novan men were running now, out of the fields and into their huts, and returning…

"Well, they have weapons now," Arcadius said. "Bows and clubs, anyway." He looked at Centurion Tacitus, seated on his massive stallion beside the Tribune, silent as always.

Arcadius looked over his shoulder at the cavalrymen, neatly drawn up in two columns behind them. "Into line behind us," he ordered. "Keep your hands off your weapons, but look sharp. Be ready for anything."

"They look as though they are expecting trouble, sir," Tacitus rumbled. As the men moved into line, Julius Spotted Horse reined his Reman pony alongside the Tribune. There were fewer people than Arcadius would have expected given the size of the village, maybe fifty in all, men, women, children, and elders.

"Want me to try to talk with them, Chief?"

"Best to try." More of the Novan men were gathering with weapons now, while the women and children had all moved off to the bottom of the fields, near the stream. Arcadius was making a conscious effort to keep his hand away from the hilt of his gladius.

Julius Spotted Horse walked his horse slowly forward, holding his right hand aloft in a near-universal gesture of peace. The Novan men looked at each other for a few moments, speaking softly among themselves, before a gray-haired man stepped forward. The guide engaged him in conversation with snatches of barely understood talk and abundant use of sign. The older man nodded and pointed off to the south several times.

After a few minutes, the guide moved back to the cavalrymen, shaking his head.

"Near as I can tell, Chief," he said, "they're tense because of some scrap they're having with the people to the south. That road," he pointed, "leads to some other people's towns in the desert out that way. Bad blood between the two groups, this old man says. Claims the other party is stealing women and children, but I shouldn't be too surprised if there's some of that going on both ways."

Arcadius frowned. "We can't get caught up in any squabbles between the locals. We've got a long way yet to go."

"There's more, Chief," the scout continued. "He gave me this. It came from one of those people to the south, and I'm pretty sure that man didn't have any more use for it." Spotted Horse handed over a small object.

Arcadius looked at the talisman. It was a carved image of a man's head, a horrible grimace on the wooden face. The crown of the wooden head was decorated with bedraggled feathers bearing a little of what was once bright red and yellow coloration.

"Mayan, sir," Centurion Tacitus rumbled. "I've seen the like around the markets in Pompeius, later in Durobrivia."

"Could they be this far west?"

Julius Spotted Horse shrugged. "Who knows? Trading parties of Rome get a long ways south, even around the Mediterranean to the people in the deserts and forests south. Mayans come north as far as Durobrivia. Who says they aren't out here in the west? After all, we are here. Then again, goods move a long ways on their own — passing hand to hand, as it were."

"If they are," Arcadius mused, "the Consul and the Senate would want to know."

The Novans were still standing at the edge of their fields, quietly watching the Romans. Novan and Roman regarded each other cautiously.

"Spotted Horse," Arcadius said at last, "ask them if they would allow us to camp nearby for a few days. I want to know more about these people to the south. If the Maya are trading in these lands, we need to report that."

The scout rode back into the town and engaged the locals in conversation again as the Roman cavalrymen watched. After a few moments, he returned to where Arcadius sat on his horse, watching. "They don't object to our camping nearby," he reported. He grinned. "The old chief, he did say we're expected to feed ourselves, though. Not a hospitable lot, these."

The Tribune thought for a few moments. "Centurion, you and Spotted Horse come with me. We're going to have a look around this little town. The rest of you, go up to that hill to the north, find a good campsite. We'll be here a few days."

"I'd send the horses up with the others, Chief," Julius Spotted Horse advised. "No point in looking any stranger to them than we already do."

"Sensible," Tacitus agreed.

"Very well. Dismount. Varus, take our horses up with the others."

Dismounted, the Tribune led the way into the town. "Not much of a town," he observed as they walked in, but what there was of the town was … unique.

The buildings under the low cliff were larger than the ones scattered about the plain. Spotted Horse pointed at the cliff. "Apparently," he said, "what passes for the quality among these people live there, in the cliff. The old man I talked to, he said he lives in there." He pointed at a narrow doorway in the center of the row of buildings.

"Let's go talk to him, then."

When they approached the building, the centurion looked at the doorway, which was obviously made for someone much smaller. "Sir," he rumbled, "I believe I will wait here."

Arcadius looked at the door, then back at the giant. "As you wish," he said. He bent and followed the scout inside.

Inside the building was dim, and there was a sour smell of

unwashed bodies. The old man the scout had spoken with earlier came out of a back room and greeted the Romans with a raised hand, then went into a stammering monologue.

"He wants to know where we come from, and where we are going. I think."

"That," the Tribune, "will take some telling." He looked around. There was a series of large earthenware jugs along the back wall, covered with wooden lids. "Fill him in, will you, Julius?"

"As you say, Chief."

While the scout and the old Novan carried on in monosyllables and gestures, Arcadius walked over to the jugs. He lifted one of the wooden lids and looked inside.

The jug was full of maize kernels.

He lifted another lid, then another. All the jugs were filled with maize.

"Julius," the Tribune said, "Ask him if they may be interested in trading for some grain."

Next morning

Ordinary activities in the Novan town had come to a halt. Instead of working in the fields or going out into the desert to hunt or gather, the villagers were gathered around the low ground between the houses and the fields, watching the strange visitors.

"This maize, it's different than the maize we grow in Rome or Tahonia." Marcus Bubonius was sifting some of the Novan grain through his fingers. In his other hand he had a small leather bag full of grain.

"It looks the same to me," Arcadius said.

"The grains are smaller," Bubonius pointed out. "They're darker, too. It is maize, no doubt, but it's a different sort of maize."

"How can there be a different sort? Surely maize is maize."

"You would think," the physician replied. "But this is maize, and it is clearly different." He thought for a moment. "This is dry country, sir, like much of the country we've passed through. If this kind of maize grows well here, and judging from what you told me of the amounts they have stored it clearly does, then we should take some with us. If any Romans move into these drier lands, they will need crops."

"Fair enough. They only seem to eat maize here by grinding it up and boiling it into a kind of gruel, so Marius and Aurelius are teaching them how to bake maize biscuits. The locals even have some honey, so they're in for a treat. And so are we," Arcadius grinned; it had been many months since they had eaten bread of any sort, even hard maize biscuits.

"That's what we're giving them in return for a supply of grain?"

"Well, that and Varus claims he can teach them how to make bows that are far more powerful than the ones they are using. He's at that now, with a couple of their toolmakers. That's the main trade. In return, we get the contents of four of those big jugs of grain."

"That must be eighty libra of grain," Bubonius said. "Enough to make bread—well, maize biscuits—for some time and still have enough to take a seed stock back to Rome."

"And a fair part of our orders here in the West is to find just these kinds of resources. A species of maize that grows well in this desert will be useful at some point, no doubt about it."

North of the Great Sister

Winter came early to the lands north of the Great Sister. Even as the men of Rome moved through the milder climates to the south, the Reman party, now afoot, had made it as far as the wandering headwaters of the Sister before a series of snowstorms forced a halt. They made a winter camp in a flat meadow on a bench overlooking the river, with a strand of small trees providing some shelter from the cold north winds.

No strangers to cold and snow, the Reman soldiers built solid wooden huts, gathered firewood, and smoked meat. Legate Malleolus brooded over the loss of the horses, but never for a moment did he think of turning back—not until many days had passed after they theft, when it occurred to him that they may have well spent the days required to walk back to Durobrivia, to try to bargain for some Roman horses to take up the journey afresh.

Too late for that now. They were committed.

The soldier who had been on guard when the horses were lost had vanished a few days afterward. He had slipped away into a dark, moonless night, presumably to seek asylum with some wandering band of nomads—or maybe simply to walk home.

Outside the legate's hut, a cold wind howled. Evening was falling. He had enough wood in the hut to see him through the night, and more stacked outside. The wind was harsher than any he had known in the environs around Terminus, and the cold seemed somehow more biting.

"Every winter ends in time," he muttered to himself. "Spring always comes. Snows always melt."

A brief lull in the wind brought laughter to his ears. Most of his men had opted to build huts housing three or four men, easier to keep warm, easier to pass the long, cold nights in the company of their fellows. As the commander, Malleolus kept to himself; he had not even an optio with whom to share a fire. He knew the men were growing restive. He knew there were a few native villages nearby, with the usual stock of young native girls. He worried about holding his men even to harsh Reman discipline in the teeth of such an attraction.

Legate Malleolus fed another stick to the low fire in its crude hearth, and wondered how late spring would come to this desolate place—and how many men he would have left when it finally arrived.

SEVEN CONFLICTS

It seems it is in the nature of people to war.

Rome's history, at least such of it that survived the great ocean crossing of our ancestors, is a history of war. The children of Nova Roma still grow up hearing tales of Africa, of Carthage, of Gaul.

Almost nobody even knows where those fabled lands may be found now, but everyone knows about General Pompey's campaign against the Alligator People and the Battle of Pompeius that ended that war. Every tutor teaches that lesson in every household in the Republic.

It should have come as no surprise that the Novan people we encountered on our expedition should likewise come into conflict with their neighbors. Their conflicts were more cautious than vicious, due to the small size of the typical Novan village, but their warriors were brave, and fights between groups were typically fast and decisive.

Representing as we did the power and glory of Rome, none of us expected to be drawn into such a conflict, much less to take any losses.

But that is precisely what happened.

—Flavius Arcadius Tahonius' Trans-Mesizibi Diaries

The southern desert

"Thank the gods for that little shit Julius Spotted Horse," Centurion Tacitus admitted. It was a considerable speech for the giant.

"Thank the gods indeed," Tribune Arcadius agreed. "I don't know how we would have gotten along without someone who could speak to the locals, even with sign."

After several days camped on a low hill just north of the village of the cliff dwellers, the Roman party had learned that the people to the south were not Mayans, but some local group the villagers called "The Old People," as they had been in the area when the villagers' ancestors arrived, several generations before. Tribune Arcadius had sent the scout south to reconnoiter the villages of the Old People, accompanied by the tracker Legionary Taurinus and the thief Legionary Minimus.

Trade had gone well. The Roman party had several heavy leather bags full of grain, one of which was to be taken back to Rome, the others used for provisioning. The Novan villagers were heavily involved in steaming, gluing and binding wood to make Roman-style laminated bows far more powerful than the simple ones they had been using. "The only thing I can't really help them with is arrows," Marcus Varus reported to his commander. "No metal to make arrowheads with. So I've got them making their normal sort of arrows with fire-hardened points, just a bit thicker to take the force of their stronger bows."

"At least we found out the people to the south, whoever they are, aren't Mayans." "As you said, thank the gods for that little shit Julius Spotted Horse." The Tribune watched as the scout talked to the other cavalrymen a few paces away, laughing and gesturing as he recounted his excursion.

"Not much to tell, Chief," Julius Spotted Horse had reported on his return minutes earlier. "We scouted a few small towns, villages really, maybe four or five families in each. The people live in mud huts surrounded by fields of maize and gourds, a few turkeys, and lots of skinny little dogs. They didn't look particularly warlike. The only weapons we saw were bows carried by the hunters moving out into the desert looking for deer and the little wild pigs that live hereabouts. We saw none of what usually passes for weapons of war, clubs and so on. That doesn't mean they don't have them, but we didn't see them."

"A hunting bow can kill a man," Arcadius mused. "And we know there has been fighting. Well, it needn't concern us. Go get something to eat," he ordered the scout.

The original reason behind the conflict between the two peoples remained unclear. Other than the one talisman evidently taken in trade, there was no sign that the Maya were operating in the area. Arcadius decided to have no further part of the scrap between locals and, that evening as the sun was setting into the low hills to the west, ordered the men to prepare to move on at first light.

The Old People struck an hour before sunrise.

Junius Marcus Aurelius was on watch when the Old People arrived. His shout of warning woke the Romans: "To arms!"

Most of the men had been sleeping with weapons close to hand due to the tenseness of the situation, and so were quickly ready. The Tribune ordered Julius Spotted Horse and the physician Bubonius to guard the horses and shouted the rest of the men into line, facing the south where a thin, ragged line of Novans was advancing through the low brush. Arcadius watched them coming with a soldier's critical eye. They moved in good order, staying more or less in line, crouching to lower their profiles. What's more, even in the dry brush of the desert, they moved quietly.

We have the advantage if they come at us, the Tribune reminded himself. He looked around. The sky in the east was brightening, casting long shadows from each and every low bush. *Whoever they are, they do know their country.* The approaching Novan warriors used the shadows to their advantage, moving from shadow to shadow, loosing arrows from the shade. The villagers, caught in the morning light, were on cleared ground around their town, and had no such advantage.

The southerners plinked arrows at the villagers who were pouring out of their low huts armed with bows and clubs; the villagers responded with a few arrows in reply, but it was obvious that the main battle would be fought in close, with only the Novan's round-headed clubs. None of the villager's new bows were finished yet.

The attackers reached the edge of the open ground, dropped bows, pulled clubs, and charged, screeching like lions. A few of them held back, continuing to drop arrows into the village.

Decent discipline, Arcadius observed silently. *Someone who knows his business planned this.*

"Stay in line," Arcadius ordered, "and hold here, behind the village. This isn't our fight. We hold the high ground. We stand on the defensive." He looked over the low fields, estimating the attacking force at twenty-five or thirty men, about half again the number of adult male warriors the village could field.

"Wish I had my bloody scutum," Arcadius heard one of the men mutter. He shared the sentiment; a wall of tall bronze and hardwood shields would be comforting.

Finally the attacking Novans noticed the line of Romans standing silently on the low rise behind the village. A few arrows started flying towards the Romans, but the range was extreme for the relatively weak bows of the desert dwellers; still, they began to land uncomfortably close. A group of about ten warriors broke off and moved towards the Romans, loosing arrows, and screeching as they advanced. The arrows began to drop closer still, some even were landing among the men.

"Sir!" he heard a shout. "Legionary Minimus has been struck!"

"Jupiter's balls," Arcadius cursed. "Very well—soldiers of Rome! In line of battle—*advance!*"

As the line moved forward, step by step, down the slight slope. Legionary Faustus Marius dropped back. He raised his powerful legion bow, drew, and sighted—there, a Novan warrior was waving his hand, motioning the others forward. He loosed an arrow that took the man in the throat. To the right, another man loped ahead of the rest of the attackers; Marius shot him in the chest, dropping him in the dust. He next turned his attention to the Novan archers, picking them off one by one. They tried to return his arrows, but his laminated legion bow was far more powerful than the Novan counterparts; he had them badly outranged.

Legionary Junius Marcus Aurelius drew both of his slim, gleaming swords, holding one lightly, easily in each hand. As the Novans gained the Roman line they sprang high, intending to smash down at the Roman soldiers with their heavy, stone-headed clubs. Aurelius struck at one, stabbing into his stomach; as the Novan fell to his knees, groaning, Aurelius reversed his swords, crossed them, caught the Novan's neck in the V formed by the glittering steel and neatly struck the man's head off.

Beside the swordsman his fellow legionaries held the line, shouting, slashing and stabbing with polished Roman steel against the wood and stone of the attacking Novans. In the center of the line stood the giant Centurion Tacitus, roaring like a bull and brandishing his gladius. The Novan attackers avoided the huge figure, breaking to the sides of the Roman line, where they were quickly and harshly repulsed.

The Novan attackers, more a rabble than a force of soldiers, had never encountered anything like the cool professionalism of trained Roman soldiers. They quickly disengaged and withdrew to the south as their losses reached half of their force. Faustus Marius picked off two more as the Novans ran south and the slinger Cominus Quintus Corvus felled one more with a well-slung round stone, that man crashing stunned into a pile of low brush. A pair of Novan defenders from the low village descended on the man and clubbed him to death.

Arcadius looked east. The sun was not yet above the horizon; the battle couldn't have lasted more than a few minutes.

"Reform!" Centurion Tacitus was shouting. "Report any wounded!"

The Romans moved back into a tight, compact line. Marcus Plancius Varus had been pinked in the upper arm by a Novan arrow, but the wound was no more than a deep scratch. Tribune Arcadius, with a commander's intuitive grasp of his men, noticed two missing. He looked around, saw Celerius Dorotheus standing a short distance away, looking down. He suddenly remembered a shout at the start of the battle…

Arcadius ran to the runner's side. Legionary Atius Lupus Minimus, the little scrounger and thief who Arcadius had saved from military punishment to bring along on the expedition, had been hit. He lay now on the dusty ground, dead, a Novan arrow implanted deep into his left eye.

"Shit," the Tribune muttered.

Next morning

The eleven Romans and the scout stood silently watching the flames of the funeral pyre leaping into the pale blue sky. A short distance away the people of the Novan village also watched, curious, talking in low tones among themselves. The bodies of the Novan dead of the village had already been placed in a series of shallow caves to the west, apparently their normal practice; the bodies of the attackers killed in the brief battle had been dragged off into the desert and left for scavengers.

Barely visible in the flames was the body of the little thief, Atius Lupus Minimus. It had taken some time to assemble a large enough pile of deadwood and the local greasy brush to make a proper funeral pyre, but there was no complaining at the effort. It was the proper Roman way to send their man to Elysium.

Tribune Arcadius was lost in angry thought. His first inclination was to ride south with his men and rain down destruction on the Old People. He knew that they could easily do so. The small farming villages described by his scouting party could only contain half-dozen adult males of fighting age at most, no match for Roman training, for Roman horses and steel.

He frowned. The pyre grow hotter, the flames more intense. The greasy bushes that grew in the area burned fast and hot. The legionary's body was no longer visible, lost in the flames that carried his spirit to Elysium. Arcadius had ordered the fallen man dressed in full uniform, minus his gladius, dagger, and helmet; he wanted no steel or bronze to fall into the hands of these tribesmen.

"He wanders Elysium's fields now," Manlus Octavian Taurinus said quietly.

Arcadius, ever sensitive to the interactions of his men, knew that the tracker had struck a strange friendship with the little thief, ever since the morning when a string of Reman ponies had appeared as though by magic next to their own horses.

Horses, Arcadius thought. *Minimus had two. We'll have to take them along with us. We traded all but one of those Reman ponies, but I'll keep these two.*

Should we take vengeance on the people to the south? Somewhere down there is the man who told them how and where to make this attack. He's a man I'd rather see dead.

We are a party of exploration, he decided, not a punitive expedition. We are not here to let these people see Roman military might. That may come later, but not today, not this year, not these men. We were caught here in a scrap between locals. I decided to stay and discover what was going on. Legionary Minimus paid the price for my error. We should have done our trading and left.

I'll not compound that mistake.

Arcadius looked up. The giant Centurion Tacitus was, like always, at his side. "When the pyre dies down," he ordered, "tell the men we'll move at first light."

"West, sir?" the giant rumbled.

"West. We've spent enough time here. We'll be on our way."

Durobrivia

The legion had raised a considerable fuss when they marched into town, accompanied by a century of cavalry; never before had the Roman trade town seen such a large body of soldiers. The Thirteenth Cisalpine Tsalesian Legion was moving west.

The cavalry were attached to the Thirteenth and therefore under the command of Legate Maximus Decimus Meridius, who stood now looking at the three flat barges available to ferry men and horses across the Mesizibi.

"It's going to take days to get the legion across," he muttered. Now, in late winter, with the river low and relatively placid, was at least a safe time to cross; the Mesizibi rarely froze over this far south, and in a few more months, the Provincial Council members told him, the great river frequently went into dangerous flood, stopping river traffic for weeks.

Maximus was an experienced commander. Short, stocky, thick of arm and back, he looked more like a blacksmith or Collegium enforcer than a senior Roman Army officer, but the Consulate had asked for him and the Thirteenth specifically, summoning him all the way to Pompeius to give him his orders—to spend a decade on the frontier.

His orders were clear, from the mouth of the Consul himself, and written orders to back them up in his personal baggage: Proceed up the Great Sister to its confluence with the next major river, which the Transalpine Tsalesian Council informed him was called the Big Sandy, and establish a major garrison there. He planned to send a century of infantry and half of his cavalry upriver to the next major fork to build a forward outpost there. Regular patrols would move west, east, and south from both locations.

"You will have overall command of all the Roman troops west of the Mesizibi. I expect you to bring the plains and their people south of the Great Sister under the eagles of Rome," the Consul had told him, "as far as the western mountains."

The Consul intended to lay claim to the Trans-Mesizibi south of the Great Sister, and Maximus was not going to be the man to fail him.

Still... "Almost twelve hundreds of men and two hundred horses," he groused.

Tribune Lucius Anneaus Seneca, his optio, walked down the muddy bank, a wax tablet and stylus in hand. "We can ferry twenty men or ten men and four horses per barge, sir" he reported.

"Juno's backside," Maximus swore. "It's going to take days."

"We have ten years, sir," Seneca replied, a weak attempt at humor.

Maximus was not in the mood for jokes. "Very well, Lucius. You go across with the first lot, then. See to setting up a temporary camp there. Tomorrow I will send a cohort of cavalry across, send them upriver to scout a good spot for a garrison. And Lucius?"

"Sir?" The Tribune had gone a tad pale.

"Take some goose grease. I am told the biting flies and mosquitoes are bad on that side of the river. If you need to send me a message, I will set up my headquarters here. I'll take a room in that large inn across the Forum from the Provincial Council building."

I may as well enjoy the comforts of civilization while I can, Maximus thought. *Ten years is a long time.*

"Seed wheat," he reminded himself. "See to buying seed wheat to take along. Some swine, perhaps. I should set the legion's supply men to obtaining barrels and casks for additional supplies."

"I wonder if we can take freight wagons across the plains?"

"We'll have to. See to the first crossings, Seneca," he ordered. Still muttering to himself, he stalked off towards the Forum.

The desert

Losing a man affected all of the cavalrymen, but Tribune Arcadius was determined not to let it slow them down. *Keep them busy*, he told himself, *keep them moving. The coast is out there somewhere.*

They passed through mille after mille of rolling desert. The land began to be punctuated by strange cactus, tall with raised arms. The men started calling them Jupiter's Priests, due to their resemblance to temple pontiffs in prayer.

"The deer," Marcus Albium Bubonius said one morning. "Have you noticed the deer?"

"The deer?" Quintus Alces Sanctus looked down at the strip

of dried venison he had been gnawing on. "They taste like any other deer."

"The deer in the mountains looked different. Remember their big ears? And their antlers and tails were different. These deer look like the deer back in Tahonia, only smaller. Same white tails"

"And so?"

"It's curious."

Sanctus laughed. "Everything is curious to you, old friend."

"You know I've always been interested in the natural world. I've been a physician long enough to know that men have the same organs, the same bones, the same muscles as any animal, only the shapes are varied. I've been a physician long enough to know the value plants and so forth can have in dealing with injury and illness. As a physician, the more I know about the natural world, the better I can carry out Meditrina's charge."

"Of course," Sanctus replied.

"Do you see what an opportunity this is? I would have given anything to have come on this expedition. The Tribune chose me because he wanted a physician along, but I came because of the chances it offered, the chances to see the gods know how many milles of new lands, new plants, and new animals." He looked ahead, where another stretch of cactus and bushes awaited.

"This," Bubonius continued, "is history in the making. Not glorious battles and conquests, perhaps, but history, my friend. Make no mistake about it."

They rode on, through the short days of winter, into higher country that was dry but at least cooler. Scattered rains again made the desert bloom for a few days at a time, before the sun returned and dried the land out.

Day by day, they rode on. In the morning they woke, ate a cold breakfast, and broke camp. Scouts rode forward while the main body loaded horses and followed at their usual ground-covering pace, walk/canter/trot. Midday they stopped when the scouts returned, reported, ate a quick meal, and rode ahead again. When the sun grew low in the sky they stopped, cared for their horses and gear, set up shelters, cooked some rations, ate, and slept.

It was a land of wonders they rode through. In one great, flat plain, they rode through great monuments of rust-red rock that rose far rose above them. Wolves and coyotes called in the night, and during the days they frequently heard the bad-tempered squalling of the little wild pigs that abounded in the desert. Early one morning, before any of the others were awake, Faustus Marius left camp with his bow, concealed himself by a small waterhole, and ambushed one of the lean, fast antelope that dotted the plains and deserts—none of the men had been anywhere near one before, in part because the lean antelope could effortlessly outrun the best horse and rider. The animal was cut up for eating once Marcus Bubonius had skinned it and removed the hide for curing and transport back to Pompeius.

After several days of non-stop travel, Julius Spotted Horse led them into a great, desolate valley. Impossibly it seemed even drier and more barren than the desert, but they crossed it in a matter of two days hard travel and finally ascended into a range of low mountains. The rocky slopes were covered with low junipers and scrub oaks, and swarming with quail, small deer, wapiti, and other game. A few bears and one lion were spotted but at some distance.

Supplies were growing low. The men were hungering to kill a bear, to gain the dietary fats that were lacking in venison. Legionary Bubonius was insisting each man drink a cup of foul-tasting juniper tea every day, claiming it would prevent scurvy; since none of the men came down with that tooth-rotting, debilitating disease, they supposed it worked. They grumbled but drank the tea, all the while wishing for any kind of fresh greens.

The fourth day in the hills they rode through a Novan village. The people of the village seemed peaceful, waving and laughing in amazement at the men on their horses. It was tempting to stop and try to communicate with the laughing, friendly locals, but Arcadius ordered the column to keep moving; the sea could not be far now.

Late in the day, Julius Spotted Horse rode to the top of one of the hills for a look around. "A couple of days and we'll be at the sea," he predicted when he came back down into the valley they were traveling through. He grinned a gap-toothed grin. "It will start getting warm here fast now that we're into spring, but it is cooler near the ocean."

"We'll find a good spot to camp for a few days," the Tribune ordered that afternoon. "Spend a few days hunting, replenishing our stores. When we reach the sea, I want to be ready to travel north. I want to identify any good harborages or ports on this west coast."

The order was met with cheers. Everyone was tired of riding; a break would be welcome.

"Kalends of Februarius," Arcadius observed, remembering his recorded notes from the previous evening. "We have been almost a year on the trail, and farther from home than ever."

On his horse beside him, Tacitus grunted his reply. Arcadius rolled his eyes. The giant's virtues were manifest, but good company and camaraderie were not among them.

Late that afternoon, they stopped in a small, grassy meadow with a clear stream nearby, made camp, and prepared to stay for a few days. On the first morning in the camp, the Tribune sent out two groups of hunters. "Find a bear!" was the order.

He had no idea how much he would come to regret that order.

EIGHT
TRAUMA

*We had thought the deserts a land of enchantment, but
the good lands nearer the coast were better still. There are great
valleys of grass and hardwoods, mountains covered in low oaks
and juniper, with many good streams and fertile lands between.
Game abounds in those lands.*

*It was not our intent to stay so long, not in a small native
encampment only a few days ride from our goal. But they say
that men plan, and the gods laugh, and that proved true for
us there, so near the goal of our journey. Fate and a great bear
would conspire to delay us.*

*It was to our great good fortune that the man who was
chosen for the challenge was not only the namesake of that great
creature, but the one man among us best suited to prevail.*

*But it was a very near thing. A blessing hides within every
trial, though; and in later years I often wondered why another
man had to pay the price for the blessing, which was mine.*

— Flavius Arcadius Tahonius' Trans-Mesizibi Diaries

Rome

"I have a report," the Consul gasped. "The Thirteenth has passed
through Durobrivia on their way west. The Legate was not at all happy
with the time required to raft a legion and the attached cavalry across
the Mesizibi."

"There are no rivers like it anywhere in the east," Senator Brutus agreed.

Moments before, when Brutus had arrived at the Consul's villa, he had been frankly shocked at Pompeius' appearance. The Consul had lost weight he couldn't afford to lose; his lips were pale blue, and his cheeks the color of ripe plums. He walked now with two sticks, slowly, haltingly.

When Brutus thought about it, he didn't remember the last time he had seen the Consul walk. The last three Senate sessions, the Consul had either been absent or already seated in the Consul's chair when the Senators filed in.

"I have a question for you," Pompeius began. "I would like you to consider taking the Consul's chair. Elections next summer; you could easily win the Lesser Consul's role, and step into the upper chair after that."

"Me?"

"You." Pompeius waved a hand over his chest. "As you can see, I doubt I'll be able to handle the responsibility much longer; there may be an emergency election. If I…have to step down, Poscus Cassius will finish out my term, but he is overly cautious for the time we find ourselves in now. I think he will leave the Consulate and return to the Senate when my normal term would have ended, and whoever wins the Lesser Consul election will step up." He casually omitted the fact that he had already confirmed this with the Lesser Consul, who had recently decided against taking the higher chair.

"I don't know what to say," Brutus replied. "I had not thought… As you say, these are critical times. Do you think I'm the man to handle them?"

Pompeius launched into a fit of coughing that left his face dark red. When he regained the ability to speak, he gasped, "I think you are the very man for it, my friend. And I think," he placed a clenched fist on his chest and paused a moment, eyes closed, "that your service may be needed sooner than you might imagine."

"Will you step down?"

"If Juno and Pluto give me enough time to do even that."

In the West

"Walk about a league up that creek," Marcus Varus told Centurion Tacitus, pointing up a small tributary to the main stream. "You'll come out of the canyon into a big open area. There is a trail leading up the hillside to the left, and just over the far side you'll see a small stand of those funny short oaks. We killed the wapiti in there."

Tacitus nodded. "Good." He wrapped his heavy robe of bison skin more securely around his shoulders and set out. Spring was well under way here in the western hills, but a damp, chilly spell had set in the day after the Romans had made their camp in the valley. "Marius and Dorotheus will be coming along. Give them directions to the kill as well."

"I will, sir." The legionary saluted and went off down the canyon, whistling.

This country, this golden land that the guide Julius Spotted Horse described, did not measure up by the centurion's standards. He preferred the deep, cool forests of Tahonia; the rivers, the meadows, the lakes teeming with fish. This country was pretty, Tacitus supposed, in its own way. The hills were rocky and steep, covered with low brush and only a few trees. Quail, deer, and wapiti were plentiful. At least the men fed well. But Ursus Tacitus would be glad to be back in Tahonia when this was over; he was, after more than a year on the trail, growing homesick.

After a brief walk the canyon opened out into a large open basin, as Varus had described. A covey of quail buzzed away to Tacitus' right, bringing a smile from the giant. It wasn't well known, but he was a man with a fine appreciation of the beauty of the natural world. He looked at the hill to the left, and saw what looked like an animal trail leading up.

Tacitus walked quickly up the slope. At least the rain had stopped, and the sun was beginning to peek through the clouds. *The wapiti kill should be just over the crest of this hill*, he told himself as he walked along. *Varus said it was just on the other side, in a small stand of oaks. I can carry twice what the others can, the better to have this done before nightfall. Wapiti liver will taste good…*

What's that?

Tacitus crested the hill slowly, cautiously. Something was moving around in the small patch of trees just thirty paces or so below him; something large enough to shake the small, bush-like trees.

Someone is trying to steal our kill, Tacitus thought. *Some local boys, probably, saw the chance for some fresh meat without having to work for it.* He stood tall, puffed up his chest and roared: "All right! Come on out of there now!"

The trees stopped shaking for a moment. Tacitus heard a huffing sound. *That's no boy. That's an animal—a big animal.*

He drew his gladius. He saw a large, broad form—impossibly broad—covered with grizzled brown hair. It was moving his way, very, very fast.

The bear roared as it charged. It was a massive old boar of the type the men called Ursus Magnus; nothing at all like the timid black bears of Tahonia. So far the men had only seen them at some distance. The big animals were thin on the ground, a fact the legionaries had remarked on and were grateful for.

This bear was not at a distance, and was not inclined to brook argument over the wapiti carcass it had claimed. It burst forth from the trees only steps from where the centurion crouched, sword held ready. Tacitus had a brief impression of a huge, grizzled animal with a humped back, dished muzzle and an impossibly huge head armed with a mouthful of yellow teeth. He had only a moment to wish uselessly for a scutum before the bear hit him.

The centurion managed a stab with his gladius, aiming at the spot where the bear's head met its neck, but missed as the bear swung a massive paw to strike at his head. Tacitus turned, managed to take the blow on this shoulder and instead of hitting the vital spot, managed only to drive the blade into the bear's side. The bear's swipe knocked him off his feet. By some miracle he managed to keep his grip on his sword; he rolled and came to his feet, staggering slightly.

The bear bit at the wound on his shoulder. He shook his head and looked at the Roman centurion. Man and bear faced each other.

"Come on, then," the centurion taunted the beast. "Do your worst."

With a roar, the bear came for Tacitus again. Tacitus met the charge with a bellow of his own. He managed to strike the razor-edged blade home in the bear's neck even as the bear's massive paw came crashing into his head. He fell to the ground, stunned.

A horrible pain accompanied by a grinding sound told him the bear had sunk its teeth into his shoulder. The bear shook him like a dog with a rat. There was something else; a stink of copper, a sticky liquid on his face…

He grasped at his belt. His stabbing dagger was still secure in its sheath. He grabbed it and struck at the bear's head, again and again.

Growling, the bear dropped him and staggered off. Tacitus rolled on his side, groaning in agony. He saw the bear, walking slowly in a semicircle; blood pumped steadily from its neck. *I struck the artery*, he realized. Even as the beast staggered back towards him, Tacitus closed his eyes. The world went red, then black.

Legionaries Celerius Dorotheus and Faustus Marius were following Tacitus' trail up the hill when they heard the bear's roar. "Did you hear that?" Marius said.

The men ran to the crest of the hill. "Juno's mercy," Dorotheus breathed.

Tacitus was lying on the ground, either dead or unconscious. An enormous bear was nosing his body. Blood stained the bear's muzzle and ran in a stream from its neck. Sensing the arrival of the two newcomers, the beast rose on its hind legs and roared a warning.

Marius reached into his quiver for an arrow, nocked it, and aimed. He loosed an arrow that slammed into the bear's throat. The beast dropped back to all fours with a gurgling noise, and started up the hill towards them in a shuffling lope.

Marius nocked a second arrow. He aimed carefully. He knew his reputation; he was supposed to be the best archer in all the Tahonian legions, possibly in the entire Roman army; now would be the test. The great beast only had one vulnerable spot Marius could see…

He loosed. The iron-tipped arrow leaped from his bow to slam home in the great bear's left eye, driving through to the brain. The bruin sank to the ground with a groan, twitching as its last breath ran out.

Marius and Dorotheus ran to their fallen comrade. Marius knelt by the giant. "He's alive." The archer looked up. "Run and get Bubonius and the Tribune."

"Eh?" Dorotheus looked stunned.

"The physician! The old owl! Get him! You're a runner, now run!"

Dorotheus sprinted away.

Marius examined the fallen giant. Tacitus' eyes opened for a moment; he looked at Marius. "About time," he rumbled. "What took you so long?"

"Oh, you know how it is, sir. We passed a village, and there were these two girls…"

Tacitus managed a stern, reproving look. "The bear?"

"Dead," Marius said. "I finished it for you, but you struck a fatal blow. It would have bled to death in a few more moments."

"Good," Tacitus breathed. "I'll wear its pelt with honor. He was brave. A worthy opponent…" The giant fell off into unconsciousness again.

"Few enough of those for a man your size, I'll wager," Marius said. He pulled the giant's bison-skin robe out from under the fallen man and covered him with it.

With that done, Marius walked over to look at the bear. "Horrible beast," he muttered to himself. "What a horrible, horrible bear."

Were the beast not laying before him, Marius would have had a hard time believing such an animal existed. He knew bears; the black bears of Tahonia and the mountains of Tsalesia could be dangerous if cornered or provoked, and the boars sometimes grew quite large.

But nothing like this.

Marius looked at the bear's neck. Tacitus had indeed struck a fatal blow; blood still oozed from the deep wound. A pool of blood spread on the ground under the beast. "How many men have ever faced a beast like this and killed it with a sword?" he marveled.

He went back, seated himself on the ground beside the fallen giant and fretted until Dorotheus, the physician and the Tribune arrived, huffing from their run up the hill.

"Caninus is bringing one of the horses," Tribune Arcadius told

Marius. "See if you can find two saplings long enough to make a travois. We'll never be able to carry him down that canyon."

"Sir." Marius trotted off into the oaks.

Legionary Bubonius was examining the big man. "Sir, this isn't good," he told Arcadius. "His shoulder was protected some by this heavy bison skin. He took a nasty bite there, but I think I can stitch him up. The bone isn't broken, and his shoulder isn't dislocated. But he took a nasty blow to the head, sir."

"How bad?"

"I may have to trepan him."

"We'll get him back to camp."

Bubonius stood up and faced his commander. "Sir, that won't do. He needs better shelter than a soldier's camp. That village we passed yesterday would be better, and the people seemed friendly enough. We should take him there."

"If you think that would be best, that's what we'll do. You and I will go on ahead with Tacitus. The rest of the men can finish butchering the wapiti, and this beast, too; a hefty gift of meat will ease the way with the locals."

Legionary Marius had just reappeared, dragging two long poles. "Sir," he said, "Tacitus—before he passed out—he said he would wear the bear's skin, sir. Said it was a point of honor."

"That's fitting. See to its skinning, Legionary."

On the Great Sister

Legate Maximus Decimus Meridius sat on his horse, watching his men work on the stockade around the garrison that they were building on a hill near the junction of the Sister and the Big Sandy.

The garrison already had two stout barracks, a small headquarters building and housing for the legion's officers. As Legate, Maximus had his own small "villa," really just a small house, a few paces from the headquarters building.

The stockade, as tall as two men and completely surrounding the hill the garrison occupied, was built from large trees that the soldiers had cut along the Big Sister and the Sandy, where large cottonwoods grew in profusion. Eventually, Maximus knew, a good Roman road would lead off to the east to Durobrivia, but for now, they were as isolated as any Roman except the party he had sent upstream to scout a forward outpost—them, and the party of cavalry he heard were even farther afield, searching for the rumored western ocean. *A fool's errand, that was,* Maximus thought. *What was the Consul thinking, sending a dozen men into a howling wilderness? They are wandering on a moonless night looking for a black dog that isn't there. I only hope they aren't dead.*

The day was chilly, cloudy, and damp. Winter was colder here than in Pompeius. A good snowfall a few days before had temporarily halted work on the stockade, but a sunny spell had melted most of the snow, and Maximus had ordered the men back to work. Now they slopped and slipped in the mud, but the work went on.

Today, as always, a few Novans were visible on a ridgeline in the distance, watching the work. A few had come around, seeking knives or axes of Roman iron, but Maximus had managed to get across to the locals that they had no trade goods.

He rode around to the side of the stockade nearest the Sister. The garrison's main gate would face the river, where a good shelf of flat land a bit above the watercourse promised good building sites should they need to expand. Tribune Seneca sat on his own horse there now, looking to the east. Maximus trotted his horse down to the optio.

"Sir," the Tribune saluted. "Look to the east, sir, down the river. A caravan."

"A caravan? Here?" Maximus followed the Tribune's pointing

finger and there, sure enough, was an inarguable Roman trade caravan, a large, high-topped wagon drawn by four lumbering bisoxen, two smaller flat-bed wagons heavily loaded with goods drawn by two bisoxen each, and behind that…

"Horses," Seneca said. "Maybe thirty horses." That was a significant investment; Rome's overall population of horses was growing rapidly from the small stock brought by the original party, but they were still highly valuable.

"Come on," Maximus said. "Let's ride out and meet them. I want to know what they're up to." The Legate booted his horse to a gallop and rode to meet the caravan.

The big lead wagon turned out to be driven by a cheerful, fat man, short and shining. He had close-cropped black hair and twinkling eyes. He wore a bison-skin cape over a rich red Roman robe. As the Army men approached, the fat man set the brake on his wagon and leaped down to the muddy ground with an agility surprising in one so stout.

"*Salve*, Chief," the short man greeted Maximus. He squelched up to the legate's horse, hand extended. "You the man in charge of the garrison here?"

Maximus shook the man's hand. "I am. Legate Maximus Decimus Meridius, commanding the Thirteenth Cisalpine Tsalesian Legion and this garrison. My optio, Tribune Lucius Anneaus Seneca. And you are?"

"Prospero, Chief," the man said. "Just Prospero. Merchant and trader out of Durobrivia. Saw your lot crossing the river a while back, and I was curious, so I asked around, and found out where you were headed. I said to myself, 'Prospero, old cock, there's going to be coin to be made out there on those plains.' So here I am with three wagons of trade goods and horses. And that's just the start."

"How long do you intend to remain here?" Seneca asked.

"You don't understand," Prospero burst out. "Chief, there's going to be a Roman town here. All of Transalpine Tsalesia is buzzing about the plains, about the Roman Army moving out here. I'm just the first caravan here—when there's a new market, Prospero always gets there first with most, that's what I always say—but there were at least three more caravans forming up in Durobrivia when we crossed the river. Three more barge services are building upstream of the city to move them across. Farmers are talking about the land, too. This is going to be a town, Chief, a good-sized Roman town, surrounded by farms. And it will only be the first of many."

"A town," Maximus mused. "A Roman town." He looked over at his optio. "Lucius, this may not turn out to be such a bad place to spend our decade after all."

"True enough, sir."

Prospero, still grinning, climbed back onto his wagon. "Well, Chief, I'll push on. I want to get a good piece of building land picked out near your fort there."

"You don't waste time, do you?" In spite of himself Maximus was impressed by the man's pluck, and by his unrepentant mercantilist outlook.

"The gods only gave me so much to spend," Prospero replied. He flicked the reins over the grunting bisoxen. "And I'll spend it as I always have, making coin, just you watch. Count on it, boys; Prospero's Trading Post will be open for business by this time tomorrow."

The Novan village

No more than forty people lived in the small collection of round huts. The Roman cavalrymen left their horses tethered in a small meadow just outside the village and walked in, looking around as the villagers emerged to see the strange newcomers returning. Caninus and Varus cut the lashings holding the makeshift travois to one of the spare horses and dragged the makeshift litter bearing the unconscious Tacitus into the center of the native settlement.

"They couldn't have anything like a large table, could they?" Bubonius complained. He stood in the middle of the village and looked around. "There," he pointed at a huge, flat-topped boulder on the edge of the village. "There's a large, flat rock. That will do. Place Tacitus on it with the injured side in the sun."

The legionaries wrestled the giant on to the large flat stone while Julius Spotted Horse found the old man who appeared to be the village chief and attempted to engage him in conversation with sign.

Arcadius walked over to watch over the guide's shoulder while Bubonius made his preparations. "Any luck?"

"I'm trying, Chief. I think we understand each other. He remembers us from when we went past the other day, and he can see we have a hurt man. I told him we brought meat to share with them. He's agreeable to us trying to help Tacitus here." The old man was nodding vigorously. He called something to some of his own people in his own tongue. Several women and young men ran forward to enthusiastically accept the offerings of wapiti and bear meat the Romans brought in. Four of the younger men helped the Romans lift the fallen centurion up on to the flat-topped rock.

Bubonius quickly unwrapped the hasty bandage tied around the giant's head. He pried the optio's eyes open, one at a time, and looked into them. He made a small grunt of displeasure.

"What is it?" Legionary Sanctus asked. The Stoic stood behind Bubonius, prepared to assist.

"His right eye," Bubonius said. "He was injured on the left side of his head, and his right eye's pupil is larger than the other. That is not a good sign."

"The box you asked for," Alces said, handing over a small wooden case. Bubonius took it, opened it, and began extracting a series of instruments. The gathering Novans let out a collective gasp of amazement when one of the instruments, gleaming, polished steel, caught a ray of the sun.

"Move those people back," Bubonius snapped. "Be polite about it, but I can't be crowded. I need light."

Alces, Caninus and Varus gently herded the Novans a few steps away from the boulder.

Overcome by curiosity, Caninus spoke up. "If he was hit in the left side of his eye, why is his right eye showing the signs of it?"

"I don't know why," Bubonius snapped. "It just does. That's how it works."

Caninus shook his head. "Doesn't seem to make any sense."

Bubonius looked up at the soldiers. "One of you go to my saddle, bring me my vinegar flask." The physician wiped off his instruments with a cloth soaked in vinegar from his flask, then laid them on a clean piece of leather. He bent to examine Tacitus' head.

"Caninus, come here. Put your hands on his shoulders. Don't let him move; don't even let him flinch."

"He's out cold," Caninus objected.

"He may flinch when I cut into him, even so. Hold him down."

Caninus stepped to Tacitus' head, placed his hands on the centurion's shoulders and leaned down.

Bubonius picked up a gleaming razor and carefully shaved the hair away from the oozing wound. Next, he took a small knife and carefully, slowly cut a semicircular incision around the wound.

"Hold him tight now," the physician breathed. He used the same knife to cut the tissue fastening scalp to bone, and laid the flap of skin down, exposing the skull.

"Pluto's arse," Sanctus breathed.

Bubonius looked over his shoulder at his friend. "You look pale. Go sit down or you'll fall, and I'll have to break your skull open as well. Now, Quintus. Go!"

Alces walked unsteadily away. He sat on a log next to a cold fire pit, bent forward and cradled his head in his hands.

Bubonius picked up an instrument he had only used twice before. It was a small bow drill with a bit formed of a small, delicate saw blade bent to form a circle, about two finger-tips across. He placed the saw carefully on the centurion's skull and began to work the bow.

The Novans gasped as the saw bit into bone. The physician worked carefully, slowly, feeling his way as the saw bite into the giant's skull. When he felt it was almost through, he slowed, then stopped.

Removing the drill, he looked at the circular section of bone. He poked it with a fingertip, then reinserted the drill and worked the bow once, twice. On his second check, the circle of skull was loose. He removed it carefully and laid it on the leather.

"Well enough so far," he muttered.

He splashed some vinegar on his finger and poked the pink tissue exposed, felt how taut it was. He took the knife he had used to cut the scalp and carefully made a small incision in the pink membrane.

A gush of black blood poured out of the wound. Bubonius made a small, satisfied noise. He picked up another instrument, this one a small forceps, and carefully removed some clots from the wound.

"Good," he muttered. "Good."

"How is he?"

Bubonius looked up to see the Tribune standing on the other side of the makeshift stone surgical table, a concerned look on his face.

"As well as can be expected, sir. He had blood and matter under his skull. I've let the blood out, which should help him heal normally. He doesn't seem to be bleeding anymore, so I should be able to close him up."

"What about the hole in his skull?" Varus asked.

"It will close up over time," Bubonius said. He picked up a small needle and some lengths of fine sinew. "Were we in Pompeius or ever a good-sized town in Tahonia, I would have had a smith fashion a small iron plate to cover the hole with, but nothing like that here. He'll have a small soft spot in his head for a few months." He carefully patted the section of scalp back over the skull and began to carefully stitch the edges down.

"He'll have a headache the size of that bear he killed as well, I'll wager," Caninus chuckled.

"He can only hurt if he is alive," Bubonius replied. "With a bit of luck, and a favorable glance from his gods, he'll survive this."

"He's strong," Arcadius said. "Strongest of all of us — strongest man I have ever seen. If any one of us could survive such a thing, he would be the one."

Tacitus lay on the stone, breathing slowly, offering no comment.

Bubonius looked into the centurion's right eye again. "Better, I think. We'll want to move him into one of those lodges — that big one in the center, if possible. Julius, will you ask that old chief if we might use it? Caninus, go round up three or four more men, we'll want to move him carefully and smoothly."

"Of course," Caninus said. He walked away, shouting for his compatriots.

Bubonius looked up to see the Tribune's eyes on him. "If we ever get back to Pompeius, soldier, I'll personally give you a hundred denarii bonus for this."

"I am tasked to this by the gods, sir," Bubonius replied modestly. "I expect no extra payment, but I would accept funds to improve my equipment and supplies."

"Done."

The Great Sister

At the bend in the big river, two small boys were wading with fishing sticks, seeking their dinner. The country around them—their homeland—was composed of gently rolling, grassy, low hills overlooking the river from which their people took much of their food. Cottonwoods and willows grew along the river. On the hills, there were only tall prairie grasses.

They knew the sound of hoof beats; they heard them from the bison that passed through their lands every summer. But these hoof beats were different, somehow. Splashing to shore, they climbed the low bank to see.

Gracchus Aquila had been chosen to lead the party of thirty cavalrymen up the river, and so he led, riding always at the front of the group.

Twenty days passed since they left the garrison and the Roman town at the confluence of the Great Sister and the Big Sandy.

Aquila held up a hand to halt the group. "This," he said. "This is as good a place as any." A good-sized creek, clean water over a sandy bottom, ran into the Sister just ahead. As he watched, two small Novan boys scrambled up the bank of the river to stare in amazement at the Romans. Aquila smiled at them. "All right," he ordered. "Dismount."

They climbed down off their horses.

Aquila stretched. He looked at the sun: mid-afternoon. "Set up camp here," he said. "Tomorrow morning, Polonius and Pulfo, you two will take my map and report back to the garrison. They'll send a century of infantry back with you." He looked around. "We'll make this a proper frontier garrison. It won't be the last."

The Novan village

Two days passed after the trepanning, and the giant still lay, unconscious, on a pallet in the great lodge. He lay there still when night fell at the end of the second day, chilly and damp. Tribune Arcadius dragged into the village from a solo hunting foray just as the last light was fading from the sky, cold, hungry, and empty-handed, although his purpose had been more to find time to think than to hunt.

When he approached his shelter, he found Julius Spotted Horse waiting for him. The scout stood up as Arcadius walked up, a questioning look on his face.

"The old chief," Spotted Horse said, "he wants to see you. He's in the big lodge with Tacitus and Bubonius."

"All right." Arcadius shrugged off his bow and quiver. "Are you getting along better communicating with him?"

"Some," Spotted Horse shrugged. "They use sign, but not all the signs they use are exactly the same. Several of them have picked up a few words of Latin, and some of the men have picked up a few words of their tongue. We'll get by."

"Good."

They walked through the quiet village, past the seemingly randomly placed collection of small, round huts. Smoke rose from the smoke holes in the top of each hut, and cooking smells emanated from them, making Arcadius' stomach growl. In the center of the village lay the large, oval lodge that served as a sort of community hall; it was there that Bubonius was caring for the mauled Tacitus.

Arcadius stopped suddenly, startled. "Oh."

"Oh, that," Spotted Horse chuckled. "Some of the village women scraped the bear's hide clean. They stretched it up on those poles with the head up like that and built that little fire under it. Near as I can tell they think the bear's spirit will watch over Tacitus while he heals, and the smoke from that fire will cure the skin."

"Who knows?" Arcadius wondered, looking at the huge bear's head where it hung from a pole at a man's eye level, eyes sewn shut but jaws open to reveal fearsome teeth. "They may have a point. One would think they know the gods of their own country well enough."

"In here, Chief." Spotted Horse was holding aside a hide drape over the lodge's entryway. Arcadius ducked inside.

Inside, the lodge was dim with smoke. The air was thick with the smell of cooked meat and something else, something herbal. Arcadius saw Tacitus lying where he had since the trepanning, with Bubonius by his side. The old chief sat cross-legged on the floor a few feet away. He stood up as Arcadius approached and said a few words, punctuating them with gestures.

"He asked if your hunt was a success," Spotted Horse translated.

Arcadius shook his head. "It was not."

Spotted Horse extended his hand, palm down, and brought it left to right in a quick slash. The old chief nodded and spoke again, briefly, again with a series of gestures.

"I think he says there is enough food in camp for now," Spotted Horse said.

"How is Tacitus?"

Bubonius stood up and stretched. "He hasn't come around yet, sir. I think he should have by now. He is slightly feverish, but not enough to be a worry. Some laudable pus from his shoulder wound. That's a sign it's healing, sir."

"It's his head that worries you?"

"It is, sir. He should have come around by now," Bubonius repeated.

Arcadius went to the rude pallet and knelt by the massive form of his optio. "Juno and Aesculapius, help him," the Tribune breathed. "We need him. Rome needs him."

He heard the door flap pull aside and fall again as someone entered. He heard the old chief say something, and a low voice — female and young — reply. Arcadius turned to see who had come in.

She was young, no more than twenty. Like most of her people, she was small, slightly but finely built, with long, raven-black hair and black eyes. She wore a deerskin shift decorated with porcupine quills and knee-high leather moccasins.

Arcadius found her strikingly beautiful.

The girl looked up and saw the Tribune's eyes on her. Embarrassed, she looked down. Arcadius heard the old chief chuckling. The old man spoke to Julius Spotted Horse.

"His daughter," the guide said, "Or his granddaughter. I think his granddaughter. He says her name is either Light on Water or Bright Water, I'm not sure which. Something along those lines, anyway."

"It suits her," Arcadius said.

"She is a pretty one," Spotted Horse agreed, and spoke to the old chief again. "She says she has something for Bubonius."

The girl pulled a leather-wrapped packet out of the basket she carried. She unlaced the thongs holding the packet closed and extended it to Bubonius; a pile of strong-smelling dried leaves lay on the soft leather.

"What is that?"

"No idea," Spotted Horse said. He raised a questioning eyebrow at the physician. Bubonius shook his head.

Bright Water spoke to the guide, motioning with one hand.

"I think it's a medicine of some kind, Chief," Spotted Horse said. "She's saying something about water; mixing it with water? Maybe boiling it? I don't know." He made a motion to the girl. "I think I just asked her to show us. I hope I did."

The girl laid the packet down on the pallet next to Tacitus. She spoke quickly to the old village chief, who nodded and walked outside. She knelt next to Tacitus and felt his brow, a concerned look on her face.

After a few moments, the chief returned, bearing a large woven basket and a small, fired clay pot. He placed the pot in the fire pit, burned down now to coals, and filled it with water from what looked to be an animal's stomach, cleaned and cured. Arcadius looked at Bubonius, who shrugged. "I suppose they know the herbs and such hereabouts, sir," the physician said. "I've done all I can. It couldn't hurt to let her try whatever medicines her people have."

Bright Water let the water come to a boil as she crushed the dried leaves to powder in her hand. She mixed the powdered leaves in the boiling water and stirred the brew with a polished stick. A thick, cloying smell filled the hut. Arcadius began to feel light-headed.

After some time, Arcadius could see the mixture growing thick as the girl's stirring slowed. She used a scrap of leather to remove the pot from the coals and set it aside to cool. While she rummaged in the basket, Arcadius and Bubonius looked into the pot; the herbs and boiling water had combined to form a thick, glutinous gel.

"Never seen the like," Bubonius said.

Bright Water produced several lengths of clean, soft deerskin from the basket. The leather was finely worked, tanned to a light yellow, and very soft. She uncovered the giant's chest and began to remove Bubonius' dressings. "Here, let me help," the Roman physician said. He knelt next to the Novan girl and quickly removed the bandages he had applied only an hour earlier.

The optio's shoulder looked worse than Arcadius had thought it would. Several large tears in the flesh were closed with heavy sutures, and there were large punctures from the bear's canines. Bright Water worked the still-warm gel into wounds, pushing it into the punctures. She wrapped the soft skins around the wounds and bound a heavier deer hide around the whole shoulder. Arcadius and Bubonius had to help lever the giant off the pallet so she could pass the skin under his back and secure it tightly around his chest.

Next, she repeated the process on Tacitus' head wound, again covering the fresh bandages with deerskin. Tacitus watched her as she worked. Her hands moved quickly, efficiently. All of her motions bespoke a quiet confidence, an ease with her own ability that Arcadius could only think of as strangely Roman. She chanted softly to herself as she worked—talking to her gods, Arcadius supposed.

While the girl was working, Julius Spotted Horse had been conversing with the old chief. When the three caregivers stood up, stretching to work kinks out of their backs, the scout spoke to Arcadius.

"The old man, he says that stuff is old medicine of his people. Says it will keep out the bad from the wounds—bad spirits, I think he means?"

"I've been a physician to soldiers long enough to know you have to keep wounds clean," Bubonius offered. "That's the most important thing in making sure wounds will heal well. But the Tahona have always used herbs in making medicine. I have some with me that are good for coughs and headaches, but nothing like that, for wounds. Sir, before we leave here, I'd like the people here to show me these herbs, and find out if they would allow me to take some leaves and hopefully some seeds. If it works, that is. No telling if they'll grow back east, but it would be worth our time to find out."

"Of course," Arcadius agreed. "That's part of our mission, after all, to find out what things of value there are in these western lands."

He looked at Bright Water, who finally smiled at him, shyly.

The old chief chuckled to himself. Turning again to the scout, he spoke quickly, punctuating his words with gestures. He inclined his white-haired old head towards the girl and grinned at Arcadius.

"What was that all about?"

Julius Spotted Horse wore an expression of sternly repressed amusement. "He says that when we leave this place, the girl will go with us."

"Eh?"

"Yes. As your wife, he says."

Tacitus looked at the girl, who was looking down at the lodge's dirt floor.

With the old man's laugh echoing in his ears, the Tribune ducked and left the lodge.

Two days later, the centurion Ursus Tacitus opened his eyes, yawned, and called for water.

COASTLINES

The long delay led to my marriage, as has been reported. It was fitting, since our purpose was to find what things of value lay in those western lands, that I came to find the one person who became of the greatest value to me — now in these later years, when I know now that my love for her would only grow greater.

The marriage was heralded on our return as a great symbol of the unification of Rome and the lands and people of the West. Perhaps that was so. I certainly would have married Bright Water in any case, symbol or no.

But a great journey still lay before us.

The scout Julius Spotted Horse, whose service was proving so valuable to our mission, knew of a river far in the north which led into the northern mountains. He also claimed to know of a route through those mountains, which would lead to the headwaters of the Great Sister. He knew little or nothing of the people who lived in those regions.

That was unfortunate, but how much more unfortunate we should have been without a man who had at least some knowledge of those lands.

—Flavius Arcadius Tahonius' Trans-Mesizibi Diaries

Summer — The Ides of Iunius, 82 Anno Novus

"Early tomorrow, then," Tribune Arcadius told the assembled men. "Early tomorrow we will be on our way. To the coast, then north."

The men saluted. There was more than one long face in the group; the Roman cavalrymen had grown attached to the people of the village, and their affection was reciprocated. The old chief, Spirit Bird, had made it plain they would be welcome to stay, to add their strength to the tiny band of nomads.

But the men of Rome had their orders, and Roman discipline was deeply ingrained in them all.

During their last days in the camp of Spirit Bird, the physician Bubonius had taken several of the villagers aside, gifted them with small bags of maize from the desert town, and showed them how to plant the seeds. With the scout translating, he advised them on caring for and harvesting the plants, and how to husband seed for the following year. "That will add a fair amount to their diet," the physician reported to the Tribune. "Better than depending on hunter's fortune. No more hungry seasons for them."

In return, the physician Bubonius had a small bag of the strong-smelling leaves Bright Water had boiled to make the curative gel, and a second bag of the plant's seeds. The two of them had scoured the surrounding hills for more examples of the plant, and Bubonius was frankly impressed how the girl carefully took only a few leaves from each stand of plants, showing great care to preserve the health of the population. "She thinks ahead," he told the Tribune. "So many of the plains folks we've encountered have little thought for tomorrow. Not Bright Water. Not her people."

Their last night with the people of Spirit Bird passed quietly. The women of the band prepared an ample meal with the last of the dried meat of the great bear the centurion Tacitus had killed along fresh greens, nuts and berries, and the evening was spent eating, laughing at stories half-understood, and enjoying a peaceful, warm night with a good fire.

In the morning, they packed their gear, made their farewells, and rode slowly west, towards the coast.

"Follow the stream down the valley," Julius Spotted Horse advised, "we aren't more than a few mille from the sea. Any stream will hit the sea soon enough." He was right; in the late afternoon of the second day the Romans arrived at the top of a large bluff, and past that was the vast blue expanse of the western ocean.

Arcadius sat on his horse, looking down at the sea. Then he looked up, looked at the two people beside him.

Their primary goal was attained; before them lay the western extent of the great continent to which their ancestors had been driven at such great cost.

It was a monumental moment for them all, and especially so for the expeditions' commander. Arcadius took a moment to glance at his men.

On his right sat the ever-loyal, ever-silent giant Ursus Tacitus, astride his big black stallion. If anything, the giant looked even more fearsome after his encounter with the bear than he had before. The centurion had lost some weight during his recovery, and his shoulder bore the puckered scars of his encounter with the great bear. On the side of his head a swath of hair had grown in white where it covered the scar on his skull. His helmet hung on his saddle, and even in the warmth of summer he wore the skin of the bear about his shoulders, with the fleshed-out ursine head over his own, ivory fangs hanging down over his broad, ruddy forehead. Tacitus knew that to an enemy, the scarred, silent giant on the back of the enormous, black, thick-necked horse would appear a horrifying sight. To Arcadius, he was a massive, comfortable presence.

To Arcadius' left, on what had been one of Legionary Atius Lupus Minimus's horses, sat Bright Water—now his wife, as her grandfather, the old chief Spirit Bird, had predicted, and thanks to the fact that the Stoic Quintus Alces Sanctus was well versed in the Roman wedding rites.

Bright Water sat the horse well now, after some weeks of practice. She rode as the Roman men rode, with her legs straddling the horse, and not seated sideways as a proper Roman woman would have done. Clad in a simple deerskin frock, she was equally comfortable now astride her horse at the walk, the canter, the trot, and delighted in kicking the beast into a flat-out run. Her tightly muscled legs, bare to mid-thigh, hung down from her rudely fashioned hide saddle in a manner that the Romans had found unsettling at first.

Now, they were simply used to it.

Bright Water had taken to Latin as quickly as to her horse. She looked at Arcadius and smiled. "The…sea, yes?" she asked.

"That is the word, my dear."

She looked satisfied. "We come here once, maybe twice a year, to catch fish and gather bird eggs."

"We'll camp here," Arcadius told the centurion. "In the morning, we'll move north."

The cavalrymen had spent several weeks in place with the small tribe of Bright Water's people, but they fell back into routine quickly. They unsaddled, unloaded, and brushed down their mounts, saw to their personal gear, and finally set up their small shelter tents and started cooking fires. The late afternoon's work went easily, punctuated by a jibe, good-natured insult, and a burst of laughter here and there. They were a close-knit group of veterans now, each man intimately familiar with every other's preferences and personality, their strengths and weaknesses.

It is a lucky officer indeed, Arcadius thought, *who is chosen to lead such men.*

As the sun sank into the sea, the Tribune dug into his own personal pack for the parchments in which he was recording the expedition's findings and activities. He dug out a roll of rough parchment—the original scrolls he had brought from Pompeius were long since filled with narratives and sketches, and the Tribune had resorted to making his own rough parchment from deer hides. In a small wooden box he had a wooden stylus with a bronze nib, and a few precious bottles of ink. He moved closer to the fire, the better to see, and began making notes of the day's events.

Preoccupied with his task, he did not immediately notice the arrival of his Novan wife until she seated herself beside them. He favored her with a smile and continued writing.

Bright Water waited for the Tribune to pause before speaking. "I have seen you do this evenings for many days," she observed. "But you have not told me what it is you are doing. Spirit Bird spoke of the talking marks you make on deer skins. Is this what he spoke of?" She spoke Latin with an odd lilt; more a manner of speaking than an accent as such. Tacitus found it charming.

The Tribune took a moment to digest the question. "Talking marks, that is actually a very apt description. This is writing, my dear." He watched as she mentally filed the Latin word away. "The marks on the parchment—the writing—does talk, in a way. You know of why my men and I came to these lands from the far east, yes?"

"I remember." She spoke as though reciting from memory, which she was. "You are on orders from your leader there, the con-sul, to explore and return with your stories of the people you meet and the lands you pass through."

"Essentially, yes. These parchments are how I keep those records, so I do not have to rely on my memory of events that may have taken place a year or two earlier."

Bright Water looked more closely at the Roman letters on the parchment. "You make the marks now, but in a year, or two years, you will be able to look at them and remember what you saw and heard today?"

"Yes," Arcadius agreed. "Your people do much the same thing. The decorations on your tools, on your houses, they are pictures of events of the past, are they not?"

"My father once killed a great bear, although not so great as the one the giant killed with his gladius. He painted his hunt and the bear on the hide of his bed's backrest."

"So it is here," Arcadius said. "Here, do you see these marks?" He indicated two sets of marks on the parchment:

AQVA LUCIS

"That, my dear, is your name." He took her hand and gently traced her index finger over each letter, pronouncing slowly as he did so: "Bright Water. Each of the marks is called a 'letter,' and each is for a certain sound." He went over her name again, more slowly, pointing out each letter as he pronounced each part of the name.

Bright Water smiled. The concept, once explained, was simple enough. "Is this something you can teach me to do?"

Arcadius sat silently for a moment, wondering why that thought had not occurred to him. Roman women were routinely taught to read and write; education for women was generally not as extensive as for men, but Roman culture valued literacy and basic mathematics as necessary aspects of living in what was essentially a merchant society.

"Of course," he said at last. If Bright Water was to live among Romans, she would have to be educated as a Roman. "Let me finish making my notes for the day, and we can begin tonight, if you wish."

Bright Water smiled. "I wish," she replied.

Arcadius had to smile back. He took Bright Water's hand and held it for a moment. "Give me just a little longer. Then we'll begin."

They moved off north the next day, riding slowly up the coast through a beautiful landscape. "You don't want to go inland," Julius Spotted Horse claimed. "Hotter than Vulcan's dick in summer if you get too far from the water. The ocean keeps these lands cool, you see."

"How far north is the river you spoke of?"

"Let me put it this way, Chief—you'd better plan on spending this winter somewhere near the coast, where the weather will be mild. We won't be able to get to the northern mountains and over the passes before winter comes. This is a big country."

"How far north does this coast go?"

"No man knows," Spotted Horse replied. "It goes as far as it goes. I've only been north as far as the river we're bound for."

"Another year on the trail," Arcadius said. "Gods beneath us."

"Plenty of time to examine the land along the coast, then."

"Plenty of time," the Tribune agreed.

On the third day, Marcus Varus, one of the day's outriders, rode back to the main party at noon with an interesting report: "A beautiful beach," he told the Tribune. "Fifty paces of golden sand. The ocean running up the beach. Lovely spot, sir."

"Well, by all means," Arcadius said, "let's go have a look. Can you swim, Centurion?"

"Sir?"

"I can!" Bright Water piped up.

Off the Mayan coast

The *Trident* was still beating south in a rough, bouncing sea, pushing to pass Mayan lands on its way to the great eastern bulge of the southern lands. The winds weren't favorable, forcing the big freighter to tack back and forth and to rely on the oarsmen more than its captain would like.

Septimus Flavius wasn't happy with the weather; he wasn't happy with the several leaks that had forced him to beach his ship surreptitiously in Mayan territory to make repairs, and most of all, he wasn't happy with the three large dugouts that were fast approaching his ship from the shore.

What bothered him most of all was the man standing in the prow of the nearest dugout; he plainly wore the red and blue feathered cape of a Mayan noble.

"Ho!" came a call from the dugout. "Parley!"

"Juno's arse" Flavius swore. He looked over his shoulder at his ship's mate. "Drop sail and heave to. Have to observe the fucking formalities. Tell that drunken lout Memio to get his men up and ready."

"Right away, Captain." Moments later, men were hauling in the canvas sails.

"What is it?"

"Ah. Sextus. Are your men armed?"

"Always," the Collegia thug Sextus Memio replied.

"Good. Have them stand ready, but keep them out of sight."

Without a word, Memio went below. A few moments later,

Flavius heard weapons rattling in the hold. "Oarsmen!" he shouted. "Keep steerageway. Keep her nose to the wind."

Moments later the Mayan boats were alongside. The Roman captain examined the men in the dugouts critically; a few of them were obviously arms men, but no more than one would expect to protect a nobleman. *Eight men under arms*, he counted. *The rest are paddlers and whatnot.*

"May we come aboard?" called a small, skinny man in an odd-looking blue tunic. He waved a hand to indicate himself and the nobleman.

Flavius thought hard for approximately six seconds. He couldn't see a way to refuse. "Very well," he shouted back. "I'll have my men lower a ladder."

"You speak good Latin," Flavius said to the skinny man in blue once the Mayans had clambered aboard the *Trident*.

"I learned in your city, Phila-delphia," the Mayan said. He had an oddly distinct accent, pronouncing the Roman name with an accent on the fourth syllable rather than the third. "I am called Meztli. I speak for The Great Chimali, cousin of our king Double Bird," he indicated the nobleman, who wrapped his cape of feathers about him and nodded gravely. The way he pronounced the noble's name, Flavius could hear the capital letters thudding into place.

Every damned Mayan noble ever whelped is some cousin of their king, the Roman captain observed—to himself. *Bastards must breed like rats.* "Septimus Flavius, master of the *Trident*. What can I do for you?"

Chimali spoke quickly, punctuating his speech with gestures. "The Great Chimali is concerned that you carry Roman weapons and tools of steel to the savages in the south. Those savages raid Mayan towns on the south of our territory. The Great Chimali wishes to inspect your cargo."

"No." Flavius snapped. "Anything else?"

The Great Chimali was astute enough not to need a translation for that. He spat out a stream of Mayan, gesturing at the boats that bobbed in the lee of the *Trident*.

"Chimali says, if you do not consent, he will have his warriors board your ship."

"He does, does he? *Memio!*"

With a thunder of boots on wood, six Roman collegium men appeared on the deck of the ship, armed with gladii and round bronze shields.

"Tell the Great Chimali, that I'd like to see them try." *Memio isn't as stupid as I thought,* Flavius chuckled inwardly. *He left half his men below decks—didn't let them see his full strength.*

The Great Chimali looked as though he'd swallowed ashes and alum. "I … we …" Meztli stuttered.

"I suggest," Flavius growled, "that you tell the *Great* Chimali to get his noble arse off my fucking ship, before I have one of those men carve out his gizzard."

The Mayans left ignobly. They backed their dugouts off fifty paces and sat, bobbing in the swells, as the *Trident* moved off. "Get those sails up," Flavius roared at his men. "Oarsmen, fastest cadence—get us the fuck out of here. You," he pointed at a crewman who wasn't moving fast enough. "Get your arse moving—my father's cock, you're slow. *Move!*" He was seized with a sudden urgency to get his ship, his men, and his cargo away from anyplace where the coast may hold a Mayan presence.

"Rome will have to hear of this," he muttered to himself, once his ship was under way again. "Mayans trying to intercept Roman trade ships, now. What's next? Will they start building proper ships? Rome will have to hear of this."

But it would be a good six months before he saw Pulcia again.

Maybe we'll encounter a northbound ship. I can always send a message back. But then, they'll likely have encountered these same pricks. Damn the Mayans, anyway.

Ten
FORESTS

We moved slowly up the western coast, knowing we would have to spend the winter somewhere near the ocean in order to attempt the northern mountains in spring and summer. As we moved north through the summer and autumn, we stopped frequently to camp, hunt, fish, gather what tubers, greens and grains Bright Water knew to be edible, and to let the physician Legionary Bubonius indulge his passion for examining and recording the flora and fauna. We saw many wondrous sights as we wandered, often far inland, then back to the sea again—great magnificent trees, vast beyond imagining. Forests birthed by near-constant summer rains, so unlike the dry lands to the south. There was a great volcano a hundred mille from the coast, one that rumbled and smoked as we passed cautiously several mille away; the men named it Vulcan's Forge.

As for the western ocean itself, the men passed many an hour on the trail debating what it should be called. Mare Occidentalis was too plain a name, all agreed. But as to a proper name for this great, peaceful western sea, we never decided.

We proceeded north, maintaining our steady yet deliberate pace, looking for a suitable place to go into camp for the winter.
—Flavius Arcadius Tahonius' Trans-Mesizibi Diaries

On the coast — autumn

A series of high cliffs lined the coast. If one of the Roman cavalrymen walked his horse to the edge a few steps away from where they rode in columns of two, he could look down the cliff to a narrow strip of rocky beach below. Julius Spotted Horse insisted that the big river they planned to follow inland was no more than a few days ride ahead. He had galloped off north the day before to confirm that fact, promising to find the Roman party again before ten days had passed, as long as they stayed near the coast. Arcadius suspected the man was long accustomed to mostly keeping no company but his own, and just wanted a few days of solitude. His service so far had been invaluable, so the Tribune was willing to indulge him.

The country they rode through was beautiful. To the east, just away from the cliffs that overhung the western ocean — no one had thought to name it yet — the land rose into rolling hills, with long grasses interspersed with scattered groves of small oaks and junipers. Arcadius planned to spend the winter near the river's outlet into the sea, the better to be able to head inland as soon as the weather allowed.

"That harbor we passed," Arcadius thought out loud, "that will be a major shipping port one day, I'm sure of it. A big, beautiful harbor like that, with a sheltered entrance and that huge, open bay to make an anchorage — it's as though the gods made it specifically for ships."

Beside him, the scarred giant Tacitus grunted an amiable agreement. Tacitus rode bare-headed, his helmet hanging on this saddle, his broad, bronze face turned up to the morning sun. His great bearskin was rolled up and stowed behind him on the horse. Arcadius fancied he saw a brief hint of a smile on the centurion's face as the sun shone on him, bringing the number of times Arcadius had seen the giant even begin to smile to no more than five.

Knowing he would get no conversation from the centurion,

Arcadius turned half an ear back to the two horses that followed him and Tacitus. There his young wife, Bright Water, was engaged in a long conversation with the physician Marcus Albium Bubonius on medical matters; Bubonius had spent several days in explaining the Roman goddess Meditrina, but Bright Water had a stubborn level-headedness borne of a youth spent in a primitive tribe and insisted on knowing the practical applications of Roman medicine. Bubonius had given up insisting that a firm grounding in the expectations and desires of the gods must come first, and was at the moment describing Roman methods for treating fevers.

Oddly, given the richness of the country, the Romans had seen no people since leaving the tribe of Spirit Bird, almost four months earlier. "It seems impossible that such beautiful lands go uninhabited," Marcus Bubonius had observed.

Thundering hooves announced the arrival of Valerius Fortis Caninus, one of the day's two assigned scouts. Flushed and grinning, the legionary rode to the column and reined in his horse as the Tribune raised a hand to halt the column.

"Sanctus has brought down a bear, sir," the legionary reported. "Not an Ursus Magnus; one of the smaller brown ones. He's about a league ahead, in a grove of trees. He sent me to tell you there's a good campsite nearby, and sir, there's an old used fire pit. He'll be watching for us from a hilltop near the kill."

"Signs of people about after all, then," Arcadius mused. "Very well then — ride on ahead, tell him we're coming."

"I would ride ahead with him," Bright Water said.

Arcadius had not heard her approach. He looked at his wife, repressing a smile; she was leaning forward in her saddle, anxious at the thought of a good gallop. She had become quite an equestrian, better than any but a few Romans Arcadius had ever seen, and loved nothing better than riding her pony at a breakneck pace. "As you wish, my dear. Do stay close to Legionary Caninus."

"I will," Bright Water smiled broadly. "If he can keep up with me!" She kicked her pony with a loud shout and galloped off. Valerius Fortis Caninus shot his commander a quick grin. "I'll look after her, sir," he said, and raced off after the Novan girl.

Shaking his head, Arcadius motioned for the column to move on.

As the line of horseman proceeded at a slow trot, the physician Bubonius moved ahead in the line to ride alongside Arcadius. The Tribune looked over at the physician, who had a strip of jerked meat in a corner of his mouth. He was chewing on it with a meditative air.

"How are the lessons in medicine proceeding?" Arcadius asked.

"Sir," the physician replied, "I'm not sure."

"How is that?"

"She's intelligent, sir; almost frighteningly so. But her background is so different than your typical Roman, that I'm not sure how to best teach her. You've seen that she has some healing skill already, as we have the Centurion's healed shoulder and head as evidence. But she has no patience for the philosophical underpinnings of modern medicine. She doesn't seem to be concerned with Meditrina's teachings and influence over the healing arts. But she is grasping the technical aspects faster than I would have thought possible."

"She learned Latin fast enough," Arcadius agreed, "and she is learning to read and write. A wonder, that; I don't think I learned nearly so fast when I was a boy."

Bubonius took the strip of jerky out of his mouth and regarded it. "I suspect, sir," he said, "she will teach all of us a thing or two before we get home again. Reading and writing, for example. We take it for granted. To her, it is something new and exciting, something she had never imagined. How will she take all of Roman society, when we do get home? If there is anything she is not, sir, it's hesitant. I suspect she will arrive in Pompeius with a large splash."

Arcadius silently agreed; but he knew that his opinion was biased. She was his wife, and he loved her. He found himself wondering what she would think of Rome, when they got there…

…And what Rome would think of her.

Centurion Tacitus may well have plucked the thought from the Tribune's head. "No one will ever have seen Rome with fresher eyes than she," he rumbled, startling the Tribune and the physician with what was for him a considerable display of loquacity.

"True enough," Bubonius agreed. He squinted ahead, and then pointed. "Look there, on that hilltop—I think that's Sanctus."

Bubonius was glad to see the lean figure of his old friend on the horizon. He had much on his mind, and the Stoic was always a good sounding board.

They moved into the grove of trees where Legionary Sanctus was already involved in skinning and quartering the bear. The men gathered around to help, and Arcadius was sure they were anxious to get some bear meat cooking; their diet of wild game was notoriously short on fats, and the rich bear meat satisfied that craving for a while.

While that was going on, Arcadius dismounted and walked over to inspect the old fire pit Caninus had mentioned. Bright Water climbed down from her horse and walked over to the old campsite with him.

Arcadius knelt by the pit surrounded by a ring of large rocks. He sifted some ashes through his fingers. "It has been months since this was used," he observed. "Maybe a year or more."

"I think people left here quickly," Bright Water said. She was walking around the area, looking at the ground. "There are still stakes in the ground, like the ones your men use to fasten down their shelters, only made of wood instead of iron. You can see where the circles of their houses were. And I found this," she handed Arcadius a small bone awl with a finely crafted wooden handle. "This is a good tool. I wouldn't leave this behind if it were mine."

"I think you are right, my dear," the Tribune said. He stood up and looked around. "But if they left in a hurry—I wonder why?"

Centurion Tacitus was walking around the area with a different set of eyes; the trees were on the crest of a small hill, and the giant's attention was—as always—focused on the terrain from the perspective of an experienced soldier: *How best to defend this place? How would I approach it to attack this hill? Where is the best place to post sentries?* He noticed the Tribune beckoning to him and walked over. "Sir?" he said questioningly.

"Look at this," Arcadius said, handing Tacitus the awl. "The fire pit has not been used for some time. There are indications that the people that were staying here left in a hurry. It's been too long to track which direction they went, but they left quickly."

"I can think of two reasons for such, sir," the giant rumbled. "Either there was some natural calamity like a flood—unlikely in this dry country—or someone drove them away."

"My thoughts precisely," Arcadius said. "Make sure the men on sentry duty are alert. We'll keep sentries all night. When we move out, the scouts are not to make contact with any people they see. Contact will be only by the full group. We'll be cautious." He looked around at the vacated campsite. "I have a bad feeling about this."

"Sir," Tacitus grunted. He moved off to brief the others.

North of the Great Sister
Legate Malleolus woke slowly. His head hurt.

He opened his eyes. Leaves fluttered overhead; yellowing autumn leaves—leaves of the great poplars that grew along this desolate stretch of the Sister. The great river was little more than a stream now, so close to its headwaters, and the land had grown high and cold, but the great trees still grew near the water, marking the river's course across the prairie.

The sun was low in the sky.

In the western sky.

"Afternoon," Malleolus muttered through thick lips. His mouth tasted full of dirt. His head pounded. "Why am I asleep in the afternoon?"

He sat up. He was alone. The tents and gear of his men were gone.

"Sons of Dis," he swore. He tried to get to his feet, stumbled once, and then finally rose. "I remember…I remember stopping for midday. I remember those disloyal bastards muttering about something. Then…" The legate stopped. He remembered now—a stunning blow, a flash of light, and then nothing.

"Fucking traitorous cunnis," he snapped. Rubbing his head, he walked around, looking for signs, but he was no tracker. His muttering, plotting, disaffected men had left for parts unknown, orders be damned.

He was alone in a howling wilderness, abandoned by his men.

"At least they left a bit of firewood." He started a fire and sat by it, wrapped in his cloak against the chill, chewing a bit of dried venison. Eventually, he slept.

In the morning, he gathered what remained of his gear and walked off west, up the river, following his orders.

On the northern coast

The kalends of November were come and gone. Julius Spotted Horse had led them to the great river that would lead them to the northern mountain passes, but that piece of the journey would have to wait until spring.

A large open meadow less than a mille from the ocean made an inviting location for a winter camp. When the Roman party first rode into the meadow, Legionary Bubonius let out a shout: "Look!"

The others followed his pointing hand: A great eagle, black with white head and tail, took off from a large pine at the upper edge of the meadow and flew slowly off. "The eagle of Rome," Tribune Arcadius exulted. "A good omen, that. This will be our winter camp."

The soldiers and the scout spent ten days constructing a series of low wooden huts surrounded by a low palisade, two rows of five huts for the soldiers to share two to a hut; the centurion and the Tribune and his wife had their own huts, separated by a short space from the others. Arcadius ordered a series of sharpened stakes to be crafted and affixed to the top of the wall, and a stout wooden gate to control entrance. "I'm still concerned about that abandoned camp we found," he told Centurion Tacitus. "Let's make sure this place can be defended."

The older men of the Evocati, Legionaries Bubonius and Sanctus, constructed a large fire pit in the center of the encampment and crafted rude chairs to surround it. "There is nothing more satisfying than a good fire on a cold night," Sanctus told the Tribune by way of explanation, "except sharing that fire with one's comrades." He was right; on a clear night shortly after the camp was complete, the older men built a roaring blaze and spit-roasted an entire haunch of wapiti, during the sharing of which there was much laughter and spinning of ever-wilder tales.

Of all the tales told that night, it was the scout Julius Spotted Horse who told them of the great mythical beasts of the West.

The scout had sat silently by the fire through the evening, chewing on a chunk of meat, smiling occasionally at the stories told by the soldiers. Celerius Dorotheus finally reached out and tapped the scout. "You're the quiet one tonight, neh? That's not like you. You must have seen a thousand times a thousand strange things on your journeys. Tell us a tale or two from your store!"

Spotted Horse looked at the runner. He leaned forward and spat a chunk of gristle into the fire. "Very well," he said. "I'll tell a tale. I'll tell of something I have not mentioned until now. I'll tell you of the great beasts of the west, the sappers of men's spirits, the beasts that ruin men's courage, the beasts that shake the earth with their steps. I'll tell you of the Great Destroyers."

The Tribune looked around at the men. They were leaning forward, listening. "Say on, then," he told the scout.

"Beasts, you say. What do they look like?" Valerius Fortis Caninus wanted to know.

Spotted Horse gestured, indicating something colossal. Arcadius realized this was the first time the scout had been persuaded to spin a tale; he had a talent for it.

"The Destroyers are huge," Spotted Horse told them. "As tall as two men at the shoulder, maybe three. Long black hair covers their bodies, hanging from their sides to the ground like tattered black skirts. They have legs like the trunks of great trees, bigger than the columns on the front of the Council building in Durobrivia. Their heads are massive, with great black ears like wings, a great long serpentine nose that can snatch you off the ground and dash you against the earth, four great white tusks like spears, and their eyes—that may be the worst of it. Their eyes are bright red, and burn with a terrible inner light. It is the eyes, you know, that drain men's courage. If you ever meet one of the Destroyers, take care! Do not look into its eyes. To look into their eyes is to be instantly unmanned. To face one of the Destroyers is to face ruin. To be taken by one is to wander the banks of the Styx forever, unable to cross, unable to return to the world of the living."

"Juno's mercy," Bright Water breathed. Arcadius smiled; his wife was even beginning to pick up Roman idioms.

"There are at least four of the Destroyers," the scout continued. He leaned forward so that the light of the fire cast flickering light and shadow on his narrow, gaunt face. "One lives on the prairie south of the Big Sandy; it roams back and forth between the junction of the Sandy and the Sister and another great river to the south. I've heard it is the oldest of the four, and its hair is black but shot through with gray, and it has a broken tusk. The people of the plains in that region call it Half Tooth. The second, it lives in the sand hills north of the upper branch of the Big Sandy. Its fur is as black as night, more than the others, and it is bigger than the other three, as tall as three men. The people of the northern plains call it the Night Spirit. The third lives in the barren country west of the southern mountains, north of the great deserts; that one roams north and south with the seasons, preying on the spirits of the nomads who live in that region. That beast is the Night Walker. And the last, well, that one is the most horrible of them all. It is the only one that is a female. She lives along the headwaters of the Great Sister, and it is said that she can call lightning from the skies and uses it to set great fires that drive all before them. She is the Night Mother."

He paused long enough to spit his wad of chewed leaves into the fire, producing a hiss and a spurt of foul-smelling smoke. "Those are only the ones I've heard of," he concluded. "That doesn't mean there may not be more."

He paused long enough to extract some more of his foul brown weed and stuffed it into his mouth. He spat another stream of brown into the fire and went on.

"When a man is lost, when the night comes close around him and his spirit falls low, that is when one of the Destroyers appears. They come out of the night, always out of the night, a shadow among shadows. They come to take what is left of a man's courage, of his spirit, and then, when that man has nothing else left, they take his soul, and leave him wandering forever between this world in the next, standing in neither, but unable to move. If this happens to you, you will be neither alive nor dead, but doomed to wander the spaces between worlds, forever."

"Bugger me, I won't sleep a wink tonight," Legionary Aurelius said. "Are there any of these beasts hereabouts? Are there any on this northern stretch of coast?"

"Who knows?" the scout replied. "I tell only of the four I've heard of."

"Juno protect us," Aurelius muttered.

"Relax," Centurion Tacitus rumbled. "It's only a story."

"Of course," Julius Spotted Horse grinned, his gap-toothed countenance suddenly strangely eerie in the firelight. "Only a story. Nothing to worry about."

"Julius here is quite the storyteller. He tells one story about a trickster god that takes the form of a wolf," Quintus Alces Sanctus observed. "Now he talks about gigantic beasts that stalk the prairies. I'm sure these stories are told many times in many ways by the people that live in these western lands, and I think that is because of the lands themselves."

"How so?" Marcus Bubonius asked.

"Think of all we have seen—the great vast lands under the enormous open sky. Herds of bison so huge they cannot be counted. Great deserts, mountains greater than any in the east or even in the old tales of Rome that was. It is a land that is made to spawn legends. And, I expect, we will hear many more such legends before we are done."

"Let's hope you're right," Caninus said. "I wouldn't care to meet one of these beasts, not without the entire Second Tahonian at my back."

Later that night, in the privacy of their sleeping furs, Tribune Arcadius curled himself around Bright Water's slim form and laid a hand on the comforting curve of her breast. "My love," he said. "Spotted Horse can certainly spin a tale, can he not?"

"He can," Bright Water said. Her voice was odd—subdued, not full of her usual confidence.

Arcadius raised up on one elbow. "What is it? Did he frighten you?"

"Not him," Bright Water answered. "Not his story."

"What, then?"

"Maybe it's a tale of the prairies and mountains and nothing more," Bright Water said. "Maybe it's not. But Spirit Bird used to tell of the same beasts. He said they ate men's spirits and cast them to walk the shadows between this world and the next, forever."

Arcadius lay back. He realized now that he, like Aurelius, may not know sleep this night.

Stories aside, there did not appear to be any of the great black beasts in the vicinity of the winter camp. There were deer, wapiti, bears, grouse, and rabbits; the streams were full of fish. The horses grew fat and lazy on the lush grass in the meadow where the camp lay and on several others discovered nearby. After a few days, the scout's story of the Destroyers was forgotten.

One chilly, damp day, Legionaries Taurinus, Marius and Dorotheus approached the Tribune with Julius Spotted Horse in tow. "Sir," Taurinus asked, "Julius here has been telling us about the mountains to the west. We'd like permission to spend a few days hunting up there."

"Your goal?" Arcadius wanted to know. "There is plenty of game around here."

"Wolves, sir," Marius grinned. "We'd like some wolf pelts."

"Very well," Arcadius said. "Bubonius has the only wolf pelt of the trip so far, and it's one of those little prairie wolves. Bring in some proper wolf pelts, then. Be gone no more than ten days," he ordered.

The men were gone for eight days, and returned with four wapiti quarters and a half-dozen rich, heavily furred wolf pelts. They immediately started to smoke-curing the skins, and Faustus Marius took to wearing one about his shoulders, with the cured head atop his own, aping Centurion Tacitus with his great bear pelt. Tacitus, wise in the ways of soldiers, said nothing.

"We found what looked like the remains of campsites," Spotted Horse reported. "Not small campsites, I'd say thirty or forty people each. We found two of them, in separate valleys, maybe ten mille apart. Looks to me to be summer camps of some folk who live in closer to the mountains, back there in that thick forest. They may be in winter camp now. Some folk do that—gather in winter, disperse in summer."

"We'll keep a watch out for them," Arcadius decided. "If they don't bother us, we won't bother them."

Thus the winter passed.

"Imagine a city here," Arcadius said one night as the Romans sat around the fire. "A Roman city. These rich lands would support a dozen cities the size of Pompeius. And who knows what we haven't yet found?"

In later years, Tribune Arcadius would recount those weeks as the most peaceful and satisfying of the entire journey.

He would also recount them as among the last peaceful weeks his party would know until they returned to civilized lands, many months later.

ELEVEN
ABDUCTIONS

I was a child of dry, open, rock-strewn mountains. Those northern lands, with their thick forests and rushing rivers, may as well have been another world entirely. In marrying Flavius Arcadius, I had agreed to leave everything I knew behind. But with my Tribune at my side, I would have happily journeyed anywhere, not just to the great western sea but beyond it — he had only to ask.

Even as happy as I was with my husband, even as familiar as I had grown with a strange man from a strange, distant, land, there were times when it was odd, being the only Novan in a group of Romans. I look back on that time now and remember it as if a dream.

It was in those northern woods that our party of wanderers encountered another Novan who would also become Roman, and who would prove as brave as any Roman warrior who ever lived. He saved my life, and my husband's, and maybe all of us.

And to think when we first came to know him the only thing I could think of whenever I had occasion to speak of him, was a sneeze.

—My Journey: From the Camp of Spirit Bird to the City of Rome, by Aqva Lucis Arcadius

Rome

"O Conscript Fathers," Consul Poscus Cassius addressed the full Senate in his new role for the first time. "It saddens me beyond description to be addressing you under these circumstances. The loss of our beloved Consul Pompeius has been a blow to the Republic, but the Republic must go on. To go on, the Republic must continue to expand. Before his untimely death, Consul Pompeius, through his unassailable logic and strength of his reasoning, convinced us to fund his western garrisons. I have said that due to health issues of my own, I will not stand to the Consul's chair in my own term, but will resign and return to the Senate when the election is held this summer, and so the people of the Republic will elect a new Lesser Consul when Senator Brutus succeeds me in the Consul's chair."

There was a slight murmur in the chamber. The passage of the measure authorizing the additional levees for the garrisons had not been without debate, some of it acrimonious.

"I would speak," Senator Publius Aquilus Aurelius announced.

"Senator Aurelius is recognized," the Consul said.

Publius Aurelius stood. His twin brother, Senator Antonius Caius Aurelius stood as well, a show of family unity and support. The "Golden Twins," Senators from the new province of Cadovia, had many supporters in the Senate.

"No man in this chamber will debate or deny the long and dedicated service of Consul Pompeius. No man in this chamber will debate or deny Consul Pompeius' status as the last in an exalted line, one that goes back to old Rome itself."

He struck a dramatic pose. "However, my friends and colleagues, no man is perfect in and of himself—not even Consul Pompeius. His western adventures have impoverished the Republic! Even now the Senate is spending every brass oboul of the levees from the various provinces to fund ever more legions, ever more weapons and horses, ever more expeditions along the rivers of the west. What trade is there in those desolate lands? Of what use can those great empty spaces be? I move that the legions west of the Mesizibi be recalled. I move further that the expansion of the legions began under the Consulship of Consul Pompeius be revoked and those added legions disbanded. Our soldiers should be at home with their families, not adventuring in a distant wilderness!"

"A motion has been made. Will anyone speak in reply?"

"I would speak," Lesser Consul Brutus announced.

"Lesser Consul Brutus is recognized," Consul Cassius said.

"Our esteemed colleague seems very concerned with the home lives of our soldiers," he began. "Perhaps he would have them all turn to shopkeeping?"

The remark was greeted with laughter—but only from about a third of the Senate.

"Senator Aurelius is correct, of course—in one respect. The western garrisons and the brave men who maintain them are an expense to the Republic. One can even honestly say that they are draining the resources of the Republic, for now, at any rate. But he is *not* correct in naming those lands as desolate and useless! Were that true, Senator Aurelius, would you be investing so much of your own resources in financing trading missions to that region?"

"You accuse," Senator Aurelius began to shout.

"I have the floor!" Brutus thundered. "And you cannot deny, my *esteemed* colleague, your investments in shipping and trading in the upper reaches of the Great Sister River!"

The debate went on into the night. In the end, the issue was not decided. Lesser Consul Gregorius Lucius Brutus was anything but confident in what the final outcome would be.

The northern mountains

The river ran fast, white water pounding over rocks, down a narrow valley surrounded by a forest of pine and spruce. The mountains they had to cross were on the other side.

"Pluto's thorny cock." Tribune Arcadius softly swore. He didn't like the look of the rapids, but the scout Julius Spotted Horse was very certain. "This is the only place within ten mille either way, Chief," he had reported after three days examining the river both upstream and down. "I can look farther if you want, but every day is one more day lost by the time we get to the high passes."

He looked up and down the river again before continuing. "And, yes, Julius, I'm anxious to get across and get on our way home. I had hoped to reach the provinces, at least, before autumn. Very well." He examined the river carefully, with the experienced soldier's eye. The banks were reasonable; the far side was steeper, where the current ran a little stronger, but the horses should be able to manage it.

He looked around. In the distance one great, snow-covered mountain dominated the skyline. There was nothing else in sight but the thick, endless forest.

It was the current that bothered him. The river was still running high from late spring runoff, and the portion of the riverbed that was visible was rocky, strewn with boulders. As he looked down, a tiny gray bird lit on a rock and, amazingly, disappeared into the torrent. It re-appeared a few paces downstream, hopping out onto a wet rock. It fluttered its wings once and flew away. *If only it were that easy for us. What a wonder, that would be — to just be able to fly over river, lake, forest, and mountain, like a great eagle. But no — we must cross this river here, now.*

Arcadius sat on his horse, thinking furiously. *Caninus is probably the best horseman among us, although I would have a hard time convincing*

Bright Water of that. If he can make the crossing, we will at least have a better idea of the conditions, what the bottom is like, how deep that far portion is where the channel runs.

"Legionary Caninus!" the Tribune barked.

"Sir!" Caninus shouted. The soldier booted his horse forward. He had been anticipating the call.

Arcadius looked at the big man. "I want you to cross the river, test out the bottom and the current. See that clump of three big spruces? Make that your mark on the far side, the bank is best there. Pay close attention to the bottom, how stable it is, take note of any big rocks."

"On the way, sir," Caninus answered. He walked his horse forward, entering the water slowly.

"Centurion?"

"Here, sir." The giant Tacitus was, as always, at the Tribune's side.

"Tell the men to rope all the horses together. Alternate the spare horses with the riding horses, one and one. If Caninus crosses successfully, we'll go on ahead."

The centurion grunted, and began bellowing orders to the men.

Bright Water sat on her horse on Arcadius' right. "Dear," he said to her, "Pass me your tether rope. I'll tie your horse to mine."

"I can control him better without him tied," she objected.

"My dear, your gelding is the smallest horse in the group. He'll have the most trouble if the water is deep." He pointed to Caninus, who was entering the deepest part of the river. His horse still had footing on the river bottom, but only just. "See Caninus there. Your horse would be very near swimming in that stretch."

"If he does lose his footing, he'll just drag you with him."

Arcadius knew a rare moment of frustration with his beautiful Novan wife. He loved her very much; he was only now discovering how much. But she was not only intelligent but independent and strong-minded.

Roman women were typically much more subservient to their men; however Bright Water was anything but submissive.

"Bright Water," he said in a tight, controlled voice, "I have ordered all the men to tie their horses together. It is the standard practice in the Roman cavalry when crossing unknown rivers. I cannot let you proceed on your own, when for their own safety I have ordered the men to do otherwise."

Bright Water relented. She was by now well aware of her husband's position as the leader of the Roman soldiers, and what that entailed. "Of course," she said. She unwound her horse's tether rope from her saddle. Instead of dismounting as the men did, she climbed forward out of the saddle over the horse's head, exposing a long length of brown thigh — her standards of modesty were much more relaxed than those of proper Roman women, as well — and tied the cord to the horse's bridle. She slid back into the saddle and handed the other end to her husband, who secured it to his saddle.

Centurion Tacitus rode forward. "Sir," he rumbled, "With your permission, I will lead."

"Of course," Arcadius agreed. Tacitus's giant black stallion was the obvious animal to lead the procession. He handed the centurion his own tether rope.

"Caninus is across!" one of the men shouted.

The big soldier had gained the far bank. He shouted across, his words barely audible over the rushing water: "The current is fast but passible. The bottom is rocks and cobbles, a few larger rocks just before the channel. Walk the horses slowly. Make your line directly to me and you'll cross with no trouble."

"Proceed, Centurion," Arcadius ordered.

The line of horses entered the water slowly. As the water rose and the current made itself felt, the horses began to protest. Bright Water's pony threw back its head and squealed in fright, but she leaned over its head and calmed it with pats and a few soft words.

Tacitus gained the far bank, then Arcadius, then Bright Water. The rest of the men scrambled their horses up the bank, one by one, until one horse began squealing in panic.

"Look!" Caninus pointed.

Quintus Alces Sanctus' horse had stepped into a hole and lost his footing. The tether rope snapped, and the horse rolled, spilling its rider into the rushing water.

Arcadius later reflected that in many years of service together, he had never seen the giant Tacitus move so swiftly. Most would never have thought so large a man capable of such celerity. Tacitus leaped from his horse, shedding his bearskin as he ran and dove into the river, swimming strongly into the current where Sanctus, clearly injured, feebly tried to keep his feet. He reached the Stoic, grabbed him, and dragged him to the far shore.

The rest of the party had made the far bank without incident. Marcus Bubonius leaped from his horse and ran to where the centurion dragged his old friend ashore.

"Are you hurt?" the physician asked.

"My chest hurts," Sanctus groaned. He lapsed into a fit of coughing.

"Help me get his gear off," Bubonius barked, once more the physician in charge.

"Sir," Caninus said, "his horse has washed up on that gravel bar yonder. It's not getting up."

"See to it," Arcadius ordered. "Take Varus with you. Centurion Tacitus, take Aurelius and find a good campsite up away from the water, a place with grass for the horses. I think this is as far as we will be going today."

Bubonius was probing Sanctus' chest. "Three ribs cracked," he reported. "Maybe four. I can wrap him up, but he shouldn't ride for a few days."

"Very well." Arcadius knelt next to the Stoic, "So, Legionary, see the trouble you've caused us?" He grinned to show his remark as a joke. "Now we'll have to camp a few days to let you recover,"

"Sorry, sir," Sanctus ground out. "I'm afraid I was just a bit clumsy there."

"Don't worry," Arcadius said. He patted the man's arm. "I'm just glad you didn't get washed away. We've lost one man. I don't want to lose another."

"I'll be fine, sir."

"I'm sure you will." He stood up. "As soon as he can move, get him up away from the river, into the trees. As soon as we have a campsite, get fires going. We'll get clothing and gear dried out."

Caninus and Varus returned a few moments later. "The horse's foreleg was broken, sir. We cut its throat to put it out of its misery. Varus has Sanctus' saddle and gear."

"Very good." He looked around. Bright Water was helping Bubonius wrap Sanctus's chest with strips cut from a cured deer hide. "As soon as he can move, let's get away from this damned river."

The Great Sister

Much to the annoyance of Legate Maximus Decimus Meridius, the rapidly growing Roman town outside the walls of the garrison had been named Prospero's Trading Post, after the fat, irritatingly cheerful merchant who was the first civilian merchant on the scene.

The garrison was complete now, and the Roman soldiers were

behind stout walls. So far the walls had proven unnecessary, but walls were Army practice, so walls Maximus would have. The local Novans had proven friendly enough. The plains people were anxious to trade furs and bison robes for Roman tools of iron and steel, and outside the garrison walls business was brisk. Fields of wheat and maize had sprung up near the river. Three more merchants had joined Prospero, and one inn was serving meals, Roman wine, and beer to all comers. Finally, a small, discreet soldier's brothel had opened to serve that aspect of the soldier's comfort and well-being.

"You can't tell me that Durobrivia merchants are funding all these trade goods to come upriver on speculation," Maximus said to his optio one warm afternoon. The two officers were on the wall, looking down at the town. A cloud of dust had announced the arrival of yet another trade caravan from the east.

"One of the men in that last caravan said that two big merchants in Philadelphia are funding a lot of the trade," Tribune Seneca said. "Looking to cash in on a piece of the profits, no doubt."

"No doubt," the Legate agreed.

"At least the garrison upriver hasn't had to deal with civilians yet."

"Give it time," Maximus groused. "That fat little shit Prospero; I would wager a gold aureus that he already has his eye on that garrison. Not that it will be easy. It's a good twenty days or more for a caravan to get that far up the Sister, and there are no roads. Of course there were no roads when he showed up here, either." Now a rough wagon trail led back down the river towards the Durobrivia crossing; a *road* only if one applied the term in the broadest possible sense.

"There will be roads, sir," Seneca said, sounding very certain. "Not this year or next, but there will be."

"There will," Maximus agreed. No doubt the man was right.

"Down the Sandy, too. Our cavalry has already identified two places along the Sandy for garrisons."

"If Rome will send the troops to man them," the optio pointed out.

"If," Maximus griped. "Always if. How can any Philadelphia merchants have the gold to fund trade missions when Rome is always crying poverty? Can the Consulate really be so incompetent on collecting levies?"

"Sir, look!" A legionary above them in the watchtower was pointing away north. A party of horseman was approaching from the north, maybe half a century of them, and as they got closer…

"Reman cavalry," Maximus said.

Their boring garrison assignment had just become much more interesting.

The northern mountains

Ochee was running for his life. He had wandered too far from his people's camp, much too far for a boy of nine summers to be wandering alone. But Ochee was an orphan, his mother having died when he was born and his father in an avalanche the winter before. A small, thin boy, Ochee now lived on the sufferance of his father's brother, and never had enough to eat. The band mostly ignored him. He subsisted on scraps, and wore only what worn-out hides were of no use to anyone else.

So he wandered the woods alone, day and night, and nobody in his small band cared.

But today he was running for the village with the sour taste of panic in his throat. Why? He had seen a monster, come face to face with a horrendous creature.

"Monster!" he screeched as he ran into the collection of low huts that made up his people's small summer camp. "Monster!"

His uncle, Pocho, appeared from his hut. "What are you screaming about, boy? Quiet down!"

"I saw a monster!" He pointed. "There, in the woods, near the river."

His uncle looked skeptically at the boy. He considered Ochee useless, small, and weak, but he admitted to himself that the child was not given to making things up; imagination did not seem to be his strong suit. "What did it look like?"

"It was big," Ochee gasped. "And black. Bigger than a wapiti. It had four legs and two heads. One head was in front like a deer or wapiti's head, but the second was like a man's head, above. It had a chest and arms like a man, its head was a bear's but with a man's face!"

"It was not Man-Of-The-Woods?"

"No," Ochee said. Every child of the band knew of the stories of the great, tall hairy men that were supposed to live in the woods to the north, nearer the great mountain, although nobody in the band had ever actually seen one. "No, it was not Man-Of-The-Woods. This had four legs."

Pocho frowned. "And where was this beast?"

Ochee pointed again. "That way. On the edge of the large meadow, near the river."

Two of the band's hunters joined Pocho. Pocho made Ochee repeat his description of the monster. "Tlinga, Ghee, get bows and knives."

"What are we going to do?"

"We will go and see," Pocho said. "If there is a monster, we will hunt it and kill it."

The three men equipped themselves with hunting bows and stone knives and headed off to the south, towards the river.

"This meadow should do nicely," Legionary Aurelius said with a note of satisfaction. "Good grass for the horses, that upper edge there looks good for shelters, lots of dry wood about. Unless I miss my guess there will be game in these woods."

Centurion Tacitus grunted an affirmative. "It will do. Go back and inform the Tribune."

"Sir," Aurelius replied. He saluted and walked his horse back into the woods.

Tacitus examined the clearing critically. Maybe three hundred paces from the river, close enough to make getting water convenient, far enough to avoid the cold damp of night air near the water. Tacitus could just hear the rushing water in the valley below.

At the lower edge the meadow was damp, so they would need to watch the horses' feet carefully for fungus or founder if they fed there, but the higher edge of the meadow was dry. He walked his horse to the northern tree line and looked down across the slight slope of the open area. *Two hundred paces north to south*, he thought, *and maybe four hundred east to west. We can stay here a while.* He climbed down from his horse and, holding the stallion's reins, walked along the upper edge of the meadow, looking for a good level place for shelters.

The sun feels good. He was still soaked, and as he walked, the sun slowly began to steam the water off his clothing. He had shucked off his bearskin to dive into the river after Sanctus, but his tunic and leggings were wet through.

"That is no monster," Pocho whispered. "See, it is a man, not a monster. He is leading that animal by a cord." The three men were hidden in the trees. Where they crouched, in a pool of deep shade under a great spruce, they knew nobody in the sunlit meadow could see them, and the slight breeze was in their faces.

"Why does the animal not run away?" Ghee asked.

"He must have some magic over it," Pocho guessed.

The man in the clearing turned and now was walking back towards them, examining the ground.

"See, he wears the skin of a great silvered bear."

"He is nearly as big as a great bear," Tlinga breathed. "What kind of people grows so big? Maybe it is Man-Of-The-Woods."

"Man-Of-The-Woods eats animals, he does not have them as friends," Pocho said, quoting the stories he half-remembered.

"Should we talk to him?"

Pocho crouched there for a few moments, thinking. The strange man obviously had great magic to control whatever manner of beast the great black animal was. But he was a man, clearly, not a monster, not Man-Of-The-Woods. A big man, but a man.

Pocho thought about killing him. He stood within bow range, brilliantly lit by the afternoon sunshine while Pocho and his companions crouched in deep shade, unseen.

But what if there are others? They will come looking for us.

"What are we going to do?" Ghee prompted Pocho.

Pocho decided. He raised his bow, pulled, sighted.

Tacitus turned at a shout from the lower part of the meadow; Legionaries Aurelius and Caninus, riding ahead of the main party. "Centurion!" the grandson of the Great Dog called. Now in the open, he booted his horse to a trot and rode towards Tacitus, grinning. "How goes, sir? Any girls about?"

"None that would be seen with the likes of you," Tacitus snapped. "Are the others coming?"

"The old owl and Bright Water are walking Sanctus up here," Caninus reported. "He can't climb up on his spare horse. Everyone else is walking the horses up. The Tribune told us to ride ahead, let you know."

"They should be along shortly," Aurelius added,

"Good. Both of you, get down off those horses. Aurelius, help me stake out a campsite. Caninus, start gathering firewood. We'll build a good big fire to dry everyone out."

"There, see, they ride on the backs of those animals. That is what Ochee saw." He spat. "Stupid boy."

"How is it that one of the animals is black, one brown, and the other brown and tan?"

"Magic," Pocho opined. "They are magic animals, so of course their colors are different."

"Some forest bears are black, others are brown, but they are both bears," Ghee objected.

"Magic," Pocho insisted. "What else?"

"So what do we do now?" Tlinga wanted to know.

"We go back to the camp. We will talk to the other men. We will decide what to do. There have been no people come into our lands since we drove off the people to the south. We will have to think how best to find out who these men are, and how to drive them away as well. There does not seem to be too many of them. That is something."

Like smoke, the three men drifted back into the woods.

Prospero's Trading Post

Out of politeness and professional courtesy, Legate Maximus invited the centurion commanding the Reman Army detachment into his personal quarters for a meal and a drop of good Roman wine. After days of dried meat, hard biscuits, and water, the Reman centurion was glad to accept.

"Gaius Vorenus, you said your name was," Maximus said after they were seated. "Are you a descendant of the famous Lucius Vorenus?"

"Not that I am aware of," the Reman commander said. "It's not an uncommon name in the Five Seas Nation. Many families name children after our heroes."

The two Caesarian centurions were infamous rather than famous in Rome, and few would have considered naming a child after one of them, but Maximus let that pass. Instead, he looked the Reman commander over carefully as an Army cook brought in bread, meat, and wine.

Vorenus was tall and thin, rather taller than the norm for the Remans Maximus had encountered. He wore the usual black tunic and leggings of the Reman Army, but as the day was warm and his mission was peaceful, he did not sport the usual black leather cuirass, greaves, and wolf-trimmed black cape of Reman officers. His eyes were the usual dark brown, almost black, but his brown hair bespoke a good portion of the original Roman blood. Out of courtesy, Vorenus had left his sword belt outside, but Maximus had no doubt that Vorenus' personal weapon was forged of good steel. If the Five Seas Nation produced anything, it was good steel.

"So, what brings you to the banks of the Sister?" Maximus asked.

Vorenus was busily cutting slices off of the chunk of bison roast with his pugio. He took a chunk of bread, sliced it almost through and stuffed the bison meat inside. Holding the mess in his left hand, he looked up to see the Legate staring.

"Standard practice in our cavalry," he chuckled. "Easier to eat while on a horse, you know." Miming holding reins in his right hand, he took a bite, chewed, and swallowed. "As for what I'm doing here, that's simple. The Imperator sent us to establish a garrison across the river, on the north side. There is a legion of infantry on the way as well. They should be here in a few more days. I'm sure their legate will visit you to pay his respects." He took another bite from his bread and meat. "There are several likely spots for a garrison on the high ground just above the river. You can see them from here—on those low hills."

Maximus thought about that while the Reman officer chewed. His orders were to place all of the lands south of the Great Sister under the eagles of Rome. That was directly from the mouth of the Consul: *Establish garrisons on the Great Sister River. Bring the plains and their people south of the Great Sister under the eagles of Rome, as far as the western mountains.*

The Reman centurion had orders to find a site to set up a garrison on the *north* side of the river.

Could Terminus have somehow known of my orders? If so, how? Could one of these merchants be sending messages across the river? Never had his exposed frontier posting seemed so fraught.

"There are no ferries across the Sister here," Maximus said, playing for time while he thought frantically. That was belaboring the obvious; the Reman party had been required to swim their horses across and had spent an hour drying out before the centurion presented himself.

"I imagine there will be in time, through," Vorenus answered. "Trade, you know. Your people already have a significant trading settlement here. I imagine some of our merchants will move down as well. Commerce, neh? It always sees through. Some of my men are already buying fresh food, down in the town." That much was certainly true. Roman and Reman coins were minted to the same standard, so trade was easy.

Maximus poured Vorenus and himself a mug of wine each, then began slicing up some roast himself. He set himself to make pleasant, nonsensical conversation for the duration of the meal; at least the Reman centurion was personable. But in the back of his mind, he was already composing the message he would have to send back to Pompeius.

Including the bit about the bread and meat. Someone was sure to find that interesting.

The northern mountains

"Would you stop fussing over me? I'm fine," Quintus Alces Sanctus snapped, for what must have been the fifth time.

"Gods beneath us," Faustus Marius said, "leave him be, Bubonius. You fuss like an old woman!"

There was general laughter around the fire. Marcus Albium Bubonius looked aggrieved. "Marius has a point," Tribune Arcadius pointed out. "Sit down, already. Eat some stew. Sanctus can look after himself for a while."

Bright Water had shown the Roman soldiers a trick from her people; a deer skin, scraped clean and cured, suspended over a good fire would boil water for stew, as long as the level of liquid in the hide pot stayed above the flames. She and Legionary Taurinus had produced a fine stew with dried venison from the tracker's last kill, pine nuts, some mushrooms she recognized from her homeland, and some salt left from their time near the coast.

"Legionary Taurinus," the Tribune said, "we'll need meat soon. Tomorrow, you and Marius go hunting, find us a fat deer or something suitable."

"I'll find something, sir," the tracker replied. He yawned. The sun had set some time before, but the party stayed gathered around the fire, still drying out. Shelters were up, the horses were staked in the meadow, grazing quietly.

"We'll stay here a few days," Arcadius decided. "Sanctus, don't object. You need a few days. I won't have you making matters worse by trying to ride in these forests. We have mountains to cross, and you'll have to be fit. We could use a few days, anyway, rest the horses and gather some food. We'll move out soon enough. Scout, what say you?"

Julius Spotted Horse spat a stream of brown liquid into the fire. "I think that will be fine, Chief. It's early enough in the year, I think we can cross in good order. We're a bit south of where I came through on my first trip, but I think the pass I crossed last time is only three- or four-days ride away—maybe six, at most."

"Very well." Arcadius yawned. "Get some rest, everyone. Caninus, take first watch. Wake Corvus when the moon reaches the zenith."

"Sir," Caninus agreed. The night had grown chilly. Caninus picked up the rolled-up bison robe he had been using as a seat by the fire. He went to his shelter and retrieved his sword and belt, buckled them on and walked off across the meadow to find a good vantage point where his eyes could adjust to the dark.

Pocho made his way slowly, carefully over where Tlinga, Ghee, and two other hunters waited. "They go to sleep," he reported. "One went off across the meadow to watch. He is under the biggest spruce to the east of their houses and their fire."

"Which ones should we take?" Ghee asked.

"The one man has a woman with him," Pocho said. "He is the only one with a woman, so he must be their leader. His house is away from the others, probably so he can enjoy his woman without angering the others. We'll take them both."

"Where is the giant?" Tlinga whispered, his tone nervous. The very sight of the enormous man was enough to inspire fear.

"Asleep in his little house," Pocho said. He grinned, showing a flash of teeth in the darkness. "He snores."

"What about their sentry?"

"Tlinga, take Fu and go around to the other side of the meadow. Move around like a clumsy man trying to be quiet. If he is not sure what he is hearing, he will investigate without calling for help, because he will not want to look foolish if he is just hearing a deer. When he is distracted, we will move on the little house."

The five men moved off silently into the night.

A few yards away, Ochee huddled against the trunk of a tree, shivering nervously. When the five men crept off, Ochee moved to where he could see the clearing.

Cominus Quintus Corvus woke when he heard his name called, softly. "I'm awake," he muttered. "How goes it?"

"Nothing worth mentioning," Caninus whispered. "Thought I heard something a while ago, but didn't find anything. Probably an animal."

"Good. Give me a moment—where did I leave my sword belt? Ah, here it is. Let me pass some water, then I'll be out. That big tree to the east, yes?"

"That's the one."

"I'll be right there."

"Remember you'll pass right by the Tribune's shelter."

"I'll be quiet. Can't disturb the Chief." They shared a quiet chuckle, then Caninus slipped back away into the darkness. Corvus followed, stepping carefully as he passed by the Tribune's dark, silent shelter. He did not notice the three men crouching silently behind the small tent.

"Now," Pocho said, "the other one will come back to sleep. We wait a little longer." They remained undetected when Legionary Caninus walked across the meadow and flung himself into his little lean-to.

"Now, we go," Pocho ordered. Two of them were dragging an inert form by its arms, while Pocho held the slight form of a girl, one hand clamped tightly over her mouth, the other holding an obsidian knife to her throat. The men of the Kobay slipped away with their captives, still undetected.

Ochee listened to them go. He relaxed a little, and settled down to wait. The night was more than half gone. In the morning, he would decide how to tell these strange men what had happened.

TWELVE
RECOVERIES

If we discovered one thing on our journey, it was that the essential nature of people remains the same anywhere. It applies to people as individuals as well as people in groups. Our forefathers passed down word of the vicious and warlike Alligator People who once lived in the southern lands that are now the province of Lustria. While no trace remains of those fierce warriors, their legend remains. Now, with our journey over half gone, we at last encountered a folk that may have been their equal.

Most of the people we met were open, friendly folk. However, our scout had predicted at the very beginning of the journey that we would encounter people of many kinds, and the insular and suspicious Kobay — with one exception of whom history has already taken note — were some of the less pleasant sort.

As Rome expands into those regions, it will take legions, not merchants, to bring the Kobay into the mainstream of Roman society, into Roman life and culture. That is my prediction, and it is not a pleasant prospect, the thought of campaigning in those distant, harsh forested mountains.

But the history of mankind has always been a history of conflict.

—Flavius Arcadius Tahonius' Trans-Mesizibi Diaries

The northern mountains

The sun was just peering over the hills to the east, sending bright beams through the trees, lighting up the far west end of the clearing when Centurion Tacitus awoke. He stretched, groaned at a few aches from his old injuries from the fight with the bear, and climbed out of his shelter.

"Let's be up!" he called to the various shelters arrayed around his. "Morning, you lot! Up, all of you."

Hearing the call, Cominus Quintus Corvus came walking in from where he had stood sentry. Tacitus looked at him, cocked an inquiring eyebrow. "Nothing to report, sir," the legionary said. Yawning, he went to the fire and poked around with a stick, trying to stir up the coals for the morning cook fire.

"The Tribune?" Tacitus asked to no one in particular.

"Haven't seen him, sir," Corvus replied. "Have you checked his shelter?"

Tacitus frowned. He never liked to disturb his superior, and since the Tribune had taken a wife, Tacitus was even less inclined to bother his superior when he had retired to his little shelter with Bright Water.

But the Tribune was normally one of the first of them up and moving, and Bright Water was a habitual early riser.

It bothered Tacitus, as did anything out of the ordinary. He walked to the Tribune's shelter, called his name softly.

No reply.

"Sir?" he called again.

The shelter was silent.

Tacitus took a deep breath. He stepped closer, put a hand on the door flap, opened it, bent, and looked inside.

Arcadius' and Bright Water's blankets lie inside, empty.

Tacitus snapped upright. "Tribune?" he shouted. "Bright Water?"

Other than the sudden silence from the men assembling around the cook fire, there was no reply.

"Centurion?" Marcus Albium Bubonius asked.

"The Tribune, and Bright Water. They aren't in their shelter."

Ochee snapped awake. He didn't remember drifting off. From where he was curled up in a stand of tall ferns, he heard the men talking, and then heard voices rising as in anger or fear. He couldn't understand any of their words, but he knew why they were agitated. He was afraid, but determined. These were the first people other than his own tribesmen Ochee had ever seen. He was an orphan. His own people didn't care for him. His own uncle, his father's brother, fed Ochee only sporadically and beat him more often than that. Maybe these people would be better, but he would have to do something for them first.

Fortunately he knew precisely what he could do for them that should win him a place among them. He took a deep breath and walked out of the trees into the sunlight.

"Who is the boy?" Legionary Bubonius wanted to know. He was pointing at someone behind Tacitus.

The centurion turned and there, a few paces form the Tribune's empty shelter, stood a small Novan boy, skinny, wrapped in an ancient deerskin so frayed as to be nearly useless. His black hair was ragged; it looked like it had been cut to shoulder length with a particularly dull knife. His feet were bare and dirty.

The boy spat out a stream of syllables and pointed to the north.

"Spotted Horse?" Tacitus asked.

"I didn't get a word of that," the scout replied. "Not any lingo I've ever heard before." He walked forward and tried to engage the boy with sign, but the lad just shook his head. "No good there either, Chief."

Ochee knew he had to communicate with these men, but their words made no sense to him. The dirty one with a feather tied to his head came forward and waved his hands, but the motions made no sense to Ochee. He was wondering if these men were either stupid or insane when an idea came to him.

Tacitus and the men watched as the boy walked over the Tribune's shelter. He pointed at the shelter, then made a fist and rapped his head lightly once. He walked around the shelter and pointed at the ground, then pointed north again.

"Taurinus," the centurion said.

The tracker came forward and examined the ground where the boy had pointed. "Drag marks here, sir." He stepped slowly towards the trees. "A little blood, too. Just a few drops."

Tacitus stared at the boy who stood, nervously shifting his weight from one foot to the other. He went to the boy and knelt in front of him. He placed his hands on the boy's shoulders. "You saw someone take them," he rumbled. "I know you can't understand me." Behind him, the legionaries looked at each other; none of them had ever heard the centurion speak to a child at all, much less in a tone so gentle. "We won't hurt you, boy. I'll protect you myself. But you must show us where they took our people." He pointed to the north. "Show us," he said. "Show us." He pointed at his eyes, at the ground, then to the north. "Show us," he repeated.

The Novan boy's face lit up with sudden understanding.

Ochee suddenly understood what the giant wanted. The scarred, forbidding man was terrifying close up, but when he spoke to Ochee his tone was soft, gentle, reminding Ochee of his dead father. The man was huge—his hands on Ochee's shoulders would make fists bigger than Ochee's head. His voice sounded like thunder far off over the mountains, but his tone was gentle. Ochee looked up; the giant was waiting for an answer. "I can show you," he said, nodding. He made to walk off, but the man held him fast.

"Wait," Tacitus said. He stood up, leaving a hand on the child's shoulder. "For some reason this boy is going to betray his own people to us, unless I miss my guess."

"I wonder why?" Bubonius asked. "Could they have treated him so badly?"

"He is a skinny little thing," Sanctus observed. "Maybe they aren't feeding him."

"Carry on with the cooking," Tacitus ordered. "Bubonius, see to it that this boy has all he wants to eat. When he has eaten, we'll have him show us where he wants us to go.'

"It might be a trap," Julius Spotted Horse pointed out.

"If they wanted to trap us all, why not just attack in the night when they obviously took the Tribune and Bright Water?" Legionary Aurelius objected. "Why send a boy to lead us into their clutches? Would you entrust such a piece of treachery to a small, hungry child?"

"Eat," Tacitus ordered, cutting the conversation off. "Then we move. Bubonius, you and Sanctus will stay with the horses and gear.

Everyone else with me. Everyone will be in full armor, swords and daggers. Archers, you will bring your bows."

The men moved quickly to their tasks.

In the Novan camp

Tribune Arcadius woke slowly. His head was pounding, his mouth tasted as though it was stuffed full of old rags.

He couldn't move his arms or legs.

Arcadius strained to look around. He was in some crude, round hut made of shakes of tree bark laid over a domed frame of branches. Strands of light filtering in through gaps told him it was morning, and his head…"Someone hit me," he muttered.

He rolled. His wife, Bright Water, laid beside him, tied hand and foot. Her eyes were wide with fear. She opened her mouth to speak, but Arcadius shook his head. "Quiet," he whispered. "Don't let them know we're awake."

Arcadius tested his bonds, but they held fast. There were voices somewhere outside, but they were not Roman voices. Some strange, unrecognized language; he wondered, absently, if Julius Spotted Horse could make any sense of it.

He turned back to look at his wife again. He tried a tentative smile; she smiled nervously back at him.

"The men will be looking for us," he whispered. "Don't worry."

"Don't worry," she whispered back. "Don't worry, you say. You may as well ask me to stop breathing."

"Did you see any of them?"

"One looked in just before you woke up. He looked Novan, but not like one of my people. His face was different—wider, somehow. And he wore his hair cut off, not cut short like yours, but cut off about at his collarbone."

"I don't suppose you can make any sense of their language?"

She shook her head. "I've been listening to them talk outside, but I don't understand a word. Whoever they are, they are not cousins to my people."

Arcadius nodded; it had been a small chance, anyway. "Roll away from me. I'll roll the other way. See if you can feel the bonds on my wrists."

After some struggling, they ended up back-to-back. "I think I feel the knot," she said after a few moments. Her small hands, so practiced and quick with medicine, proved equally capable with knots. After a few moments Arcadius' hands were free. He bent quickly and untied his ankles, then freed Bright Water. While she rubbed her hands and feet to get the blood moving, he looked quickly around the hut.

Dirt floor. No weapons in sight. There were only some old hides and a rawhide satchel, which turned out to be empty. Arcadius had nothing but his light cotton tunic he wore for sleeping; Bright Water was also in her night attire, which (normally to Arcadius' delight) consisted only of a buttery soft sleeveless deerskin tunic which stopped just above her knees. Arcadius felt his head; he had a knot raising on the back of his cranium, but his head was clear. He closed each eye in turn: His vision was clear. *Nothing serious, then*, he thought, remembering his training in battle injuries. *Just a headache.*

Outside the hut the voices continued. Arcadius stepped carefully, quietly to the low wall of the hut and peered through a small crack in the bark wall.

Five men. Two boys. They're just sitting around the fire, talking. Looks like they are trying to decide what to do with us.

Nearby

Tacitus was betting on the Novan's arrogance, on their confidence in their knowledge of the thick woods around their camp. But Tacitus and all the men with him were also children of the thick forest. They had grown to manhood hunting and wandering the deep, dark forests of Tahonia, and had practiced the soldier's arts in those same forests.

They were as accomplished in their woodcraft as the locals, and far more accomplished in the arts of warfare.

The boy led them straight to the Novan camp. Tacitus halted them some distance away, when he smelled smoke from the morning fires, and sent Celerius Dorotheus and Faustus Marius forward to reconnoiter.

The two returned quickly. "Maybe a dozen huts," they reported. "One fire in the middle, in the open. Some smoke coming from several of the huts. Five men and two boys were sitting at the fire, talking. While we watched, a woman came out of one of the huts carrying a child, spoke to one of the men, then went back inside. The men had bows close to hand, but we didn't see anyone keeping watch; they were all just sitting at that fire talking. We didn't see either the Tribune or Bright Water."

"Good," Tacitus grunted. He spent a useless moment regretting the death of the little thief Atius Lupus Minimus back in the desert the winter before; the man would have been invaluable today.

He stood for a few moments, thinking. "Taurinus, Caninus, Marius, move around to the right of the camp. Take up a position on the east. Spotted Horse, Corvus, Dorotheus, move to the left, take position on the west side. Make sure you are all in a position to move into the camp quickly. Varus, Aurelius, you two are with me."

"Sir," the men agreed.

"When you see one of the Novans take an arrow, move in.

Swords and daggers. If they surrender, let them live. Otherwise, kill all the men. When the men are down, search the huts. Find the Tribune and his wife. Whoever finds them, call out. We get them out, then move back to our camp down the hill."

He turned to the skinny little Novan boy and squatted down before him. "Stay here," he said. He pointed at the boy, then pointed at a down log. "There," he said. "Sit."

Ochee understood. He went to the down log and sat. He composed himself to wait. He saw the men preparing what were obviously weapons, and had a good idea of what was coming.

His uncle Pocho had starved him, and cuffed and kicked him when it amused him to do so. Ochee would not be sorry if he was killed.

Tacitus stood up and walked back to the men. "Any questions?" The men shook their heads.

"Very well. One more thing: When you charge, yell. Yell like Furies. Move."

The six men moved off, slowly, carefully. Tacitus began counting, silently. He would give the men time to move into position. When his count reached a century, he would strike.

Pocho was growing angry. He knew they couldn't talk to the two strange people they had taken. He wanted to keep the girl for himself, but Ghee argued that since Pocho already had one wife, that he should be allowed to keep the girl. "After all," Ghee said, "You struck the man and captured him, and that was brave. But I took the girl. She should be mine."

"It was my idea to take them in the first place," Pocho snapped. "You can have the man, if you can control him. I think we should kill him. He looks strong, and he will be nothing but trouble. But the idea was mine, and so is that girl. Keechee would like to have a sister wife to help her with her work, so I will keep the girl."

Ghee stood up. "No," he said. His tone was that of a challenge. "I took the girl. She is mine."

Pocho stood as well. "If you fight me, you will lose, and I will still keep the girl."

In the woods, nearby, Centurion Tacitus whispered one word to Legionary Varus, who stood with his heavy legion bow at the ready. "Now," he said.

Pocho felt the heavy strike on his back. In shock, he looked down to see something bloody protruding from his chest: an arrow. He had a moment to wonder at the perfectly symmetrical arrowhead made of some strange substance, before the world went dark. He fell forward, face-first into the fire.

Ghee grabbed for his bow and arrows. Two men were racing towards him from the trees, howling like wild animals. *Someone should have been watching*, he thought, too late. A big man was running at him, a strange man wearing heavy leather on his chest, some shiny objects on his arms, a heavy skirt of leather strips and some strange helmet of yellow-brown on his head. He raised his bow, but the man was too fast; he leaped over the fire and stabbed at Ghee with a long, shining knife. Ghee dodged but the man turned with him, slashing with a short knife in his off hand. The knife caught Ghee in the throat. He fell.

In the low hut, Arcadius heard Roman voices shouting. "Come on," he said, grabbing Bright Water's hand. They went to the hut's low door and looked out.

By the fire, Legionaries Caninus, Corvus and Dorotheus were making short work of the Novan men. One more man burst from a hut, a club in his hand, screaming a war cry, but before he took five steps an arrow came hissing from the right to take him in the throat. Centurion Tacitus roared into the camp with Legionaries Varus and Aurelius at his side.

"Search the huts," Tacitus bellowed.

"Here!" Arcadius shouted. "We're here!" With Bright Water at his side, he ran to the Romans. "We're unharmed." He looked around. "Not like this lot, it seems."

"Sir," Tacitus saluted. "You're well. Good."

Four women and six children, one an infant, were hiding in the huts. The legionaries dragged them into the center of the village.

Tribune Arcadius looked them over. "Leave them be," he decided. "In fact, set them to work dealing with their dead. We'll move camp up here so we can keep an eye on them until Sanctus is fit to move. Can't have them wandering around—who knows what mischief they may get into."

Tacitus frowned, but assented. "As you wish, sir." He looked around. "The huts aren't much, but I suppose they are better than soldier's tents." The camp sat in the middle of a clearing, smaller than the one they had spent the previous night in but big enough. "There's enough grass to keep the horses for a few days."

Arcadius noticed Caninus and Marius eyeing the captured women. "No taking any of them by force," he ordered. "Their men are freshly dead, and we'll observe the decencies." Then he grinned. "If you can persuade any of them to warm your beds voluntarily, that's a different matter."

"Caninus, Varus, guard the women and children," Tacitus ordered. "The rest of you, go back to camp, move everything up here." He turned to his commander. "Sir, if you will excuse me a moment?"

"Of course," Arcadius agreed. "You did just save my arse, after all."

Tacitus walked away into the forest, returning a few moments later with a small, skinny Novan boy.

"This boy, sir," Tacitus said, "He led us here. I'm not sure why."

"Has anyone spoken with him?"

"We can't. Julius Spotted Horse tried, but he doesn't speak any language the scout recognized. No sign, either."

"How did he get you to follow him here?"

Tacitus shrugged. "He's a smart boy."

Arcadius squatted down before the boy. He tapped his chest. "Flavius," he said, realizing as he did so that he hadn't used his own prenomen in some time; only his wife called him by his first name, the rest of the party being soldiers under his command.

The boy understood. He patted the top of his own head and made a sneezing sound.

"Ochee?" Arcadius repeated. "Well, Centurion, it seems he has a name."

Ochee went back to the giant. The giant had spoken gently to him, the first adult to do so since his father perished. Ochee felt safer standing in his shadow. He looked towards the fire, and saw the body of his uncle Pocho laying in face-down in the fire pit. Someone had kicked some dirt over the fire, but Pocho's hair was still smoldering. A nasty stink of burnt meat arose from his corpse.

Ochee scooped up a handful of dirt and threw it on Pocho's dead body. He spat on the ground, then leaned up against the comforting mass of the giant.

"Well, Centurion," Bright Water laughed, "it seems he's your boy now."

"Quite so," Arcadius agreed. "Very well, then, we'll take him along with us. He can hardly stay here, after all. Tacitus, you're in charge of him. Teach him to speak. Have Spotted Horse help if he can. I'm curious to find out why he betrayed his people so easily."

"My boy, sir?" Tacitus's shaggy black eyebrows were trying to climb off the top of his head.

"Centurion, in all the years I've known you, this is the first time I've ever heard you sound uncertain. Yes, your boy. I'm sure you'll raise him to be a fine young man."

Tacitus looked down at the boy, uncertain for the first time in many years. Of all the things he expected to happen to him on this journey, becoming a father was the last.

In the woods to the north, Fu peered cautiously around a tree. He had gone into the woods early that morning to hunt grouse, and was just returning when he heard the shouts of the strange men. He saw his fellow hunters slaughtered; their women captured.

In winter camp, all of the people of the southern branch of the Kobay came together, and more than ten hands of hands of hunters and their families were gathered. There were other winter camps, but the southern branch of the Kobay was large and powerful. In spring, as now, they scattered into summer camps. But Fu knew in which valleys the other summer camps of the Kobay were, and he knew they would want to strike back at these men who had just killed their kinsmen.

It would take many days to gather them, but Fu was a fast and tireless runner. He turned and slipped away into the forest.

THIRTEEN
FLIGHT

The mountains of that northern country are rough and harsh, the spring comes late. We had been made to understand early on that the southern route was more open, warmer, but we had the desert to pass through. The northern route was richer in many ways; the mountains fifty mille or so the coast, where we had to cross the first of several passes, were heavily forested and rich with game. It stood to reason that there would also be more people in the area, but we were expecting no more than the same sort of scattered wanderers that lived in the south. We were soon disabused of that notion.

Our scout Julius Spotted Horse had warned that the pass he sought to lead us through would not be open before the kalends of Maius at the soonest, but after our incident with the Novan kidnappers I was determined to be up and moving as soon as Legionary Sanctus was fit to travel. There was the issue, of course, of not being able to take the word of a notorious Stoic as to his own fitness for duty — and Legionary Sanctus was as staunch a Catonian as ever drew breath — so I relied on the physician Bubonius to determine when the older man was fit to sit a horse again.

As it happened, we moved out none too soon.

— Flavius Arcadius Tahonius' Trans-Mesizibi Diaries

The Novan camp

Five days had passed, and Quintus Alces Sanctus was insisting he was fit to travel. It was time to go.

Early on the sixth morning in the camp they saddled horses to follow Julius Spotted Horse towards the mountains, towards the pass he had used before. The women of the camp stood impassively, watching them mount up to leave. Legionary Caninus walked over to one of the younger women and chucked her affectionately under the chin before he climbed on his horse. The woman just watched him impassively, but her eyes were shining. Judging from the cries that had come from her hut the three nights previous, Caninus had persuaded her to let him help assuage her grief over the camp's men.

When Celerius Dorotheus teased him about it, the grandson of the Great Dog just grinned. "That's just me," he said. "Women in four provinces cry out my name by night."

"All right," The Tribune said. "Let's be on our way."

The Romans walked their horses slowly away through the heavy forests, leaving the Novan village behind.

"Slower going than on the prairies or even along the coast," Tribune Arcadius observed on the first afternoon.

"We'll have a few more days like this," the scout replied. "Heavy woods through here—it rains a lot, as you've seen." There was a heavy drizzle falling at the moment, dripping down through the trees, making travel damp and unpleasant. "The pass I remember is a narrow one through the mountains east of here, but it's passable once the snows have cleared, and on the other side we'll have more open, dryer country again."

"Good," the Tribune muttered. "Dry will be good."

"Getting anxious to get home again, Chief?" the scout grinned.

"Anxious only to get out of this damp, cold place. Jupiter's balls, if

I wanted to live in cold and damp I'd have gone north to the Five Seas Nation, not all the way out here." He sneezed—the last few days in the cold, damp woods had left him with a bad head cold.

"Soon enough, Chief. Warmer lands, sunshine that will clear your head right up."

They moved on, following the same routine as they had in all the months of traveling: Scouts out at morning, the main party following, excepting only that now the scouts stayed closer in, due to the heavy forests.

Day by day they moved on, pushing east, climbing slowly into the mountains. They followed the big river up its valley for several days, through a narrow gorge into higher country, then left the big river to follow a smaller one east, then two days later left that one to proceed into the foothills.

After three more days Julius Spotted Horse rode to the top of a bald ridge for a look around. He returned after an hour and advised a slight turn south. "I think we've gone a little farther north than I planned. The pass is in those hills to the southeast there," he said, "where I crossed last time. The trail opens out into dryer, open country after that."

"Good,' the Tribune said. "Lead on. Dryer country would be desirable." He sneezed.

Prospero's Trading Post

"Well, it didn't take them long to get set up."

Legate Maximus Decimus Meridius stood on the wall, watching the Reman legionaries working across the river. Their own garrison was a near copy of his—not surprising, as both Roman and Reman militaries had only two to three generation's time to diverge. There was one key difference: Instead of the eagles of Rome, the red banner of the Five Seas Nation flew over the other garrison: Red with two black ravens.

"I don't see any Reman civilians," Tribune Seneca observed.

"Nor will we," Maximus predicted. "Not anytime soon. The Five Seas Nation doesn't allow their citizens as much freedom of action as does Rome."

"Their legate," Seneca pointed; the man had uncommon eyesight.

"Unpleasant bastard," Maximus muttered. As he had predicted, the Reman Legate Artorius Atricolus had paid a courtesy call soon after his arrival with his legion of infantry, accompanied by the centurion Vorenus, but whereas the centurion remained unfailingly polite and pleasant, the legate was just the opposite, suspicious to a fault, sour, and unfriendly.

"Will you return his call?" Seneca asked.

"I'd love nothing more than to ignore the bastard," Maximus snapped. "Let him rot over there. But, I suppose, we must observe the customs. Besides, I want to get a better look at their fortifications and the layout of their garrison, and maybe see how his men look."

"If centurion Vorenus is any indication, then the Five Seas Nation's Consul—no, wait, they call him their Imperator, is that right? Anyway, it would seem the men they sent are rather better than the normal run of soldiers. When you go, sir, you should have an interesting visit."

"Oh, it will be," Maximus smiled cruelly. "For us both."

"Both, sir?"

"Of course! You don't think I'd go over there alone, do you? No, Tribune; you'll be coming with me." He leaned down and shouted for a messenger. "May as well send a note across the river to him now, request an audience with his exalted arse. Best to get it done quickly. I'm almost due to send another report back to Rome, anyway."

The northern pass

"People have feet," Ochee said.

Tacitus grunted an affirmative. The boy Ochee grinned and stood up on the saddle behind the giant centurion, bracing himself with his hands on Tacitus's shoulders. Tacitus frowned but indulged the boy.

"Wolves have paws," Ochee went on.

Tacitus grunted again. On his own horse beside the centurion, Legionary Caninus chuckled. Tacitus shot him a severe look.

"Deer have feet," Ochee said next. He wasn't as gifted with language as Bright Water had been, but his command of Latin was improving—and he practiced almost constantly, leading the Roman soldiers to start calling him Ochee Loquax Minimus—the Little Chatterbox.

"Deer have hooves," Tacitus corrected. Ahead, the trail was growing steeper, where it climbed up an increasingly narrow canyon. Tacitus wondered where the scout was; Julius Spotted Horse had ridden ahead earlier that morning to have a look at the pass.

"Deer have hooves," Ochee agreed. "Deer have hair. People have hair. Snakes have scales."

"Yes," Tacitus allowed.

"He is your son," Caninus jibed. "In every way. Except for being tiny, and talking constantly, and being worthless in a fight, of course."

"Fight!" Ochee shot back at the legionary. "I can fight. Father fights better than you!" The Latin for father was one of the first words the skinny little Novan boy had picked up, and he immediately associated it with Tacitus.

Were he forced to admit it, the boy's attachment pleased the giant.

"He can at that, little one," Caninus agreed. It was true, after all—even after his fight with the great bear, Tacitus was by far the strongest of the Roman party.

"He fight a great bear. He fight my bad uncle Pocho."

"Fought," Tacitus corrected Ochee's tense. "I can fight. I have fought."

"Fought," Ochee repeated, committing the tense of the verb to memory. "Fighting, fight, fought," he conjugated.

"He'll be a tutor in no time, just you wait." Caninus found the whole thing very funny.

Tacitus scowled. "Just you wait, *sir*," he snapped.

"Of course. Sir. As you say, sir." The legionary's grin never faded.

"Birds have feet. Birds have feathers. A grouse is a bird that is good to eat. A raven is a bird that is not good to eat." The language lesson went on.

At the head of the column, Tribune Arcadius held up a hand to signal a halt. The scout was returning at a gallop.

"Spotted Horse," Arcadius greeted him. "What news of the pass?"

"Snow," the scout said. "Lots of snow. Forget that, Chief; snow or not, we have to go. Fast. As fast as we can!"

"What? Why?"

"From higher on the trail, you can see them. Come on, Chief, get everyone moving—at the gallop! We have to get across as quick as we can!" The man was close to panic.

"What is going on? You can see who?"

"Warriors, Novan tribesmen. His people, I'm guessing," Spotted Horse said, pointing at Ochee. A hundred or more! Coming up the approach to the pass, at the run. They're after us, Chief! We have to go *now*!"

"How did they get this close without us hearing them?"

"They are creatures of these woods, Chief. They know how to pass unnoticed, bet on it."

Arcadius shouted orders. "Bubonius, Sanctus, Bright Water, take the spare horses, to the front! Tacitus, let the boy ride behind Sanctus." Tacitus spoke quickly to Ochee, who slid to the ground and ran to clamber up behind the Stoic. "At the gallop—go! Everyone else, form up behind them. Gallop—*hah*!"

He risked a look back. The first Novan warriors were just cresting the low rise they had just passed, maybe a hundred paces back. One ran ahead of the others, shouting angrily now that the Romans were in sight. To the left, Legionary Marius halted his horse, raised his bow, aimed, and loosed an arrow that took the man in the chest. He kicked his horse to a gallop and joined the flight. Arcadius let the men go on ahead of him and then, with the giant centurion as always at his side, galloped for the pass.

"Ambush at a narrow spot in the trail?" Tacitus asked as they galloped behind the others.

"Not if we can outrun them," Arcadius shouted back. "Too many of them. Come on!"

Fu lay on the rocks of the trail. He couldn't breathe. He didn't understand it. He was well out of bow range of the strange men, and yet somehow they had struck him. His last vision was of the other men of the Kobay running past him chasing the strange men who fled now on their beasts. *Run*, he sent the thought after them. *No man can outrun the Kobay.*

Then he never thought anything, ever again.

The trail to the pass grew narrower and rougher as they climbed. "About a mille to the crest," Spotted Horse shouted. "Come on!"

The snow deepened. The horses slowed, unable to gallop in the hock-deep drifts. Arcadius risked a look back; the snow was slowing the Novans, but not as much. They were gaining. They pushed on, passing under a steep cliff. The path bent around the cliff, turning to the right. When Arcadius passed the cliff and made the turn, he could see the crest of the pass. *Not far now.*

"And what then?" he wondered. "We'll be able to move faster. So will they."

"Corvus!" he heard the centurion shout. "What are you doing?"

The slinger had dismounted just past the cliff. He pointed up. Arcadius and Tacitus followed the man's pointing finger, to a cornice of snow at the top. Above the cornice was a long, sloping field of heavy snow. Water was dripping from the underside of the cornice, splashing on the rocks below.

Corvus bent and scooped up a rock. With a smooth, practiced motion, he whirled the leather strap over his head and let fly. The rock plopped into the underside of the cornice.

Arcadius looked up the slope, up at the thick snow above. *I see what he's trying to do*, he suddenly realized. *If this works…*

The legionary grabbed another rock. The Novan warriors were close now; several of them stopped and began to plink arrows at Corvus. He slung the second rock. It struck a few feet from the first.

Corvus waved the Tribune and the centurion to move on. They galloped a few paces farther on, then stopped to watch. They drew their swords and waited. The rest of the party pushed on, reaching for the pass. "Keep moving," Arcadius shouted after them. "Don't look back."

The slinger grabbed a third rock. The Novans were almost to

the cliff. He wound up, whirled, and slung the last rock. It struck the cornice a long pace past the first two.

A long, rumbling groan came from the top of the cliff. Shouting in alarm, the Novans stopped and turned back, running away from the cliff.

"Move!" Corvus shouted at the officers. "Up the trail!" He grabbed his horse's reins, but waited—he had to be sure—

The cornice collapsed. A mountainside's worth of snow fell onto the trail and cascaded down the mountain, drowning out the screams of the warriors of the Kobay.

Corvus looked down. A Novan arrow had struck him in the thigh, somehow escaping his notice until he felt the pain of the penetrating wound. He gritted his teeth and pulled it out. Some blood flowed. *Not so bad*, he thought. Slowly, painfully, he climbed on his horse and followed the others.

They reassembled at the top of the pass. The Tribune quickly filled the others in on what had happened at the cliff as Bright Water quickly, efficiently bandaged Corvus' leg. "That," Arcadius concluded, "was one of the greatest acts of bravery I've ever seen. Novan arrows falling all around him, and Corvus just stood there, slinging stones at that cliff, until the avalanche swept the enemy away. Legionary Corvus!" he barked.

"Sir?" Corvus said through gritted teeth. His leg was really beginning to hurt now. Bright Water had made him sit on a large rock while she bandaged his injured leg. He started to get painfully to his feet, but the Tribune motioned him to stay put.

"Everyone, listen. Legionary Cominus Quintus Corvus, you are henceforth *Duplicarious* Cominus Quintus Corvus. Your pay will double from this day forward, and you now are third-in-command of the expedition, after myself and Centurion Tacitus."

His leg still hurt, but Corvus grinned anyway. He could almost feel the extra coins in his pockets — not like he'd see any of the coin until they returned to the Republic, but still. The other cavalrymen greeted the news with cheers and applause.

"Chief," Julius Spotted Horse said after the shouting died down. "We should keep moving."

"You think so? Surely the avalanche swept them away?"

"It gained us time, yes, Chief," the scout said. "Maybe a few hours. But those people are people of these mountains. They knew just where we'd try to crest the pass. They knew the trail. They'll be familiar with avalanches, and I'd bet my pay for the entire journey that most of them survived. Once the snow settles they'll be climbing over it, after us."

"But why? Why are they so set on killing us?"

Spotted Horse pointed again at Ochee. "I'd wager they are of his people. We wiped out all the men of one of their summer camps. They'll want to pay us in kind for that, Chief, and they won't stop anytime soon."

"They were Kobay," Ochee confirmed. "My people. I know them by their hair."

"Julius? How far before we're out of their territory?"

Spotted Horse frowned. "Honestly? I've no idea. Maybe just being over the pass is enough. Maybe not. Best to be safe."

"Ochee? How far do your people live? If we continue on through the valley below this pass, will we be safe? Will they follow us?"

"They will keep coming," Ochee predicted. He frowned. "I do not know where all the camps of the Kobay are. There are many. But if they chase us, they will keep chasing us until they catch us, or we kill them."

Arcadius didn't like the sound of that. "Centurion?"

"Best move on as fast as we can, sir."

"I agree," the Tribune decided. "To the others. We move."

Once they were moving, the Tribune spoke to his optio. 'Centurion, how much has the boy told you of his people?"

Tacitus shrugged. "His Latin is not yet adequate, sir. He has told me that they are called the Kobay, and that his camp was one of many of their people. They are hunters and nomads, although they gather in a winter camp each year."

"Find out more. Anything he knows — their numbers, how often they go to war, any other people in the region. We know nothing of them now. Anything is more than nothing."

Four hands of hands and four of the Kobay had set out after the strange men and their beasts. Two hands of hands, three hands and two were left after the avalanche.

Yap was the oldest and most experienced of the men that were left, so the others looked to him for a decision. "Do we chase them over the pass?" a young hunter asked.

"No," Yap said. "We cannot cross the pass. The snow now blocks our way, and we cannot wait for it to melt. We will go now north into the country of Man-Of-The-Woods and cross at the pass in that country. We can easily do that in a hand of days and pick up their trail on the other side."

"What of our summer camps?"

"Our wives and sisters are gathering food, and we will have time to hunt when we return." Yap looked at the men around him. "If any of you wish to return to the summer camps, go now. I will continue to follow the men who killed all of the men of Fu's camp. If you wish to revenge our brothers, come with me." He struck a defiant pose. "If none of you are brave enough, I will go alone."

The men of the Kobay gathered themselves and turned to go back down the mountain trail. When they reached the deep forest, they turned north. Not a man of the Kobay left for their summer camps.

Four days later — In the foothills east of the pass

Reman Army Legate Marcus Malleolus was at the end of his endurance.

"Jupiter Capitolinus and Martius Paternis, how has it come to this?" he muttered. He looked around him. The Great Sister had dwindled to a stream long before, and still he walked. He had passed through the hills and long since noted that the streams and growing rivers flowed mostly west, not east, and still he walked. He had used the last of the arrows he had scavenged from the camp where his men had abandoned him, and eaten the last of the venison he had taken with the arrows, and still he walked. He abandoned the legion bow and now subsisted on rabbits caught with snares, and fish grubbed from small streams, and even frogs and ground squirrels, and still he walked.

Now, he knew it was the end. He had no more strength to go on.

"At least it's a beautiful place to die."

Malleolus had reached his end in a small valley leading up to a rampart of low mountains. Snow still glittered on the peaks above him. At least he wasn't dying of thirst; a painfully cold stream of crystal-pure water ran only feet from where he had lain down to rest for the last time and awoken unable to rise.

On what he expected to be his last morning, he managed to crawl to the stream and drink. He crawled back to the big aspen he had been leaning against and composed himself. He murmured a brief prayer to Venus Lifegiver and closed his eyes.

The Kobay men knew they were close to the strangers who had killed their brothers. "This valley will lead to the valley they should be in," Yap had said that morning. "We will find them there."

Instead, they found a man, almost dead, sitting in the long grass, his back against a tree.

"He is one of them," Weyo said. He bent down and looked closely. The stranger's eyes opened slowly, then opened wide. "We should kill him." He drew his obsidian knife.

"No," Yap said. He knelt beside Weyo and touched the strange man's cheek. "Look at what he is wearing. He wears black. The others wore red and brown. And he is starving. The others were well fed." He stood up. "I want to know more about this man. I want to know how he came to be here alone and starving."

Yap looked around and took count of the men still with him. "Weyo," he said, "you and Klee stay here. Feed this man until he can walk. Talk to him if you can. When he is strong enough, follow us." He looked again at the stranger. He bent to take the long, strange knife the man wore at his side. "I will take this with me."

Legate Malleolus thought his eyes were failing. A large group of Novans with the look of warriors approached from the west. They approached him slowly, cautiously, finally gathering around him. He thought about reaching for his gladius, the one weapon he had managed to retain, but decided not to bother. *So my death will come a few hours sooner*, he thought. *It does not matter now.*

But the Novans didn't kill him. They gathered around him and talked for a while. One of them, an older man with a few streaks of gray in his cropped black hair, bent and took his gladius. Malleolus was too weak to resist.

Then, finally, another man knelt in front of him. He held out something.

A piece of dried meat.

Southeast

"I swear, Julius," Manius Octavius Taurinus jibed, "six days since we've been over that pass, and you're still as nervous as a mouse in a bag of weasels."

Julius Spotted Horse had only moments before caught up to the party, having dropped behind a mille to watch their back trail. "Better to be nervous than dead," he said. He pulled up his tunic to reveal the scar on his leg. "Believe you me, if one of these bands has their hearts set on your blood, they don't give up so easy."

"So you keep saying," Celerius Dorotheus said, "and I think you're right—but do you honestly think they can catch us, even so? We are a-horse, they are on foot, and we've kept up a pretty good pace since the pass." That was true; the Tribune had kept them moving from sunrise to sunset, and sometimes a bit past that. They had made only cold camps, no fire to give them away by night, and by day had moved as fast as the horses would stand.

At the rear of the formation, Spotted Horse looked nervously over his shoulder, as he had been doing for the past few days. The Roman party was riding in an open formation, with the soldiers in a loose oval and Bright Water in the middle. Ochee rode on Bright Water's horse; he was not happy with being separated from his adopted father, but a sharp word from Tacitus had quieted his complaining.

The day was bright, warm, and clear. "Summer at last," Taurinus said with some satisfaction.

"Look alive," Dorotheus said. "The Tribune."

Arcadius left his place at the front of the formation and trotted back to where the scout rode with the tracker and the runner towards the rear of the formation. "What news?" he asked.

"No sign of anyone after us, Chief," Spotted Horse reported. "Doesn't mean they aren't out there."

"Even now, after six days?"

"Some of the lads I grew up with could run for five, six days at a stretch, stopping only to nap an hour here and there. They may be out there." He pointed ahead. "See where that valley up there branches off to the north? I'd not mind taking a look up there a mille or so. Take the rest straight on down this stream's course. I'll catch up before nightfall."

"Very well. Taurinus, go with him." The tracker saluted, and both men booted their horses and galloped off.

"You are bloody nervous," Taurinus called after Spotted Horse as they rode.

"I have a bad feeling," Spotted Horse replied. "The way that lot, the Kobay, came after us at the pass. We must have missed one of them when we took the village and now he's turned out the whole tribe." The scout frowned, an unusual expression for the normally cheerful man. "I made a bad mistake. Most of these little groups, they're just nomads and little family groups like on the plains, see? This bunch is different. The boy Ochee says they are a big clan, like, that spreads out in summer to hunt and gather. There are groups on the plains that make winter camp in one place, two or three clans come together to share fires. Ochee has no idea of their numbers, but these folk, I'll bet a gold aureus that there are enough of them to form a bloody great winter camp, and some bastard has turned them all out."

He leaned off his horse and spat. "He also said they drove off those people to the south, near where we camped for the winter. Only lucky they didn't detect us there in the winter camp as well, or they would have come at us with their whole tribe. They don't like neighbors," the scout concluded, "and we just went and wiped out one of their summer camps. We managed to start a vendetta."

"They started it," Taurinus objected. "They tried to steal Bright Water and the Tribune."

"I'm sure they don't see it that way," the scout said.

Yap had led the men of the Kobay at a killing pace, day and night, stopping only to drink from small streams and pools, and snatch a few moments of sleep. Even though Yap was one of the older of the men several others had fallen out, unable to keep up with him.

But now the punishment was rewarded. Two of the strange men were just ahead, riding their great beasts. Yap shouted, waving his captured weapon above his head. "There!" he roared. "Kill them!"

"Fuck me sideways," Taurinus pointed at the oncoming rush of natives. "That one has a sword!"

There were far too many of them, sword or no. "Flee!" the scout snapped.

Both men wheeled their horses and ran, back towards the main party, the howling horde of the Kobay in pursuit.

"Well, you were right," Taurinus shouted.

They reached the bottom of the valley having outdistanced the Novans, but only by a few hundred paces. The main party was just ahead. Arcadius had heard the approaching hoof beats and halted the group.

"Right behind us!" Spotted Horse yelled as they rejoined the group. "Fifty or more!"

"How close?"

"A few hundred paces, no more," Taurinus replied. Behind him, the excited screams of the attacking Novans could be heard.

No time to run. No time to set up any kind of ambush. No time even for a proper defensive formation.

Well, enough of this. If it's a fight they want, a fight they shall have.

Arcadius began shouting commands. "Corvus, Marius, Varus, stay here with Bright Water and the pack horses. Use your bows and slings. Keep them at a distance. Protect her and the boy. If you must, flee down the valley. Everyone else, swords! Centurion, take Caninus, Bubonius and Dorotheus, flank them on the left. Everyone else, on me! We'll take one slash through them, and then we turn and head back down the valley. *Charge!*"

Whirling swords, the Roman cavalrymen charged the approaching Kobay…

…who melted away before them like a flock of birds swirling around a diving falcon. The Kobay swirled around, dodging the charge of the cavalrymen and hurled their clubs at the Roman horsemen as they passed. The speed of the Roman horses caused all but one of the clubs to miss; that one struck Centurion Tacitus a glancing blow on the leg, doing no real harm.

The Romans reformed a hundred paces up the valley and watched the warriors of the Kobay. "Now that's clever," Marcus

Aurelius observed. "They have long thongs tied to their clubs. See them drawing them back in."

"Sons of whores won't come to blows," Valerius Caninus complained.

"They aren't stupid," Arcadius agreed. Striking at their flanks hadn't worked. The Kobay were advancing again, slower now, loping at the horsemen in small groups of three and four.

"Into line," the Tribune ordered. "When we charge, bend the flanks forward. Leave them nowhere to dodge. Charge!"

They booted their horses to the gallop again. "Come on, you slick little cunnis," Caninus taunted as they charged. "Let's see what you're made of!" He managed to catch one Kobay as they passed, striking deep into the man's neck with a perfectly timed stab. Two other Kobay fell to Roman steel in the second charge, but Legionary Dorotheus took a painful blow along the ribs from a thrown club. "Back to the others," Arcadius shouted.

A whistle sounded from somewhere behind them.

Yap raised a carefully carved wooden whistle to his lips and blew a long blast. When the Kobay hunted, the whistles were used to signal a waiting ambush. The Kobay used the whistles in war as well.

"Look to the flanks!" Tacitus roared. From either flank, a dozen or more Kobay warriors charged, screaming. They ran to the front, attempting to block the Romans' retreat down the valley. Arrows began to drop among the Roman soldiers who, for the moment, slowed and milled about on their horses, confused.

They have numbers on us, Arcadius thought quickly. *They have the advantage of terrain—archers on our flanks on high ground. Our only advantage is speed.*

The Tribune pointed with his sword at the Novans, who had formed a ragged blocking line across the valley only paces away. "Wedge formation! Split their line! *Charge!*"

At the point of the wedge, Arcadius led the men straight at the Kobay blocking the valley and managed to split their line, breaking through into the clear. They fled down the valley at the gallop as the Kobay closed ranks neatly behind them and pursued.

"Are you all right?" the physician Bubonius called after Dorotheus as they galloped away from the Kobay.

"I'm fine," the runner replied. "I can ride. I'm fine." He looked down at a streak of blood running down his leg.

They rejoined Bright Water and the others moments later. "We got three of them."

"Four came at us," Duplicarious Corvus reported. "We killed them." Arrows from the Roman legion bows proved much harder to dodge than the swords of the cavalrymen.

The shouts of the Kobay were coming nearer again. "They don't sound so enthusiastic now," Arcadius noted. "We've stung them. Now let's make them run after us. Down the valley—at the gallop! *Haaah!*"

Yap stopped and watched the strangers riding swiftly away on their animals.

"Seven dead," one of the others reported.

"They are too fast," Yap said, as much to himself as to the others. "They can strike too well from a distance."

"What shall we do?"

"Kachee, Taday," Yap called two of the younger men who were

known as fast, tireless runners. "Follow them. Find out where their land is. Find out where they come from. Then come back. The rest of us will think of a way to beat them despite their animals, in spite of their speed. They are strong, but the Kobay are quick and clever. We will see them again."

When Arcadius finally allowed a brief stop, Bright Water and Bubonius quickly dressed Dorotheus' leg. "He should be all right," the physician reported to the Tribune when that was done. "A glancing blow, really, just took off a strip of skin. Bright Water promised to boil up some of her herbal concoction when we stop for the night, if it works as well as it did on the centurion, it should help him heal cleanly. Caninus took a knock on the head that raised a welt, but other than a headache he should be fine. Three horses injured—Sanctus' horse took an arrow in the flank, and two others were hit by clubs."

"Anything that will slow us down?"

"I hope not, sir. I'll keep an eye on them."

"Good. Well done. We'll keep moving."

FOURTEEN

PASSAGES

The Kobay proved to be persistent, if nothing else.

With the exception of one scrap in the southern deserts in which we lost the only man to perish on our long journey, the Kobay were the only people who required our men to act as soldiers. It was always the intent of the Consul that we should be a party of discovery, to find new peoples, new trade routes, and new sources of wealth. We knew there was a possibility that some of the people we encountered would be hostile. In retrospect, it is amazing that out of all the thousands of milles we traveled, the Kobay were the only people we met with the potential and the willingness to become enemies of Rome.

After the dramatic crossing of the pass, we moved down into the drainage of the Great Sister. We knew we had a long way yet to travel, but the end was in sight. It was still early summer, the country was open and clear, and our horses were healthy and strong. Civilization seemed close at hand once more, and we were all more than ready to see Rome once more.

—Flavius Arcadius Tahonius' Trans-Mesizibi Diaries

Rome

"Those bastards," the new Consul swore. "Those damned Golden Twins."

"Calm yourself. You're only Consul a few days, and you're already making yourself agitated. You'll do yourself an injury—trust me, I know."

The changeover of the Consul's office was nearing its conclusion. The transition required a series of meetings and conferences between the outgoing Consul and the incoming. This was the final meeting, between old Consul and new, in Brutus's villa on the Catonian hill.

Consul Brutus drained a cup of wine at a gulp. "I know, friend Cassius, I know. It's just the short-sightedness of some is too much to bear. I grant you we have barely enough Treasury to maintain roads and troops here in the provinces. But would those Cadovian bastards rather see all of the trans-Mesizibi under the ravens of the Five Seas Nation? That would be the only other option, unless the Mayans take it in their heads to move into those empty lands."

Poscus Cassius, now again a Senator from Lustria now that his brief term as Consul was over, laughed. "Be careful. You know that when you name an evil, you give it power."

Brutus slammed his cup down. "I have enough gold allocated to keep the western garrisons fed and paid another year, maybe two, if the soldiers don't eat over much. After that?"

"After that, we withdraw the garrisons," Cassius completed the thought for the Consul.

"And surrender the West," Brutus snarled. He refilled his cup and drained it again. "Surrender the West and all of its resources to whoever is strong enough to take it."

"I take it there is no word of your western expedition?"

"None," Brutus said. "None whatsoever. Two years now they've been gone. Who knows what has happened? They may all be dead."

"Perhaps they found some locals and settled in with them out there, somewhere in the West."

The Consul shook his head. "No," he said. "Not Arcadius. I know my cousin, Cassius. No truer Roman than he, and that's a fact. No, if Tribune Arcadius lives, he will return."

"If we're lucky, he'll return with news of the West that will entice the Senate to look favorably on more expansion."

"If he returns with news of resources, of riches, of fortunes to be made, there will be nothing the gods themselves could do to stop Romans from moving into the trans-Mesizibi and beyond."

The former Consul Cassius raised his cup. "Let's hope that he returns with good news, then."

The West

Several days had passed. The valley the Romans had moved down following the Kobay attack had opened into another, larger valley. The thick forests west of the pass gave way to more open, drier country, as the scout had promised. "We keep moving downstream," Spotted Horse had told them. "We are in the high end of the Great Sister drainage. Any stream will lead us down to the Sister in time."

Arcadius kept the party moving, sunrise to sunset.

Then, on the sixth day after the Kobay attack, Legionary Aurelius halted his horse and pointed. "I swear I saw a Novan watching from that ridge to the north." It wasn't the first time the sharp-eyed youth had made such a claim.

"Aurelius," Legionary Varus said tiredly, "you're seeing things. It's been ten days. Those bastards couldn't still be after us."

"It would hardly be the first time some local has watched us from high ground," Valerius Caninus added. "To be fair, we must look pretty odd to the folk this far out. Not like they've ever seen horses before."

"Country is opening up some, anyway. That's good. You can see further."

"I'm sure I saw him," Aurelius insisted.

"I saw the man on the ridge," Ochee told his adopted father.

"You did?"

"He had Kobay hair," Ochee added. He was on the back of Tacitus's spare horse, learning—slowly—to ride. The Kobay boy patted his head. "Like mine was."

"Was, little chatterbox?" Legionary Caninus asked.

"I will let my hair grow," Ochee said. He pointed. "Like Father. Only I can't make my hair grow a white stripe."

"You have to fight a bear first, little one," Caninus advised him.

"Ochee," Tacitus rumbled, "stay with Caninus and the others. I have to talk to the Tribune."

"Yes, Father," Ochee agreed.

Tacitus dropped back to where the Tribune and his wife rode towards the rear of the formation. "Sir," he began.

"The man on that ridge?" Arcadius asked, pointing north.

"Yes, sir. Ochee said he has Kobay hair. They did have a distinctive haircut."

Arcadius frowned. "They did. And Ochee does have quite the set of eyes. Remember a few days back, he sighted those three deer a good mille off on the hillside?"

"It is possible they sent scouts after us."

"Why?" Arcadius thought aloud. "To see where we came from? To see where we're going? They must be quite some ways out of their own country by now. Julius? What do you think?" he asked the scout.

"I didn't see him, Chief," Julius Spotted Horse replied, a little sullenly. He had finally run out of his nasty chewing weed a few days earlier, and it was affecting his mood for the worse. He had a juniper twig stuck in his mouth now, chewing on it absent-mindedly, but there was obviously something in the weed that he needed.

The Tribune turned back to Tacitus. "So you think they are Kobay?"

"I think it's possible, sir. They may be locals—the Kobay, they are a people of the forest on the western side of the pass. This is open country, fewer trees, more grass. Look at the peoples of Rome. Tahona stay to their forests in the north. The former Tsalee stay in Mesizibi valley and the tributaries. The original tribes of B'kou stay around Rome. People tend to stay in country they know."

"What about us?" Arcadius grinned at the giant. "Apparently we have no such good sense."

"Sir, we are under orders. Orders from the Consul himself," Tacitus replied, as though that explained everything.

And Arcadius had to admit, it did.

But there was still the problem of their trailers.

Tacitus looked up at the ridge and went on: "There is this, sir: If those are Kobay following us, they're scouting us out for the rest of their tribe. That means the rest of the tribe is somewhere behind, still hoping to learn our whereabouts."

"Centurion," Arcadius said softly. He looked around. Ochee was ahead in the formation, talking with Varus. "Take Caninus, Taurinus and Aurelius. Go find those men that are following us."

"Yes, sir. When we find them?"

"Convince them to stop following us," the Tribune ordered. He looked at the giant, one eyebrow cocked. "If they are in fact Kobay, deal with them. We don't want them following us. Understand?"

"Yes, sir." Tacitus saluted and rode off to gather the others, thinking as he went: *They are persistent. The best way to make sure they stop following us is to make sure they can no longer follow us. Fortunately, the Tribune gave me latitude to do exactly that.*

"The Tribune wants us to find the man Aurelius saw and any

others with him," he told the other three once he had them gathered. "We will also make sure they don't tell their people where we've gone. Is that clear?"

Legionary Caninus grinned wickedly. "Clear as ice, sir."

They rode up to the top of the long ridge to where Aurelius had seen the watcher. Legionary Taurinus dismounted and examined the ground, walking back and forth until…

"Here, sir," he pointed. "Two of them. They're moving east." He looked up. "Towards that group of trees." He pointed to a small copse on the crest of the ridge, a few hundred paces away. "I'd bet a hundred sesterces that they're still in there, watching the valley for us to pass. It's too good a vantage point not to use."

The giant nodded agreement. "Caninus, you and Aurelius drop down the south side of the ridge. Taurinus, you come with me up the north side. Move at the gallop. We'll come at those two from both sides."

"Are we making any special effort to capture them?" Caninus asked.

The centurion looked directly at Caninus. "No," he said. "Move."

"As you say, sir." The legionary drew his sword. "Just making sure. Come on, Junius. Let's have at them." He kicked his horse and galloped off. The giant and the tracker rode off to the opposite side of the ridge.

Kachee and Taday had stopped in the copse to eat a handful of the ground dried meat mixed with berries that made up their travel ration. They heard the hoof beats approaching, but failed to immediately associate it with the men they were following until the Romans burst into the small grove of pines.

"Hah!" Caninus shouted as he spotted the two Novans. He whirled his sword, but beside him, Aurelius already had drawn one of his blades. He threw it, transfixing the nearer of the two Novans with the thin, glittering steel.

Taday saw Kachee fall, a long blade through his chest. He turned to run, but two more of the strangers were entering the grove from the other side. One of them had a bow, already up and drawn…

"Looks like there was only the two of them," Taurinus reported.

"Food for worms now," Caninus complained, "and I never got to strike a blow."

"You're far too slow," Aurelius teased the big man. "Maybe you're getting old."

"Oh, piss off," Caninus said, laughing.

"Enough, both of you. Back to the others," Tacitus ordered. "And not a word of this to Ochee. He's had enough of these people to last him, no point in upsetting him any further."

"Yes sir!" the others chorused.

That evening, the party stopped as usual, cared for their horses, set up shelters, and built up a fire. Once the entire party was finished with the evening's work and was sitting around the fire eating the evening meal, Taurinus and Aurelius recounted the attack on the Kobay scouts in the copse of trees, especially Aurelius' sword throw that took out one of the Kobay warriors. "Who ever thought of throwing a sword?" the tracker concluded.

"My swords are lighter than the usual issue gladii," Aurelius reminded them. "I've practiced throwing them from time to time, but this is the first time I've tried it in battle."

"Well, it worked," Caninus complained. "I was all set to run the little bastard through when I saw your sword come flying in."

"You'll have to be faster next time," the swordsman said. "Still.

It would be nice if we had more ways to strike a foe from a distance. Bows and slings are all well and good, but limited to what, thirty or forty paces? In these great open spaces, it would be better to hit from, say, a hundred paces or more, like a siege trebuchet or an onager."

"Well, when you come up with a way to carry a trebuchet around with you, let me know," Caninus replied.

Marcus Bubonius sat by the fire, listening with half an ear. There was something hovering around the back of his mind…

He stood up suddenly and went to where his packs lay on the ground near his saddle.

"Marcus," Quintus Sanctus called. "What are you doing?"

He finally found what he wanted: A leather bag, about the size of his two fists clenched together. He opened it and looked at the white powder inside—the powder given him by an old Novan shaman, in the deserts far to the south, many months earlier. He walked back to the fire, staring into the bag.

"Marcus," Sanctus said. "What is it?"

"I don't know." He took a pinch of the white powder and tossed it into the fire. He watched as a bright, hot flare of purplish flame burst out of the campfire. He watched the mushroom of smoke rise into the air.

"I don't know," he repeated. There was something about that puff of smoke—about that flare of flame…

"I don't know," he said again. "But I'll figure it out."

To the west

The Reman legate was still weak, but he could walk, albeit slowly. The Kobay didn't push him, seeming to understand his weakness, but they did keep him moving with the group, bound west. Malleolus didn't object. Communicating with his new friends was coming along much more slowly than his physical recovery.

At least they were moving west, up a broad valley towards a distant mountain range. *I'm still following my orders*, Malleolus thought, *even if I am a prisoner.*

He wasn't entirely sure that was in fact his status. The Kobay escorting him west did not tie his hands, or seek to bind him in any way. They gave him food and water, and although one of them had taken his sword, they let him retain his pugio and all of his remaining gear—as the mountain nights grew chillier he was glad of his warm, heavy, wolf fur-trimmed cloak. None of the Novans threatened him or shouted at him, although he wasn't sure what would happen if he tried to leave their company.

Since he was depending on them for sustenance, staying with them seemed the wisest course of action in any case.

The old man who was leading the group, Yap, was making regular attempts to communicate. The legate was learning the language of the Kobay faster than the old man was learning Latin, which did not surprise Malleolus; the Kobay were a sheltered, primitive people with no formalized education system. The Reman knew how to learn and extract meanings from context, where Yap did not.

Still, the Novan's Latin was improving—slowly.

One day towards evening, as the group was moving into the foothills of a range of low mountains, Yap called a halt. Without orders, the Novan warriors began setting up what passed for their traveling camp: A common fire for cooking and warmth, some low shelters hastily constructed from branches and tree bark.

Malleolus made his own shelter as he normally did, with his last scrap of heavy cloth propped up with some short poles. He built his own personal fire, which as usual elicited some comments from his Novan traveling companions, who preferred their communal fire.

Malleolus warmed up some venison left over from the day before and sat on a rock by his fire, wrapped in his now badly worn legate's cloak, staring into the flames.

Someone approached his fire. Malleolus looked up to see Yap standing a few feet away, his eyebrows raised in an unspoken question. The Novan gestured to a fallen log near the fire. Malleolus nodded, motioning for the native to take a seat; he hadn't expected that sort of display of courtesy from a savage.

Maybe these people are more civilized than they let on, he thought.

Yap handed him a small rawhide pouch. Malleolus looked inside; it contained the mixture of chopped venison, berries, and herbs that the Kobay frequently carried as a traveling ration.

"Eat," Yap said in his poor Latin. "If not…" he trailed off and switched back to his own tongue, motioning towards his mouth. "If you do not eat that, if you eat just plain meat, you will get the sickness of rotting teeth. Your skin will turn black, your teeth will fall out, and you will die."

Scurvy, Malleolus thought. *Roman and Reman alike were familiar enough with that malady.* He looked into the pouch. Apparently the Kobay believed something in their traditional fare prevented the disease. He nodded; *it wouldn't hurt to go along with the man.* He searched his memory for the Kobay words for a moment: "I you thank," he managed.

Yap nodded. He produced another pouch of the mixture for himself, hooked a mouthful out with two fingers and chewed companionably for a few moments. Once he had swallowed, he spoke again.

"The men you called Ro-man," he said in his own language.

"They are from the east, you say?" He pointed to the east to emphasize his words.

"Yes," Malleolus nodded. He tapped his chest. "My people also. Many, many days walk to east, on other side of a great river."

"Your people and Ro-mans, you are enemies," he observed. It wasn't the first time he had mentioned that.

"Yes," Malleolus agreed. It was more or less true; the Five Seas Nation had always been on touchy ground when dealing with their larger, more powerful cousin to the south.

"Ro-mans are our enemies," Yap added. "They killed all of the men of one of our summer camps. They stole a child of the Kobay."

"Yes," the legate agreed again. *Where is he going with this? And why does he keep going on about that attack on the camp? There has to be more to it—whatever you think of Roman soldiers, they don't just attack people with no reason.*

Then again, these are the same bastards that stole our horses and left my party stranded on the prairie. They have to be.

Yap motioned east again. "The Ro-man soldiers, they have fled east. I have two men watching them …"

Malleolus cut the man off. "You have men following them?"

"Of course," Yap said. "We must find out where they live."

"Can you call them back?" the legate snapped in Latin, forgetting himself for the moment. He fought for the Kobay words: "Send a man. Tell them to stop follow. Come back!"

"Why?"

He shook his head. "Dead, probably, already. Romans are great warriors. See them, no matter how quiet. Kill them. T'achee." *It can't be helped.*

Yap did not appear overly concerned. "If so, then so. But you are here. You can tell us much about Ro-man soldiers."

"I can," Malleolus said thoughtfully. "Rome is now your enemy. Rome has been my enemy. Your people and mine, friends that makes us."

Yap sat for a moment, digesting that. "Yes," he said finally. "Yes, that would be a good thing."

"When I speak better, more talk will we," Malleolus said. "Stronger I get for walking. I can tell you many things of Rome."

Yap nodded and took another mouthful of chopped meat from his pouch. He sat silently, staring into the legate's fire, his face registering an eloquent display of deep thought.

An alliance of convenience, Malleolus told himself. I may well be overstepping my authority—but the Imperator's orders included seeking out possible allies, possible new peoples to join the Five Seas Nation. These people appear to be fierce fighters, and they put a fair number of warriors into the field on short notice. Good auxiliaries, perhaps, for the Reman army.

He sat silently for some time, staring into the flames as the night fell. Yap stayed where he was, eating slowly. Oddly, Malleolus was glad of the other man's company. He was evidently a leader among his people, a man of some authority even as Malleolus was—had been—and they were more or less of an age. *Things held in common can make for friendships*, he mused, *for men and for nations*.

Malleolus was reminded his mother. She had been a small, dark woman with some Tahona blood, originally from the country around the Three Sisters. The border between the Five Seas Nation and Rome in that region was nebulous, and there were scraps between Roman and Reman soldiers as each tried to keep hunting and fishing parties from each side out of their own poorly demarked territory. The exact placement of the border was long argued in both Rome and Terminus by representatives of each people. *It will take a war to define that border at last,* the legate told himself, *and Rome is larger than we are. Allies could prove useful—a strike from an unexpected direction could help us seize our share of the Tahona lands, maybe even gain a place on the Atlantic coast.*

Eventually his fatigue overtook him, and he rolled up in his cloak to sleep.

In the morning, Yap woke Malleolus. "We go," he said, and walked off. Malleolus sat up, rubbing his eyes. The sun was barely up, but around him the Kobay were rolling up sleeping hides, dousing the fire, and preparing to move. The legate followed suit.

They moved off to the west as before, climbing steadily as they went.

The headwaters of the Sister

"I think that's a branch of the Sister," Julius Spotted Horse opined. He sat on his Reman pony next to Tribune Arcadius, looking down from the crest of a low ridge at the dull sliver of a river.

A few days had passed with no more sign of Kobay followers, and at last the Tribune had seen fit to reduce their travel agenda back to its normal tempo. The hills around them this warm early-summer afternoon were covered with a waving sea of tall grass, while a small band of cottonwood trees traced the course of the river. As they watched, a flight of ducks lifted off from the edge of the river and flew away downstream.

Arcadius looked at the scout. *At least his disposition has improved some over the last few days,* he told himself. *Must be getting used to doing without that weed he chews.*

"It is a good-sized river. If, as you say, we are in the Sister's drainage now, any river we follow downstream will take us to the main body of the Sister, yes?"

"And from there to Durobrivia," Spotted Horse agreed. "And I'm sure you boys can find your way back to Pompeius from there."

"I've been meaning to speak to you about that," the Tribune replied. "I wish you would come on to Pompeius with us. This mission would not have succeeded as it has without you, Julius; we may have made the ocean and found our way back, but we wouldn't have learned anything about the people of the plains and mountains without you to talk to them, and we wouldn't have covered half as much territory without someone along who knew something of the country. Your service has been invaluable, and I am certain the Consul of Rome would like to personally reward you for it."

The scout looked thoughtful. "I'm a creature of the prairies, Chief," he said slowly. "I haven't been east of the Mesizibi since I was in the legions. I'm not much of a one for towns, much less cities."

"Nobody is asking you to move there. Just come and receive your duly earned recognition and reward."

"Reward, now there's a thought," the scout grinned his stained, gap-toothed grin. Somewhere during the flight from the Kobay he had lost the turkey feather he had worn tied to a thong around his temples as his only headgear, but he had found a long black wing feather from a vulture to replace it, making his appearance even more disreputable. "I know we negotiated my coin for the trip, and I'm duly grateful to you for that, Chief. You were generous there and I know that. But if the Consul wants to reward me further, that might be worth the ride east."

"You'd be feted in the city," Arcadius continued. "You could always return to the prairies afterwards, but seeing Pompeius, that would be something to tell your grandchildren about."

"Grandchildren," the scout said. "Well, there's a thought." He squinted at the river. "Chief, want I should ride down the river some way, see if there's anything in our way?"

Arcadius inclined his head towards the river. "By all means," he agreed.

The scout kicked his horse and galloped off.

The Tribune shook his head. *Grandchildren*, he scolded himself. *Why did I mention grandchildren? He doesn't even have any children he ever mentioned, and he must be in his fourth decade. He's probably going to die alone in some prairie hovel with nobody behind to remember him. Well, all the more reason to get him to Pompeius, where he can give some of his own accounts to the scribes. At least history will remember him. That's something.*

He motioned the main column forward, down the ridge, towards the river that would lead them home. As they rode, the giant centurion, Tacitus, moved forward in the formation to ride alongside his commander. Arcadius looked back; as was often the case, Bright Water was a few paces back, engaged in another discussion of medicine with Legionary Bubonius. The physician was explaining something and tapping the side of his head as he did so.

Arcadius looked sidelong at the centurion. The man had changed over the trip, first after the battle with the great bear, and again following his adoption of the Kobay boy, Ochee. He was as serious as always, but also seemed more attuned to the beauty of the wild world around them. The greatest change had to do with the attribute implied in his name; he was more talkative. Still a quiet man, since the bear he had been more talkative around the evening fires, was quicker to offer opinions on a variety of things, and had even told a story or two of his life before the legion.

A few days earlier, the Tribune had asked the physician about the changes. "A good hard hit on the head can sometimes change a person," the physician Bubonius had told his commander, "but if you ask me, it was the near brush with death that's made the difference. Approaching that closely to the next world can make a man more appreciative of this one. For that matter, sir, there is not a man—or woman—among us that has not changed in some way over the course of this journey."

"So, Centurion," Arcadius began, deciding to take advantage of Tacitus's more open outlook. "The end of our odyssey is in sight. What will you do when we return to Rome? You are reaching the end of your second decade in the legion, are you not?"

"Yes, sir," Tacitus replied. He fell silent then. Arcadius thought he was returning to his usual silent ways, but a glance showed the giant's huge, lantern-jawed face registering an expression of thought. After a few moments, Tacitus spoke again.

"From the time I was a boy, my father, myself, and everyone around presumed the gods intended me for the Army. When I was no more than ten summers of age, I was bigger and stronger than most of the men in my village. I joined the legion when I was sixteen summers of age, as you know, sir."

"True enough. And you made Centurion when you signed on for a second decade as an Evocati."

Tacitus nodded. "Yes, sir. And I have loved the Army. I have served proudly."

"And your service has been exemplary," Arcadius agreed. "You are a scion of the Second Tahonian Legion, Centurion—however, I sense a 'but' coming here."

"Sir," Tacitus said, "With respect, I do think I will take discharge on our return. I have a son now," he shot a glance back to where Ochee rode on Tacitus's second horse, chattering away at the other soldiers. "All my life I have thought of nothing but my suitability for war.

But is it possible the gods intended me for something else? One god or another put Ochee in my path. And, sir, I think they did so for a reason."

"Have you determined what that reason might be?"

"I have, sir. I have been thinking about how I will have to see Ochee educated when we return to civilized lands, just as a proper Roman boy should be educated. And when I thought of how a proper Roman boy should be educated, I began to think that I should start an academy for boys. A Roman boy should learn a wide range of arts, from swordplay to horsemanship to woodcraft to mathematics and literature. That will be the purpose of my academy, sir; to produce young Roman men the like of which we have not yet seen. I will build an academy to provide a wide range of arts in one place, to produce well-rounded young men of ability and confidence."

"I have no doubt you will succeed," Arcadius agreed. "You will turn out boys that will be as fine as the best men of old Rome that was, I am certain of it."

Tacitus nodded. He looked back for a moment at Ochee. "A man must have a purpose," he mused. "This will be mine."

"You should have no trouble finding investors for such a venture," Arcadius pointed out. "A great hero like you, just returned from the greatest journey of discovery in the history of Nova Roma? You'll not lack for students, either; every family of quality in all of the provinces will want their sons to find a place in your academy." The Tribune thought about that for a moment. "In fact, I may be interested in investing in your academy myself."

"It would be improper, sir," Tacitus rumbled, "to speak of such matters while we are both under the eagle of the Second." He shot a glance at his commander. "Perhaps, though, sir, I will speak with you again on the matter when I am mustered out."

"I look forward to that," Arcadius said.

They made camp that evening in a meadow that lay cradled in the inside of a wide bend in the river, framed by cottonwoods. After shelters were set up and horses tended to, Bright Water came to her husband with a request.

"Two long straps of leather?" Arcadius asked. "I'm sure Varus has some, he keeps a stock of leather and such for crafting. What do you need leather for?"

"I want to make something for my saddle," Bright Water replied. "Something for my feet."

"For your feet?" Arcadius frowned. "What do you mean, for your feet?"

"My feet just hang down when I'm on my horse," Bright Water said. "It's not comfortable. When we're galloping or running, it's very uncomfortable. I want to make something to hold my feet."

"As you wish, my dear," Arcadius said. "I'll be interested to see what you come up with."

Bright Water spent the next few evenings working on her idea. When it was finished, the entire party gathered to see what she had made. She had just finished her project and, with the last daylight fading from the sky, re-saddled her horse.

"Interesting," Legionary Varus said. "What do you call those?"

"I don't call them anything," Bright Water said. "They are there. What would I call them?" At times her Novan background came through; she lacked the Roman compulsion to assign a label to everything.

"I have no idea," Varus replied.

Bright Water had fastened two long straps of leather to the saddle. The straps hung to the horse's belly, and at the end of each strap was a loop of thick leather. "Your feet go in those?" Valerius Caninus asked.

"Yes," Bright Water agreed. "Watch." She put a foot in the near loop, swung easily onto the horse's back, and found the other loop with her off foot. She stood up in the loops, looking around theatrically; then she booted her horse into a gallop, rode to the far end of the riverside meadow, almost disappearing in the growing dusk. When she reached the far side of the clearing she wheeled her horse around and rode back. She bounced off the horse and stood, grinning, as the Roman cavalrymen applauded.

"Did you see how standing in those loops gives her greater vantage to look around without having to stand on the horse itself?" Caninus observed. "I'm going to have to make a set of those myself."

"I think they make it easier to control the horse, too," Bright Water added. "I feel more … secure, somehow, when the horse is running."

"My dear, I think you have something there. Something nobody has thought of before. I really think so."

Bright Water smiled at her husband. These men of Rome were amazing in many ways, but she had thought of something no one from Rome had ever considered.

They are amazing in all they know, she realized, *but even they don't know everything.*

FIFTEEN
REUNIONS

History will note the amazing transformation of the cisalpine regions of the Trans-Mesizibi in that narrow space of three years. Not only the expansion of Roman legions and Roman trade onto the plains, but the increasing influence of Roman society and Roman ways to the people of that region, all happened so quickly.

The transalpine regions of the west may well prove to take long to civilize. But the plains, with the great rivers enhancing travel and trade and the great herds of bison providing sustenance—not to mention the millions of square milles of excellent farmland—proved irresistible to Roman citizens looking for opportunity.

As for our party, by this point in our journey we were simply happy to be returning to Roman territory, even if we entered the protection of Rome rather sooner than we had suspected we would.

But we still had many milles yet to travel before returning to what we had learned was the renamed city of Rome. Our adventure was not over yet; far from it. We were about to be reminded that Rome was not alone in exploring opportunities in the west.

—Flavius Arcadius Tahonius' Trans-Mesizibi Diaries

The Sister

"Well," Tribune Arcadius said. He waved for the column to halt. "Isn't that something?"

Beside him, Centurion Tacitus grunted agreement.

"What is it?" Bright Water asked. Then she followed her husband's gaze. "Oh."

A few hundred paces ahead, at a bend in the river, sat a large wooden structure. Tree trunks, sawed off and planted in the ground, formed a wall around several wooden buildings, square instead of the round huts favored by Bright Water's people. At two corners of the wall stood raised towers. Men were visible on the towers, and from one of the towers flew a large red banner. Outside the wall, a herd of horses grazed quietly in a large enclosure that appeared to be made of split wooden rails.

"That," Arcadius said, "is a Roman garrison. It seems things have changed some since we left."

"Small," Tacitus agreed. "An outpost."

Arcadius pointed. "And there are our forward scouts," he said. "On their way back, and they have company."

Faustus Marius and Celerius Dorotheus were headed back at the gallop. With them were two Romans on horseback. One of them wore a centurion's helmet. Arcadius spent a moment wishing he had time to dig out his uniform and make himself presentable. He was suddenly painfully aware of his appearance; he had managed to keep his hair cut short in the Roman manner and still shaved regularly, although he had not done so for two days. He wore a rather faded red soldier's tunic, his sword belt, and leather moccasins made for him by Bright Water. He was bare-headed; his Tribune's helmet hung on this saddle. Still, there was no time; he would just have to meet this Roman officer as he was.

In a few minutes, the Tribune was looking at the first Roman he had seen outside his party for almost three years.

"First Spear Centurion Pollux Vulpes Argentus," the man said. He looked at the bedraggled party. "I hear you have been on the trail for a while."

"That is Tribune Arcadius," Marius pointed.

"My apologies, sir!" the centurion snapped. He saluted smartly. "I didn't realize…"

Arcadius gave a dismissive wave. "Never mind, Centurion. As you say, we have been on the trail a long time. As my man said, I am Tribune Flavius Arcadius, former commander of the Second Tahonian Legion, now Tribune of Mars from that province. We didn't expect to see a Roman garrison clear out here."

"This?" The centurion looked over his shoulder at the stockade. "This is just the forward outpost, just my century of cavalry for now. At the junction of the Sister and the Big Sandy, that's the main western garrison. A full legion of troops, the other century of horse, and a trading post run by a fat Roman merchant named Prospero—there will be a good-sized town there soon, sir, just you watch."

"All that in three years," Arcadius marveled.

"Bring your men in, sir," Argentus said. "How long has it been since you've had bread, wine, and a proper meal?"

"Bread?"

The centurion goggled at the feminine voice; he hadn't noticed Bright Water in the formation. "Of…course."

"My wife," Arcadius said, amused at the look on the centurion's face. "Bright Water. She came from a tribe far across the land, near on to the western ocean. We have had many adventures, Centurion, and met many new people. It would take more time than we have to tell you half of it."

"Well. Come on in, then, all of you. Welcome back." He raised his voice to address the whole formation. "Welcome back, all of you. You are under the eagles of Rome again. Welcome home!"

Arcadius grinned. "I thank you, Centurion. Men — Bright Water — forward!"

Later that evening

"If there is anything as wonderful as bread," Valerius Fortis Caninus was saying, "I can't imagine what it might be." He stuffed another chunk of course brown bread into his mouth, followed by a slug of vinegary wine. The fare was only fair, this being a forward outpost: Bison stew, hard bread carried from the main post, coarse, vinegary wine carried in earthenware jugs all the way from Durobrivia. When the outpost was built, Centurion Argentus had ordered his men to construct this huge dining hall, which now was overfull with laughing, celebrating men — and one slightly overwhelmed Novan girl, who sat now very, very close to her Roman husband's side.

"Women?" Faustus Marius grinned.

Caninus looked around the big dining hall theatrically. "Since I don't see any hereabouts, I'll settle for the bread."

"Speaking of which," Tribune Arcadius asked the garrison commander, "How far is it to Durobrivia?"

Centurion Argentus swallowed a mouthful of stew. "How far? It's a good twenty-day's ride down to the main garrison, another ten-day past that to Durobrivia. Things have changed, sir, as you said, but Durobrivia is still where real civilization starts. But that won't last. There are trade barges carrying goods up the Sister and the Sandy now, and that will only increase. The tribes are bringing all manner of goods in to trade — everything from bison robes to herbs and venison. There will be a fair amount of coin made on these plains now. And there's more—there are at least two Reman garrisons on the north banks of the Sister. That seems to be the border now, the Sister—north of that is Reman, south, Roman. West of the headwaters of the Sister are still up for grabs."

"Those lands will take some grabbing," Arcadius said, remembering the Kobay. "There are hard people there."

"As you say, sir," Argentus said. "Hard enough to stand against Rome?"

"Rome has always spread through trade and commerce," Arcadius mused. "If we want to move into those lands, it may have to be through conquest. I hope not to see it myself, mind you. I'm a soldier, but I'm no Caesar."

Bright Water leaned close to her husband. She had been very quiet, taking in the big wooden building, the oil lamps that seemed so bright, and all the people—all the men, laughing, eating and drinking. She had tasted the wine and set the cup aside. Bread was interesting, but she wasn't hungry.

For the first time since leaving that distant camp near the western ocean, she was a little homesick.

So this is Rome, she thought. *It's so … loud.* That afternoon had been a revelation. Once they entered the garrison's stockade, it seemed noise was everywhere—men shouting, horses neighing, carpenters hammering, blacksmiths clanging. The noise only shifted to clattering dishes and laughter when the evening meal started. Bright Water looked over at Ochee, knowing he would be feeling much the same—and there he was, attached to Centurion Tacitus as tight as a tick in a rabbit's ear. His eyes were huge and round; he clutched a chunk of bread in both hands, holding it under his chin like a chipmunk, nibbling on it from time to time.

Flavius said this is just a small outpost, she remembered. How much bigger and noisier will a real city be? It couldn't possibly be much bigger than this—could it?

Bright Water knew she would have to adjust. In truth, she knew she would.

It will take time, she thought.

"So, what news from Pompeius?" Arcadius asked.

Centurion Argentus took a final sip of wine, grimaced and set down his cup. "That's right," he began, "you won't have heard."

"Heard what?"

"The city was renamed," Argentus said, "at the request of the late Consul Pompeius, before his death…"

"Consul Pompeius is dead?"

"Some months back. Senator Poscus Cassius is in the Consul's chair now. Or he was, last news we had. That word is some months old now. News doesn't travel quickly all the way out here, you know."

"There should have been an election since. Can you tell me who was Lesser Consul in Cassius's place?"

"Senator…Brutus, is that it? Yes, sir; that was the name. Brutus."

My cousin is rising in the world, Arcadius thought. "To what was the city renamed?"

"Rome, of course," the centurion said. "Fitting, neh?"

"They city and province of Rome," Arcadius pondered. "Well, that won't be confusing."

"It won't?" Bright Water asked. "I don't understand."

"Said in jest, my dear," Arcadius assured her; like her people, Bright Water didn't seem to grasp sarcasm. "But that's not for us to worry about."

"Sir, I suppose you'll be anxious to be on your way back to civilized country?" Argentus asked.

"I plan to leave at first light," Arcadius agreed. "We have a report to make to the Consulate, and a long, long way yet to go to deliver it."

Tribune Arcadius politely refused Centurion Argentus' offer of his personal quarters, preferring to set up his and Bright Water's usual shelter just inside the garrison's walls. Since the night was clear and warm, Centurion Tacitus announced he would prefer to sleep where he could see the stars. He and his adopted son Ochee wrapped up in their bison robes and went off to sleep in the grassy field behind the barracks.

The rest of the men spent the night in the garrison's barracks, drinking the sour wine, exchanging stories, and laughing late into the night. Arcadius woke once well past midnight with the urgent need to pass water, and heard raucous laughter coming from the barracks on his way to the latrines.

Let them laugh, he thought. *They'll be a sorry lot in the morning, but they've been too long away from anything like civilization — and they have performed wonders these three years.*

Come first light the men were indeed a sorry lot. To a man, they winced and grimaced when Centurion Tacitus roared at them: "You drunken louts! Get yourselves straightened out! Saddle your horses and stand to! We move out at once!"

Arcadius suppressed a laugh. He caught Bright Water's gaze; she was already on her horse and ready to move. Her eyes were twinkling. Bright Water had found the sour wine unappealing, but when she and Arcadius had retired to their shelter the night before, she had come up with her own ideas on how to celebrate their return to Roman lands.

Centurion Argentus walked over to bid them farewell, looking a little the worse for wear himself. "Sir," he said, saluting, "I wish you a safe and swift journey. Be well. I envy you more than a little; we're here for five years. It will be a long time before I see a real Roman town again."

Arcadius returned the salute gravely. "I suspect, Centurion, that a Roman town may come to you before that many years pass. In any case, my thanks for the good wishes. I will pass a commendation on the state of your garrison to your commander downriver. You've done a fine job here, and you deserve some recognition for that."

"Thank you, sir." Argentus saluted again as Arcadius climbed on his horse.

The Tribune looked around; his men were in their saddles now, pale and shaky to a man, but ready to move. "Farewell," he called, and led his men out of the garrison's gate. "Caninus, Varus, take scout duty today," he ordered, and as the two men trotted their horses ahead, led his party off downriver.

Pulcia

Ten years earlier Manius Gracchus Macrinus had been a boy, twelve summers of age, playing with toy boats on the shore of Pulcia harbor. Whenever he could break away from the drunken lout of a tutor his merchant father had hired for him, his steps always led him to the waterside, to see the ships coming and going, the drills of the soldiers at the small fort on Pulcine Island and the larger fort on the big island in the bay.

It was the ships that caught and held his attention.

Roman shipbuilding in the new world was something of an inexact science. When Pompey Magnus led his original party of outcasts ashore there were no experienced shipbuilders in the lot. There were many ship's masters and experienced sailors, but not one man knowledgeable about the building of ships. So the budding

Roman fleet was built by scrupulously copying the various triremes, quadremes, and quinquiremes that had survived the crossing.

Now, in his twenty-second year, Manius Macrinus aimed to change that.

He was a lean, quick young man, with sharp, piercing black eyes and close-cropped black hair. His mother claimed Alligator People blood, and Manius had a sharp, aggressive manner than seemed to bear the claim out.

Today he was on a mission to revolutionize Roman shipbuilding.

"It's a long ship, but broader in the beam as proportion to her length than current ships. That will make her more stable in open seas," he was telling the Tribunes of Mars from the provinces of Rome and Lustria. The two Tribunes were in Pulcia on an inspection tour of the shipyards and docks, checking on the progress of the late Consul's plan to place armed Collegia thugs aboard Roman trade ships.

Macrinus continued: "She will be built of stout oak, not cedar or cypress. Heavier, stronger wood will make a stronger ship. She will have a sharp keel on the bottom to help hold a course and three masts, not one. Flat on the back, and the steering oars will be lower, straight into the water from a lower deck. They will be controlled from the top deck by a system of cables and a windlass, rather than directly." He pointed to a large-spoked winch handle raised to chest height on the ship's raised weather deck at the aft end.

He had rolled out his scrolls on the flat top of a low stone wall along a walking path overlooking the harbor. Behind them bustled a prosperous inn; Macrinus had borrowed enough coin from his grumbling father to buy the Tribunes a meal and some wine in return for their consideration of his ideas on ship design.

"Interesting," Tribune Secundus Sollemnis of Rome said, looking closely at the detailed plans Macrinus had drawn out on his scrolls.

"Where are the rowing decks? The oars?" Gallus Gavros, Tribune of Mars from Lustria, wanted to know.

"There are no rowers and no oars. This ship will move solely by sail."

"Impossible," Gavros objected. "How will the ship move if there's no wind? How will it dock when it comes to harbor? Ships have always used oars."

"Not my ships. Not anymore." Macrinus pointed to the drawing. "See the two ship's boats? They are half again the size of any small boats carried by Roman ships now. Worst case, the boats go in the water, secured to the ship by long cables. Oarsmen in the boats can move the ship a short distance, say into a dock or away from one. But this is a dedicated sailing ship, Tribunes. The likes of this ship have not been seen before."

"And why is it in our interest to go fund you to build one of these ships now?"

Macrinus rolled up his scrolls. "Why? There is a vacuum of shipbuilders here in Pulcia, because no fewer than three shipwrights have packed up and left in the last three months. They haven't gone north to Ostia or south to Philadelphia, either. Smart money says they have gone farther south still, south of the Mediterranean. There have been Mayan nobles snooping around this port since last year, and you know the Mayans—plenty of gold and to spare. I am certain you have heard the reports of several ship captains who have had Mayan parties stop their ships and attempt to board. Now the Mayans have Roman shipbuilders working for them. Would it not be wise for Roman shipbuilding to stay one step ahead? Would it not be wise for Roman ships to be faster, stronger, and more capable than any others? My ship," he tapped his rolled-up scrolls, "Will be faster, stronger, and more capable. With onagers mounted fore and aft, with archers in the rigging and a good bronze ram at the front, they'll be the best warships mankind has ever seen."

"Sure of yourself, aren't you boy?" Tribune Gavros snapped.

"When I'm right, I am," Macrinus shot back.

"Relax, Gallus," Tribune Sollemnis said to his colleague. "Son—Macrinus, was it? Yes, we know the Mayans are looking for men to build them ships. But think—there are over a hundred Roman ships working the Atlantic coast and the Mediterranean even now. Some of those ships are armed, and most of them are carrying armsmen aboard—men of the Collegia of Rome, Pulcia and Ostia. The Mayans are hiring malcontents and grafters away from the Pulcian docks—I don't think we need to worry too much about the Maya building a dozen or so leaky freighters of their own."

"That's the problem, Tribunes," Macrinus said, disappointment manifest in his voice. "We never have to worry about trouble—until we do."

He picked up his scrolls and stalked off towards his father's small villa, which stood on a low hill overlooking the harbor. He stumped angrily through the neighborhood of modest homes—mostly owned by the various traders, factors and ship-owners that made up most of Pulcia's population. To his surprise, Macrinus found his father, Marcus Macrinus, at home when he arrived. The elder Macrinus was shorter, stockier than his son, but the elder Macrinus had a keen eye for business.

"How did it go?" the older man asked his son.

"Not well." He dropped his scrolls on a table.

"Come on outside. Have a cup of wine with me." The elder Macrinus led his son out onto their small patio, where several chairs sat behind a two-foot stone wall. The patio provided an excellent view of the harbor. Marcus Macrinus poured cups of wine for himself and his son before plopping himself down in a chair. He motioned to another chair. "Sit down, boy. Talk. What went wrong?"

"The Tribunes weren't interested, not in the slightest." Marius waved a hand at the harbor. "Look out there, father. See, out there, you can see all the reasons the Tribunes don't pull a hair for new ships. We have plenty of the old sort, they say. We've always done things this way, they say. Why change what already works?"

"I told you as much," Marcus Macrinus observed.

"You did," Marius agreed. He drained his cup of wine and wordlessly extended his cup for a refill, which his father obligingly provided. "So what shall I do now?"

"You just provided your own answer."

Marius sat upright in his chair. "I did? What do you mean?"

"In business," the elder Macrinus explained, "the better part of any deal lies in knowing what the other party wants. You want to know their interests, where they might be able to profit from whatever you're proposing. That's what motivates men, boy—profit. Make no bones about it. Now, your Tribunes, they won't show any profit from a newer, better sort of ship. But those people down there," he motioned towards the harbor just as his son had, "the ship owners, ship masters, the factors that fund the movement of goods—I promise you; those men are concerned about the Maya stopping our trade ships. A few Collegia thugs won't keep our ships safe forever—the Maya will just start putting their own thugs on their new ships. Those people down there at the harbor, if you convince *them* they need bigger, better ships, you'll have them clamoring for you to build them. If you convince them you can build faster ships, tougher ships, ships that can carry more goods and get them safely to their destination—boy, you'll have them eating out of your hand."

"Do you suppose," Marius Macrinus asked his father, "you could provide introductions to some of these men?"

"That thought," Macrinus the Elder said, "had occurred to me."

The Sister

On the third day after leaving the garrison, Arcadius halted the party on a low hill above the Sister for the midday meal. As was practice, the scouts for the day rode back to the main party, but when Legionaries Aurelius and Varus appeared, they had two Novans with them—on horses.

Arcadius strode over to greet the scouts as they clambered down from their horses. "Sir," Varus reported, "we met these two men a mille or so ahead; they were on the river trapping beaver. They say their folk are set up in a summer camp a ways downstream, and that we'd be welcome to pass the night with them."

Arcadius turned to the two Novans, who still sat on their horses. He raised a hand in the universal greeting of the people of the Trans-Mesizibi.

The two men seemed somehow familiar. He looked at the older man, who still sat on his horse; he was a skinny man, sharp-faced, lean, and rangy. He wore worn leather trousers and moccasins; his skinny chest was bare in the warm summer sunshine. He had a single long braid of black hair beginning to show streaks of gray, and wore a single turkey feather tied to a thong around his head…

Arcadius was about to speak when a shout came from behind him:

"Primus!"

The older Novan looked over Arcadius' head. His face split into a wide, gap-toothed grin. "Julius," he called, followed by a stream of syllables in his own tongue.

The guide Julius Spotted Horse pushed forward through the gathering soldiers as the Novan climbed down from his horse. The two men embraced, laughing and exchanging bursts of their own language. After a few moments, Spotted Horse turned to the Tribune.

"Chief, this is my older brother," he said, "Primus Long Dog. I haven't seen him, in, what, a decade and five?"

"At least," Long Dog replied in fluent Latin; he was obviously comfortable with the Roman lingo, which made Arcadius wonder where all this band of wanderers had been. "Not since you took it in your pointed head to wander off and join a Roman legion." He finally released his brother and returned Arcadius' gesture of greeting. "Tribune. Men. As I told your scout, our folk are set up in a summer camp down river a ways. You're welcome to pass the night if you like. We just finished a bison hunt and are smoking meat, but tonight we have plenty of fresh hump steak left."

"We would be proud to accept your hospitality," Arcadius said formally. He quickly introduced the Novans to Bright Water and the other soldiers, smiling inwardly at the wide-eyed expressions the two Novans wore when meeting the giant Centurion Tacitus. Then his curiosity overcame him: "How long have your people had horses?"

"We only have a few. There are a lot of beaver along the Sister, and we've made something of a business of trapping them for the pelts, although they aren't bad eating if you're hungry enough. There's a Roman merchant Prospero, he runs a trading post down the fork of the Sister with the Big Sandy. He trades a horse for a full bale of beaver pelts, or for twenty wolf pelts, or ten bison robes."

"We've heard of Prospero," Arcadius agreed.

"Three other men besides Payo here and me have raised Prospero's price for a horse. We have five men with horses in camp now." He laughed. "Makes hunting much easier. All five are mares, and that fat-arsed Prospero, he wants double the usual price for a stallion—says he only has a few. That's what has us out on the river. We want to start raising our own horses."

"Sensible idea. And I'm sure the horses do make your hunting easier. I can't imagine hunting bison afoot." He gestured to his men. "We were just having our midday meal. Would you care to join us? No fresh hump steak, I'm afraid, just dried venison and some hard bread from the Roman garrison upriver, but you're welcome."

Long Dog spoke quickly to his man Payo, who grinned and dismounted. "We will," Long Dog accepted. "Dry or not, we don't get bread very often. Prospero is planning to plant wheat around the big Roman garrison, and I hear from one of our other men that a couple of Roman farmers are setting up in that area as well, so maybe we'll be able to trade for bread soon."

"You should be able to grow wheat hereabouts," Marcus Bubonius said as the group walked back to where the Roman party had settled down for the meal.

"What about maize?" Bright Water asked. She had grown fond of hard maize biscuits in her brief exposure to that standard Roman travel ration.

"Maize would grow well here too, especially near the river," Bubonius agreed.

Primus Long Dog frowned. "I doubt you'll have much luck turning our lot into farmers. We're wanderers, hunting in summer, holing up somewhere along the river in winter. Julius here," he slapped his brother's back, "he got a little more than the usual amount of wanderlust but to be honest, I don't think any of us could settle in one place for too long."

"This is good land for farming," Bubonius objected. "It's only a matter of time until someone decides to plant crops. You are in what would seem to be Roman territory here, after all, with a garrison downstream and an outpost upstream. What will your people do then?"

"We'll cross that river when we come to it," Long Dog observed. "Until then, why worry?"

"Something to that," Quintus Sanctus said with a low chuckle. "Things change whether we would or no; best just to take changes in stride. A wise man knows not to worry about things he can't change."

As they walked back to where the grazing horses were staked, Valerius Caninus had a question for the guide's brother: "Most of your plains folk, your names seem to have some story behind them. You and I, we have something in common in being named after one sort of dog or another. What's the story behind your name, if I may ask? Long Dog seems an odd name."

"Not so odd," the Novan laughed. He slapped the crotch of his heavy leather trousers. "Long Dog—it's a polite way of saying Long Cock."

Arcadius shot a glance at Bright Water. Her face flushed dark red as she realized what the Latin words meant. It wasn't a subject the men had broached around the Tribune's wife.

"Women in five tribes have competed for the touch of my brother's manhood," Spotted Horse agreed. "I suppose you've settled on one by now, brother?"

"I have. Remember Gaya's daughter Pretty Eyes? She shares my bed now. We have six children."

"Jupiter's balls! Six!"

"You've been gone a long time, Julius, and winter nights out here are long and cold."

"That's true," Spotted Horse said. "So the Long Dog has been tied down to one woman? That's a surprise."

"I didn't say that." Long Dog winked outrageously. "You know how dogs are. Sometimes they are content to stay in camp. Other times, they like to run."

Valerius Caninus laughed. "I like your brother, Julius. I think we'll be good friends." He thought for a moment. "Too bad my grandfather isn't alive now. He's probably looking down at us and having a right good laugh. He was the Great Dog of Nova Roma, after all," he explained to the Novans.

"Maybe it's just as well he's not here, then," Long Dog said. "Two big dogs in one pack are enough."

"Just what we need," Tacitus rumbled. "Another horny bastard."

Bright Water whispered to her husband: "I don't understand … what do horns have to do with …"

"Later, my dear," Arcadius said, suppressing a snicker. "I'll explain later."

That evening

It was nearing evening when they arrived at the village.

The homes of Julius Spotted Horse's people were not the usual dome-shaped oblong huts of hide and bark. Instead, the village of maybe a hundred residents lived in odd-looking conical structures of poles covered with heavy cured bison hides, with a flap at the apex as an outlet for the small fire each family kept going in the center of the interior.

"They don't take much wood to heat, and they stand up well in the heavy snows we get in the winters around here," Primus Long Dog explained.

In the center of the village several smoky fires were burning under big wooden racks covered with strips of bison meat. A large group of women were engaged in grinding some of the meat to mix with berries, herbs, and wild grains, which mixture they stuffed into cleaned bison intestine for storage. "Good winter food," one of them grinned up at Tribune Arcadius.

Legionary Bubonius squatted next to the woman and began quizzing her on the ingredients that went into the mixture. The rest of the soldiers gathered around a large fire in the open area where several bison humps and one entire hindquarter spitted for roasting were sending up delicious odors. The people of the village began to lay down their various tasks and gather around to meet the strangers.

"Feast night," Julius Spotted Horse explained. "You must have had a good hunt," he said to the young man Payo, who stood nearby inhaling the smell of the meat.

"A good hunt," Payo agreed. His amiable face split into a wide grin. "The horses helped. Hope to never hunt bison on foot again. Too easy to take a horn through your guts." He mimed a man being gored in the stomach, staggering about clutching his abdomen and groaning, which sent the gathered village children off in gales of laughter.

The evening quickly took on the air of a festival. The Roman soldiers filled their brass mess trays with cooked meat, pine nuts, and cattail tubers that the village women had prepared, while their Novan hosts ate from wooden bowls. There was much laughing, storytelling and several pipes filled with an acrid-smelling concoction of hemp and prairie grasses were passed around, following which the laughter got louder.

Arcadius contrived to seat Bright Water and himself near Julius Spotted Horse and his brother. "Let me ask you," he addressed the older man, "have you been in the country north of the Sister much?"

Primus Long Dog swallowed a chunk of fatty bison hump meat and wiped his mouth with the back of his hand. "A few times," he replied. "Not so much this last year or two. Those Five Seas folk, they are making it unpleasant up north of the river."

Ah ha, Arcadius thought. "Unpleasant? How so?"

"They make it pretty plain that they don't want anyone following the bison herds north of the river—as though there weren't enough bison to go around! In the last year we've been north of the river twice, and both times we ran into Reman cavalry patrols. If they cut a trail, and our lot leaves a pretty good trail, they come and find you. 'Get out,' they say, 'stay south of the river if you know what's good for you.' They are usually in parties of twenty or thirty horse, well-armed, too. That's too many for a bunch of families to take on."

"They are moving up the river," Arcadius mused.

"They are. Did you know they have a big garrison across the river from the Roman fort where the Sister meets the Big Sandy? Some of our men went over last time we were down at the Roman fort, went over to see if the Remans were open to trade, but they got sent away pretty smartly. There aren't any merchants down from the Five Seas Nation like the Roman merchants at the fort down there, and the Reman army folks aren't doing any business. You ask me, Tribune, most of the folk on the plains like Romans a lot more than Remans. Your folk, they're sharp traders, but in a good trade, both sides come out ahead, or think they do, anyway. Those Remans…" Long Dog spat a chunk of gristle into the fire. "Bunch of cock-suckers, if you ask me. They don't want to share the plains with anyone."

He took a good grip on a chunk of bison hump with his front teeth and sliced the bite off with a knife—a Roman knife, forged of good Roman steel—chewed for a moment, swallowed, and went on: "I wish you Romans could do something about them. Send some more men out here; chase those Reman bastards off the plains. You'd find plenty of plains folk willing to help."

The Republic had not fought a real war in eighty years, but Arcadius remembered all too well the written accounts of the Battle of Pompeius, and he and all of his men had engaged in a scrap or two with Reman troops along the ill-defined border in northern Tahonia. "My friend," he told Long Dog, "a war here on the plains—you don't want to see that. You really don't. Nobody does."

Primus Long Dog looked at the Tribune keenly. "Maybe the Remans do. And if they want one, it doesn't matter what you or I want."

Arcadius sat in uncomfortable silence. He hadn't expected that kind of insight from a plains nomad, no matter how smart the man was—and Julius Spotted Horse's older brother was nobody's fool.

The observation made Arcadius more uneasy than he cared to admit.

Next morning

"I wish you'd stay, brother. Will you come back after you see these people to Rome?"

Julius Spotted Horse smiled and clapped his older brother on both shoulders. "I will," he promised, "in time. I'll make sure it isn't another decade and five."

"You'd better not. You know where to find us—somewhere between the Great Sister and the Big Sandy. North in summer, south in winter."

"I'll find you." Julius Spotted Horse embraced his brother one more time, then turned and climbed on his horse. He looked at Tribune Arcadius, then at the rest of the party he had guided for so long, for so great a journey. Everyone was packed, mounted, ready to move—even the boy Ochee, who sat comfortably on Tacitus's spare horse.

"Ready to go, Chief," the guide told the Tribune.

"Very well. Let's be off—down river."

The village was turned out to watch the Romans leave. As they moved off down the river, Julius Spotted Horse stopped once and looked back.

His brother, Primus Long Dog, stood with his wife Pretty Eyes, surrounded by children. He raised a hand in farewell.

Spotted Horse raised his hand. *Until I see you again, brother.*

He turned his horse and rode off.

SIXTEEN
HARBINGERS

*All in our party were relieved to enter what was supposed
to be Roman territory, even though Roman towns and Roman
citizens were still few and far between.*

*We followed the Great Sister downstream. The Roman
cavalrymen manning the garrison had informed us they had
made rough maps of the area, but our physician Bubonius was
also a reasonably skilled cartographer, and he kept detailed notes
of the course of the river as well as the flora and fauna.*

*The Roman troops at the garrison warned us that the land
north of the Sister was claimed by the Five Seas Nation. We were
soon to have that warning confirmed by soldiers of the Five Seas
Nation themselves. Still, the placement of the border on that
river yielded one advantage over the situation in my own home
province: In Tahonia, in the thick forests, the border was not
well-defined, and there has been fighting over those lands along
the boundary. But in the West, the border was clear, defined by
the great river. It was a considerable advantage for those western
garrisons.*

—Flavius Arcadius Tahonius' Trans-Mesizibi Diaries

The Sister

"A few days ago, we could have crossed the Sister easily enough,"
Tribune Arcadius observed. "Not so easy now."

Beside him, Centurion Tacitus grunted in agreement.

"I count twenty-one men and horses," Arcadius said.

"Yes, sir," Tacitus agreed.

"Reman cavalry, well. It seems Spotted Horse's brother was right. They are making their claim to the north bank of the Sister. I should have kept scouts out. This is only nominally Roman territory, after all."

Tacitus tactfully remained silent.

"I think two of them are coming across."

The Remans had to swim their horses part of the way, and ended up reaching the south bank a few hundred paces downstream. The Romans rode down the bank to meet them, finding two rather bedraggled Reman soldiers wringing water out of their clothing.

One of them came over and introduced himself: "Centurion Gaius Vorenus, commanding the first cohort, Second Five Seas Cavalry." He smiled. "And my man here is Legionary Commodus Vulpes. I'm afraid you're not catching us at our best. I didn't expect the river to be so bloody deep. And cold."

Arcadius signaled his men to stay on their horses. He and Tacitus dismounted. "Tribune Flavius Arcadius, former commander of the Second Tsalesian Legion, Tribune of Mars from the province of Tahonia," Arcadius replied. "My optio, Centurion Ursus Tacitus."

Vorenus cast a nervous glance at the giant Tacitus, who stood silently holding the reins of his huge black stallion, glowering down at the Remans. The Reman centurion politely saluted Arcadius—a courtesy he was not really required to render. "When I saw you over here, sir, I thought we'd better have a talk."

"Indeed."

Vorenus looked uncomfortable, and Arcadius expected it wasn't just because of his wet undergarments. "I am obligated to tell you, sir, that you must remain on the south bank of the Great Sister River."

"Is that so?" Arcadius asked coldly.

"Yes, sir. With respect—I am under orders. The Imperator of the Five Seas Nation himself has ordered the Reman army to lay claim to all the lands north of the Great Sister, as far as the western mountains. These lands are now under the ravens of the Five Seas Nation."

Arcadius forced himself to relax. It wasn't as if it was a surprise. "If you say so. I will tell you this, Centurion; if you want to move west of the mountains, you will find those lands occupied by a harsh and powerful people."

"You've been that far west? There are civilized folks west of the mountains?"

"We have, and farther, even to the western ocean. As for those people: Civilized? I wouldn't go so far as that. Dangerous? Yes. Your folk would do well to be cautious of the Kobay, Centurion. Rest assured that Rome will not be taking them lightly." He looked up and across the river, where the rest of Vorenus' party was waiting. "Nor will we be taking your Imperator's establishment of the border here at the river lightly. Now, I'll take you at your claim, and ask that you get yourself back to your side of the river."

Vorenus looked down at his sopping-wet tunic and sighed. "As you wish, sir. You are certainly within your rights to insist."

The Remans climbed on their horses and entered the muddy river. "Well," Arcadius looked over at his optio, "at least they saved us the trouble of crossing the river to talk to them."

Tacitus frowned at the Remans, who were now swimming their horses across the river's main channel. "There will be trouble over this, sir. Maybe not this year or next, but there will be trouble."

"Centurion, I think the continent is big enough for everybody. We just need to keep our heads, that's all." He looked back at his men, then downstream. "Well, let's be on our way. I wasn't expecting this to be part of my report to the Consulate, but there you are."

Prospero's Trading Post

"I'd be willing to bet a gold aureus that someone will open a brothel down there within a month," Legate Maximus Decimus Meridius opined. Beside him on the watchtower by the front gate of the Roman garrison overlooking the rapidly growing town of Prospero's Trading Post—some were already just calling it Prospero—his optio Tribune Seneca repressed a snicker. The legate wasn't kidding; he had a strong affinity for what he deemed "proper Roman virtues" and was utterly humorless on the topic.

"You have to admit, sir, it is getting to be a proper town."

Prospero's Trading Post was indeed becoming a proper town, and then some. Bustling under the afternoon sunlight, it was a long crescent of a town hugging the inside of a shallow bend in the Big Sandy, a mille upstream from where that river flowed into the Sister. Near the water were a few warehouses and shops, a blacksmith that was busily engaged in shoeing horses and making tools, and a small cloth-making and leather-tanning works that had the entire district smelling of piss. On higher ground above the river stood a few barracks for workers and even a few private homes, of which Prospero's rambling stone and wood villa took pride of place. On the hills behind the town, farms were starting up—Maximus could see four farmhouses from where he stood on the watchtower.

Maximus nodded in reluctant agreement. What the town *was*, was a distraction to his soldiers, but he could overlook that in return for having some of the comforts of civilization closer to hand—not to mention fresh food from all the farms that were springing up. A horse breeder had even taken up residence, competing with Prospero for the trade in furs, meat, and hides coming out of the plains. Demand for horses was strong; all the plains nomads wanted mounts and the Legate was certain they would be breeding their own horses before long.

"Give this place five years, and it will be a city," Seneca observed.

"Five years? Three," Maximus said. "Look over there, down by the riverbank—see those men hammering away? They're building a dock for barges coming up the Sister. Plenty of water to float heavy cargo barges up this far, even in midsummer. And, according to that prune-faced bastard of a Legate over in the Reman garrison, they'll soon be bringing supplies for their men down the Mesizibi and up the Sister as well."

"And what of the Mesizibi?" Seneca wondered. "The headwaters of the river lie in the Five Seas Nation. According to their claims, they hold the western bank of the river to the junction with the Sister. Thereafter it passes through Roman territory. How will that affect navigation? The Remans trade with the Maya, sending goods as far downriver as Philadelphia."

"That," Maximus said, "is not our concern, and fortunate for us that it's not. If there is ever trouble and the Consulate tells us to close the river, then I suppose we'll close it—how to close off traffic on a river like this, I've no idea. But until then, it's the politician's problem. I suppose there will be some sort of treaty regarding the two navigable rivers that form parts of our borders," he said, referring to the Mesizibi and the Sister.

"Sir, do you suppose the Remans will set up a garrison near ours on the upper reaches of the Sister?"

"Wouldn't you? I would," the Legate replied.

"It would make good tactical sense," Seneca agreed. "I suppose a town will spring up there, too."

"Most likely." Reman towns were not what concerned Maximus. He looked across the river towards the Reman garrison; no town surrounded their high-walled stockade, no farms were operating in the area. It was purely a military operation. *How will they feed their men? An entire legion of infantry, a century of horse, and already they are sending patrols up the river. I don't like what I'm hearing from the plains people here that come in to trade, either; they want those lands north of the Sister for themselves and themselves alone.*

"When is our party of cavalry due to return from their upstream patrol?" he asked his optio suddenly.

"Tomorrow, sir, or the day after."

"Send out two more patrols, a dozen men and horses each. I want one up our bank of the Sister, and the other down the north bank of the Big Sandy. They are to ride out for ten days, then back. Their mission is to find any signs of crossings by Reman soldiers into our territory."

"And if they find any, sir?"

"Then they are to send those Reman bastards howling back across the border like a coyote with its tail on fire," Maximus snapped.

Seneca saluted. "I'll see to it at once, sir." He clambered down from the watchtower and headed off to the small building that served as the legion's offices. Maximus stayed where he was and continued to brood over the town from the watchtower. Beside him, the two soldiers on duty continued their vigil in stony silence. Maximus knew his presence made them uncomfortable; he didn't care.

The Consulate's orders are to secure the lands south of the Sister, to place them under the eagles of Rome. Well, if those are my orders, that is what I will damn well do.

He made a mental note to send a message back to Durobrivia with the next scheduled post rider. *I need more infantry. We should have*

*at least one more outpost on the Sister, and one on the Sandy. I don't have
enough men for all this country.*

It was small comfort that the Remans had the same problem.

The northern mountains

Legate Malleolus was finally feeling like he had recovered his
health and with it, his strength. Almost as good as that was the fact
that Yap had returned his sword to him.

Malleolus was now speaking the Kobay language fluently. Yap
had abandoned his efforts to learn Latin, understandable since the
Kobay were an entire tribe and Malleolus but one man — and he was
going into their homeland, and not vice versa.

As the Kobay war party entered the thick green forests west
of the mountains, they split up into smaller parties again and again.
One afternoon as they were walking down a deep, V-shaped valley
following a rushing river, Yap explained to Malleolus that they would
return to their scattered summer camps. "When winter comes," he
said, "we will meet again in winter camp. Ten hands of hands and
more of the Kobay are in our winter camp."

Malleolus was learning how the Kobay math worked. It was
a logical system, once you got used to it; a hand was five, a hand of
hands was twenty-five. Ten hands of hands would be two hundred and
fifty.

"How many winter camps are there? Just yours?"

Yap shook his head. "No, ours is only one winter camp. There are
at least four hands of winter camps."

"How many Kobay are there in all?" Malleolus asked.

Yap shrugged. "Who knows? There are as many as there are."

Twenty winter camps, Malleolus estimated, *two hundred and fifty
to a camp. Five thousand Kobay. Maybe more.*

A substantial auxiliary to the Reman army, perhaps.

Three days later they arrived at the summer camp where Yap was headman. Malleolus saw the camp as they descended a hillside into a valley; in a meadow in the bend of a small creek lay a dozen round huts in a rough circle. A fire in a large pit in the center of the village was sending up a plume of smoke. As the men descended the hill, women and children started emerging from the huts.

"The women will make you a house," Yap told Malleolus. "You will help us hunt. There are now many women here without men, since we lost many men when we fought the Romans. You will have no trouble finding a wife or two from among them."

Or two?

Malleolus spent an uncomfortable night sleeping on the ground near the central fire, wrapped up in his ever-more tattered cloak. The next morning the camp's women set to building his house. The dwelling took shape rapidly: A large, round hut of wood, bark and hide, with a smoothly swept earthen floor and a large stone-lined fire pit in the center. One handsome woman with long black hair brought in a large bed woven of limber pine branches, with a high woven backrest. She positioned it to the rear of the hut, away from the hide-flap door. As she was arranging sleeping furs on the bed, Yap tapped on the doorway and entered.

"This is Tlee," he said, indicating the woman. "Her man was killed by the Romans when we attacked them in the valley where we found you. She will stay here with you and take care of you."

Malleolus looked the woman over. She was tall, strong, and lean, with the sharp face, thick black hair, and piercing black eyes typical of the Kobay. "She is now your wife," Yap added. "I am sorry to tell you she has no children yet, but she is still young."

"Very well," Malleolus agreed. Apparently Tlee had either

agreed to this in advance or realized she had no say in the matter. It made little difference to Malleolus. If she was now his wife under the traditions of the Kobay, that was that; he could see no reason to not take advantage of all that entailed. He looked the woman over again with fresh eyes, with a man's eyes; she would do.

"Would you ask her to bring us food?"

They are strangely well-mannered people for savages, the legate—no, former legate, he was forced to admit—thought. *She is now my wife, so Yap does not feel it fitting to ask her himself.* "Bring us food and water," Malleolus ordered.

"I will," Tlee said. She ducked out of the narrow doorway.

Malleolus sat on the bed. It's a crude home, but it will do. I wonder how far the western ocean is from here?

Yap sat on the dirt floor near the bed. "Now," he said, "tell me about the men of Rome."

The Sister

"We should be nearing the place where the Sandy meets the Sister," Julius Spotted Horse opined. "I think I remember the country…" His sentence was cut off by pounding hoof beats; Duplicarious Corvus, riding back to the main party from forward scout duty.

"Sir," Corvus saluted the Tribune. "I think you'll want to see this. Best bring Bright Water and Bubonius, as well."

"Was someone hurt? Aurelius is scouting today as well as you—is he all right?"

"He's with the man we found," Corvus said. "An old, old man, left alone on the prairie. Maybe two mille ahead, in a small stand of trees by the riverside."

"Lead on." Arcadius turned to the rest of the party. "Legionary Bubonius to the front! Everyone, at the trot, follow me!"

At a brisk trot, it only took a matter of minutes to cover the distance. Arcadius signaled a halt when he saw Legionary Aurelius standing under a big cottonwood, waving.

"Bubonius! Bright Water! Someone needs help," Aurelius called.

The Romans gathered around where a skinny old Novan man lay in the grass. The old man looked around at the group and managed a weak smile.

"Bugger me, I know this man," Julius Spotted Horse said. "You should remember him, Chief. This is Leaves-in-Wind. I was staying with his folk when you found me on the way west."

"I do remember him," Arcadius agreed. Bubonius and Bright Water knelt by the old man, looked at his eyes, listened to his heart and his breathing. "Ask him if he's sick or hurt."

The guide spoke with the old man quickly. Leaves-in-Wind answered slowly, haltingly.

"He says there's nothing wrong with him," Julius Spotted Horse reported, "other than being old. He says it is his time to die. He left his people in the middle of the night to find his place to die."

"He just walked out into the prairie to die?" Bright Water asked.

"Some of the plains folk will do that," Spotted Horse explained. "My people prefer to go surrounded by their family, but some of these smaller bands, the old folks go out into the prairie when they think it's their time. Leaves-In-Wind's folk usually build platforms in the trees for their dead, but I don't think he had the strength to build himself one." He bent and spoke to the old man again, then looked up at the Tribune.

"What did he say?"

"He wants to know if you will help him die."

There was really only one answer possible. "Tell him yes."

The rest of the afternoon was spent cutting small trees and building a sturdy platform ten feet off the ground in the big cottonwood. They covered the platform with soft grasses. Centurion Tacitus gently lifted Leaves-In-Wind up to Arcadius and Bubonius, who helped the old man on to the platform. Bubonius handed the old man a silver denarius, without explaining the reason; the old Novan didn't know about the ferryman he'd soon be meeting, but at least he'd be able to pay the toll. Leaves-In-Wind examined the coin briefly, wordlessly, before tucking it in a small pouch on the cord that served as his belt.

Legionary Caninus dug through his packs and extracted a red blanket. He climbed up and covered the old man with it, tucking the edges in carefully. "My mother insisted I bring that along," he explained, "said it would be good luck. It was. Now I reckon this old man could use some of that luck in the next world."

"Well done," Arcadius praised him. "Well done indeed."

Leaves-In-Wind turned his head and spoke to the Romans.

"He says, 'thank you'," Spotted Horse translated. "He says, he thinks Man-Above smiles on the men of Rome. He says, now he sees why. You are all good men."

"Tell him we thank him. Tell him we wish him a safe journey to the next world."

The guide passed the message on. As the old man smiled down at them, Arcadius barked an order bringing his men into formation. Bright Water held Ochee's hand, standing to one side of the formation, watching.

As one, the Roman soldiers saluted the old man. Bright Water burst into tears.

"It will be dark soon," Tacitus observed.

"Let's be on our way," Arcadius ordered. "We'll move on a mille or two. A man should have some privacy at a time like this. To the horses, everyone."

Leaves-In-Wind turned his face to the setting sun. *It is fitting*, he mused, *that these men of Rome came along to help me die. It is fitting that it was the men that came to our camp three summers ago. I sent that wanderer with them to show them the way, and he did so. The men of Rome are coming into the plains, more every day, and it is clear that the future of the plains lies with the men of Rome. But they are men like any others, and they may have been badly lost if not for that man Spotted Horse. It is good that one of my last acts was to help show them the way.*

He smiled. *The future lies with Rome. Man-Above surely smiles on them. But Man-Above smiled on me in my time, too. My time is of the past. My people will be part of that future to come, but I will stay here.*

I hope Man-Above will smile at me again when I take the road to the life after this.

He turned his head and looked to the west. The sun was setting. He smiled once more, and closed his eyes.

CIVILIZATION

After three years, we were all relieved to return to what we reckoned was civilized country at last. My wife Bright Water and the Kobay boy Ochee were the only ones among us with no knowledge of the comfort and safety of established Roman territory. The comforts of good wine, fresh bread, and decent beds were calling to all of us strongly as we grew nearer the Roman city on the Mesizibi.

As we neared Durobrivia I observed that while Bright Water was excited to finally see Roman society, the boy Ochee was nervous and clung ever closer to his adopted father, Centurion Tacitus. The soldiers had taken him on as a group of brothers may take to favored nephew, a metaphor that was particularly apt, for the men had truly become a band of brothers over the course of our long, difficult, trying journey. As we approached the city, I felt certain that Ochee would adapt quickly.

After all we had been through it was somewhat anticlimactic that our first indication of our return to civilization was something as prosaic as two little girls herding a flock of ducks.

—Flavius Arcadius Tahonius' Trans-Mesizibi Diaries

Prospero's Trading Post

Legate Maximus Decimus Meridius spent the morning going

over patrol reports from his cavalry. He was just starting a late lunch in his office in the cramped headquarters building when Tribune Lucius Anneaus Seneca burst in.

"Sir!" he blurted. "At the front gate! You should come at once!"

"I should? Why?"

"That party that was sent west, three years ago! By Consul Pompeius—remember, sir, we were told about them when we received our orders to come out here?"

Maximus punished his memory for a moment; he had quite forgotten. "Ah, yes. The missing Tribune of Mars from Tahonia and his men from the Second Tahonian Legion. It's been three years—are you saying they are here?"

"At the gate, sir! The men themselves! And three Novans with them."

"Well, by all means, Tribune, let's go and welcome them home."

Maximus led his optio to the gate. A tall man in a worn Tribune's uniform and a tall, massive man wearing the uniform of a centurion and what looked like a bear pelt over his shoulders strode forward to meet them. Maximus saluted—the man was a Tribune of Mars, after all—and introduced himself and his optio.

"It is good to see you, Legate," the man said. "I am Flavius Arcadius, Tribune of Mars from the province of Tahonia, former commander of the Second Tahonian Legion. My optio, First Spear Centurion Ursus Tacitus."

"I am honored, sir. If you will permit me to say so—we thought you were dead."

Arcadius laughed. "Not hardly." He motioned for a small, finely built Novan woman to come forward. "My wife, Bright Water. She comes from a village near the western ocean. The boy clinging to my centurion there is from a land of deep forest far to the northwest, beyond a mountain range past the headwaters of the Sister; his name is Ochee."

Maximus shook his head. "Sir, I cannot begin to imagine the tales you must have to tell."

"You have no idea," Arcadius laughed. "But, if you would happen to have some bread and wine, I may tell you a few of the better ones."

"Bread and wine? Sir, I will do better than that. Seneca, go to the kitchens—I want the Tribune and his party to have a proper feast to welcome them to—uh—Prospero's Trading Post. We are well supplied. I'm sure you noticed all the farms on the grounds above the river? Those farmers are coining money selling to this garrison, as well as to the shopkeepers closer to the river."

"Indeed—our first encounter with proper Roman society was when we came around the bend in the river and happened on two little girls herding a flock of ducks away from the water. It's amazing how much has happened while we were gone. You have a proper town here, where three years ago there was nothing but grass and trees."

"And we aren't alone," Maximus said, inclining his head towards the Reman garrison across the river."

"Here or anywhere else along the Sister," Arcadius confirmed.

"So I've heard. Have you met the notorious Prospero himself yet?"

"We have not. Your men at the outpost upstream told us much about him, though."

Maximus waved to one of his men. "Gather a party. I want these men's horses tended to and their gear safely stored. Show the men to the barracks, make sure they have food and drink. Tribune, would you and your wife and the Centurion care to join me in my headquarters for the midday meal? Bring the boy, too—he looks hungry."

"Trust me—he always is."

As they followed the Legate towards a small, square building, Arcadius said quietly to Tacitus: "We'll plan to stay here for a few days. The men will probably be in no condition to travel tomorrow."

"As you say, sir," the giant rumbled. He frowned, disapproving as always of the men's tendency towards debauchery but, for once, kept his opinion to himself.

Across the river

The fuss on the Roman side of the river had not gone unnoticed. The Reman Legate Artorius Atricolus had his sources of information in the shops and warehouses on the Roman side of the river, and word reached him yet that day of the return of the long-lost Roman party of exploration.

Atricolus summoned his clerk. "Assemble five men to accompany me across the river. Centurion Vorenus has not yet returned from patrol, has he?"

"No sir," the clerk confirmed.

"Bring Second Spear Centurion Horatius and three or four legionaries. I want to pay a call on Legate Meridius."

"As you command, sir." The clerk saluted and withdrew.

Prospero's Trading Post

Once the men had eaten some roast duck and fresh bread—the first warm, fresh bread they had eaten in three years—Tribune Arcadius had Tacitus gather them in formation in front of the garrison's barracks.

"Men," he addressed them, "I regret that I am unable to provide for you all of the back pay that you all so richly deserve. That will have to wait until we return to Rome." He nodded to Centurion Tacitus, who began to pass through the ranks, handing each man a small leather purse.

"What I am able to do, however," the Tribune continued, "is to issue to each of you the sum of one hundred denarii. Legate Meridius has graciously offered to extend this advance from his own accounts. Bear in mind that we will be passing through Durobrivia as well and I cannot guarantee you another advance prior to that, so exercise some restraint. It is now shortly past midday—you are at liberty to explore the town until sunset, when Legate Meridius has promised you all a feast that will make your ribs groan. Soldiers of Rome! Men of the Second Tahonian Legion! Enjoy yourselves! That's an order! Dismissed!"

Hooting and cheering, the men broke up and ran for the garrison's gate. Only the two older men of the Evocati hung back.

"What about you two? Not going into town?"

"Sir," Legionary Quintus Alces Sanctus said, "I thank you and Legate Meridius for the consideration. But I have no needs that are unmet. I had thought, though, to climb one of the hills over the town, sit in the grass and enjoy a quiet afternoon in the sunshine." He chuckled. "It will be nice to spend an afternoon without a horse between my legs."

Arcadius laughed. "Always the Stoic, eh Sanctus? Very well—suit yourself. What about you, Bubonius?"

"I may go down to the town, sir, to see if there is a chemist and a grocer. I have been out of vinegar for some time, and I have other medical supplies running low. Then, I believe I will join my old friend Sanctus on that hilltop."

"You are men of uncommon good sense, both of you."

Bright Water stood nearby, smiling. Arcadius walked over to her. "My dear, would you like to explore the town yourself? Legate

Meridius' advance extended to Centurion Tacitus and me. You are welcome to take my portion into the town and see if anything appeals to you. Take the boy Ochee with you if he wants to go."

"I would love to, but…" Bright Water's voice trailed off in a rare lack of confidence. "You taught me to read and write, and I know that you use money for trading, but, Flavius, I don't know how to use it. I don't know how to count money or how trading with money works."

Arcadius stood stock-still for a moment. He had taken some pains to prepare Bright Water for Roman life, but the idea of buying goods with coin had not occurred to him. "I'm sorry, my dear," he apologized. "I never…Well, perhaps tomorrow I can accompany you into the town. I have a great deal to discuss with Legate Meridius on the state of affairs up the Sister and beyond, but…."

"Sir," Centurion Tacitus cut in. "As you have not requested it, I presume my presence is not required this afternoon?"

"Well, no," Arcadius admitted. "I intended to give you your liberty as well."

"And I will be glad to take it. You know I am not interested in drinking and…other sports that the others will get up to, but I would like to show Ochee the town. I would be honored to have your wife accompany us, and to provide any assistance she may require in dealing with the merchants."

"Bright Water?" Arcadius asked.

"I would be glad of Tacitus' help," Bright Water smiled.

"A fine idea. Centurion, I thank you." He handed Bright Water his own small leather purse. "Best you get used to handing coin, but defer to Tacitus if you have any questions."

"I will." She reached up and kissed her husband, making Tacitus look away and cough, embarrassed. "I will be back before sunset."

"Enjoy the afternoon," the Tribune said.

Later that afternoon

"I'm surprised that young whelp Vorenus was that far upriver," Maximus said. He sat a cup of water down on the table in his office, which was covered with rough maps. "If it was about here," he pointed at the spot Arcadius marked as his estimated position when he had encountered the Reman officer, "that's well over half-way to our forward outpost. If they want to lay claim to all the land north of the Sister, they are going right about it."

"Vorenus didn't seem too enthusiastic about enforcing his Imperator's no-crossing policy. He seemed almost apologetic about it."

Maximus snorted. "It's a fine bunch they have over there, sir. Their Legate, Atricolus, is a prune-faced prick. Vorenus is a friendly ass. There's a Second Spear Centurion named Horatius, he's a favorite of Atricolus—gods know why—and he's angling to undercut and replace Vorenus as commander of their cavalry."

There was a knock at the plank door. "Come," Maximus called.

Tribune Seneca stuck his head in the door. "Sir, Legate Atricolus is here. He requests to speak with you and Tribune Arcadius."

"Speak of the prick, and who should appear but the creature himself. Very well, Lucius, show him in."

Moments later Seneca ushered in an older man. The Reman legate was stocky, short, and broad-shouldered, with a craggy face, and close-cropped hair turning to gray. Even in the summer heat he wore his entire retinue: Heavy black leather cuirass, black gauntlets, black linen leggings, and heavy black leather boots. He even wore his heavy black cape with the wolf-fur trim, and carried his polished iron helmet with its fore-and-aft brush of raven feathers. His expression was sour, but his manner proper. "Legate Meridius," he greeted the Roman garrison commander. "And you must be Tribune Arcadius. Legate

Artorius Atricolus, commander of the Reman Army garrison." He extended a rough-callused hand; Arcadius shook it.

Probably no point in asking just how he knew who I was, Arcadius mused.

"Well, Artorius, what can we do for you?" Maximus asked.

The Reman's face turned a little sourer at the Roman's use of his first name, but he let it pass. "I was hoping to speak with Tribune Arcadius on a matter of some importance to the Reman Army and the Imperator himself."

"Say on," Arcadius prompted.

"Three years since, the same summer you and your men were sent west by the Consul in Rome, the Imperator sent a party west. There were twelve men and horses, commanded by Legate Marcus Malleolus, commander of our Third Legion. There has been no word of them since they were rafted across the Mesizibi at the Roman city of Durobrivia. I was hoping you may have some knowledge of their whereabouts."

Arcadius was caught short for a moment; all he could think of was the morning three years past when a string of Reman ponies had suddenly appeared tethered next to his party's horses. *Now that entire expedition has gone missing, and it may well be my fault.*

"Legate," Arcadius decided to answer truthfully, but not completely, "We did see them immediately after we crossed the Mesizibi ourselves. We sighted them once or twice proceeding up the north bank of the Sister. But we left the Sister to follow the Big Sandy west, and did not see them again after that. Of their current whereabouts, I've no idea."

"I noticed your party's horses when I entered the garrison. At least one of them, Tribune, looked very much like a Reman horse.

You know our horses tend to be smaller and more heavily furred than yours—an adaptation to our colder weather, no doubt."

Arcadius nodded. "It looks like a Reman horse because it is a Reman horse. Our guide, Julius Spotted Horse, whom we hired in the Trans-Mesizibi, he traded for that horse the year before we departed to go west." *And thank the gods we traded off all of the other Reman horses.*

Legate Atricolus scowled. "As you say, of course." He could not very well insult a Tribune of Mars from Rome by disbelieving him, and besides, the man may well have been telling the truth. "I appreciate your time, Tribune. Legate Meridius." He nodded to his Roman counterpart, spun on his heel, and marched out of the room.

"See?" Maximus said. "As I said. A prune-faced prick."

He is, indeed, Arcadius thought. *But a suspicious prune-faced prick, and he does not know it, but he has reason. Gods beneath us, I need to get back to Rome.*

Two days later

It was a motley-looking lot of soldiers that Tribune Arcadius beheld early on the morning they were to leave Prospero's Trading Post. Julius Spotted Horse had only just appeared, having been absent from the barracks the previous two nights. He was happily chewing a cheekful of his usual weed; he had obviously found a substantial resupply.

The sun was just peeking over the eastern horizon, and some of the men obviously had not slept. Only the two older men of the Evocati appeared to be fit to leave. Sanctus and Bubonius looked well rested and fit to travel.

One man was particularly miserable, and so had drawn the wrath of Arcadius' optio: "You mean to say you spent every oboul of your advance?" Centurion Tacitus was demanding of Legionary Valerius Caninus.

"I did, sir," Caninus admitted. His face was a delicate green, and when he walked out of the barracks that morning, he had done so as though every footfall threatened to jar his eyeballs loose from their sockets.

"I suppose you found a brothel or some other such depravity," Tacitus demanded. Arcadius, watching in some amusement, noticed several of the other men wincing at that comment. "You didn't deserve the Legate's generosity—pissing it away on whores and wine!"

"As you say, sir," Caninus responded miserably.

"Sons of Dis," the centurion swore. He stomped away from Caninus and turned to regard the men where they stood, holding their saddled horses by the reins. "In your saddles, all of you! The Tribune wants to move at once!"

Arcadius turned. Legate Meridius and his optio were there at the garrison's gate to see them off. Arcadius shook the Legate's hand, then his optio's. "My thanks to you both," he said. "Maximus, I appreciate everything you've done for me and my men."

"And mine as well," Bright Water smiled. The Legate took her hand and bowed over it formally.

"I'm sure you are anxious to get back to Rome," Tribune Seneca said.

"I am," Arcadius agreed, "for a number of reasons. I'm sure your reports have kept the Consul aware of what all is happening out there, but I nevertheless have an extended report to give him. The lands west of the mountains have enormous potential. And there are people in those regions we'd best be prepared to face." He frowned. "It's been a long, strange trip. But not entirely without its benefits," he added, taking his Novan wife's hand.

"Well, safe journey to you all," Maximus told them. "It's still a bit wild between here and Durobrivia, but there is at least a trail, if not a road, most of the way. And once you're in Durobrivia, you're in the provinces again. Civilized country."

"At last," Arcadius smiled. "Well, again, my thanks. We'll be on our way."

A shout from the gate distracted them: The fat, oily form of the merchant Prospero shot into the garrison like a projectile.

"What in the name of Dis do you want?" Maximus demanded of the merchant. He was obviously not enamored of the fat man; Prospero, however, was oblivious. He ignored the Legate and addressed Tribune Arcadius.

"I'm so glad I didn't miss you!" he exulted. "I wanted one more chance to pay homage to our brave soldiers, but mostly, I wanted—with your permission, of course—to present your lovely wife with a gift."

"Of course," Arcadius said, a little bemused.

Prospero came forward with a parcel wrapped in linen, tied with a string. "As you are going back to civilized country, I wanted you to have a good Roman dress to wear. Sandals, too."

Intrigued, Bright Water took the package and opened it. "Oh," she said. "I do thank you!"

She held up the dress. It was fine linen, dyed deep blue, still a rare color in Nova Roma. It was the current style for fine women in the provinces: A clean, evenly wrought sleeveless dress with a low neckline, a high waist, and an ankle-length pleated skirt. In the package under the dress was a pair of fine leather sandals that laced up to the knee.

Arcadius was surprised and pleased, and told the merchant so. Prospero actually blushed. "I could not allow such a lovely young lady to enter Roman society wearing deerskin," he said. "Especially not since she is the wife of a hero of Rome." He shook Arcadius's hand and blushed again when Bright Water kissed him on the cheek. "Thank you again," she said. "It's beautiful."

Prospero grinned. "And now, if you'll excuse me—I have a business to run. Safe journey, all of you!" he shouted, making Legionary Caninus flinch visibly. With his characteristic energy, he bustled back out the gate, headed for his warehouses along the river.

"Bugger me," Maximus said. "There's more to that fat little bastard than I thought."

"He is a man of parts," Arcadius agreed. "Well, let's be off." He climbed on his horse. Bright Water almost bounced into her saddle. With his wife at his side, Arcadius rode to the front of the formation. "No scouts today," he ordered, "not on a decent Roman trail. Caninus, if you fall off your horse I'll have you tied to one of the pack animals. We're too close to home—I won't be delayed again. Let's be off! At the trot! Haah!"

"Oh, fuck me," he heard Celerius Dorotheus mutter miserably.

Arcadius was not a harsh disciplinarian, but he believed a horseman should always be ready to travel; if some of the men ended up vomiting off the backs of their horses, they would think the idea over before entering into their next debauch. He grinned tightly to himself as he kicked his horse into motion.

On the last leg of their incredible journey, the party rode out of the garrison gate and onto a well-trodden dirt trail leading downstream.

Across the river

Legate Artorius Atricolus stood on a watchtower in the Reman garrison and watched the Roman exploration party depart, riding off downstream. He turned to Second Spear Centurion Horatius.

"Vorenus should be back within the next ten days," he said. "When he returns, I plan to send him on to Terminus to ask for another legion of troops. You will take over as commander of the cavalry here."

"Sir," Horatius saluted. "You honor me."

"You are now First Spear," the Legate went on. "Your mission will be to take your century of horse upriver to establish a forward outpost. I want you to go to the foothills of the western mountains, past the headwaters of the Sister. We will push the boundaries as far as we can. When Vorenus returns with the reinforcements, I will send a century of infantry upriver to reinforce your outpost. The Romans will *not* outflank us in the West—do you understand that, Centurion?"

"I do, sir."

"Good. We'll see how you frame at this assignment, Horatius. You've been pushing for it long enough."

The Sister

For the first time in almost three years, the country the Romans rode through was familiar—and at the same time, it was not. Late on the first day they encountered a trade caravan, bound west. "We hear Prospero's Trading Post is filling up fast," the merchant leading the caravan told Arcadius. "So we're bound farther upriver—as far as the forward outpost we hear about, if we can make it. If not, some other friendly spot along the river will do."

There was another sign of the increasing Romanization of the plains: The man had his wife and three small children with him.

On the fourth day they came across a century of infantry out on what their weathered Centurion described as a "toughening expedition." Arcadius halted his column long enough to answer some questions the Centurion had about the plains. "We were mustered in Cadovia," he explained, "these children have never seen this kind of country before—nor have I, for that matter."

"Not your first stint, I take it," Centurion Tacitus observed.

"No, I signed on for a second decade with the Evocati—as, I suspect, did you. You have the look."

"You are correct," Tacitus confirmed. The two men were—except in size—two of a kind, Arcadius had to admit.

As they rode off, Legionary Bubonius commented to his friend Sanctus, "Juno's mercy, Quintus, they were just boys."

"As were we when we joined the Second Tahonian," Sanctus pointed out. He laughed. "I don't think you had even had your first woman yet."

"You mean he has now?" Valerius Caninus joked.

"Yes, your mother among them," Bubonius said, and laughed to show it as a joke.

With Caninus quite recovered from his hangover at last, a series of jokes resulted, growing increasingly bawdy until the Centurion had had enough. "Shut up, you horny bastards. You're not in the wilds anymore. Comport yourselves as though you were still civilized men." He looked at the sun. "Another mille or two, and we'll make camp," Tacitus snapped, cutting off the conversation.

"As you say, sir," the men chorused.

EIGHTEEN
DOMI ITERUM

It was an amazing thing, coming into the country of Rome.

I had crossed a great land, together with my husband and his band of heroes. In my sheltered youth, I knew much of my own lands, the plants and animals, the rocks, and mountains. But in the months we spent traveling, I saw amazing things, including great rivers, deep forests, and the great open prairies.

But nothing I had ever seen, or even imagined, could have prepared me for the sights, sounds and smells we encountered after entering the provinces. Roads paved with stone! A great city spanning both sides of an impossibly huge river, with people in their thousands shouting, trading, and crafting. Huge flat barges of wood hauled by great cables across the huge brown river! Domestic bison and strange animals called "swine" that people kept for eating; while I later grew fond of pork, at first I could not bring myself to eat any animal whose living area smelled so bad.

So this, then, was Rome; my husband Flavius was fond of speaking of the power and glory of Rome, but until I saw it for myself, I could not have imagined it.

—My Journey: From the Camp of Spirit Bird to the City of Rome, by Aqva Lucis Arcadius

Durobrivia

"Well," Arcadius said. "Isn't that something? *Both* sides of the river."

The Tribune had halted his party on a low rise. Before them at last lay the great boundary river—the enormous, slow-moving brown mass of the great Mesizibi. On the far bank, barely visible in the late-summer haze, lay the bulk of the city of Durobrivia—but a substantial settlement had grown up on the west side as well. At least five ferries were moving people and goods across the river, and a large flat-bottomed trade ship was tacking slowly upstream under the power of two triangular sails and a bank of oarsmen.

"It's so big," Bright Water breathed. "I know you told me that a real Roman city would be much bigger than anything we've seen, Flavius, but I could not have imagined…"

Ochee moved his horse up alongside Centurion Tacitus. "Father," he asked, "that is the Mesizibi?"

"It is," Tacitus said.

"How much longer until we get to Rome?"

"Many days yet."

Ochee sat staring at the city. Even from the distance the clamor of a boom town was audible: Hammers clanging on anvils, the clatter and bang of carpentry, the shouting of merchants and work-gang bosses. Tacitus shot a glance at his adopted son. *At least he's a competent young horseman now,* the Centurion mused. *The beginnings of his education. He will be a man to reckon with one day.*

Arcadius looked at the sky. "The sun is not quite yet at the zenith. With a bit of luck, we may be able to cross yet today. It looks like most of the traffic is coming this way, we may be able to take advantage of un-laden ferries going east."

"Flavius," Bright Water asked, "could we stop here for a few moments? I'd like to go behind those trees and change." She held up the wrapped package containing her Roman dress, the gift from Prospero. "If I am to enter my first Roman city, I would do so as a Roman woman."

"A sound idea," Arcadius agreed. "Everyone," he ordered, "dismount. Clean yourselves up. I know our uniforms are in a sad state, but let's get them sorted out. We'll ride into Durobrivia looking like Roman soldiers. If anyone comments on the state of our gear, we will simply tell them we have been in the wilderness for near unto three years. We look this way for a reason."

Bright Water dismounted with her parcel and went into the nearby grove of cottonwoods. Arcadius watched her go, then began digging through his packs for greaves and helmet.

He was as presentable as he could be when Bright Water appeared. The entire party stopped what they were doing and watched her approach, entranced.

She had left her thick black hair in the usual pair of braids hanging to her waist. The dress fit her perfectly, from her smooth brown shoulders to her small brown feet, a flowing sculpture of deep blue that seemed to float about her legs as she walked.

"Venus Lifegiver," Arcadius breathed. He had always found her beautiful, but the transformation was amazing. *All that with only a dress?*

"The Tribune, he's a lucky man, he is," he vaguely heard Legionary Caninus mutter to one of the others. Even Ochee was, for once, silent.

Bright Water walked up to her husband, beaming. "It is lovely, isn't it? I'll have to hike it up to ride my horse, but I think I love it."

I'll eventually have to tell her how proper Roman women ride — I suspect she'll have none of it.

"It is beautiful," Arcadius told her, "and so are you. So, let's go introduce you to Durobrivia."

As the Tribune had predicted, they were able to cross the river well before nightfall. Barges were running continually throughout daylight hours, and Arcadius' bedraggled but still legible orders from Consul Pompeius was able to win them passage on two large flat-bottomed ferries crossing from west to east.

There was a slight breeze blowing from the bank as they approached the docks. Arcadius was suddenly given to remember something about a large Roman town, something he had forgotten until he saw Bright Water's nose wrinkle: The smell of a city. Raw sewage, stale piss used in tanneries and cloth-makers, and smoke from a thousand cooking fires. Before, Arcadius had not noticed the stench of a big city, but after three years in the wilderness, it seemed almost intolerable. "Well, I suppose I'll get used to it again," he muttered.

When they had reached the eastern bank, Arcadius had Centurion Tacitus assemble the men in formation. He spoke to them as a small curious crowd gathered.

"We aren't staying here long, so no debauchery," he warned his men. "We'll leave at first light. We still have the Tsalesian Alps to cross, I'll remind you, and many days travel to Rome. You can leave your drinking and womanizing until then. That means you, Caninus."

Caninus threw back his head and laughed.

"Centurion Tacitus has found us quarters in the barracks of the Fourth Transalpine Tsalesian Legion," he announced, "they seem to have room to spare, as they have a century of infantry on patrol down the river. So see to your horses and rest well. I have to report in to the Provincial Proconsul, and then I'll be back to share the evening meal. Men," he said, "we're back in the provinces!"

The men replied with cheers.

Centurion Tacitus took over. "See to your horses, see to your gear. Prepare to move out early."

"Centurion," Arcadius said as the men went about their tasks, "I intend to take Bright Water with me to the Proconsul's offices; I'd like to take Ochee as well. I would like to introduce them as the first Roman citizens from the Trans-Mesizibi."

"Of course, sir. Ochee?" The boy appeared as if by magic. "Go with the Tribune and Bright Water. You will see some of the city and meet some of the people who run this province."

"Yes, Father," the boy agreed.

On impulse, as they walked through the city's Forum, Arcadius stopped and bought the boy a proper Roman tunic—a knee-length garment of simple cotton, dyed a dark yellow—a simple leather belt with a pouch, and some leather sandals to replace the moccasins Bright Water had made him. "Do you have a place the boy can change?" Arcadius asked the merchant.

"He is welcome to use the back room," the man agreed. As Ochee disappeared into the rear of the small shop, the man went on: "Are you part of the party that has been in the west for two years?"

"Closer to three, but yes. How did you know about that?"

"Tribune, the whole city knows about you. A messenger from Prospero's Trading Post brought the news four days since. Newsreaders have been shouting about little else."

"I suppose he went on to Rome?"

"I wouldn't know about that. But I'm sure someone is taking word there. That's how it works—ah, here is your boy now." Ochee appeared, looking like a good Roman boy.

"You look very fine," Bright Water told him.

"The shoes pinch my feet," Ochee complained. "I like the moccasins Bright Water made me."

"You'll get used to them. Sooner or later, you're going to have to get used to looking like a respectable Roman boy. You are the son of a hero of the Roman army, after all—son of a First Spear Centurion and all, talk about respect!"

Ochee looked at his feet. "I still like the moccasins better."

Arcadius cut the discussion off. "Come along, it's getting late."

They discovered that the Proconsul and the Provincial Council had been waiting for them. The meeting consisted mostly of the officials fawning over Arcadius and Bright Water; the Proconsul insisted on kissing her hand repeatedly, causing Bright Water's eyes to widen in alarm; Arcadius had neglected to inform her of this custom.

The Proconsul also spent some time assuring Ochee of what a fine young Roman man he was; by the time he was finished, Arcadius was suspicious that nobody had paid much attention to his abbreviated report. At last, as the sun was growing low in the sky, they managed to break away.

"Bloody hell," he muttered as they walked through the crowded streets on their way back to the barracks. "I never thought I'd be happy to be back on the trail again." After their years in the wilderness, Durobrivia seemed impossibly crowded and noisy; it was making Arcadius a little claustrophobic.

Next morning, as the eastern sky was growing light, they left the city and followed a solidly paved Roman road east, into the Roman province of Transalpine Tsalesia. The Tribune noticed Centurion Tacitus glowering suspiciously at Legionary Caninus as they trotted along the road. Caninus had a look of insufferable smugness; the man had obviously gotten away with something during the night.

"After all, you saw how she was looking at me when I was unsaddling my horse," Arcadius overheard the big man saying *sotto voce* to Legionary Marius. "I knew the moment I saw her eyes. She wanted me. She wanted me bad. I can always tell. And when I got her back into the stable…wet as October."

Marius sniggered. "Well, I…ssstt, the Tribune."

Arcadius wisely decided to let the whole thing pass. "We'll move as fast as we can push the horses," he said to Centurion Tacitus. He was growing anxious to be home.

"We will be slowed by the approaches to the Tsalesian Alps," Tacitus pointed out.

"Yes," Arcadius agreed. "But once we pass into Cisalpine Tsalesia, it's all downhill."

They moved at the usual walk/canter/trot, but pushed it all the same, walking the horses only so long as they absolutely required the easier pace. After a few days they climbed into the mist-wreathed Tsalesian Alps, and eventually on the side of the road they passed a large stone marker denoting the border.

"Cisalpine Tsalesia," Arcadius exulted. "Then we pass through Attepia, then on to Rome!"

They began to see names out of history: After they crossed into Attepia, a sign at a crossroads pointed the way to the Roman town of Ursineius, the birthplace of the Nova Roman hero Ursus Quadrus Tranquilus. Increasingly, signs bore the legend of the new name of the primary city of the Republic: Rome.

They camped for their last night afield in the shadow of the Primus Magnus aqueduct, the great construct of stone that bore water from the Attepian hills to Rome itself. "Home tomorrow," Arcadius told the men. "Home at last."

The Kobay summer camp

Former Legate Marcus Malleolus woke early, as usual. He finally felt back to full fighting strength. He propped himself up on his elbows on his bed of woven wooden laths and looked down at Tlee, his Kobay wife. She was still asleep; the furs had spilled off her chest, which was rising and falling slowly as she breathed. Malleolus reached out to tweak a brown nipple and was rewarded with a small, sleepy groan, but coupling was not really on his mind at the moment. He let Tlee sleep on.

Malleolus had improved his dwelling some since taking it over, covering the floor with sheets of bark from aspen trees and constructing a small wooden chest with a fitted lid to store his few possessions. One innovation had made him a man of some stature among the Kobay, and that was a small aqueduct of hollowed-out logs that brought fresh water from a mille upstream to a basin in the camp itself, saving the camp's women the daily chore of bringing water from the river.

The Reman officer was becoming a man of consequence among the Kobay. He was even teaching reading and writing to any of the Kobay who showed interest, mainly the young men; Yap had sat in on one lesson before losing interest.

He sat up, pulled on his black Reman tunic, his knee-high leather moccasins and buckled on his sword belt. He swigged some water from a cleaned wapiti-stomach water bag that lay on his storage chest, and, thus fortified, went out into the early morning sunlight.

Yap was up and about also, sitting on an upturned chunk of firewood near the camp's central fire pit. Malleolus went over and sat on the ground near the summer camp chief. Yap nodded a cordial morning greeting.

"Cold this morning," Malleolus observed.

Yap nodded. "Soon it will be time to move to winter camp, nearer the smoking mountain. Some of the men are talking of going to the ocean to collect shellfish and make salt. This would be a good thing. There has been no salt in our camp for two winters."

Malleolus nodded. "Salt is valuable. If we make a lot of salt, we can trade some of it to the other summer camps of the Kobay for other goods, like meat, or furs."

Yap looked at him keenly. "That is a good idea. Do you Remans always do such things?"

"Trade? Yes. It is the foundation on which our people live. And, as I have told you, so do the Romans."

Yap digested this silently. After a few moments, he spoke again: "You bring many new ideas to the Kobay, my friend." That made Malleolus's eyes open wide; that was the first time the Kobay chief had ever referred to the Reman as his friend. "Your water device has made you very admired among the women. I do not doubt you could have three or four or five wives, with the finest of the available girls to choose from."

"One will do," Malleolus demurred. "Tlee suits me. We get along well. She takes good care of my house."

"You have a good time in the furs?"

"I am happy with her in that as well," Malleolus agreed. A Reman man asking that of another's wife would have started a fight, but as Malleolus had to constantly remind himself, he was no longer in Reman society, and the Kobay were much more open about discussing such things. "She is a woman of great…I am sorry, I do not know your word. *Passion* is what my people would say."

"I know what you mean, I think," Yap answered with a sly grin. He had two wives himself, the first since his boyhood, the second a much younger extra wife to help his first wife with the work and to add to his stature among his people. Malleolus knew Yap had fathered ten children, only four of whom had survived their first year: not an unusual statistic among the Kobay.

They sat silently for a few moments. Malleolus dug into his belt pouch and found a strip of dried meat to break his fast.

"I have been thinking about what you asked me two days ago," Yap finally said.

"About my going back to my people?"

"Yes." Yap looked up at the sky. "I think I will bring it before the council of chiefs at our winter camp. It is too late in the year for anyone to travel across the mountains now, but in the spring it would be possible. But I do not think it seemly that a man of stature among the Kobay such as yourself should risk such a journey."

"But I …"

Yap held up a hand. "I do not mean we should do nothing. But you have been teaching some of the young men to make the marks that speak, and I have seen you do it myself. It seems to me that we could send two or three young men who are fast runners east to your people, and you could prepare a …scroll, you say? On it you could make the marks for your story before and since we found you." Yap picked up a stick and began to stir around in the coals. "A man of age and wisdom should not risk himself on such a journey. Two or three young men, running fast, could take your message to your people and bring their message back."

"That is a good idea," Malleolus admitted. In truth, he was not looking forward to walking all the way back to Terminus. *By providing a small team of runners with a good map, perhaps showing how to follow the rivers…* "Yes, this is a good idea. I can tell them how to find my home, and they will know how to get back. And when this is done, your people and mine will be good friends, I think."

"My people are yours now," Yap said. "You are here. You have a

Kobay wife. You are a man of the Kobay now. You stand with a foot in each of two worlds, my friend. I think your gods have great plans for you."

"I think," Malleolus said, "you are probably right."

The Attepian Gate — the ides of October

A crowd quickly gathered to watch the strange procession coming through the gate. They rode their horses at the walk through the gate in rows of two, each horse and rider leading a second horse loaded with gear. Over the previous five days, rumors had shot through the city like wildfire, rumors of the band of heroes that had ridden all the way to the western ocean.

Leading the procession was a man in a battered Tribune's uniform, with a strange, beaded vest over his leather breastplate. He was the most Roman looking of the group, still — after over three years, still clean-shaven in the Roman manner, his hair cut short.

Beside him rode a scarred giant. He wore leather leggings and a red soldier's tunic, his gladius sheathed at his side. The skin of some giant bear was draped over his shoulders, the bear's preserved head still attached but thrown back to allow for the worn centurion's helmet. Long black hair hung down from under the helmet, a long, wide streak of white on one side marring the black. A skinny Novan boy in a yellow Roman tunic sat on top of the packed gear on a second horse led by the giant.

Behind the two walked a single horse, bearing a small, slim Novan girl with long, braided black hair. The girl looked around her in unabashed wonder at the Roman capital. She wore a long blue dress, but had it hiked up above her knees the better to sit the horse. Her long brown legs hung bare, and her moccasined feet pushed into some odd arrangement of leather loops that depended from the rude leather saddle. Her demeanor was striking; there was a measure of amazement showing on her face but in spite of her entrance into strange surroundings she showed also confidence, assurance, and most of all, a manifest intelligence.

A pair of older men rode behind the girl. Both wore their hair in braids, and both wore an odd mix of Roman army gear and Novan clothing. One of them carried a physician's bag with a white owl feather tied to the carrying strap.

Behind the two older men rode four more pairs of horses, each bearing what was, presumably, a Roman soldier. Like to two older soldiers, each man wore an odd mix of clothing—pieces of worn Roman army uniforms, and garments crafted of leather or rough cloth. Each man led a second horse loaded with gear.

First Spear Centurion Lucius Atius met the party just inside the gate and motioned them to halt.

The party's leader, the man in the Tribune's helmet, dismounted. He turned to his retinue and motioned them to do likewise. Removing his helmet, he turned to the centurion and spoke, his tones strangely formal for one so bedraggled: "I am Flavius Arcadius, Tribune of Mars from the province of Tahonia, former commander of the Second Tahonian Legion, leader of the mission of discovery to the western sea and its environs. I ask to be presented to the Consul of Rome." He paused, and smiled, slightly. "And, if I may ask, is it still Senator Brutus who sits in the Consul's chair now? We've been gone for some time, and last news we had was in Durobrivia."

The centurion came to attention and saluted. Tribune Arcadius gravely returned the salute. "First Spear Centurion Lucius Atius, sir, at your command. We heard you were coming; the city will turn out to welcome you, be sure of that. The Consul is indeed Gregorius Lucius

Brutus," he informed Arcadius. "He was not Consul when you left, was he?"

"He was not. Our task was set by Consul Pompeius."

"That long ago? Consul Pompeius died some time before his term as Consul would have ended," Lucius Atius replied. "He was mourned deeply—the last of a great line, he was."

"We had heard," Arcadius said. "As we have heard of the renaming of the city at his request. Rome, then. It's fitting. Centurion, can you tell me where the Consul may be found?"

"The Senate is in session," Atius told the Tribune. "Your men are welcome to refresh themselves and rest at the barracks. And…" he looked at the Novan girl, who had walked over to stand next to the Tribune.

"My wife, Bright Water," Arcadius introduced her. "My dear, this is Centurion Lucius Atius. He will take us to see my cousin."

"Your cousin, sir?"

"Consul Brutus is my cousin," Arcadius explained. "And I'm sure he will be glad to see us. We have much to tell him."

"I'm sure you do, sir. Oh—I am given to understand there will be a Triumph for you and your men as well."

"A Triumph? Oh, for…Sons of Dis."

EPILOGUE

Rome — a month later

"I tell you, cousin, we had almost given up on you. It has been three years, after all. And here you are with a wife, and quite a lovely one, too."

Tribune Arcadius had to agree with his cousin the Consul on that last, especially now, still bemused as he was in Bright Water's quick assimilation into life in Rome. She stood now on the other side of the open courtyard in Consul Brutus's Catonian hill villa, in conversation with the Consul's wife Claudia.

The Novan girl from the tribe of Spirit Bird was gone now; in her place stood a composed, confident Roman woman. For the visit today Bright Water had chosen to wear a deep red linen robe that left her smooth, brown right shoulder bare. She had wrapped a black woven belt around the robe to emphasize her slim waist, and finely worked leather sandals graced her small feet. Her thick black hair was braided and wrapped into a coil at the back of her head. That slim waist wouldn't last much longer; Bright Water was had informed the Tribune only the night before that she was expecting a child.

Every inch a Roman woman of quality, Arcadius thought proudly, *even if her outspoken independence shocks some of the older matrons of the city.* Bright Water was something of a sensation in the town; her forthright demeanor, obvious intelligence and finely wrought beauty made her one of the most sought-after guests at levees in the finer homes of the city.

In truth, he was proud of her for that, too, even if at times he felt relegated to the role of 'Bright Water's husband.'

Then there was the matter of the parade: "And, you had to go for the Triumph, I suppose?"

"Please, cousin, we had to give the people a show." The Triumph had been, well, a triumph; a parade through the city, wherein Arcadius and his men, outfitted in new, clean uniforms, rode their horses from the Attepian gate to the Forum, through streets lined with cheering throngs. Bright Water and Ochee rode with the Tribune and Centurion Tacitus; all were received as heroes. Each man was presented with a thousand denarii bonus to go with his back pay, and all were allowed to keep their horses as an added reward.

"You and your men are the heroes of the hour. Have you not seen 'Arcadius and His Twelve Heroes' at the Pompeian Theater?" He laughed. "The actor portraying you is quite good, although they struggled to portray your Centurion Tacitus; they ended up putting one man on another's shoulders and draping a long tunic over both."

"Ugh. Well, cousin, I'm gratified you find it entertaining, at least."

Brutus laughed again and sipped at his wine cup. "So, how are you adjusting to life back among the civilized?"

"Well as can be expected," Arcadius replied. He took a sip from his own cup of blackberry wine and picked up another small loaf of fresh bread — he was still rediscovering that Roman staple, and had grown fonder of fresh loaves than ever. "Most of my men have finished recounting their stories to the scribes and have gone home to Tahonia. Our physician is planning to spend his retirement from the legions writing a description of the flora, fauna and lands we discovered. Centurion Tacitus and his adopted son Ochee are still in the city, but they will be leaving to go home soon, as well. It seems incredible, but he intends to open an academy for boys in Tahonia, and is seeking tutors here in Rome before he goes home."

"And you, cousin?"

Arcadius frowned. "Of course, being back in Rome at last is wonderful. But I confess, after three years afield …" His voice trailed off as he remembered — the vast prairies, the enormous herds of bison, the snow-covered western mountains, the deserts, the rolling hills, the peaceful western ocean, the great forests of the north, the headwaters of the Sister lined with great cottonwood trees — and not least, the rainy night in a tiny, dark, smoky native hut when he first looked into the eyes of the Novan girl who became his wife. He shook his head and continued. "Yesterday I spent half the day in the Senate arguing with three Senators about a proposal to raise another legion from Tahonia to expand the western garrisons. They are here, worried about gold and trade, while in the West … Well, it all seems so mundane, here in Rome. Can you understand that?"

"Understand?" Brutus replied. "No, I don't think I can. How could I? I was here in Rome these three years while you, cousin, unlocked a continent. I have heard your descriptions and have started reading the accounts of your men, but living for three years in those distant lands? No, I can't imagine how that may have been, much less understand it. But I could not be any more grateful, for myself and for Rome, for the impossible feat you have just completed."

"I grew to love those lands," Arcadius mused. "There is a majesty there that makes these eastern environs seem so … small."

"Would you be interested in command of one of the western garrisons?"

"I don't think so," the Tribune said, "although I am grateful for the offer. No, I will remain in Rome — for now. This is where the future of those western lands will be decided, and I would be a part of that decision."

"A wise choice," Consul Brutus agreed.

'There's more," Arcadius said.

"There is." Brutus stood up and began to pace. "There is, cousin, and as with most things, it begins and ends with one thing; gold."

"Gold," Arcadius repeated.

"Indeed. You have heard of the Golden Twins from Cadovia?"

"I've crossed paths with them, as it happens. They are of the opinion that I've been wasting my time these last three years."

"And they have friends. Many friends in the Senate, and as you know, the Senate holds the purse. The Consulate cannot spend a single sesterce without the Senate's say-so, and the Golden Twins' faction is preventing any more expansion into the West."

"Gold!" Arcadius snapped his fingers. "In all that I related to you, that's the one thing I left out—until I could tell you privately." He reached for the small satchel he routinely carried around with him, dug into it, and extracted a small object. He handed it to the Consul.

"Is this?" Brutus began.

"Gold, cousin. From a small stream in the mountains past the Trans-Mesizibi."

"It may be enough to sway the Senate," Brutus mused. "If we propose to send more parties to the West, to explore for gold…Do your men know about this?"

"They do," Arcadius allowed. "I asked them to keep it quiet. Asked, not ordered; most of them are discharged now, but I persuaded them that it was in Rome's best interest that this be conveyed directly to you alone."

"Wise, cousin, but gold is a powerful draw."

"Excuse me," said a soft voice.

"My dear," Arcadius said. "I don't …"

"Please, go on." Brutus was still bemused by his cousin's Novan wife; she spoke up where most proper Roman women would keep silent.

"I didn't mean to interrupt," Bright Water said, "but you said you were concerned about the cost of sending expeditions west, yes?"

Both men nodded.

"And you said gold was the problem."

"Yes," the Consul agreed.

"And all that is Rome, all that drives the Roman people to do all that they do, all they achieve, has gold at the heart, yes?"

"Of course," Arcadius said.

"Then why should the Senate pay for parties of soldiers to go west? It seems as though plenty of Romans from all of the provinces would go on their own, if they knew there was gold for the taking in the West. Just let it be known that the gold is there. Have every newsreader in every town spread the word of the gold in those mountains, and I think you would see a rush of people seeking that gold. And where can they spend that gold? Many more will go west to build towns for the gold seekers to spend their gold. Many will start caravans to take supplies west. Let the Roman people engage in private enterprise in the West, and the region will become Roman by default."

Arcadius smiled at his wife. "Without costing the Senate anything!"

"And with many Romans in the west, the Senate cannot deny but that the western garrisons will have to be supported to protect the trade from that region," Brutus said. "And since they go west to protect Roman trade, then the Senate are within their rights to levy the folk there to pay for the legions."

"Of course." Arcadius jumped from his chair. "And I know just the man to start things off. Our scout, Julius Spotted Horse—you met him just days ago, cousin—he is still here in Rome, probably debauching himself in some tavern or another. He knows those Western lands as well or better than anyone."

"Many fortunes will be made," Brutus laughed. "And Rome will expand across the continent. Even the Golden Twins, with their fingers in every pocket on the lower reaches of the Mesizibi, will probably be enriched even more by the new trade."

"If you want the pig," Arcadius observed, "you have to take the squeal."

Brutus laughed. "Very well. We'll have our squeal, and the pig in the bargain. Cousin, tomorrow, you and I are going to start by talking to a few people here in the city. We'll get that news out."

"We'll have our gold rush, and we'll have the West."

The Aventine — next evening

"See, I told you we'd find him in one dive or another, and here he is." Valerius Fortis Caninus announced.

"So you did," Manius Octavius Taurinus agreed.

"Here he is," Marcus Plancius Varus chimed in.

"And why not?" the scout Julius Spotted Horse slurred. He was well into his cups. The once and former scout for the great western expedition was sitting on three year's pay, had all of Rome at his disposal, and was now ensconced in a comfortable seat with a cup of wine and an Aventine popsy under each arm. "The Raven's Roost is the best inn on the Aventine. Try the dandelion wine, it's very good."

"We will." Caninus shouted for three cups.

"We three, we have a proposition for you," Caninus told the scout. "A private sort of proposition."

"You can talk in front of Octavia and Adela. They're good girls."

"Unless they're deaf and mute, they can wait. Here, girls," Taurinus said, tossing them each a silver denarius. "Wait for him at the bar, if you don't mind."

The girls made the coins disappear and sauntered away. Spotted Horse glowered at the discharged soldiers. "All right," he said. "Tell me what it is you want, so I can get back to my wine."

They waited in silence as the ash-blonde proprietor brought three more cups of clear, bright wine, collected coins and went back to the bar.

"Do you remember that valley in the near slope of the western mountains?" Caninus asked once the four men were more or less alone. He looked around; there were people seated all about, but the general tumult of the rowdy Aventine inn drowned out their conversation.

"What valley?" the scout asked.

Caninus looked at his companions, then back at the scout. "You know."

"Oh," Spotted Horse said slowly. His eyes widened. "*Oh*."

"Yes. *That* valley, neh?" Varus grinned.

"Think you could find it again?" Caninus asked.

"Easily," Spotted Horse agreed. "Easily." He looked blurrily at the three Tahonians. "Discharged, are you now? Free to come and go as you please?"

"That is so," Taurinus said. "Free to go exploring again."

"Even free to go back to the Golden Valley," Caninus said softly.

"What did you have in mind?"

"Four-way split of whatever we find," Varus said. "The old owl, he found a big old nugget right off, without even knowing it was there. Stands to reason there would be more. Maybe a lot more. Maybe a fortune."

Spotted Horse looked owlishly at the three discharged soldiers. "Rome is a crowded place," he said after a few moments. "It has its good points," he cast a look at the two girls where they stood at the bar. One of them waved at him. "But it's a busy place. I was just thinking, it is about time I was on my way, back to the plains. Wouldn't be a bad thing, having you boys along to help with the hunting and so forth. The Consul, he let you keep the horses, neh? Same as me?"

"He did," Caninus said. "They're all rested and fit, too. It would take, say, two days to buy supplies: bows, arrows, swords, camping gear, dried meat, corn and the like. On the third day, we could be on our way."

"Well," Spotted Horse mused. "Well."

"You will go along?" Taurinus pressed.

It wasn't a hard decision for the scout. He liked to think of himself as a creature of the plains and mountains, but he also liked the comforts gold could bring as well as any man—and he wasn't getting any younger. *I can't wander forever. With a good haul of gold out of those mountains, I could set my brother and myself up as horse breeders. We could make a fortune.*

"Why not?" he decided. "It's not like I'm doing anything else at the moment."

"Girl!" Caninus shouted. "Four more cups!"

"Octavia! Adela!" the scout called the girls back over. "Would you have two friends that might like to meet my traveling companions here? Yes? Suppose you go find them, bring them here?"

The girls nodded and walked away, giggling.

"Here's to another adventure," Caninus raised his fresh cup of wine.

"Here's to gold," Varus added. They raised their fired clay cups in salute and drank.

At the bar, Drusilla Secunda noted the quiet conversation and nodded to herself. *I'll have to have a talk with Octavia and Adela before they take up with that lot again. They'll have some idea what that little conference was all about. Or they will, after the night passes. I'll see to that.*

Tahonia

"Three decades in the legions," Marcus Albium Bubonius mused from the back of his horse. "One as a common solider, two in the Evocati. Three more years on the journey west. Old friend, it has been so long since we saw home, will we even recognize it? Will anyone there recognize us?"

Beside him, Quintus Alces Sanctus stretched, leaning forward over his saddle to ease a crick in his back. He looked back to check the pack horses they led; their loads of camping gear, oddities and souvenirs from the western odyssey were secure. "If they do, it will be well. If they don't, it will be well. You can't step into the same river twice, Marcus. It is highly unlikely anyone in our home village will even remember us."

Bubonius shrugged. "Perhaps. But I still have my work to occupy me. There are always people who need medicine, and I still have other interests." He thought of the bag of white powder that even now rested in the packs on his second horse. He had purchased other materials in Rome: Charcoal, hard coal, flowers of sulphur. "I have some other things in mind to keep me occupied in my retirement."

"How goes the writings?"

"Better than I had hoped. After all, it's just a matter of compiling and organizing the notes I made on the journey. Perhaps it will bring me some coin to ease my old age."

"No doubt you'll live in luxury," Sanctus chuckled.

"And you as well, were that to happen," Bubonius added. "We

have been through too much together, Quintus; you are as my brother. I won't see you in poverty."

"You know my needs are few," the Stoic replied. "A few plain robes, a small house, a good fire, perhaps a wife. It was good enough for old Cato, and it is good enough for me."

"Good enough for both of us to live the rest of our days in peace and quiet."

"Indeed." Sanctus looked around at the trees that lined the narrow path. "It is good, to see the forests of Tahonia again at last."

Bubonius silently agreed. The old familiar trees, the old familiar bird songs, it had been so long since he had seen Tahonia, it seemed like no more than a long-lost fragment of a dream.

But here they were, two old friends, on the last leg of a long, long journey.

The two old soldiers rode on through a warm summer afternoon. Around them was a chorus of birdsong. In the distance a wolf howled, and farther away another answered.

Late in the afternoon, the two men arrived at a narrow stone marker beside the trail; carved into the stone were two words:

BLACK CREEK

A Roman town lay just beyond, a small hamlet carved out of the deep forest.

"Home," Bubonius said. "Three decades and three, and finally, we are home."

A shout from the village welcomed them. Children and adults poured out of the houses. Small towns in the woods, Roman or not, didn't see many visitors.

An old woman stumped out of a house near the road, leaning on a stick, her long white hair trailing in the slight breeze. She walked up to the mounted men.

"Quintus," she breathed. "Juno's mercy, it *is* you."

The Stoic looked down at the old woman, then slowly climbed down from his horse. He stepped forward; tears suddenly spilled down his weather-beaten face. He embraced the woman. "Mother," he said, softly.

Still on his horse, Bubonius looked away and smiled.

Terminus — The Five Seas Nation

To say that the Imperator Marcus Aquilonius was unhappy was something of an understatement. His ambitions for much of the Trans-Mesizibi were stalled; his initial expedition to the west had disappeared without a trace and the Reman Army held only the land north of the Sister. Roman garrisons were now sprouting like weeds south of that river, as far as the first range of mountains.

General Hirtius Varus was only the latest to feel the pointed end of the Imperator's anger, but he was not overly concerned; the Imperator needed him to run the army, and besides, for once he had good news.

Once the Imperator's standard complaints of the western failures was exhausted, Varus spoke. "Imperator, the mission I sent north has only this day returned to Terminus."

"Have they now? Over a year gone, in fact. What news?"

"There is much to tell, and it will be days in the telling, but the initial news is good. Vast forests lay to the north; that much we knew. But there is more — a great bay that opens into the Atlantic, more iron in the hills in that region, and traces of gold in the streams. The men brought back a bale of furs: fox, marten, beaver, and fisher-cat. Elk and deer abound, and the lakes are full of fish. There are lands that, properly managed, will make the Five Seas Nation wealthy."

"Wealth," the Imperator said. "Now, that is good news. Wealth will bring us strength. Strength, General."

"Sir," the General said, wondering suddenly where the Imperator's thoughts were going.

Aquilonius walked across his office and poured two cups of Roman wine. He crossed to where the General sat, handed him one of the cups. He sipped from the other. In the distance, the ever-present hammering of the furnaces provided the usual background noise of Terminus.

"Strength, General. Our ancestors contended with the Romans, and were driven to these cold northern lands. We hold the Five Seas, which connect west and east as much as the Mesizibi connects north and south. Our Five Seas border on the Roman province of Tahonia, this is true, but we have as great a claim to the lands of northern Tsalesia and Tahonia as does Rome, and only their greater numbers held us from those lands. My father and grandfather said as much, and it remains true today. But in time, with gold and iron from the Terra Borealis, we can redeem the losses of our forefathers."

General Varus chipped off a few inches of frosty grin. "I have no doubt we will, sir."

Uukil Abnal — the Mayan Capital

"And so, we have our start," the Mayan king Double Bird stated. "We have Mayan gold in the pockets of Roman merchants. And the Romans treasure gold above all else."

Before him, his brother Smoke Monkey kneeled. The king's nephew Pacal kneeled at his father's side. "It is so, my king," Smoke Monkey agreed.

Double Bird sat on a small stool in the great hall of his home. The Mayan royal palace was a grand affair of stone and gold, but the king's personal chamber was modest; Smoke Monkey understood the value of grandiosity, but for himself, he preferred comfort over splendor. "Stand up, brother," he ordered. "You as well, Pacal. We are family, after all."

Smoke Monkey stood slowly. Of late, his knees had been troubling him.

"So, brother," the Mayan king continued, "your plan is well started. This is good."

"It is the plan of a generation, perhaps more," Smoke Monkey reminded the king. "But it will work. The Roman merchants will in time owe allegiance not to their consul, but to us. We will make them wealthy, and they will do anything to keep that wealth."

"Good," the king smiled. "Good, brother. And our other efforts? Pacal?"

"Gold again is our best asset, my king. I have hired five Romans who worked in their ship building yards in their cities of Pulcia and Ostia. They are teaching artisans of ours how to build the great boats they use to travel the seas even now."

"What about soldiers?"

"There are some that remember the training young men once received to go to war," Pacal answered. "We are starting now to select young men from each city. They will be our warriors, and as they grow experienced, they can train others, building strength on strength. My king, our thoughts were to send them first against the savages in the south, to beat them back away from our borders and away from the coast, to deny the Romans a reason to take their great ships past our borders. That will also deny Roman steel to those savages."

"Sound thinking," the king complimented them.

"All of this gives us time," Smoke Monkey pointed out. "Time to grow to our full strength. The Maya have not faced a challenge like this in many years, but we can grow to meet it."

"Even better. Time, my brother, my nephew. We hold the lands south of Rome, and our friends the Remans hold the lands to their north. All we need is time, and we will overmatch these Romans yet."

"Of course, my brother, my king," Smoke Monkey agreed. "Time."

POSTSCRIPT

As in the first book in this series, there are a few items I had a little fun with, and there are a few Easter eggs.

First, some locations: The Roman city of Durobrivia, being at the confluence of what we call the Mississippi and Missouri rivers, is at more or less the same location as the city of St. Louis in our timeline. The first major Roman garrison in the west is at another key river junction, that of the Missouri and the Platte. This is a short distance from the location of Omaha, Nebraska today.

The cavalrymen crest two mountain passes on their initial journey west. The two passes will be familiar to anyone who lives in Colorado and has driven Interstate 70; they are Loveland Pass and Vail Pass. The golden stream is a feeder to Clear Creek, long a known gold-bearing stream. The Chasma Maxima is, of course, the Grand Canyon.

A bit of California arcana: In Chapter Seven, the centurion Ursus Tacitus almost dies in a fight with what the legionaries refer to as an 'Ursus Magnus,' or 'Great Bear,' which is obviously a grizzly. What is not obvious is the location of the fight, but it is a real place. If you take Highway 33 north out of Ojai, California into the Los Padres National Forest and hike up the Potrero John trail into the Sespe Wilderness, you will proceed about a mile up a canyon to a place where the canyon opens out into a large basin. This is the open area described in that scene.

An astute reader may note that some of the Latin names are starting to take on a distinctly non-Roman flavor. For example:

Ursus Tacitus: Quiet Bear.

Marcus Albium Bubonius: Marcus White Owl.

Cominus Quintus Corvus: Cominus Five Crows.

Atius Lupus Minimus: Atius Little Wolf.

And so forth. This trend, along with the growing adaptation of language to take in native terms and grammar, is personified further by the scout Julius Spotted Horse, who initially gives his name in the native tongue of his people's nomadic prairie tribe, and thereafter is referenced in plain text as a reminder of the adaptation of language and culture. And speaking of the scout, the "filthy weed" he chews through much of the journey is, of course, tobacco, one of many New World crops—maize, potatoes, and so forth being only a few more.

While we're on the topic of names, the astute reader will have noticed the name of the Legate commanding the garrison at Prospero's Trading Post: Maximus Decimus Meridius. Yes, this is paying a bit of homage to Ridley Scott's movie *Gladiator* and the main character therein, played with tremendous *gravitas* by Russell Crowe.

Latin was not known for the tendency to borrow (or steal) grammar and terminology to the extent that English is; it has famously been said of English that it does not so much borrow from other languages as it chases other languages down dark alleys, mugs them, and goes through their pockets for loose grammar. Latin did not always do so, but Latin was never subjected to the stress of having a few thousand Latin-speakers cast ashore in a new continent peopled with locals who spoke non-Indo-European languages with a completely different map than Latin. While the characters in Nova Roma still refer to their common language as Latin, in reality it would have become a *lingua franca* of Latin and the various Novan languages it encountered. I hinted at this by introducing a common Tsalee saying used in the Five Seas Nation: "T'achee," meaning "it can't be helped." There is a term with the identical meaning in Russian, *nichevo*, which like the Tsalee term is deeply ingrained in its home culture.

Finally, at the time my Romans landed in the New World there were many more people living in North America than fifteen centuries later in our timeline, when the Europeans we are familiar with first came to the Americas. Nobody is certain as to why the North America population crashed; it may have been disease, it may have been warfare, it may have been some environmental crisis, it may have been a combination of the three. But in 49BCE when I have my Roman refugees arriving in what we call the Carolinas, the American continent was home to many people, and they were not all stone-chipping primitives. The Maya had their great cities in the Yucatan, as we have noted; the Anasazi were building pueblos in the

Southwest, and the Hopewell culture (who I have identified in these works as the Tsalee) were building cities and great earthen pyramids in the Mississippi river valley. These were people who were ripe for assimilation by a new culture that brought only a few new things to the mixture, but they were key things: Metalworking, horses, commerce, and an organized military.

In *Nova Roma II* we see not only the exploration of the new world by the people of Rome but also the beginnings of the assimilation of Roman ways by many more people in the West—and also, we begin to see the shape of future conflicts between Rome, the Five Seas Nation, the Maya and even the Kobay. There is a truism that 'only the dead have seen the end of war,' and the introduction of a new, vibrant, expansive culture into a land already occupied by many and varied peoples will eventually lead to conflict.

Human history has always been one of exploration. Many of history's great heroes have been explorers, from Marco Polo to Lewis and Clark to Neil Armstrong. Now with most of our home planet's land area explored, we can only look outward to the stars (see my earlier, unrelated novel *The Crider Chronicles* for my ideas as to how that may happen.) Even when that happens, there will have to be firsts; the first brave few to take those first steps into the unknown.

As a species, we must not ever lose that urge to explore, to look outwards, and to strive to see new places and new things. If we lose that urge, I fear for what will happen to Mankind. But for now, in this piece of fiction, the power and glory of the new Roman Republic is only starting out.

About the Author

Anderson Gentry grew up in the hills and trout streams of northeast Iowa's wooded uplands, gaining a keen interest in wildlife, camping, hunting, fishing, and the outdoors.

Gentry served in the U.S. Army in the last years of the Cold War, including service in the Persian Gulf War. Captain Gentry concluded his military career by serving on the staff of the Command Surgeon, U.S. Army, Europe. Along the way, he obtained a bachelor's degree in Biology.

Anderson Gentry's first major novel, *The Crider Chronicles* received a 2005 Preditors & Editors Reader's Choice Award for Top Ten Science Fiction Novel. The Galactic Confederacy series continued with the 2008 release of *Sky of Diamonds*. A spin off work, *Barrett's Privateers* was released in 2008.

His fast-paced, hard-hitting style combines a unique blend of outdoor savvy, real-world military experience, and realistic character development.

Learn more at https://andersongentry.com

Other Books by Anderson Gentry

Barretts Privateers

The Galactic Confederation Series:

The Crider Chronicals
Sky of Diamonds

Nova Roma Series
Nova Roma 1:De Itinere in Occasum

Find more about

Crimson Dragon Publishing's Books,
sign up for news, sneak peeks,
giveaways, and more!

https://crimsondragonpublishing.com